Tina Reilly, now writing as Martina Reilly, is the author of six successful novels: *Flipside, The Onion Girl* and *Is This Love?* published by Poolbeg in Ireland and *Something Borrowed* and *Wish Upon A Star* published by Time Warner Paperbacks. Her most recent novel, *All I Want is You*, and the brilliant forthcoming *The Summer of Secrets*, are published by Sphere. She is a mother of two and in her 'spare' time she teaches drama at the Maynooth School of Drama, writes plays and helps out with her son's under-11s soccer team!

For more information see www.martinareilly.info.

Praise for Martina Reilly

'Clever, frank and funny' – *Bella*

'Hard to put down, laugh-out-loud funny . . .
perfect holiday reading' – *Woman's Way*

'Reilly is a star of the future' – *Belfast Telegraph*

'A rollicking good yarn' – *Irish Evening Herald*

'Reilly has a wonderful comic touch, both in the way
she draws her characters and in her dialogue . . .
A brilliant read' – *U Magazine*

*Also by Martina Reilly*

Flipside
The Onion Girl
Is This Love?
Something Borrowed
Wish Upon A Star
All I Want is You

# *Wedded Blitz*

## TINA REILLY

sphere

SPHERE

First published in Great Britain as a paperback original in
March 2005 by Time Warner Paperbacks
This edition published by Time Warner Books in January 2006
Reprinted 2006
Reprinted by Sphere in 2007

Copyright © Martina Reilly 2005

The moral right of the author has been asserted.

*All characters in this publication are fictitious and any resemblance
to real persons, living or dead, is purely coincidental.*

All rights reserved.
No part of this publication may be reproduced, stored in
a retrieval system, or transmitted, in any form or by any
means, without the prior permission in writing of the publisher,
nor be otherwise circulated in any form of binding or cover
other than that in which it is published and without a similar
condition including this condition being imposed on
the subsequent purchaser.

A CIP catalogue record for this book
is available from the British Library.

ISBN 978-0-7515-3845-8

Papers used by Sphere are natural, recyclable products made from
wood grown in sustainable forests and certified in accordance with
the rules of the Forest Stewardship Council.

Typeset in Baskerville MT by
Palimpsest Book Production, Polmont, Stirlingshire
Printed and bound in Great Britain by
Clays Ltd, St Ives plc
Paper supplied by Hellefoss AS, Norway

Sphere
An imprint of
Little, Brown Book Group
Brettenham House
Lancaster Place
London WC2E 7EN

A Member of the Hachette Livre Group of Companies

www.littlebrown.co.uk

For Olive

# Acknowledgements

Thanks to all my family, friends and well-wishers who have been thanked before.

Thanks to all my writer friends for understanding how boring and obsessive writers can be!!

Thanks especially to the *Evening Herald* gang – Dave, Sheila and Anna – for their lovely words the last time around.

Thanks also to Ciaran Nevin – fantastic hairdresser – who checked all my hairdressing chapters for me – any mistakes are mine.

Thanks to my agent Ali Gunn and to all at Time Warner – Joanne Coen, Sheena-Margot Lavelle and Rebecca Gray. Thanks to Time Warner too for sponsoring the soccer kit of the Maynooth under-10s. They are top of the league as I write – as long as my book does the same!! Thanks also to Margaret Daly who made the PR for *Something Borrowed* so easy and to Jim Binchy for all his hard work.

Thanks to you, all my loyal readers, for buying my books – hope you like this one.

# Prologue

NO MATTER HOW many times Jane dusted the mantelpiece, she always had to stop whenever she came to the photo. Matt, with his big wide grin and his tousled black hair, laughed out at her from the frame. It was the sort of photo that made noise. His black hair, the green grass of Phoenix Park and his red Man United jersey all produced a joyous clash of vibrant colours that made her smile. Jim had taken it – one of the few he'd ever taken of Matt. Jim was a good photographer with a great eye for a picture. She was glad he'd taken that one.

It had been a great day, she remembered. Jim had taken his camera out to the park to do some shots of greenery for an ad project he was working on. She and the kids had accompanied him. They'd pulled up in the park, tumbled out of the car and begun walking. Owen had taken his skateboard and was whizzing along in front of them. Matt ran alongside him for a bit, begging for a go, while Di snuggled up to her dad. She was a real Daddy's girl and had yet to discover her love of all things black. Jim had wrapped one arm around his daughter and the other around her. No, he'd put his hand into the back pocket of her jeans, she remembered. And she had put her hand into the back pocket of his. They'd walked along like that, hip to hip, him nuzzling the top of her head and turning her on something rotten.

Then Matt had wrestled the skateboard from a laughing Owen and had stood shakily on it. 'Don't', she'd called out, trying not to laugh, knowing he'd fall.

1

And he had.

Right onto the grass.

And snap! Jim had left her side and taken the picture. Then he'd snapped her. And he carried that one in his wallet.

Or at least he used to.

'Jane?'

She jumped. Guiltily put the picture back in its place, before turning around. Jim stood, framed in the doorway, his dark hair falling across his face. His eyes flicked to the photo and darted away again. He looked like Matt, she thought suddenly. The notion caused her to wince. 'Yeah?' She made her voice over-bright.

'Look,' Jim swallowed. Moved from one foot to the other. 'I've been thinking.'

'Yeah?' A sort of dread began in the pit of her stomach. Jim was not one for thinking about things, as far as she knew. 'Thinking? About what?'

'Us.'

'Oh.'

'And, well,' Jim swallowed again. 'It's not working, is it?'

She didn't answer. Instead she felt her heart swell up inside her and her stomach gave a weird lurch.

'I think, and well, maybe it's for the best, I think I should move out.'

Move out? She stared at him. 'What?'

He met her gaze for the first time. 'D'you think that would be best?'

Best? Did she think it would be for the best? What kind of a stupid question was that? The memory of that day in the park was only one memory. There were so many more. Like the time they'd bought the house and christened every room. The birth of Di when he'd picked up the wrong baby in the nursery and brought it into her. The time he'd phoned her to tell her that he was coming home early so that they could 'get some decent sex in' before the kids came home from school, only to find he

2

was talking to his mother-in-law, who informed him that she wasn't in the least attracted to him, though thanks for the offer. The time she'd cooked a birthday dinner for him and he'd got food poisoning. The funny times. The erotic times. The bloody wonderful times. And of course the sad times.

'Do I think it would be for the best?' she asked, her tone sarcastic. 'Is that a joke?'

'No.'

'So you actually want me to tell you if you moving out would be for the best?'

'Oh forget it!' He turned around.

'Just like you're trying to forget, is that it?' She was gratified to see his shoulders stiffen. 'There are some things you can't forget, Jim. Leaving is not going to change that!'

He turned around. His dark eyes looked hopelessly at her. 'It's because I can't forget that I'm leaving,' he said, and his voice rose too, though he didn't sound as aggressive as her. He never could. 'We had good times Jane, great times. That's why I'm going – we don't have that any more.'

'But if we tried, we could have.' She hated pleading with him, but this was the only man she'd ever loved.

'We *have* tried,' he said flatly.

'*I've* tried, you mean,' she said. 'You haven't talked to me once. You've never told me what went on in your head that time when—'

'That doesn't matter!' He closed his eyes and bit his lip and when he looked at her again, she knew that no matter what she said, even if she told him that it wasn't for the best, he was still going to leave. But damn it, he wasn't going to take her dignity along with everything else.

'What about the kids?' she tried to hit him where it hurt most. 'What will they think?'

Jim bit his lip again. She used to love seeing him do that.

'I'll tell them – OK? They might be happier anyway.'

She didn't know what to say to that. She never knew what

3

to say to Jim any more. He wasn't the same person that she used to know. She reckoned that he wasn't the person he used to think he was either.

'And where will you go?'

'Fred said he'd let me stay for a bit.'

Fred. *Jesus.*

She must have rolled her eyes because Jim said, a bit sharply, 'Yeah, well, I won't have much money, will I? I mean, I think we should keep the house for the kids' sake, don't you?'

'I dunno,' her tone was sarcastic. 'Do you think it would be for the best?'

'Jane. Stop.'

She bowed her head. 'Right,' she snapped. 'Let's keep the house.'

'Good.'

'If that's what *you* want.'

Jim winced. It wasn't what he wanted. Of course it wasn't. He wanted things to be the way they used to be. He wanted him and Jane to be happy. He wanted her respect again, but he'd lost that. He glanced briefly at the photo she'd been holding when he'd come into the room. His best shot ever. Bloody photo. Every time he looked at it – which wasn't often – it seemed to mock him. 'It's not what I want Jane,' he said. 'But, I guess it's just the way things are.'

She was about to tell him that the way things were was because they were acting the way they were, but it was too late. He'd turned his back and walked out.

Their marriage was over.

# 1

*Three months later*

J ANE PARKED HER car and grinned – twenty minutes to get to work had to be some kind of record. Since Jim had left, she was driving to work late in the morning, which meant that the traffic had eased. Patrick, her business partner, had insisted that as she was now a broken marriage statistic it was important for her to be there to see her kids off to school. Jane smiled, thinking that being in work was sometimes preferable to dealing with her daughter's sulks first thing in the morning.

Pulling her bag from the boot, she flicked on the car alarm and began the short walk to the salon. Fifteen years ago, her father had lent her the money to invest in a salon of her own. Jane had thrown her lot in with Patrick, a mate from hairdressing college. Together they'd slowly built up the business. She'd cut and Patrick had coloured. And then, when one stylist wasn't enough, they'd taken on Mir. Much to her mother's horror, however, they'd put Patrick's name over the door. Patrick Costelloe's sounded so much classier than Jane D'arcy's.

Jane hoisted her bag over her shoulder and sighed. It was going to be a quiet morning. They'd closed the salon to do interviews for a new trainee and a quiet morning was not what she was after. Cups of tea and meaningless chat would be the order of the day. But she was good at that. Hadn't she been doing it for the last four years of her marriage?

\* \* \*

His back was killing him. That was Jim's first thought as he woke up. Sleeping on Fred's sofa bed was torture. Not only because the bed was lumpy and small, but because he had to share the room with a manic African Grey parrot that screeched 'Fuck' at least every half-hour. Fred was very proud of the parrot, claiming that it was a real conversation ice-breaker with girls. Jim knew he'd been out of it too long. Girls being fascinated with cursing birds was not something he could envisage.

'Sleep well?' Fred, fully clothed, and stinking of cologne, walked into the sitting room. 'I was going to wake you, but hey, you looked so peaceful there.'

Jim glanced at his watch. Christ! He jumped off the bed and picked up his clothes from the floor. His boss would freak at him being so late. As he shaved and washed he wondered if he'd be stuck with Fred for a long time. The thought chilled him.

It had been crap looking for a flat to rent. Prices everywhere were so high that he'd have had to take out a mortgage on the house just to afford a month's rent. And he definitely didn't want to share with a load of people he didn't know. It had been brilliant when Fred, a mate, had mentioned that he was stuck for someone to share his rent with. At the time, Jim was convinced that it had been heaven sent. He and Fred went back a long way, they got on great and Fred was decent enough, even if there was a major personality clash between him and Jane.

The thought of Jane made him feel a bit sick. He tried not to think of her too much these days. Thinking about her only made the pain worse. When he'd first left he'd thought about her all the time – the Jane of the early years: the warmth of her body beside his in bed, the way she whirled about the house in the morning getting the kids ready for school, the sound of her laugh. He'd loved her laugh. He'd loved *her*. He didn't miss the awkwardness of the last few years but God, he really missed just *seeing* her.

Fred rapped on the bathroom door. 'Listen Jimbo, I'm going!'

'OK.' Jim bit his lip. The whole idea of sharing with Fred didn't seem so brilliant now. For one thing, if he had to sleep on that sofa for much longer he'd be crippled by the time he was forty.

'I'll see you later,' Fred shouted through the door. 'I vote, right, that we have a few beers and make a plan of action – get you circulating in the world again. No point in being free if you're gonna mope like you've been doing – right?' Without waiting for an answer, he called out a 'bye' and a slam of the flat door followed.

Jim looked at himself in the small bathroom mirror. How the hell had it come to this? OK, it was nice not to have that awkwardness every time he tried to talk to his wife, but Jesus, he wondered if he'd ever get over her. She was the only woman he'd ever loved.

'FUUCCKK!' the parrot shrieked from the sitting room.

'Yeah. Fuck.' Jim laid his head against the cool of the glass. 'Fuck,' he said again.

MIRANDA, THE OTHER stylist, was on the phone when Jane walked into the coffee room of the salon. Miranda was sitting scrunched up in a chair with her back to the door. She spoke in a low threatening tone into the receiver. Jane smiled. It was kind of reassuring to know that she wasn't the only one with man problems. Mir's love life could have had a regular spot on *Oprah*. If there was a useless waster out there, Miranda would find him. Her latest fella was a musician. He was dead good apparently and his band was called The Condemned. They sang Beatles' numbers and stuff they wrote themselves. How Miranda did it, Jane hadn't a clue. The girl could have had anyone. Miranda was thirty-two, three years younger than Jane, but she looked like a girl in her early twenties. Her jet-black hair was cut short and tight, showing off her perfect oval face and wide brown eyes. Her clothes always had a label whether it was Levi or Calvin Klein, and no matter what she wore it always looked good on her.

Lately, Jane had envied Miranda's free and easy life. There were no kids, no mortgage and if her relationships broke up on a regular basis, at least it didn't impact on anyone else. Mir could still head out the following week and find some other loser, while Jane had spent the last couple of months see-sawing between a sort of grief that her marriage was over and relief that it was finally over. It was only when Jim left that she'd realised how her heart had broken a little bit every day at their inability to laugh and talk together. Every stilted word had been like a piece of glass cutting her open. She wondered if Jim felt that too.

Walking past Mir, Jane hung up her coat and began reviewing the letters from the job applicants. The first one was due in at ten-thirty.

'Bastard,' Miranda said loudly into the receiver. She sniffed a bit. 'No I *won't!*' Slamming down the phone she muttered 'Bastard' again.

'Trouble?' Jane looked up from one particularly badly spelt letter. In normal circumstances the letter would have been thrown in the bin, but these days, for some reason, trainees were very difficult to find. She had to interview anyone who was interested.

'You said it.' Miranda rooted around in her Gucci handbag and pulled out a packet of fags. 'D'you mind?' she asked.

'Just one, right?' Jane replied. 'And keep the window open.' The last thing Jane needed was a stylist grumping and biting the heads off all the applicants.

'That fecker,' Miranda pointed at the phone, 'stood me up last night.' She lit her fag with shaking fingers. Inhaling deeply, she blew a long stream of smoke towards the ceiling. 'He was meant to pick me up at eight and I waited in for him until after ten.'

'That's bad.' Jane braced herself for the details. Miranda shared her problems in the same way that Jesus had shared out loaves and fishes. Most days it was entertaining, and at least today it meant that she could keep her own problems on hold.

'You think *that* was bad!' Miranda exclaimed. She waved her cigarette around and ash fell everywhere. 'When he *eventually* showed up – at around eleven – he was totally locked and reeking of smoke.'

'I hope you told him where to go.'

'Fecker was swaying all over the place, like he was after stepping off the waltzer in Funderland or something. He could barely string a sentence together.' She paused and sighed dramatically.

9

'Well, I couldn't have him acting like that outside my apartment, sure I couldn't?'

'No. So you told him where to go?'

'Yeah,' Miranda nodded. 'I told him to come in.' She flicked her cigarette in the general direction of the ashtray. More ash fell on the floor. Her face softened a bit. 'Aw Jane, even though he was tanked up he's as cute. He's got this little dimple right here,' she pointed to her left cheek, 'and when he smiles it goes in.'

'That's what dimples do all right,' Jane said, half-amused. 'So what did you do then?' She could guess the rest of this story.

They'd talked.

'Well, we talked for a bit. Straightened things out.'

They'd kissed.

'Had a bit of a snog.'

One thing had led to another.

'A bit of a shag.'

And then he'd pissed off, like they always did.

'Anyway, he fecked off this morning and never even said "goodbye" or "good morning" or anything.'

Jane tried to look as if she hadn't heard the story a million times before. 'So . . . what? He rang you just now to apologise?'

'No, I rang him to see if I could see him this evening,' Miranda bit her lip, 'but he says he's busy.'

'Oh, Jesus, *Miranda*.' Jane couldn't help it. The girl was hopeless.

Miranda shrugged. Gulped. Took another drag on her cigarette. 'Don't gimme the lecture, Jane. Don't tell me what I should have done.'

'I wasn't—'

'It's OK for you. Well,' Mir looked pained, as if she'd just put her size three stiletto in it, 'it *was* OK for you. You've done the great guy bit.'

Jane flinched. 'And look where that got me.' She tried to keep her tone light, to bite down the hurt. She stared hard at one of the applications.

'Yeah, but at least you *did* it,' Mir made a face. 'I don't think I'll ever get a guy to love me the way Jim loved you.'

'*Loved* being the operative word.'

'You have no idea what it's like out there now,' Mir went on, ignoring Jane's bitter comment. 'The whole scene is a fecking cattle mart. Everyone parades about like . . . I dunno . . . like big heifers hoping to get bought up by the highest bidder.'

Jane said nothing. When Miranda began equating dating to anything to do with animals, it was best to keep schtum.

'And when they pick you out they want some action, you know? No one buys a cow and gets milk in the local shop.' Miranda viciously stubbed out her fag.

'Jesus, Miranda, that's awful!'

'Awful world out there,' Miranda said wearily.

There was no hope for her, Jane thought. Every guy she was ever with had done the same thing to her. 'Will you shut up – you're like an auld wan.'

'I feel like an auld wan.'

'Come here and gimme a hand with these CVs.'

'What? All three of them?' Miranda snorted. She stood up and brushed the ash from her clothes. 'I wouldn't mind so much,' she said thoughtfully, 'only he was great in bed. Very considerate.'

'That was nice.'

'I betcha your Jim was like that. I betcha he cared about what you wanted.'

Jane flinched. Mir could be so insensitive at times – not that she meant to be.

'Well?' Miranda looked at her expectantly.

'Mir – I am not going to discuss my sex life with Jim with you.' He'd been great though. *No*, she corrected herself, *they'd* been great. Couldn't keep their hands off each other. And even though the last few years had been bad, and the sex had declined, it had still been explosive when it had happened. 'I'm not!' she said sharply as Mir poked her in the arm. She picked up the

11

second CV. Coffee stains adorned it. Something that looked like jam had stuck to one corner. Her stomach did an involuntary roll.

'I betcha,' Miranda poked her again. 'I betcha Jim didn't do a Koala bear on you.'

'What?'

'You know; eats, shoots and leaves.'

It took a second for the joke to register and when it did, Jane laughed. 'Where do you get them?' she giggled. 'You're disgusting.'

'Not as disgusting as that CV.'

The only person out of the three applicants to show for the interview was the owner of the revolting CV. By the time she turned up, Miranda had worked herself into an even more foul humour.

'You'd think they'd cancel, wouldn't you?' she said as Jane placed a cup of tea in front of her. 'I mean, it's only manners now, isn't it?'

'You're right, but there's not a lot we can do about it.'

'No one has manners any more. I mean, take that fecker last night – did he even thank me for the use of my bed? Did he?' She shook her head. 'Did he fuck! That's everyone these days—'

The doorbell rang and Jane went to answer it. Her head was going to explode if she had to listen to Miranda any longer.

There was a girl of about eighteen outside. She was dressed in what might have passed for an interview suit if it had been ironed: a blue skirt, blue jacket and red blouse. Dark brown tights and heavy shoes did nothing to add to the overall effect. The girl's hair was caught back in an untidy ponytail and she sported oversized glasses through which she peered anxiously at Jane.

'Hiya,' her voice was high and nervous. 'Am I in the right place? I'm looking for the "Patrick Costelloe Hair Saloon"?'

'That's us.' Despite her sinking heart, Jane managed a smile and pointed at the sign above the door. 'Come on in.'

The girl stepped through the doorway and looked around. 'I went to the place up the road, the sort of empty shop where there's loads of work going on, that's where I thought it was.'

'Well, you've found us now.' Jane tried to hide her dismay at the state of the girl behind a frazzled smile. 'Come this way.'

'Yes, yes I did, didn't I?' the girl giggled nervously. 'They said that they were Cutting Edge and that they were opening up next month. They said that you were down here.'

Jane froze. The girl banged into her and her glasses slid off her nose and on to the floor. 'What did you just say?' Jane hoped she'd heard wrongly. Her mouth was dry as she asked, 'Did you say Cutting Edge are moving in up the road?'

'Uh-huh,' the girl located her specs and stood up. Nodding eagerly, she said, 'Cutting Edge is really the business, isn't it? It'll probably get you some customers too.' She looked around the place. 'Isn't it awful quiet?'

'What?' Jane could barely register what the kid was saying now. All she could see was the Cutting Edge hairdressing empire muscling in on her territory. A sort of slow sick feeling spread right through her.

'It's very quiet, isn't it?' the girl repeated. 'I mean, very, very quiet.'

'We're normally busy, it's just that we've closed for the morning to conduct the interviews.'

'Oh.' The girl gave another giggle. 'Ooohh, right. I just thought that . . . well . . . you were . . . well . . .' she paused, unsure. 'Oh, never mind.'

'This way.' Jane's heart had now sunk so far into her boots that she felt as if she was squishing it with every step that she took.

'Interview candidate here,' she announced to Miranda.

Miranda quickly stubbed out her fag and shoved her mirror back into her bag. She folded her hands in front of her on the desk and put on her serious face.

The girl gazed around the office before sliding into a seat. 'Hi,' she beamed. 'Sorry I'm late. I was waiting for the bus and didn't a car come and splash me and I had to go back home and dry myself with a hairdryer and then, after I got off the bus, I lost my way and had to run all the way here.' She stopped and beamed.

'I see,' Miranda muttered.

'So, er . . .' Jane pretended to look through loads of papers, no longer in the mood for talking now. 'You are . . . Rosemary?'

'Rosemary Dalton, that's me.'

'And what experience have you work-wise, Rosemary?'

'Well,' Rosemary licked her lips and frowned. 'I wrote it on my job application.' She smiled and blushed. 'I've got, well . . . none, really. I, er, I just left school and I've always wanted to work in a hair saloon.'

'Have you?'

'Oh yes. I love doing people's hair. I cut all my mates' hair. Your hair,' she gazed in open admiration at Miranda, 'now, that's *fab*. I'd *love* to make people look like you.'

Miranda rolled her eyes and muttered something that Jane couldn't quite catch.

Rosemary didn't seem to notice. She kept going. 'I'd do anything. Like, I know you won't let me loose with a scissors, for like, ooohhh . . .' she bit her lip, '. . . *ages*, but in the meantime, I'll do whatever you want.'

'Well, at the start, Rosemary,' Jane said gently, 'it'll be just sweeping and cleaning and washing the odd head of hair.'

'Yeah yeah, I know,' Rosemary nodded.

'Sometimes the odd head of hair is *very* odd,' Miranda said darkly.

'What?'

'She's joking,' Jane confirmed.

'I'm bloody not,' Miranda hissed.

Jane kicked her. Just because her fella had dumped her there was no need for her to carry on like she was.

14

'You'll get used to Miranda if you work here,' Jane smiled.

'Ohhhh,' Rosemary gave a few very unconvincing giggles. Then she gave some more. And then some more. Her hands twisted themselves into fists on her lap. 'I know loads about hair. I've got loads of hair books at home. I read all the time about hair, I do.'

'Good,' Jane wondered if maybe she might be suitable. 'Are there any questions you'd like to ask us?'

Rosemary looked at her with huge eyes. 'Any questions I'd like to ask yez? Oooh.'

'It's not a trick question.' Miranda's voice was brittle. 'Any time today now.'

Rosemary giggled again. 'You're funny.' She giggled some more before saying, 'Well, no, that's it really. Is my interview over now?'

Jane couldn't think of anything else to ask. The girl had no experience at all; her average exam results were on her CV, her CV was a mess. But, hey, she read books on hair, she was available, she would do anything and they were desperate.

'Well, thank you for coming Rosemary,' she said as she got up.

'So, when will I know?'

'Soon,' Jane said. 'Maybe tomorrow – we'll call you.'

Beside her, Miranda let out a long slow breath.

'OK,' Rosemary got up too. She smiled brightly at them both as she hitched her glasses up her nose. 'I'll work *really* hard. I promise. Are there many in for the job?'

'Loads,' Miranda answered quickly. 'We'll let you know.'

Rosemary nodded. 'Thank you. Thanks.'

'I'll show you out,' Jane said. She tried to ignore Miranda who was rolling her eyes and pretending to gag. She'd tackle her later. As far as Jane was concerned, beggars couldn't be choosers. They needed a trainee and Rosemary would just have to do. She wondered if, in a few months, they would still be in business.

Patrick was going to flip when she told him about Cutting Edge.

## 3

JIM FINISHED WORK early that day. His new campaign ideas for Twizters crisps had just gone belly-up and staying in the office and pulling his hair out over it just didn't appeal. He dumped his laptop and his files in the back of his car along with a few packets of the crisps and, flicking on the radio, he drove out of the car park.

Boy, Jim thought, was he glad to have the day over with. All he wanted to do was get back to the flat, order a pizza and have a few cans with Fred. Maybe do a little work. He wasn't going to think beyond that.

The Declan D'arcy radio show was on as he manoeuvred his car on to the M50. Declan was interviewing a guy who'd managed to have sex sixteen times in one night.

'Aw,' Declan said, 'I've never managed that meself now. The auld wife got tired after ten.'

Jim laughed and wondered if Jane was listening.

'So,' Declan went on, 'have you a super-turbo-charged dick or what?'

Jim laughed again. Jesus, Jane was going to go mad. She hated when her dad went on like that on air. She'd be in a foul mood when he got home.

But he wasn't going home.

This was the third time he'd done that this week. Jim indicated and took the opposite lane to his normal one.

The grin disappeared from his face.

\* \* \*

He got a giant-sized pizza and some chips in a little place just up the road from where Fred lived. The food smelt delicious as he carried it to the door of the flat. This was home now, he'd have to learn to love it.

Fred was already inside, sprawled on the sofa, drinking a can of lager and watching the news. 'Aw, Jimbo,' he stood up and looked approvingly at the food. 'Sustenance. Good man.'

'Should still be hot.' Jim put the pizza and chips on the table as Fred handed him a can.

'Cheers.'

'Cheers.'

They ate in silence for a bit, commenting now and again on what was on the news. Jim, though he was hungry, found that he couldn't eat. It was sort of unreal, being here with Fred. Almost as if time had reversed itself and he was still a young lad who'd just left home. He missed the noise of his kids squabbling, the sound of Jane yelling at them to stop, the buzz of the heating system, the way Jane's cold feet always found their way between his legs when she got into bed. All the little things that he'd never really thought about before. The things he knew he shouldn't think about if he was to stay sane.

'So,' Fred asked after a bit, 'what's the story? You left her for good?'

Jim flinched. Fred was a good mate, he'd taken him in without asking any questions but he certainly wasn't going to lay it all out for him now. And, to be honest, even if he'd wanted to, he wasn't sure that he could. 'I guess.'

'Why?'

'Aw, you know, just wanted a younger model.'

'Yeah, figures. What age is she, about thirty-four or something?'

Jim was about to laugh until he realised that Fred was actually dead serious. 'Jesus,' he said instead. 'I was only jokin'.'

'Yeah yeah. I *knew* that.' Fred retorted, blushing. He took a swig of his can. So – did you have an affair? She find you wearing her knickers – what?'

Jim shrugged. 'Na. Nothing like that.' He took a slice of pizza and bit into it. Fred was still staring at him. 'Look, it doesn't matter, right. It's over.' He hated the sound of those words but he guessed he'd have to get used to them. 'Over.'

Fred gulped. He wasn't much good at all this nursemaid crap but his girlfriend, Gillian, had told him to be understanding. 'He's going to be upset, Freddie,' she'd said. 'And maybe he might want to talk about it.'

'Yeah, but what about me? Maybe I *don't* want to talk about it,' he'd said. 'He's better off without Jane. She's an awful bossy bitch.'

'This guy,' Gillian had said emphatically, 'is your *friend*, Freddie. He might need you.'

Sweat broke out on Fred's forehead. He hoped desperately that Jim wouldn't need him. He didn't like being needed. But Gillian had been pressuring him for weeks to talk to Jim and if he didn't report something back to her soon she might dump him. So tonight was to be the night, he'd promised himself, as Gillian, with her huge breasts, was the best lay he'd ever had. So he took a deep breath and asked, 'And how do you feel about it being over?'

Jim almost choked on his drink. Lager came out of his mouth and down his nose. He coughed and his eyes began to water. 'What?'

'Forget it.' Fred shifted uncomfortably in his chair. 'Here, is there anything else on?' He pointed the remote at the telly and began flicking from station to station.

Jim mopped his nose with his sleeve. *How did he feel about it?* He looked at Fred's red face and couldn't help being amused. He'd known this guy for years and they'd never talked about anything. They'd just *done* stuff.

'Have you done a course in the new man experience?' he asked.

Fred's flush deepened. 'I was going to say,' he muttered, still not looking at Jim, 'that if you want a shoulder to cry on, you can piss off out of here.'

Jim laughed.

'And secondly,' Fred, now that he'd managed to save some face, added, 'I'm heading out on Saturday night. You can come if you want. We have to get you circulating again Jimbo – throwing some body shapes.'

'I have piles of work on and I've got to take the kids out that day too.'

'Oh right.' Fred made a face. 'Bummer.'

Fred's momentary lapse into a caring sharing man had been only fleeting, Jim thought. He resisted the urge to tell Fred that he didn't think he'd ever want to go out again. How could he when he'd had it all once? There was no way Fred would ever get his head around that one. For Fred, life was one big party.

Lucky bastard.

# 4

'I HEARD,' DI SAID nonchalantly, as she sidled up beside Jane, 'that Granddad had sex with Grandma ten times in the one night.'

'Mmm.'

'Imagine,' Diane went on, '*ten* times.'

Jane said nothing, just continued to mash the spuds.

'Is it possible to have sex ten times in a row?' Di asked, plucking out some potato with her finger and eating it.

'I don't know and I don't care.'

'God, there's no need to be so narky – I'm only saying . . .'

'Well don't. Your granddad just makes these things up.'

Diane folded her arms and cocked her head to one side. 'If Dad was here, *he'd* laugh – not like you.'

She'd been hearing this for the last three months. According to Di, Jim laughed at everything. Jane couldn't help her sharp tone as she replied, 'Well he isn't here – is he? He's left us.'

'He hasn't left *us*,' Diane's eyes sparkled with tears. 'He's just left *you*!'

'Thanks.' Jane turned back to the spuds. Di's words hurt her more than anything else she might have said. She gulped hard so that she wouldn't blubber.

'Sorry,' Di said, sounding sulky. 'I guess that wasn't very nice.'

She *was* going to start blubbering. Di issuing an apology was a rare and touching event. 'No it wasn't nice,' she agreed, 'but it was true though.' She attempted a smile. 'He hasn't left you. I'm glad you know that.'

'And he wouldn't have left you if you hadn't been horrible to him,' Di said, sounding hopeful. 'I mean, Ma, you don't have to cry over it, it can be fixed if only—'

'He's not coming back,' Jane said gently. 'It wasn't working. You know—'

'I don't want to talk about it.' Di flounced out of the kitchen.

Jane heard her stomping upstairs before finally slamming her bedroom door. Jesus, she hoped things got easier. Still, they couldn't get much worse.

*Dong!*

*Dong!*

Jane dumped the plates on the table and wondered who could be calling at dinnertime. It couldn't be the milkman, he never came on Thursdays, it couldn't be Libby, Di's mate, as Di had come straight from Libby's after school, though Jane, seeing her daughter's rumpled shirt, had wondered, and it certainly wasn't anyone for Owen, because as far as she knew, Owen didn't have any friends – none that called to the house anyway – and it couldn't be . . . She stopped dead halfway to the door. Through the frosted glass, she made out the shape of someone quite tall. Someone quite thin. And if it was who she thought it was, someone quite unwelcome.

'Please God, don't let it be my mother,' she whispered. 'Oh God, don't do this to me, not now.' She opened the door a fraction.

'Oh God—'

'Jane. Dahling!'

It *was* her mother, standing in the porch with two enormous suitcases, four or five plastic bags, and her fur coat draped over her shoulders. Her hair was caught up in a rather elaborate bun and her flawlessly made-up face was spoilt by a sulky pout which pushed her lips out and showed all her fine lines off to perfection.

God was doing his best to really piss her off, Jane thought. The last person she needed to see right at that minute was her mother.

'Mam.' She didn't attempt a smile. 'This is a surprise.'

'Jane – dahling,' her mother said again. She blinked rapidly and tossed her head. 'I've . . .' she gave a big lick of her lips '. . . I've just had the most awful time.' Stepping into the hall, she wrapped her arms around her daughter.

Hairspray stung Jane's nostrils and the stench of perfume made her eyes water. She hoped this display of anguish didn't mean what she thought it meant. Reluctantly she patted her mother on her fur-lined back.

'I've left him,' her mother sighed.

'Again?' Jane wriggled out of her mother's embrace. This was not happening. 'What did you leave him for *this time*?'

'Don't say *this time* as if I'm always doing it,' her mother chastised.

'Mam, you *are* always doing it. Ever since I was a kid you've been doing it. Now, forgive me if I don't take you seriously . . .'

'There's no need to be so cranky, dahling.' Her mother gave a big false smile. 'No need at all.'

'I think there is.' Jane folded her arms and glared at her mother. She was not moving in. There was *no way* she was moving in.

'Did you *hear* your father's show today?' The smile disappeared from her mother's face and the pout returned. 'Did you hear what he said?'

'Nope. You know I don't listen to him.' Jane didn't move. If she went back into the kitchen, her mother would be sure to follow her, bags and all. There'd be no getting rid of her then.

'Well,' her mother closed her eyes. 'He told the whole nation that we,' she shook her head, 'I won't say "made love" because that barbarian wouldn't know the *meaning* of the word, but he told the whole nation that we'd had sex ten times in one night.'

'And?' Jane tried to look as if it wouldn't bother her.

'Oh come on, Jane.' Fluttering hands crept to her mother's throat. 'How would you like it if Jim went into work and bragged about you and him in bed – huh?'

22

Jane couldn't help it, she flinched at the mention of Jim. Then said ruefully, 'Well, that's not going to be too likely, is it?'

'Ohhh,' her mother flapped her hand about, 'you know, if he'd said it *before* he left. Well, you wouldn't have been too pleased, would you?'

'Mam – I don't see what—'

'That father of yours needs therapy,' her mother went on. 'Huh, he'd need a scaffold to keep it up for ten rounds.'

She really didn't need to hear this. 'Look, Mother—'

'So I'm moving in with you for a while until I decide what to do. Your father knows all about it.'

'You're moving in with me? Like – who decided that?'

'Well,' her mother tossed her hand in the air, 'you'd hardly see me out on the street, would you? You've always been a very good daughter.'

'Mam, my kids have been through enough lately without you dumping your problems on us as well.'

'I'm not dumping my problems on anyone! Just say it – if you don't want me here, just say it.'

Oh for Christ's sake! Jane clenched her fists. 'Where will you sleep?'

'Well, Jim has gone, there's sure to be room, isn't there? Anyway, I don't mind, dahling. Don't worry about me. I'll sleep anywhere. Put me on the floor if you must.'

She'd love to do just that. But she knew she wouldn't. 'OK. But I'm warning you, Mam, you can't go upsetting the kids – right?'

'You are a star, dahling. A star.' Her mother turned and began tugging at her suitcases. 'I'll just leave them here – I'll bring them up later.'

'I'm still not sure this is a good idea, Mam.'

'OK, we'll get Owen to bring them up. He's a big strong boy. Now,' her mother smiled brightly, 'something smells nice. Is that chicken?'

*   *   *

Diane and Owen accepted the fact that their granny was staying for a bit without so much as a bat of an eyelid.

'So, Gran,' Diane began. 'Have—'

'Less of the "Gran" there now,' Sheila D'arcy said briskly. 'Nana Sheila sounds *so* much *nicer*, doesn't it?'

Jane rolled her eyes.

'So, *Nana*,' Diane stressed the 'nana', 'have you left Granddad *again*?' Even more stress was placed on the 'again'.

Sheila tittered and looked to Jane for guidance.

Jane shot Diane a look which she ignored.

'Well, have you?' Diane demanded.

'Maybe for a little while,' Sheila said. 'Me and your granddad – we're not getting on too well.'

'Oh.' Diane gave her a cheeky grin. 'That's not what he said on the radio today.'

Owen spat out his dinner and started to laugh.

Sheila went bright red.

Suppressing a grin, Jane ordered Di to leave the table.

'I only—'

'Get upstairs and stay there for the night!'

Diane threw her knife and fork on to the table. 'Fine. I *only* asked.'

'Sorry, Mam,' Jane said, unable to stop grinning.

Diane slammed the kitchen door and Sheila winced. 'It's OK.' She mopped her face with her palm. 'That's only the beginning. Things will get worse, mark my words.'

If Diane had anything to do with it, Jane felt like saying, she was probably right.

Her mother went to bed at nine o'clock.

'At my age,' she said, 'I need all the sleep I can get. Twelve hours a night stops one fine line every ten years.'

Where on earth had she heard that load of rubbish? Jane wondered.

'Your father, the barbarian, had a beauty expert on his show last week. She said lots of sleep was a wonderful thing. So I'll say goodnight.'

'You can have my room,' Jane said. 'I've changed the sheets.'

'All right, thank you, dahling. You are a star!'

Jane watched her mother leave. The least Sheila could have asked her was where she'd be sleeping. But that was her mother all over. Once she was OK no one else mattered.

'Oh, and Jane,' her mother poked her head back round the door, 'if your father rings, tell him I've gone out, all right?'

Her dad wouldn't ring. He always let Sheila stew for a week or so before telling her he loved her. He normally did it on his radio show and the audiences loved it. But Jane nodded and agreed.

'Good girl. Tra-la.'

'Where does she get those sayings from?' Owen whispered. 'Tra-la?'

Jane grinned. 'She thinks it sounds posh.'

Owen smiled back at her.

'Don't let your gran see you smiling,' she warned.

'Don't you mean me nana?' he joked.

He really was a great kid, Jane thought.

'So,' he asked, 'are you sleeping with her tonight?'

'Nope.'

'Are you on the sofa?' He looked at her anxiously. 'You can have my room if you want.'

'It's fine. I'll be in . . . ,' a lump formed in her throat before she continued, '. . . your brother's old room.'

'Oh.' He turned away. Stared hard at the telly. 'OK.'

'So I'll be fine,' Jane said.

He didn't answer and she didn't press him. Owen, like them all, found it hard to talk about Matt.

She waited until everyone was asleep before going up herself. There was something about looking in on her kids when they were sleeping that made her happy. Di was in her black bedroom,

25

with her black duvet thrown aside and her long legs sprawled across her bed. An enormous pink teddy, which took up a whole corner of the room, spoiled the Goth effect she was trying to create and Jane smiled. Di looked angelic when she was asleep, no sulky pout, no sneer, just a good-looking fifteen-year-old kid. 'Night Di,' she whispered.

Jane closed the door gently and padded to Owen's room. She knew by his breathing that he was still awake, though she let him think that she thought he was asleep. 'Night Owen.'

Finally, she turned to her own room, well, Matt's room. It was the smallest room for the smallest kid. Painted red for Manchester United, scarves and posters adorned the walls. She'd put a United duvet on the bed. Sometimes it hurt her to come in here, other times it gave her comfort. As she snuggled up under the duvet and found Keano, Matt's old brown teddy named after Roy Keane, she felt close to her child. Burying her face in the soft brown teddy, she imagined that she could still smell the scent of her youngest son. 'Night Matt,' she murmured.

## 5

THE BUZZ OF the doorbell woke him. Jim rolled over and fell on to the floor. 'Shit,' he muttered as he picked himself up. If he wasn't going to end up crippled from the sofa bed, he was going to end up with concussion. Every morning since last week, he'd rolled over to look at the alarm clock and fallen out on to the floor.

'Shit!' the parrot shrieked.

Jim grimaced. That bird was too clever. Say anything remotely crude and he would pick up on it. It'd be screeching 'shit' the whole day long now. Just as well he wasn't going to be here, he had to pick up his kids at lunchtime.

He tried to focus on what had woken him.

*Buzzz!*

Yeah, right – the buzzer. He padded barefoot towards the door. It was probably Fred, he hadn't heard him come back last night, and knowing Fred, he had probably lost his key. Jim opened the door without bothering to see who it was.

'Hiya, is Freddie here?'

Jim started at the female voice and then became aware that he was wearing an old T-shirt and boxer shorts. He knew he was blushing as he stammered out an embarrassed, 'Eh, sorry? What?'

A small girl with brown fluffy hair gave him an amused smile. 'Gillian,' she said in what was an unmistakable New York accent. 'Hiya,' she extended her hand towards him, 'pleased ta meet ya.'

Jim shook her hand and gave her a sheepish grin. 'I thought you were Fred,' he mumbled. 'I would've thrown on some extra clothes otherwise.'

Gillian flapped her hand at him and came further into the flat. 'Naw! You look *great*. Men's legs are always nicer than women's. Less fat on them, don't ya know?' She rapped smartly on Fred's bedroom door. 'Hey, you in there! Ged up! Ged up!'

There came a sort of whimpering sound from within.

'He's gonna be in major pain today.' Gillian stalked over to the press and took some Disprin down. 'The guy couldn't even stand up last night. I drove him here and shoved him outa my car. I mean, no way was I gonna carry him up to this place – d'ya know what I mean?'

Jim nodded. Jesus, he must've been totally out of it if he hadn't heard Fred coming in. Maybe the cans of lager before bed had helped.

Gillian poured some water into a glass and dropped in the Disprin. She carried them towards Fred's room. 'Make us a cuppa tea, will you, honey?' she yelled over her shoulder at Jim.

While she was gone, Jim hastily shoved on a pair of jeans. By the time she came back out, he had made a pot of tea.

'Whoever had you, had you well trained,' Gillian smiled, sliding into a seat and watching as Jim poured her a cuppa.

'Sugar?' Jim asked.

'No thanks.' Gillian patted her stomach. 'Dieting – don't ya know.' She picked up her cup and smiled at Jim.

He smiled uneasily back. He knew it was mad, but suddenly, being semi-single again made him really self-conscious about talking to women. He'd always been a bit of a disaster at it before, but with Jane he'd gained more confidence. He used to be a right eejit, taking stuff too seriously and getting tongue-tied, and now it looked as if he was reverting to type. He managed another silly smile at her before turning away.

'So,' Gillian said, 'Freddie tells me you're . . . ,' she lowered her voice and spoke sympathetically, '. . . separated.'

'Uh-huh.' He stared into his tea. He wasn't going to discuss his personal life with a stranger when he still hadn't got used to the idea himself.

'That's tough,' Gillian said. 'And Freddie tells me you've . . . what?' She screwed up her face. '*Piles* of kids?'

'Yeah, well Freddie thinks one kid is too much.'

Gillian cackled and clapped her hands delightedly. 'You're right. You're absolutely right. He hates kids, just hates them,' she giggled. 'I have a niece living over he-a and I take her out with us now and again. Freddie can't talk to her, can't relate to her. He asks her stupid questions.' She nodded and grinned at Jim. 'You're absolutely right.'

Jim grinned. At least the girl was under no illusions about Fred the way that all the millions of others he'd dated had been. 'So, do you want toast?' He stood up from the table. 'I'm just about to make some.'

'Mmm, better not. Fighting the flab, don't ya know?'

Jim shoved some toast under the grill and stood with his back to her. He prayed that Fred would appear soon.

'I hope Freddie is treating you well,' Gillian went on. 'I said to him that if you eva need a night out, to come out with us, there's no problem about it at all. I've loads of girlfriends so it's not as if you'll be, you know, a *spare* or anything.'

'Thanks,' Jim grinned at her complete lack of tact. 'Being a spare would be one of my major nightmares.'

'Yeah. Mine too.' Gillian agreed, missing the irony. She held her nails to the light and said, 'So, anytime – it's no problem.'

'Ta.'

'Now, where is he?' Gillian stood up. 'Freddie,' she said loudly, 'if you don't ged up now, I'm leaving.' She spoke to Jim. 'We're meeting up with some friends and then going hiking.'

'Hiking?'

'Oh yeah, best way to spend a Saturday. Keeps ya fit.'

Gillian must be some girl, Jim thought. Fred on a hike – it didn't bear thinking about.

Just then Fred, dressed in combats, came out of his room. He looked pretty crap, Jim thought. He must have really hit the bottle the night before. 'Hi yez,' he muttered.

'You betta hurry,' Gillian looked at her watch. 'Debbie and Liz and Edmond are leaving in half an hour. I told them we'd bring the food and stuff.'

Fred turned bloodshot eyes on his girlfriend. 'Listen baby, just don't mention food, OK?'

Gillian giggled.

'I hear you're going on a hike,' Jim grinned.

'Yeah,' Fred nodded.

'Freddie loves the outdoor life, don't ya Freddie?'

'Yeah.' Fred shot Jim a look, begging him not to disagree. 'There's nothing like it.'

'Yeah, he always did,' Jim began to butter his toast. 'Sky diving, he loved that more than anything. He was great at it.'

'No way!' Gillian looked impressed.

'Yeah. *And* he was a mean marathon runner, weren't you,' Jim paused and added, '*Freddie?*'

'Aw, no I wouldn't go so far as—'

'Oooh,' Gillian interrupted, wrapping her arms around Fred and snuggling her face into his hair. 'You never told me that – you are just the most modest man eva!'

'Aw, yeah, well—'

'Wait till I tell the others about you. A real marathon runna. Wow!'

Fred disentangled himself from Gillian's embrace. He sneered over at Jim. 'Don't go telling any more of my secrets, OK?'

'Fine by me.' Jim bit into his toast and grinned at his mate. Jesus, the guy must be in love.

When Fred and Gillian eventually left, Jim had a shower. He was picking the kids up at one o'clock and taking them out for lunch. Then they were going to head off somewhere for the afternoon.

He felt weirdly nervous as he drove to the house. Every Saturday and Sunday, before picking them up, he felt the same way – it was almost as if he expected the place to have changed. Of course it hadn't. It looked exactly the same as when he'd left. It was still painted white, the gate going up the driveway still creaked when he pushed it open and the front door was still red. The bell jangled when he pressed it, just like it had for the past fifteen years.

He felt sick as he waited for the door to open. He wondered if Jane would answer. She hadn't answered the door since he'd left, always leaving the kids to do it. The most he'd heard her say was a 'goodbye' to them. He really would like to see her.

From inside the house, he heard an unmistakable voice. 'Diane, Owen, your father's here.'

Oh shit. Jim nervously rubbed his hands through his hair and patted himself down. What the hell was his mother-in-law doing here? That was all he needed – her looking down her haughty nose at him. It was ridiculous, he knew, but Sheila D'arcy always made him feel like a kid with his fly open.

The door opened and Sheila, dressed and made up to perfection as usual, stood looking down at him. 'Hello, James,' she said, a big stiff smile on her face.

'Sheila,' Jim nodded to her and attempted a smile.

'I suppose you've come to collect your poor children from your abandoned wife.'

'You were always dead clever.'

Her big stiff smile stopped and sort of hung on her face like a dirty piece of washing and Jim felt like laughing. But before she could make a retort, Diane pushed past her and flung herself on him.

'Oh, Dad, it's awful here without you!'

Jim was startled at the display of affection. Diane was not normally a hugging type of girl. She had now wrapped her arms

31

around his neck, almost strangling him, and had her head buried in his shoulder.

'That's a fine thing to be saying,' Sheila sniffed. 'And your poor mother working her fingers to the bone to put food on the table.' She looked accusingly at Jim as she added, 'She's working a half-day today.'

'That's because Mir is sick,' Diane retorted, her arm still around Jim's neck.

'She needs the money too!' Sheila snapped.

Diane scowled at her. 'Only 'cause *you're* here,' she muttered.

'What?' Sheila frowned at her. 'What was that?'

'Is Owen ready?' Jim asked quickly, giving Di a dig in the ribs to shut her up.

'I'll go check, Dad,' Diane said. 'Back in a second.' She gave him a huge smile and without looking at her grandmother, sauntered up the stairs.

Sheila glared after her, then turned and glared at Jim. Eventually she said, 'I hope you're proud of yourself, abandoning my daughter.'

'I'd hardly—'

'Goodbye.' She turned and left him standing at the door.

Anne Robinson had nothing on his mother-in-law. Still, he guessed that she was only sticking up for her daughter. He'd often thought that it must be nice to have someone who'd do that.

Unconditional love. He'd never experienced it until he'd met Jane.

The tramp of feet on the stairs made him look up. Owen and Diane stood there.

'Hiya Dad,' Owen muttered.

Jim smiled at his son and daughter. He'd gladly confront ten Sheilas just to see them.

Diane danced out the door, pulling on her black, tattered coat. 'So, where to?' she asked.

'Lunch first?'

32

'Great.'

Owen said nothing, just followed Diane.

Seeing them together, one so bubbly, the other so quiet, Jim realised how much he was missing them.

## 6

'THANK THE LORD those two have left for school!' Sheila exclaimed, coming into the kitchen on Monday morning. She wore a nightdress made from yard upon yard of flimsy material that floated behind her as she walked.

She looked like a jellyfish, Jane thought – a big poisonous one with loads of little tentacles floating about all over the place.

'I could murder a cup of tea,' Sheila said wanly, as she massaged her temples. She sat down gingerly on a chair. 'The noise of those two getting up has started a migraine. I mean, *really*,' she gave a humourless laugh, 'does Diane have to shout *all* the time? And the way you scream at them from the bottom of the stairs is quite unnecessary, Jane. I don't know, all this stress and fighting is really getting to me.'

'Stress? What stress? Was it stressful being rude to Jim on Saturday?'

'I wasn't—'

'Diane told me.' Jane pushed a cup of tea in her mother's direction and said firmly, 'It's none of your business, Mam, so keep out.'

Sheila pursed her lips. 'Well, you are my daughter and I have to stand by you.'

'No you don't – I have to apologise to him now!'

'You'll do no apologising on my account.'

'So you'll do it yourself then?'

'I said nothing to him that wasn't true. He abandoned you.'

Sheila picked up her tea and took a sip. 'Mind you, it's not the first time he's abandoned you – is it? He was a disgrace . . .'

'Mam, stop!'

'I'm only saying that I *know* what it's like to be abandoned, dahling. I mean, I'm forty or so years old and all alone. That's no joke.'

'Mam, *you* left Dad. You weren't abandoned.'

Sheila sniffed. 'Well . . . I'm abandoned *now*. Your father hasn't even bothered to pick up the phone.' She emphasised 'your father' as if it was all Jane's fault.

'He'll ring.' He had to, Jane thought. She hadn't time to sort out her mother's life as well as her own. That's if she could even sort her own out.

'I suppose so,' Sheila said, not sounding particularly interested. She focused her gaze on Jane. 'So,' she asked sympathetically, 'how are *you*, dahling? It must be terribly hard for you. I couldn't cope on my own with two children.'

No surprises there then, Jane thought, smiling suddenly.

'What's so funny?'

'Nothing.' Jane picked up her bag. 'Listen, Mam, I've got to go. See you this evening.'

'Oh, I'll be on my own all day again, will I?'

'The kids will be back for lunch.'

'Oh.'

'And if you get too bored, you can do a bit of hoovering.'

Sheila laughed. 'And what would the cleaner say – me hoovering?'

'Mam,' Jane said patiently, not knowing whether to laugh or cry, 'I don't *have* a cleaner. I live in the real world. You should visit it sometime.' She ignored the dismay on Sheila's face as she picked her coat up from the back of the chair. 'I'll be back around six. One of the kids will start dinner.'

She was about to leave when from the kitchen Sheila called, 'But you're only joking about the hoovering, aren't you dahling?'

'Nope,' Jane shouted back, grinning. 'The Hoover's under the stairs. Plug it in, press a button and Bob's your uncle. Bye now.'

When she arrived into work, Mir was puffing madly on a fag and disregarding the anti-smoking ban as usual. She was also grouching about something. Patrick, who normally made clucking noises and provided her with tissues, was instead mincing up and down the coffee room, shaking his head and alternately opening and fastening the top button of his indigo shirt.

'Hi yez.'

'They've *polished* the windows,' Patrick said frantically as he scurried across to her. Then taking a deep breath, he blurted out, 'They've also put up their shelving and, Jane,' he swallowed, '*you want to see the decor.*'

Momentarily confused, Jane looked to Mir for guidance.

'Cutting Edge,' Mir barked. 'Patrick has been nosing around the competition.'

'And so have you.' He turned back to Jane. 'Go up there now and have a look.'

'Will you let me get a cup of tea first?' Jane flicked on the kettle.

Patrick flicked it off again. 'No, go now, go now. Go on.' He made whooshing motions with his hands. 'You'll be *suicidal* when you see it.'

'And that's supposed to inspire me to go?'

Mir snorted back a laugh then said, 'Fag, Patrick?'

Patrick whirled on Miranda. 'This is not the time for insults – we have to stick together!'

'Naw, I was asking you if you wanted a fag.' Miranda held out the box to him. 'It'll calm you down, stop your frillies getting in a twist. Though with the weekend I've had, I'm the one who needs calming down. It was fuckin' awful.'

Patrick ignored her. 'Jane, I'm telling you, they're going to,' he paused and hissed dramatically, 'put – us – under.'

'No they won't,' Jane flicked the kettle back on. 'Our customers are very loyal.' Even to her own ears she sounded a bit freaked.

'Please, Jane?' Patrick gave her another push. 'Please just go and have a look. For me? I'll have tea made for when you come back. Mir has already seen it. Isn't this going to be a disaster for us, Mir?'

'Not as fuckin' disastrous as my weekend,' Mir said sharply. 'Now, if yez think being put out of business is bad, you should have been there when Drew, that's the musician I was tellin' yez about, left me for a complete bimbo on Saturday.' She made jabbing motions towards them with her cigarette. 'I swear to Christ, I couldn't score if I was a friggin' drug addict.'

Jane did not want to hear about Mir's weekend. It couldn't have been as surreal as hers: sitting watching *Coronation Street* while her mother clipped her toenails and complained about her father, while her daughter went out saying she was meeting a friend and came back with her hair all over the place and love bites on her neck. Nope, maybe heading up the road to view the competition would be preferable.

'A nice strong cup, right?' she ordered. 'And no sugar.'

'I dunno,' Patrick was already getting her cup down. 'Sugar is good for shock and you might just need it.'

The Cutting Edge logo was emblazoned across the window. The C and E intertwined against a neon-blue lightning streak. It was very striking. Not classy like theirs, Jane thought, just striking.

She put her palms up to the window and, pressing her nose against the glass, peered in. Inside, as Patrick had said, stainless-steel sinks gleamed on black marble pedestals. The floor tiles were a mixture of enormous white, black and steel grey triangles. The walls were white as was the ceiling. But what on earth was that yoke hanging from the ceiling? Attempting to get a better look, Jane put her knees on to the window sill and pressed closer to the glass. It looked like the Starship *Enterprise*. It was some sort of light fixture.

37

'Any more leaning on that window and you'll smash it,' an amused male voice remarked behind her.

'Aw, wouldn't that be a pity,' Jane scoffed, turning slightly. 'It'd ruin the lovely logo.'

'It certainly would.'

Looking back inside, she went on, 'I'm just trying to figure out what that yoke is that's hanging from the ceiling.'

'It's a—'

'It reminds me of something that gave me nightmares when I was a kid.'

'Really?'

'Uh-huh. It's like a giant fungus. Come here and look.'

'No, I've—'

'I mean, honestly, who would put something like that in there?'

'I would.'

The shock of his words and the fact that he obviously had something to do with Cutting Edge, caused Jane to lose her balance. She tumbled off the sill and on to the ground.

The stranger stood looking at her as she clambered to her feet, her ankle throbbing. Huh, she thought, he *could* have offered to help.

'Um, sorry about that.'

'What?' He didn't sound amused any more. 'Falling over or slagging off something I paid a fortune for?'

She couldn't look him in the face she was so mortified. 'Both,' she muttered, making a big deal of brushing down her jeans. 'I was only joking though.' You spineless git, she mentally cursed herself.

'So you didn't have nightmares about giant fungi?'

'Well, no . . . what I mean is . . . well . . .' her voice trailed off. 'Look, I'm sorry, all right?' she said ruefully, finally plucking up the courage to look at him.

He was, as Mir would say, a waste out of bed. Tall and attractive with dark brown hair cut military short. His face was tanned and weather-beaten, which made the pale blue glint of his eyes even more startling. Yet it was his eyes that spoilt his handsome-ness. They were, Jane thought, shivering slightly, ice-blue and very cold. They belied the grin on his face. He would have been madly fanciable otherwise.

'No problem.' There was a flash of white teeth. He jangled some keys in his hand, 'You can come in and have a look around if you want. It's always nice to get a female perspective. And I promise, right, that the light won't attack you.'

'Aw, no.' Jane backed away, suddenly wanting to leave. 'I'm late for work now. I'd better go.'

'Hope you're not some kind of fashion-magazine guru, are you?'

Jane gave a weak laugh in response.

'Naw, thought not,' he said and she wasn't sure if it was an insult. 'Anyway, if you do work around here, maybe we'll see you coming in some time for a cut. We're opening up in a week and all cuts will be half-price for the month of February.'

'Half price?' She felt like puking.

'Uh-huh, and we'll be having a big opening, with radio and press and free glasses of wine all day, so do come to that. Tell all your workmates to come too.'

'Oh,' Jane gave a brittle smile, 'I'll be telling them *all* about it.'

'Pete Jordan by the way,' he thrust out his hand.

Pete Jordan? *The* Pete Jordan? Jane gulped. He of the Cutting Edge empire. Shit! Shit! Shit! 'Jane McCarthy,' she muttered with bad grace. This guy was out to bury her and he didn't even know it. Well, she certainly wasn't telling him who she was – it was the only advantage she had over him, so far.

'Nice to meet you, Jane, see you around some time then?'

'Aw, I shouldn't think so.' She couldn't resist it. 'I go to the place down the road. They're very good. Very talented.' She stressed the 'talented'.

'What place?'

'Patrick Costelloe's.'

'Oh, *that* place.' He spoke with disdain. 'Sure all they do is OAPs.'

OAPs? *OAPs?* The nerve!

'Actually,' her voice had an indignant edge, which she couldn't curb, 'they do all sorts of people.'

'Do they? That's—'

'They've a loyal clientele,' Jane carried on, unable to help herself. 'Everyone loves the cosy atmosphere there.'

'Aw, sure, well if ever you want a change, you know where we are.'

'I won't be changing.'

'Eh, right.' Pete sounded as annoyed as she felt. 'Well, it's up to you. Anyway, we'll be around a long time. This'll be our flag-ship store.'

Which meant that her place would probably be the *Titanic*; the thought came unbidden and she quashed it. No way. No bloody way! She'd worked too hard to let him come and mess it up for her now.

Pete started unlocking the door. 'Sure you won't come in?'

'Yeah. Thanks. Bye.'

Without even waiting for him to reply she left.

'Good luck,' he called after her.

Good luck? She'd need a miracle.


A miracle was what they all needed when Rosemary started work. Jane had done her best to explain to Patrick that Rosemary was the only applicant to turn up for the interview and that she wasn't exactly what they had been looking for. Patrick had been OK about it, but Jane got the feeling that he hadn't completely grasped the situation. He was so caught up with Cutting Edge moving in on their doorstep that when Rosemary arrived with her crazy ponytail and disastrous clothes, he mistook her for a customer.

'Sorry honey, can't fit you in today, we're fully booked. You'd need a good two hours, minimum.'

'No,' Jane heard Rosemary giggle uneasily, 'I'm Rosemary. Rosemary Dalton – your new person.'

'My new—?'

'She's the trainee,' Jane tried to sound unfazed. She wished she could stop Patrick from gazing in such horrified amazement at Rosemary's hair and clothes.

'The new trainee,' Patrick muttered. 'Oh, right.'

'Rosemary, this is Patrick,' Jane tried to cover up the awkwardness, 'he's my partner.'

'Hiya,' Rosemary grinned brightly, 'pleased to meet ya.'

'Yeah. Sure.' Patrick was having difficulty getting his composure back.

'Listen,' Rosemary went on, 'Thanks a *million* for giving me this job. No one believed me when I said I'd got a *real* job. My dad laughed and everything.' She stopped. 'But now I'm the one laughing, isn't that right?' She didn't wait for a reply. She took off her coat and looked around. 'Is there somewhere I can put this?'

'Don't tempt me,' Miranda whispered, coming up behind Jane.

'In the office.' Patrick still couldn't tear his eyes away from Rosemary's hair, though he was attempting to smile at her. 'Jane,' he said faintly, 'show her, will you?'

'Sure.' Jane was glad to get away from him. She knew he'd have something to say to her later.

She smiled at Rosemary. 'This way.'

The girl followed her so closely that Jane could feel her breath on the back of her neck when she talked. And she talked non-stop.

'Thanks. Wow.' On entering the office she gave a squeal of recognition. 'This is where I had my interview, isn't it?'

'Yes.' Jane hung her coat on the coat stand.

'And it's really an office, is it?'

'Office-cum-coffee-break-room.'

'Right, I see.' Rosemary nodded sagely. 'An office-cum-

41

coffee-break-room,' she murmured as if committing it to memory. She gave another bright smile. 'So – what will I be doing? I can't wait to start. I've been looking forward to it all weekend.'

'Well, you'll be sweeping the floor,' Jane said, leading her back out into the salon. 'It's important to do it at least after every haircut.'

'No problem. I can do that. I like sweeping floors.'

'And we need fresh towels for every customer. And eventually we'll let you shampoo hair.'

'Wash hair. Wow!'

'The towels are in here,' Jane showed her a large press at the end of the room. 'Every evening we take them down the road to the launderette and then we collect them again in the morning. You can do that from now on.'

'Yes, yes. Brilliant.'

'And you can work out front too.'

Rosemary's face dropped. 'Oh . . . oh, right.'

'Is something wrong?'

'Well, I . . . you know . . .' Rosemary winced. 'I want to be a hairdresser – not a billboard. I mean, if I have to, I will, but it's not, not me, really. I get cold easily too.'

'Out front,' Jane repeated, trying not to grin, 'on the reception desk. Taking appointments?'

'Ohhhh. Right.' Rosemary blushed. 'Oh OK.' She nodded. 'Fine.' More nodding and blushing. 'I mean, that's brilliant. Glamorous even.'

Her enthusiasm was kind of endearing. Jane smiled at her. 'We'll try not to work you too hard.'

'Oh right. OK. Yes. That's fine.'

Jane handed her the brush. 'Off you go then.' She pointed to where Mir was just dusting a customer down. 'Sweep up over there.'

Rosemary giggled. 'Oh, this is going to be brilliant, I just know it.' She held the brush to her and sighed happily.

42

'It'll be the best job in the world. Everyone seems so friendly. And so *glamorous*.' She stared at Miranda. 'With my first pay packet I'm going to buy a pair of the jeans that Miranda's wearing.'

Four of Rosemary's pay packets would hardly pay for a pair of Miranda's jeans, Jane thought.

Patrick beckoned Jane over a little while later.

'There you go,' he said to June Rodgers as he helped her on with her coat. 'Enjoy your bridge party.'

'Thank you,' June croaked, smiling at him. 'You do a lovely colour, Patrick.'

He smiled as she left, and then turned to Jane. 'Jane,' he said quietly, 'I don't know what it's going to take, or how much it'll cost us, but for Heaven's sake, do that child's hair.' He looked sorrowfully in the direction of his new trainee. 'She'll put us out of business quicker than you can say "Cutting Edge" walking about with a head like that on her.'

'I think we've more important things to discuss,' Jane said, ignoring him. 'Like what are we going to *do* about Cutting Edge?'

Patrick looked stricken. 'I don't know yet. We'll have to talk about it.'

'When?'

'Ooooh.'

'How about Sunday? My place?'

He nodded. 'Right. We'll draw up a plan of action.'

A plan of inaction more like, Jane thought in amusement. Patrick was useless when he was panicking.

'Around two or so all right? Jim'll have the kids and my mother's heading into town.'

'She still with you?'

'Yep.'

'Poor you.'

'Aw, she'll be heading home soon anyway – Dad'll start begging her to come back any time now.'

43

'So Sunday's fine then?'

'Yep.'

'And Rosemary's hair?'

'I'll have a word.'

'That's my girl.'

They grinned at each other and then turned their attention back to Rosemary. She looked over at them and started sweeping vigorously. Miranda's customer tripped over the brush.

'Ooohhh, sorry!'

Patrick sighed resignedly and went over to apologise. 'Soon, sweet cakes,' he begged as he left.


Patrick left work at four. The minute he went, Rosemary scurried over to Jane. 'Can I ask you something?' she whispered.

'Yeah.' Jane wondered how to broach her own question.

'Is he *gay*?' Rosemary whispered.

'Who? Patrick?'

'Uh-huh.'

'Yep. Eh Rosemary?'

'Wow!' Rosemary shook her head. 'Wow! Imagine. A real gay person. Wow!'

'It's not such a big deal, you know.' Really, Jane thought, Rosemary was exhausting. She was like a two-year-old kid the way she went on. Every experience appeared to amaze her completely. There seemed to be no bored cynical teenage side to her at all. 'Rosemary, I was wondering—'

'It's not a big deal to you 'cause you're *old*,' Rosemary was almost hyperventilating with excitement. 'You've seen loads of mad stuff. But like, I haven't. I didn't think gay people were really like that. I mean,' she said, as she leaned on her brush, 'he's good-looking, right? That's a dead giveaway. *And* the way he dresses. It's cool and yet it's too nice for a *real* guy.' She shook her head. 'Wow.'

Jesus, Jane thought. She couldn't remember the last time she'd been that amazed by anything. 'Look, Rosemary, about your hair—'

'Yeah, it's nice, isn't it?' She began to fiddle with the elastic band that tied it up, making Jane wince as it got caught time and time again. 'I got it done at Cutting Edge a few months back. I saved my dole for two months to get it done, but it was worth it. It's held its shape well, hasn't it?'

Once free of the band, her hair, which had appeared dishevelled, fell across her shoulders in glorious curls. In parts it was frizzy but it was still possible to see how it must have looked when she'd had it done.

'Wow,' Jane said.

Rosemary went to tie it up again.

'No, leave it.' Jane took the band from her. 'It looks well and maybe I can trim it for you and do a conditioning treatment on it.' She touched the ends of Rosemary's hair. 'It'll stop the frizz.'

Rosemary looked doubtful. 'Aw, I dunno. You might mess it up.'

'What?' Jane almost laughed.

'Well, I sort of trim it myself, you see,' Rosemary went on. 'Like, I don't want an old person's style.' She gazed around at the four waiting customers. 'I'm not after a blue rinse.'

'I know how to do hair,' Jane gawped at her. So much for thinking that the kid would jump at the offer.

'Yeah. Yeah. I know you do.' Rosemary smiled a big bright false smile.

Jane watched her hair as it caught the light. Bright, vibrant, slightly frizzy hair. Her fingers itched to style it. Still, if Rosemary wouldn't let her, she couldn't force her. Well, not for the moment anyhow. 'Just don't go telling the customers that you got it done at Cutting Edge,' she said. 'It's not good for business.'

Rosemary giggled and rolled her eyes. 'I'm not *stupid*, you know.'

'Wear it like that in future, it's nice.' Again she wanted to touch it. She'd always loved good hair.

'OK.' Rosemary blushed with pleasure. 'I will then. Yez are all so nice here.' Off she waltzed with the brush.

## 7

'WHAT THE HELL are you doing?'

What the hell was he *trying* to do more like, Jim thought in irritation. It was impossible to bring any work back to the flat, what with the noise of the parrot – who was currently screeching 'Fuck me sideways' courtesy of *Father Ted* – and the constant bombardment of talk from Fred.

'Well?' Fred asked as he buttoned up a lurid green shirt. 'What the hell are all those pieces of paper?'

'Statistics,' Jim muttered.

'Boor-ing!' Fred gave a giant yawn and plonked himself down beside Jim. 'Statistics on what?'

'On boring things,' Jim snapped.

'Ouch.' Fred made a face. 'Honest Jim, you are such a dry arse. Where's the craic in you gone? Jaysus, all you ever do is work. You never used to be like that.'

'I have two kids, half a mortgage and rent on a flat to pay.' Jim didn't look at Fred as he spoke. He studied the data for Twizters crisps and tried to stop himself from groaning. Philip, his biggest client, was going to flip unless he came up with a new angle pronto.

'I vote,' Fred was nudging him on the arm, 'that we head out on the town and get locked. I'll ring Gillian and cancel. It'll be just you and me – right?'

'Naw.' Jim shook his head and indicated his papers, 'I have to analyse this stuff.'

'Tonight? You have to do it tonight?'

Jim shrugged. He didn't, but working kept his mind off other things.

'Well?' Fred asked.

Maybe going out with Fred would be a blast. It always had been in the past, but they'd been a decade and a half younger then. Still, a few gargles wouldn't hurt and maybe getting drunk would be more fun than sitting in the flat. It might open up his mind too.

'Just for the one, right?' He folded away his papers. Grabbing a few packets of crisps, he said, 'I might bring these with me – leave them on a few tables – see what the reaction is.'

'Aw, sure, fuck it, bring the laptop too.' Fred rolled his eyes in exasperation.

Jim ignored him. 'Where to?'

'That's the Jimbo I know,' Fred grinned. He pulled his mobile from his pocket. 'Hang on till I give Gillian a ring. She'll be cool about it.'

'Na, it's OK,' Jim shrugged. 'Tell her to come too. The more the merrier.' Plus, if he wanted to leave, at least Fred would have Gillian for company.

'Great.' Fred gave him the benefit of his shiny smile. 'Let's head, shall we?'

The pub was hopping when they arrived. Fred was a master at pushing people out of his way and Jim trailed in his wake. He felt a bit out of it in his good suit trousers and shirt. At least he'd taken his tie off and worn a denim jacket instead of his suit jacket. If he hadn't, he'd have been completely overdressed. They probably wouldn't have served him because he looked too old or something mad stupid like that. Jesus, it was ages since he'd been out. Fred was king of everything. He ploughed towards Gillian's table hailing people along the way, slapping others on the back and roaring with loud laughter over the most inane comments.

'Hey,' Fred elbowed Jim, 'get a load of Gillian's mate Debbie – is she like Catgirl, or what?'

Jim looked. Jesus, what was that girl like?

'Catgirl', who was beside Gillian, was poured into and pouring out of a low-cut, skintight leather catsuit. Black hair cascaded over her shoulders.

'Hi,' she said. She gave Gillian a nudge, 'Hey, Gill, it's Freddie.'

'Aw, hiya baby,' Gillian blew him a kiss across the table. Her voice rose, 'And hiya Jim. Good for you. You finally came out!'

'He's not bleedin' gay,' Fred squeezed his way in beside Gillian. 'You want to watch what you say.'

People laughed.

Gillian patted the seat on the other side of her and wriggled towards Fred. 'Hey, Jim, sit down here.'

The last thing he wanted to do was to sit beside the catsuited girl, but he hadn't much choice. He sat down gingerly between them. 'Hi,' he muttered to her.

'Hello. It's Jim, is it?'

She had a deep, husky voice – very sexy. Jim gulped and nodded. 'Uh-huh.'

'Hey everybody, quiet.' Gillian clapped her hands and waited for people to look at her. 'This is Jim – Freddie's friend. He's staying at Freddie's for a while.'

'Hiya,' someone said.

More people introduced themselves and Jim promptly forgot their names. He just grinned self-consciously and wished that he'd told Fred to cancel with Gillian. He thought it was just going to be the three of them. His head was spinning. He hated crowds.

'News flash ov-a,' Gillian announced. She leaned towards Jim. 'So, whatcha having?'

'Na, it's OK, I'll get it.' Jim stood up and dug his hand into his pocket.

'No!' Gillian pulled him down. 'Freddie is going to the bar – it's ya first night out wid us, he'll buy.'

'The bitch has me broke,' Fred grumbled good-naturedly. 'Carlsberg, is it Jim?'

'Yeah. Thanks.'

Jim watched Fred leave and wondered if he'd get away with having just the one pint before heading back. It was stupid, but he felt guilty about being out.

'So, Jim,' Catgirl spoke, startling him, 'I'm Debbie. It's nice to meet you.' She extended a perfectly manicured hand.

Jim took her hand in his and stammered, 'Nice to meet you too.'

'So, how come you're with Freddie?' Debbie asked, releasing him and studying him with dark eyes.

'Well, I, eh—'

'Things that desperate?'

His bumbling reply shuddered to a halt. He looked up to see her smiling at him. He grinned back and nodded, 'Pretty much, yeah.'

Debbie laughed. She didn't look quite so vampish when she did that. 'Poor you. What happened? Did you take a vow of masochism or something?'

Jim grinned again, then saw that she was looking expectantly at him. 'Well,' he shrugged, 'it was more the "or something".'

'Yeah?'

Jesus, she really wanted an answer. He guessed that he'd better say it. Saying it made it awful real though. He began threading the beer mat in and out of his fingers.

'I, eh, I'm separated.'

'Oh. Right.'

Fortunately she didn't seem to know what to say to that. He wondered when Fred was coming back with the drinks.

'I think your reply has just stalled our conversation, huh?' Debbie said. 'I thought you were gonna say that you'd been evicted from your flat or that you'd lost your job or something.'

'No such luck.' He hadn't meant it to come out sounding so

50

bitter. Attempting to get things back on a less personal level, he muttered, 'I hate me bloody job.'

'You do?' She angled her body towards him. She had long, slim legs that seemed to go on forever. Jim wished he'd sat beside someone else. 'What is it you do?'

'Market crisps.'

'Sorry?'

'You're not the only one.'

She laughed. Her laugh was like her voice, deep and husky. 'No, I meant, what exactly is involved in marketing crisps?'

'Believe me,' Jim shook his head, 'you don't want to know.' He reached into his pocket and pulled out a few bags. 'I've got to market these. They want them to be called Twizters. Here, try a pack.'

'Is he fucking working again?' Fred's booming voice cut in on the conversation. He dumped a pint in front of Jim. 'Here, drink that up and forget about those bloody twistery things.'

Debbie had opened her packet and was busy examining the crisps. They were tight spirals. She took a nibble of one. 'Tastes fine.'

Jim nodded. 'Yeah, but would you have bought a packet of crisps called Twizters? Or would you have stuck to your Tayto or Hunky Dorys?' He looked eagerly at her.

Debbie shrugged. 'Stuck to what I know I guess.'

'That's what I figured,' Jim said glumly as he observed the others messing about with the bags he'd brought. One of the guys, whose name he couldn't remember, was making funny shapes out of them. He'd joined a few together and had the crisp chain dangling from his nose. Everyone was laughing. Jim grinned. Philip Logan would not be at all impressed to see his sophisticated snack being abused in such a way.

'So,' Debbie said, breaking into his thoughts, 'besides giving out freebies to a load of drunken adults, what else do you have to do to make these the next big thing?'

'You sure you want to know?' Jim looked at her doubtfully.

51

It was one thing not knowing what to say to women, but it was even worse boring them stupid.

Fred elbowed him in the ribs. 'Whoa Batman,' he whispered. 'You're away there.'

There was no way that Debbie could have failed to hear. Jim took a gulp of his drink so that he wouldn't have to look at her for a second. 'Don't mind him,' he eventually muttered.

'He's an asshole,' Debbie said loudly.

Fred didn't hear, he was busy regaling the table with his mad days at school. Gillian was clinging on to his arm and giggling frantically.

'I don't know what she sees in him,' Debbie said, quieter this time.

'Aw, he's all right.' Jim felt he had to stick up for Fred. 'He's been a good mate to me.' And he had. He'd rescued him more than once. 'I've known him years, he's good fun.'

Debbie shrugged, obviously not convinced. 'So, tell me about marketing these things,' she said. 'What do you do? Design cool new foil-wrapped packets for extra freshness and give them extra-strength onion flavour, or what?'

'Now you're attempting to trivialise my job,' Jim said in mock annoyance. 'I'll have you know, marketing the latest Cheese and Onion is damn hard work.'

'Cheese you off, does it?'

Jim laughed.


Debbie was good company. Jim talked to her for most of the night. She was easy to talk to, not at all as scary as he'd imagined. By the time he left, he was quite drunk. He'd had more than he'd had in ages and his head was spinning nicely.

'Thanks for the chat,' he smiled.

'Thanks for telling me all about crisps,' Debbie said back. 'I'll definitely buy your ones in future. What are the company called again?'

'Incredible Crisps.'

'Inedible Crisps?'

Jim grinned. 'Bye.'

'Nice to meet you. See you again maybe.'

'Maybe.' Jim nodded.

Debbie walked off. Jim couldn't help noticing the looks that she got as she walked through the pub.

Such a body.

She'd make some fella a very happy man.

He pulled on his jacket and left the pub.

It was later that night when the idea struck. He was just dozing off when it came to him – one of the best bloody ideas of his career.

## 8

H ER MOTHER HAD finally gone out. Jane heaved a sigh of relief as she heard the door slam. Sheila had been hard work this past week, monopolising the bathroom and leaving her false eyelashes in the sink. Jane had been forced to draw up a bathroom rota, much to her mother's chagrin.

Flicking on the television, Jane decided that she needed a break. The sounds of her two kids squabbling upstairs, she decided, was not going to interfere with her enjoyment of the Sunday film. They'd be heading out with Jim soon, so she figured she could put up with the noise of their arguments until then.

The title *Calamity Jane* appeared on screen. *Wonderful.* Doris Day had just begun to sing about her secret love being a secret no more when the doorbell rang.

She glanced out the window and saw Jim's Volvo at the gate. It sort of shocked her, seeing the car like that. Normally it was parked in the driveway with her car blocking it in. Jim used to tease her that the sight of her car would frighten any would-be thieves away. She smiled sadly as the memory washed over her.

The bell rang again.

'Di! Owen! Your Dad's here!'

'Just getting my jacket, Mam. Owen has hidden it,' Di yelled.

'Have not!'

They continued to fight and once again, Jim rang the bell. Jane willed one of the kids to come downstairs.

Nothing.

'Owen!'

'Down in a sec.'

It'd be pure childish not to answer the door, she thought, as she uncurled her feet from under her. After all, it was *only* Jim.

The sight of his tall silhouette through the glass made her realise quite suddenly how very weird things were. When she'd married Jim it was for ever. There was nothing about him that she hadn't loved. And even though she'd been expecting Di at the time, it had only made the two of them happier. She remembered him proposing to her in a McDonald's car park and when she'd said yes, he'd shoved an onion ring on her finger. It had been one of those rare moments when happiness is recognised and enjoyed and she wouldn't have traded it for anything. Even then, she hadn't really realised how lucky she was. But then again, neither had he.

Heart thumping, she plastered a smile on her face and opened the door. 'Hi.' It was the first time she'd seen him in months. On weekends she normally made sure she was out of the way when he called. Damn, he looked good, she thought before she could stop herself, his dark hair clean and shining, his liquid brown eyes, even the way he half-smiled.

'Hiya,' he nodded back.

'The kids aren't ready yet,' she gabbled, opening the door wider and catching a whiff of his familiar aftershave. 'Step in for a sec.'

'Ta.'

Another attempt at a smile as he brushed by her. She wanted to touch him all of a sudden, just to feel the warmth of his hand interlocking with hers. It took everything she had to stop herself. Instead, she let him walk to the bottom of the stairs and stand facing her. His eyes were fixed firmly on her face. She wondered if he was trying to show that he wasn't uncomfortable with the situation. Then he shoved his hands into the pockets of his jeans and his jacket fell open, revealing his shirt.

A new shirt.

A new *bright orange* shirt.

Huh, she thought, as her semi-sad feelings were washed away by a tide of indignation and hurt, there *she* was looking after his kids and there *he* was out gallivanting and buying new clothes. And bloody bright orange clothes at that. *And* he hated shopping – she'd always had to do it for him – but now, they were barely three and a half months apart and he'd reinvented himself. She'd never have bought that shirt for him.

'How's things?' Jim asked. His eyes drank her in. He hadn't seen her in months and it was like seeing her for the first time. He didn't want to stare at her but he couldn't help himself.

'Things are great,' she answered and he thought that he detected an edge to her voice. 'Just great,' she repeated.

'Why – has Sheila gone home now?' He meant it as a joke. He wanted to see her smile.

Instead she glared at him and said, 'No. She's staying for a while. I enjoy the company.'

He flinched. It was a barb and aimed straight at him. His heart sank. He knew when he'd moved out that it was for the best. He'd hoped that at least they could stay, well, maybe not friends, but he didn't want her to hate him. He didn't think he could bear that. So he ignored her dig and forced his voice to sound glad. 'That's good then.' The light from the hall window was catching the auburn glints in her hair, forming a sort of halo around her face. He wished that he could touch her, just one more time.

'Yeah. Great.'

More silence. Where the hell were the kids?

'Down in a sec,' Diane yelled, breaking the tension that seemed to have arisen between them. 'I have to get my Docs.'

Jane shrugged apologetically at him.

He shrugged back. Wondered what to say.

She broke the silence. 'I hear my mother was a bit abrupt with you last week.'

He forced a grin. 'No more than usual.'

It was the grin that did it – it made her realise that he wasn't hers any more. It hurt. She had to swallow the huge lump in her throat and force her voice to be normal. 'Sorry anyhow.'

'You don't have to apologise,' his voice and his smile were like the Jim she'd known before the edgy silences. 'You never did before.'

She couldn't answer him. Instead, she turned away and yelled up the stairs for the kids to come down. When she turned back, she was glad to see that his gaze was now directed at the floor. She didn't like the way he had been staring at her.

'Dad!' Diane appeared at the top of the stairs.

The smile she gave Jim was so bright that Jane felt irritated.

Diane flung herself down the stairs as if she was welcoming the Messiah into the house. 'Hi!' She gave him a big cuddle. Then pulling back, Diane nodded approvingly. 'Hey, nice threads, Dad.'

'Sorry?'

'Your shirt, Jim,' Jane said nonchalantly, delighted to know what her daughter was talking about before he did. 'She likes your, er,' she tried to sound slightly amused, but it didn't quite come off, '*tangerine* shirt.'

'Yeah, it's cool.' Diane gazed at him adoringly.

Jane rolled her eyes behind Diane's back, as if to say, 'Huh, kids, what would they know?' Jim looked, Jane was gratified to see, very alarmed at the eye-rolling. He obviously wasn't *that* confident in his choice of clothes just yet. 'Well,' she said, knowing she was being awful, but unable to help herself, 'I'll leave you to your children, Mr Tangerine Man.'

She closed the kitchen door and tried to block out the happy-sounding voices of her kids as they left with their father.

'Hey, I have a life.' That's what Jim's shirt said, Jane realised. He had a life: he'd been shopping, he'd been out hunting for things to make himself look good. And what had she done? Worked. And worked. And worried.

Damn him anyway.

Damn him and his new shirt.

She opened the fridge to get the bottle of wine she knew was in there. She felt like getting drunk.

The wine was gone. Typical. Her mother had probably drunk it in bed or something. She'd kill her if she'd taken the red too. But, nope, it was in the press. Uncorking it, she poured herself a glass and took a huge slug.

The fecker had even looked good. Maybe he'd wanted to leave. Maybe he was relieved it was over. She squeezed her eyes shut to block out that thought.

But then again, *she*'d been relieved when he'd moved out.

Not relieved enough to go out and buy new clothes though. She hadn't been *that* relieved.

There was a fuzziness in her head and a huge lump in her throat, and the lump hurt when she tried to swallow it. She was damned if she was going to cry over such a waster.

But he *wasn't* a waster, the fair-minded part of her tried to say. Not always.

Not always.

Something plopped into her wine glass. And then something else.

Tears, she realised. Tears.

Closing her eyes, squeezing them tight shut, she tried to make herself stop. There was no point – just like there had been no point when—

*Dong! Dong!*

Jane froze.

'Jane!' Patrick's voice came through the letterbox. 'It's meeee!'

She stayed very still, willing him to leave. Maybe she could pretend that she had forgotten their business meeting? She put down her wine glass and hastily wiped her face. Jesus, her eyes must have been leaking like mad. There was no way she could answer the door when she looked like this.

'Jane!' There was more tapping on the door. 'Open up!'

58

Outside Patrick began to mutter to himself. 'Television on, that's a sign she's in. Mmmm.' He began to walk around the house. 'Windows open, definitely in. There is no way Jane would leave windows open and go out. A security freak, that's what she is.' He tapped on the door again. 'Jane! Jane! Hello!'

He was not going to go away. In fact, knowing Patrick, he'd call the police if she didn't answer. The kettle was stainless steel and hastily she studied her reflection in it. Her eyes looked red. Sort of tired. Maybe she could get away with saying she had a headache or hay fever or something.

She kept her head down as she answered the door. 'Hiya. Come in.'

Patrick, dressed to kill in a big orange mohair jumper and red jeans, bent down anxiously to look at her. 'Ohhh, have you been crying? Your eyes are all red and swollen-looking.'

'Hay fever,' she mumbled, reddening.

'Really? At this time of year?'

Jane shrugged.

'Isn't it unusual to get it at this time of year? I hope that's what it is and that it's not the flu or anything. The last thing we need is you sick.' He turned from her. 'Hey, great wallpaper. Did you get that in Habitat?'

'Yep.'

He smiled. 'I can tell, you see. An eye for good quality, that's me.' He held up a briefcase 'Plan of action,' he grinned.

Jane held up her wine glass. 'Plan of action.'

Patrick giggled. 'Is there some for me?'

'Loads.'

He ruffled her hair and walked past her into the kitchen.

After Jane had topped up her own drink and poured a generous glass for Patrick, he opened his briefcase. 'I've just jotted down a few ideas that might work. You've probably done the same.'

'Well, jotted down, no,' Jane admitted, 'but I've been thinking about the best way to market ourselves.'

'And here they are.' Patrick ignored her as he drew a tatty little notebook from the depths of his case.

Jane would have smiled only it was hard to get the image of Jim in his orange shirt out of her head, especially as Patrick was wearing orange too.

Patrick coughed and she smiled.

*Jim had looked great.*

Patrick smoothed out his notebook and after a small silence began, 'We're going to have to up the profile of the salon somehow – are you with me?'

Jane hoped that the rest of his stuff wasn't so blindingly obvious. She nodded, only half-listening. *And the gentle way he'd said that she didn't have to apologise. She loved his voice when he sounded like that . . .*

'Firstly,' Patrick said smugly, 'I'm going to spy on Cutting Edge – see what sort of shampoos and colours they use and then do something with that information.'

As if on cue the tune to *Mission: Impossible* began on the telly. Jane smirked.

Patrick didn't seem to notice. 'The next stage involves your father, Jane.'

'Sorry. What?'

'The next stage involves your father, Jane. Are you listening at all?'

'Yeah. Yeah. Sorry.' She took a gulp of wine. 'Fire away.'

'Are you all right? You don't seem your usual sunny self. Is there something wrong?'

She shook her head. The concern in his voice was making her weepy and she was not about to cry in front of Patrick, especially as the future of the salon was at stake. This was probably the most important meeting of her life so far.

'Right.' Patrick sounded doubtful. 'If you're sure.'

'I'm fine – go ahead.' *Patrick had an orange jumper on.*

'I was wondering if he'd give us a plug or two on his show.' Jane had thought of that idea and immediately discarded it.

60

She managed a grin. 'Patrick, if we'd topless lap dancers prancing about as we cut hair, he'd mention us, but otherwise . . .'

'Mmm,' Patrick bit his lip, 'yes, I suppose it *is* that kind of show.'

'And if he did mention us,' Jane continued, 'we'd get every pervert in town coming through the door.'

'Business is business.'

He meant it too, Jane knew. 'I'll see what I can do.' She bit her lip. 'It might be difficult though, seeing as Mam is still here.'

'I thought you said that she was going back soon?'

'Yeah, well, I don't know about that.' Her dad had phoned the night before just for a chat and to ask how she was coping without Jim. At first Jane had been convinced that it was a cover for asking about Sheila, but her dad hadn't mentioned her once. The signs for an early reconciliation were not looking good.

'Ohhhhh, you poor duck.' Patrick squeezed her hand. 'I did think you looked a bit down today, and I thought that maybe you'd been told you only had a week to live or something, but I never envisioned anything this bad!'

Jane smiled weakly. Tears pricked her eyes again.

Patrick noticed. 'Heeey, it's not *that* bad, is it?'

It was no use. His big orange jumper was making her cry. His kind, sympathetic face was making her cry. The way he was squeezing her hand was making her cry.

'Hey.' His big scratchy orange arm wrapped itself around her. 'Hey, what's wrong honey pie?'

Tears were plopping into her wine, her nose was running, her shoulders were shaking and her sleeve was getting wet. Damn it! Attempting to swallow the hurt only made things worse.

'Cry, pet,' he whispered. 'Get it out.' He pulled his hanky out of his pocket and pressed it into her hand. 'This isn't hay fever at all, is it?'

'No.'

'Well, then, what is it? Is it . . .' he hesitated, 'Jim?'

61

She nodded. 'He's wearing new orange shirts that I didn't buy for him.'

Patrick had been great. Their business meeting had gone by the board as he'd listened to her sniff and snuffle her way through the miserable story of the last four years of her marriage. Of course, he'd known some of it, but not everything, and anyway, half of what she'd said hadn't made any sense but it didn't seem to matter. She just couldn't pretend that it was fine to be separated any more. OK, so it was a relief not to have the silences or to be walking on eggshells all the time, but she felt like a failure.

'No,' Patrick handed her a cup of coffee. 'You're not a failure. You and Jim, well,' he sat beside her, 'you've had it tough, you know. At least you both tried.'

'Not hard enough though.'

'And what is hard enough?' He pushed her hair behind her ear. 'Suits you better,' he murmured. 'You were together for a long time. You had good times. You've done well, honey pie, to be where you are today.'

Jane shook her head.

'You've got your own business, two kids, me and Mir. Some people would have given up, but not you, you kept going.'

'I had no choice.'

'You did, you know.' Patrick hugged her. 'You could have given up, but you didn't. You are a fighter, Jane. Always will be – that's what I like about you. *Love* about you,' he clarified.

Jane said nothing. She was a fighter all right. She bloody well seemed to fight with everyone these days, her daughter and mother included.

'And,' Patrick went on, 'have you considered the possibility, Jane, that maybe Jim *needed* the orange shirt?'

'He needed an orange shirt like I need smallpox.'

Patrick laughed loudly and for the first time that day, she smiled too.

\*　\*　\*

62

At five, he left. They hadn't managed to discuss any of Patrick's other plans for the salon, but he'd told her there were more important things to worry about.

'We'll discuss them another time,' he tapped his folder and smiled. 'Meantime, I'll work on them and then when you're emotionally stronger you can see them come to fruition. There's loads we can do. And you,' he pointed a stern finger at her, 'don't go getting drunk. That's the worst thing to do. Have a lie in tomorrow – I'll go in for nine. Give yourself a nice bath with some smelly candles and you'll feel a lot better.'

'Maybe I will,' Jane watched him leave, feeling sort of lonely when Patrick drove up the road and out of sight. But it had been nice to confide in him. It had been a long time since she'd talked so frankly to someone and it left her feeling lighter, more able to cope.

# 9

'THANKS FOR THE shirt.' Jim peeled the orange shirt off and threw it on top of the stack of other stuff that he had to take to the laundry.

'No probs,' Fred grinned. 'Jaysus, I can't believe you forgot to get your washing done.' He grinned at the mountain of clothes in the black sack. 'What sort of a moron does that?'

'The sort that keeps forgetting to go to a laundry,' Jim said sheepishly.

'So wifey looked after you well, then?'

Jim shrugged. He didn't like discussing Jane with Fred. The two had never liked each other, mainly because Fred had advised Jim not to marry Jane under any circumstances. 'She'll turn out just like her mother,' he'd warned.

On that count, Fred had been dead wrong.

'Tell ya what,' Fred went on, cutting into his thoughts, 'I'd rather do me own laundry than be stuck with a woman for ever. Couldn't stand that.'

'And that's what you tell Gillian, is it?' Jim grinned.

Fred shrugged and searched around for his jacket. 'Gillian knows the score. She's cool.'

'And you'd never consider her as potential wife material?'

'Listen, Jimbo, I'd never consider any woman as potential wife material. The shine doesn't last, you know what I'm saying?' Fred pulled on his leather jacket. 'Things go great for a while and then it's . . . bang!'

'Lots of bang,' Jim grinned again.

'Dirty fucker!'

They laughed.

'Anyway,' Fred said, 'Gillian knows how I feel. And while you're here, she can't move in, can she?' He smiled at his brilliance.

'I can move out.'

'Don't even think about it! D'you want to ruin me life?' He grinned, poked his finger into the bird cage where he was given an affectionate nip and then, giving himself the final once over in the mirror, he left the flat.

So that's why Fred had asked him to stay, Jim realised – to stop Gillian from trying to get him to commit. He felt oddly let down. He wondered, not for the first time, how a guy could go through life without caring for anyone. Still, maybe Fred was one of the lucky ones. He'd never be in this mess if he'd listened to Fred all those years ago.

But then again, he wouldn't have had eleven happy years with his kids. He wouldn't have woken up with Jane beside him every morning. He wouldn't have seen her all tousle-haired and sleepy-eyed as she stretched like a cat under the covers. He wouldn't have kissed her until she cried out.

He wouldn't have had a life, he realised.

But he wouldn't be in such a mess now, either.


Jane got the call just as she was about to step into her camomile-scented bath. For a second she thought of ignoring it, but the fact that her mother hadn't yet arrived back from her shopping spree decided her. Sheila loved shopping, but there was nowhere still open at nine on a Sunday night. Maybe, Jane thought hopefully, as she picked up the receiver, she's gone back to Dad and she's ringing to tell me.

It *was* her mother.

'Jane, dahling,' she whimpered. 'Come and get me, please. I'm in Pearse Street Garda station. Oh, come quickly, dahling. Please.' Without further explanation, Sheila hung up.

Jane, sick with worry, abandoned her bath, told the kids to be good and raced across town to her mother.

Apparently, from what Jane could gather from the guard on duty, Sheila had been arrested for using a stolen credit card.

'Honestly,' her mother said, pale-faced, as she tottered out of the station behind Jane, 'they didn't even know who I was.' She glared at the policeman on the desk. 'I told them I was Declan's wife and they just kept sniggering at me.'

'Come on.' Jane took her mother by the arm and began to lead her to the car which was double-parked outside. 'You'll be fine.'

'I'll never get over this,' Sheila gulped. 'The *humiliation*.' She clutched her daughter's hand. 'Not being believed is the worst ordeal that anyone could suffer.'

Jane grinned. In her mother's life, it probably *was* the worst ordeal she'd ever suffered.

'I mean,' Sheila continued, 'I must have said about a hundred times who I was, but they just kept saying, "Of course you are, dear."'

'Maybe they didn't recognise you because the photo the press use of you is about twenty years out of date.' She unlocked the car.

'That's the best photo that's ever been taken of me.' Sheila sank into the passenger seat and pulled down the mirror. 'I got it professionally done. It was the time they did the big spread on our house in that celebrity magazine. D'you remember?'

Did she remember? She'd been fourteen and the slagging she'd got at school for having a picture of her bed in a national magazine had been awful. And the picture of her parents lolling across their bed with her dad in his boxers and her mother in her baby doll haunted her to this day.

Jane knew that she should have been annoyed with her mother. After all, the lovely bath she'd prepared for herself was growing cold at home, her bubble bath was wasted, her precious store of scented oil gone, and all because her mother had been arrested. But God, it had almost been worth it to see her sitting in all her finery in a holding cell.

Sheila began to examine herself in the mirror. 'Well, at least my make-up stood up to the stress of the day,' she murmured. 'Thank God I looked well through my ordeal.'

'That's the important thing,' Jane said drily.

'But my hair now,' Sheila began pulling fistfuls of hair out of position, 'that's very untidy. That hairspray didn't do a good job at all. I'll never buy that again. This,' another bit of hair was yanked out of place, 'shouldn't happen with a really good quality spray.'

'So tell me, what *did* happen?' Jane was still unclear on the details.

The subject change caught Sheila off balance. 'I already told you,' she snapped. 'Your father reported a stolen credit card. Stupid man didn't realise that I'd taken it.' She brushed a tendril of hair from her face. 'Of course, if he'd bothered to ring me, he'd have known. So there I was, in the middle of BT's, buying some fabulous clothes – oh, dahling, you'd just die for them. There was this exquisite cerise top with the most gorgeous beading on the sleeves. And some of the shoes were really lovely.' She looked pointedly at Jane's trainers. 'Much nicer than those things you wear, dahling.'

'So, what? You went to pay and . . . ?'

'I went to pay, and this gangly girl on the till – I don't know how she got the job, really, you should have seen her, dahling – working in a supermarket would be too good for her. She had an awful voice and her make-up was moving all on its own. Awful.' Sheila shuddered.

'And?' Jane prompted.

Sheila looked blank for a second and then gave a brittle laugh. 'Oh, yes. Well, this horrible girl tells me to go to the manager's office. And when I get there, I'm told that I'm under arrest – I mean, can you imagine it, dahling?'

'Must've been a shock,' Jane murmured, trying to sound sympathetic.

'A shock!' Sheila rolled her eyes. 'I didn't believe it. I laughed. I asked them if they knew who I was. I said, "I'm Sheila D'arcy", and they said that *of course* I was. Then I was taken away. And then, hours later, I was told I could go.'

'Did they ring Dad?'

Sheila shrugged. 'I don't know. I don't even want to think about it.'

'Well I do,' Jane said. 'I mean, did Dad know they'd arrested you? What's happened to the credit card?'

'Gone.' Sheila sighed. 'It was his card as it happens. Mine is in the red. I can't pay it now.'

Wonderful! Jane clenched the steering wheel tightly. 'Well, Mother,' she said, through gritted teeth, 'maybe you should ring Dad tomorrow and find out what you're going to do about money now.'

'Ring him?' Sheila laughed. 'You have got to be joking. He'll have to ring me – to apologise. He'll be on that phone quick smart tomorrow, I can tell you.'

'How can you say that?' Jane demanded. 'He hasn't rung you at all, he had you arrested for using his card and he's left you with no money – *you* have to ring him!'

'I don't *have* to do anything,' Sheila said. 'The man is a barbarian, I'm always telling you that. And please don't rub in the fact that I was arrested, I thought you were better than that, dahling.'

Jesus, the woman was impossible!

Jim liked the silence of night-time. He found it easier to work when everyone else was asleep. It hadn't always been like that, but for the past few years, he'd done his best work at night. It was far better, he figured, to work productively, than to lie in the darkness trying not to think. It had been a good day, first he'd had the kids and they'd been great and then after he'd dropped them home – without seeing Jane – he'd gone back to the flat. Gillian was there with her six-year-old niece in tow and she'd let Jim study her as she played with the Twizters crisps. Fred hadn't been impressed. He'd spent the whole time yawning and complaining loudly about how bored he was. But Gillian, much to Jim's amusement, had ignored him. She knew how to handle Fred all right.

'Don't ya mind him,' she kept saying to Jim. 'Selfish, that's whad he is. Ignore him.' Then, blowing a kiss in her boyfriend's direction, she said, 'Why don't ya make yourself useful honey and put the kettle on?'

So Fred had made them all coffee and been sent out to buy biscuits. When Gillian left, Fred had gone to bed, but Jim was still up at four in the morning, contemplating perhaps the biggest idea of his career so far. The preliminary artwork was completed; the idea was beginning to take shape. He reluctantly decided that maybe he should get some sleep, he was running on empty by this stage, so he lay on the sofa, fully clothed, with the duvet thrown over him. It was no use – ideas were pounding his brain. He finally conked out around five, but by seven-thirty he was washed, shaved and ready for the off.

Philip Logan was expecting a great campaign and if Jim had anything to do with it, a great campaign he would get.

## 10

' AW, HERE SHE is,' Diane called as her grandmother came down to breakfast. 'Owen, have you got your valuables locked up?'

Owen half-smiled but said nothing.

Sheila looked wearily at Diane as she sat down. 'Honestly, dahling, have you so little in your life that you have to make the same silly comments every morning?' She poured herself some tea. 'I feel sorry for you.'

'Huh,' Diane muttered, 'if you felt that sorry for me you'd go home.'

'Diane,' Jane caught her daughter's eye across the table. 'Stop it!' she mouthed.

Di gave her a cocky look in return, which made Jane smile. Jesus, she was as cheeky as hell, but you had to admire her spirit.

'Haven't you your school books to organise?'

'Yep,' Diane agreed. 'Better make sure they're all still there. After all,' she threw mock-dark looks in her nana's direction. 'We've a thief in our midst.'

Owen started to laugh, which made Jane laugh. Owen was normally so quiet that it was good to see him laugh at something. Spotting her mother's anguished look, she spluttered out a 'Sorry, Mam,' and turned from her mother's martyred face to Owen. 'Come on Owen, will you get a move on? You'll be late.'

Owen stood up. 'I'll go now. Me bag is ready.' He found his coat amidst the tangle of clothes hanging on the end of the stairs and, with a brief nod at his mother and nana, he left.

'You've very strange children, dahling,' Sheila observed. 'One attacking me constantly and another who hardly talks at all.' She took a slice of toast from the plate in the middle of the table and examined it. Putting it back, she took some fresh bread out and looked around for the toaster.

'What's wrong with the toast that's already there?' Jane asked, her smile disappearing. 'You're wasting food.'

'I like a nice crisp toast,' Sheila explained. 'That slice is too thick. Bad for the digestion,' she said. 'Very bad.' She busied herself trying to figure out how the toaster worked, then she sat staring into it, as if willing it to hurry up. Jane tidied the kitchen, picking up cups and saucers and stacking them in the dish-washer. She then wiped the table down. She wondered how to broach the subject of her father with her mother. It was best to wait until her mother was sitting comfortably.

It took about five minutes. Sheila got her toast, buttered it, poured herself some fresh tea and began to nibble the crust very daintily.

Even the way her mother ate was beginning to get on her nerves.

'Mam,' Jane slid onto the seat beside her, trying to ignore the little crunchy sounds she was making. 'Dad still hasn't rung, has he?'

Sheila stiffened. She swallowed hard and drank some tea. 'Too busy trying to impress the nation with filthy comments,' she said airily.

'But he must know you're still here?'

'Well of course he knows.' Sheila rolled her eyes. 'The news-papers saw to that, didn't they?'

Jane took a deep breath and said the words she swore she'd never say again: 'Maybe I should go and see Dad, try and sort this thing out?'

'Maybe you should just mind your own business,' Sheila said smartly. 'If I were you, I'd sort your rude daughter out. Honestly, I've never met such a cheeky child. You were never like that.'

71

'I'm surprised you noticed,' Jane said. 'It's not as if you were around much.'

'Well *of course* I noticed.' Sheila was offended. 'You were such a good girl. Really good.'

Jane rolled her eyes. 'Anyway, we're not talking about me,' she got the subject back on track. 'We're talking about you and Dad.'

'No, dahling,' Sheila gave a bright, brittle smile, 'you are the one talking about Declan. I most certainly am not.' Without finishing her toast, she left the room.

'Well, the nerve!' Patrick, who had just collected the post from the door, was waving a bright red and white envelope about. 'Honestly, I can't get over it.'

'The nerve of what?' Jane was studying her appointments for the morning and to her dismay Eileen Simms had booked a cut. Eileen's hair was the pits to style as she couldn't keep her head still for more than two seconds and she constantly talked about her dogs.

'The nerve of this!' With a dramatic flourish Patrick laid a flashy card down in front of her. 'An invite from Cutting Edge to their big opening today. I mean *really*.'

'From Cutting Edge?' Rosemary sounded excited. She abandoned her towel folding to peruse the invite. 'Can you not go, Pat – is that it? I'll go if you want – I think the place up there is deadly.'

'No one from here is setting foot in that place,' Patrick said sternly. 'Not unless they want to lose their jobs, that is.'

Rosemary giggled. 'Sure that'd be unfair dismissal, wouldn't it?'

'Yes,' Patrick nodded, 'indeed it would, but that's never stopped me before.'

Rosemary gaped at him as he stalked past her. 'Grumpy knickers,' she muttered, copying Mir's expression. She adjusted her glasses and, with a sulky pout, returned to her towel folding.

Jane idly studied the invite. It was a no-expense-spared gold embossed card. Addressed to the staff of Patrick Costelloe's, it invited them to share a celebratory drink at the opening of Cutting Edge's flagship store. Pete Jordan had signed it himself, his signature scrawled across the page like a man in a hurry. Such a wanker, Jane thought. Did he honestly, *honestly* think that they'd amble up the road to wish him success in his business when he was in direct competition with them? Even more, did he think they'd have *time* to amble up the road? Crumpling the card up, Jane fired it at the bin.

'That's where you and your stupid salon belong,' she smirked.

The card missed the bin and rolled on to the floor.


Cutting Edge's opening started at noon. It was loud and noisy and seemed to be achieving the desired effect of being hugely noticeable. Jane, on her way up the road to grab a paper from the local shop, hurried past it, not wanting to be seen to be interested. The local radio had a broadcast unit set up outside and was asking queuing customers why they liked Cutting Edge.

To Jane's horror, Eileen Simms was being interviewed. The traitor. 'Ohhh,' she was simpering, 'Cutting Edge is the business and with everything half-price for today—'

The DJ interrupted her. 'That's half-price folks!' he boomed. He thrust the mic back at Eileen. 'Yo!'

'Well, with everything half-price for today,' she went on, giggling, 'it's good value.'

'Did you hear that?' the DJ announced. 'Good value!'

A cheer went up from the crowd waiting outside.

Jane felt sick. Cutting Edge were welcome to Eileen Simms. She'd like to see them cut her hair when she couldn't sit still.

'Some wine, madam?'

Jane hardly heard. Her eye had been caught by Cutting Edge's window. Where it had once been blank, now it was covered with classy framed prints of fabulous-looking hairstyles. Every style that they'd ever entered in competition was there.

Jane remembered some of them from her own visits to the IHF competitions. Most of the styles had won too, she thought faintly.

'Wine, madam?' the offer was repeated.

She shook her head.

They'd won the IHF championships four years running. Pete Jordan himself had won last year with a fantastic fantasy style.

'Canapé, madam?'

'No!' Jane abandoned any thoughts of getting her paper and headed back down to Patrick. Something drastic would have to be done. And fast.

'Ohhhh, I dunno.' Patrick bit his nails. 'My own ideas were going down other avenues. You know flyers and . . .' he paused. 'Well, flyers, basically.'

'Yeah, well, we can try everything,' Jane said, pacing furiously up and down. 'But for now, if we can't beat them, we have to join them. I vote that we enter the IHF championships this year ourselves.'

'With what?' Patrick squealed. 'We've no model.'

'Rosemary,' Jane said. 'Have you seen her hair?'

'Yes,' Patrick gave a semi-hysterical nod. 'It's frizzy and out of shape and she won't let you touch it.'

'It's fab hair,' Jane replied smartly. 'Secondly, are you forgetting that I won Trainee of the Year when I entered years ago?'

Patrick stopped his agitated nail-biting. 'I could never forget that, honey cakes,' he said affectionately. After she'd won, Jane had been beset with offers from big salons all wanting to offer her work, but instead she'd gone it alone. Well, alone with him. He'd been in her debt ever since. But it had been at least sixteen years ago.

'It was a long time ago though,' he reminded her gently.

'Yes, I'm probably a little rusty, but I'll do a few courses beforehand. They've a great one with Julian Waters this year – I can book myself on to that.' She looked pleadingly at him. 'I need you in on this Patrick. I need you to advise me about colour. I can't do it on my own.'

'What if we make a balls of the hairstyle?'

'Then we say it's a bun.' She cracked a grin. 'Come on – they'll,' she nodded in the direction of Cutting Edge, 'they'll wipe the floor with us, otherwise. And Patrick, they can't do that. That man is so arrogant. If you'd met him, you'd know what I mean. I'll bet he bullies other hairdressing salons into liquidation, but not us. Come on!'

Patrick hopped from foot to foot. 'You've your mind made up, haven't you?'

'Almost.'

'Oooohhh,' he winced and waved his hand about. 'Fine. OK, fine.'

'Great!' She hugged him. Tried to do a little dance around the room with him, but he pushed her off, laughing.

'You've to persuade frizzy-head first.'

'Don't call her that – she's our model.'

There was a second's silence, before Patrick asked, 'And it won't be too much for you – what with home and everything?'

Jane shrugged. 'I won't have a home if I don't do something soon.'

'That's not what I mean.' Patrick said gently.

'I *know* what you mean.' Jane bit her lip. Patrick had not mentioned their chat yesterday, knowing that if she wanted to talk she would. 'To be honest, it'll be a diversion. Something to keep me going.'

'Well, if you're sure . . .'

'I'm sure.'

He smiled and nodded. 'And while you organise that, I'll organise something more short-term.'

'Like?'

'Flyers. They're a surprise.' He tapped his nose. 'I think you'll be pleased though. Now, go,' he whooshed her away. 'Talk to frizzy-head – see what she says. She's washing hair at the moment.'

\* \* \*

75

Rosemary was thrilled. 'A model?' she gaped. 'Me?'

'A hair model,' Jane clarified. 'You'll be modelling your hair. Of course, we'll provide you with the clothes and shoes and accessories that you'll need to go with your final style.' Rosemary didn't look so certain now. 'All free,' Jane added.

'Ooooh.'

'Would you like that?'

'And would *you* cut my hair?'

Jane braced herself. For some reason, Rosemary had got it into her head that she was a crap stylist. It was a bit annoying actually. 'Well, initially I wouldn't.' She pretended not to see the relief on Rosemary's face. 'I'd condition it and trim off the split ends – just basically get it into peak condition for the competition. Then, as the time gets nearer, I'd try out a few ideas, play around with a few styles.'

'Like?'

'I don't know yet. I'd have to see what inspires me. For instance . . .' Jane tried to think of what Rosemary might like, '. . . I could do a colour and some highlights, stuff like that.'

'In a cool way, though?'

'Well, yeah.' Jane felt insulted. 'Rosemary, I am a qualified hairdresser, I have won competitions before!'

She must have sounded annoyed because Rosemary flushed, then attempted to explain. 'You see,' she sat down on a chair and frowned. 'I like my hair a lot.'

'You've good hair.'

'Yeah, and I don't have good much else.' Her forehead wrinkled as she tried to explain. 'I mean, I'm a bit spotty and my glasses are awful, but they're the only ones I can afford, and my clothes make me look fat, but my hair see,' she ran her fingers through her hair and her face softened, 'well, that always looks good no matter what.'

There was something so vulnerable about her that Jane's eyes filled up. She thought of Di stalking about in the latest Goth fashion and wondered if the girl ever thought about how lucky she was. Most likely not.

'Well, when I'm finished with you,' Jane put her arm around Rosemary, 'you'll look like a princess.'

'Getting a head transplant is she?' Mir asked sourly, as she led a customer to the basin.

Rosemary giggled nervously.

'No,' Jane said, eyeballing Mir firmly. 'Rosemary is our model for the IHFs this year.'

Mir gawped. 'No way!'

'I am actually.' Rosemary sat up straighter. 'No joke.'

'Well, can you wash Mrs Boylan now please?' Mir snapped.

Mrs Boylan sat down. 'Hello Rosemary,' she said brightly. 'How's the boyfriend?'

'Great, Mrs Boylan and how's your boyfriend?'

Jane left her to it. Rosemary was great with the auld ones.

## 11

'JIM? JIM? JIM, are you with us?'

Jim jerked awake at the abrupt voice. He looked around and the whole table was staring at him.

'Yeah? What? Sorry.'

Dave, his boss, was looking annoyed. 'I was just explaining how much work we've put into designing a concept to market Incredible Crisps' new Twizters crisps, Jim. It'd be nice if you could contribute something.'

'Oh yeah. Right.' Jesus, what on earth was he thinking, nearly falling asleep on what could turn out to be the most important meeting of his life? Well, either that or the meeting that would end up with him losing his job. With the strain of it all, he hadn't bloody slept the last few nights.

'And Jim has been researching the campaign for us, haven't you, Jim?' Dave spoke loudly, his face fixed in the chummy smile he seemed to think the clients went for. 'Jim?' Dave was staring at him again.

'Yeah. Sorry.' Jim gave a bright false smile. 'Just getting my thoughts together, you know?'

Dave continued to glare at him. Thoughts were meant to be gathered prior to meeting clients. Incredible Crisps were big. Westbury Marketing's biggest client, in fact. Jim had come up with a brilliant angle on their first foray into the crisp market and as a result they wanted him to head all their campaigns.

'Well, Philip,' Jim nodded to Philip Logan, the brain behind the crisp empire, 'I commissioned a report for you.' He took a sheaf of papers from his folder and handed them around the table. 'Basically, it's not good news. If you cut out all the jargon, the bottom line is that Twizters is about the crummiest name for a packet of crisps you can get. All sorts of connotations there, you know – only twizters eat Twizters crisps, that sort of thing.'

Philip nodded, looking slightly pissed off. 'Oh, shit. Yeah. I see where you're going.' He folded his arms. 'So, what? What happens now?'

'I decided to brainstorm a couple of the lads in the marketing department and we've come up with a few names you might like. We've a few rough ideas for the packets too.' On autopilot, Jim began showing Philip the concept behind what the designers had come up with: blue packets calling them Spirals, green packets calling them Incredible Edibles.

'And mine.' Jim took out a bright-yellow design. 'Now hear me out, right? When the report came in a few weeks ago, it was really depressing, I kept thinking that there had to be some way out of it. And well, I only have the tiniest proof on this, but it kinda dawned on me that kids would go for the crisps in a big way.'

'Kids?' Philip didn't look impressed. 'They're an *adult* party snack.'

Philip Logan's men nodded and mumbled.

Dave gave Jim a dig. 'Jim, this had better be good,' he hissed.

Jim ignored him. He knew when he was right. OK, so it was suicide to suggest a campaign with very little research to back it up, but he'd got that tingly feeling up his spine when the idea had struck. Tingly feelings meant that he was on to a good thing, and Gillian's niece had kind of confirmed it for him.

Everyone was gawking at him. He took out a sample packet of the Twizters. 'Gimme a sec to demonstrate.' He opened the bag and began to join the spirals together. 'Crazy, isn't it? Cool too. Crisps that make chains, necklaces, bracelets. Kids, girls in particular, will go mad for them. See,' he held up a necklace and grinned. 'Great piece of jewellery, isn't it? And when I get bored,' Jim popped a couple of the Twizters into his mouth and with supreme effort, his stomach turning somersaults, he chewed them, 'I can eat it.'

Some of the guys around the table laughed.

Philip looked confused. 'But they were meant to be a sophisticated snack,' he protested.

'They'll sell better this way,' Jim explained. 'And as for the name, they could be called "Incredible",' he made a big production of holding out his design, "Chains Bond".'

There was more laughter.

Jim grinned. When clients laughed, you were just about to nab them.

'And the name, being similar to James Bond, will appeal to the boys, so you'll get both groups buying the crisps,' Dave explained unnecessarily. He kicked Jim under the table again.

'Mmmm.' Philip jabbed a finger at Jim. 'Once again, you have totally disregarded what I wanted.'

'I didn't.' Jim held up the other two designs. 'If you want boring, it's right here.'

Dave sucked in his breath. He could never get used to Jim showing such disrespect for clients, but Jim called it honesty. He was a funny guy, Dave thought, he was so quiet that sometimes he was easy to overlook. He was hopeless at general chit-chat, but give him an abstract concept and ask him to come up with an angle and the man was a genius. Philip was going to buy. Dave could smell it.

'And you think these Twizters would sell if we went after the kids' market?' Philip asked.

'Like hot cakes.'

'I'm not interested in the hot cake market,' Philip snapped.

'They'll outsell hot cakes,' Jim amended. 'If you go this way, you'll be on a winner.'

Philip stood up. 'I'll think about it. I'll need more research done, though.'

'Gimme two weeks.'

'Done.'

Philip shook hands with Jim and Dave, then Dave saw him and his entourage down to the front door. Jim was suddenly on his own in the big office. He looked out of the huge glass windows at Dublin. The city looked so orderly from where he was standing, he thought. He packed all his papers back into his folder. Standing up, he poured himself a black coffee from the pot on the table and stood for ages just staring down on to the street.

When he got back to his office, Jim buzzed his secretary. 'Maud, will you come in here for a sec?'

'I will, angel face.'

Jim grinned. Maud had started calling him that about two months after she'd begun working for him. She was in her sixties and needed someone to baby. 'And you'll do,' she'd clucked. 'You'll do.'

She walked in now, grey hair in a bun, ample bosom and a wide smile. 'Yes?'

'Maud, will you take that box of Twizters and give a few packets out to anyone here who has kids under ten? Tell them they've to give the crisps to the kids and then fill this form out. Will you do that?' Jim handed her a sheet of paper.

'I will.' Maud took the form from him. She cocked her head to one side. 'You're very black-looking under your eyes. Are you sleeping all right?'

'I'm sleeping fine. Now how about—'

'You're pale too.' She lowered her voice. 'Now look, I know it's not my business, but leaving your own place takes its toll. It makes it hard to sleep at first. You should get yourself a tonic or something.'

'A gin and tonic, maybe.'

Maud clucked disapprovingly. 'I don't know how you can make light of the situation. It's no joke. You work too hard, you know. Always have. You need to relax now and again.'

'Yeah. I know, Maud. Now look, can you please just give out the crisps?'

'I already said I would.' Maud was not pleased. She threw him a withering look before exiting.

Jim rubbed his hand over his face. Jesus, he was wrecked. He laid his head on his desk and closed his eyes.

'Tired?' Dave startled him as he closed the office door. 'Not a good idea when meeting our biggest client, Jim.'

Jim could feel his face flushing. He glared sullenly at his boss. 'So, what is it you want?'

Dave walked slowly towards his desk. Placing his hands on it, he leaned towards Jim and said slowly, 'Never, ever, pull a stunt like that again. You only tell clients what you know, not what you think. Is that clear?'

'It's a good idea. He'll buy it.' Jim kept his voice even.

'But it might just have easily been a crap idea,' Dave said. 'And we can't afford that.' He was silent for a second before saying, 'You get away with a lot of shit here, Jim, but don't cross the line like that again.'

'Sorry.' Jim gave a half-shrug. 'You're right.'

'And another thing, don't tell Philip Logan his ideas are boring ever again.'

Jesus, Dave was really milking this. Jim decided to ignore him. He indicated his computer. 'Dave, I've two weeks to get a survey together, so can I start now?'

'Yeah, start now,' Dave ordered. 'If you're sure you don't want Maud to bring you in a cup of cocoa.' Laughing to himself, he left.

'Asshole,' Jim muttered. 'Bloody asshole.'

# 12

ROSEMARY ACCOSTED HER before she'd even taken her coat off. 'Jane. Hi. I'm all set for today.' She stood in front of her, beaming.

'Are you?' Jane smiled. 'That's good.'

'I thought I'd bring you this in,' Rosemary said triumphantly as she produced a tatty book from her bag.

'Did you?' She wondered idly if Rosemary was on drugs.

'Here!' The book was shoved at her. 'It's my favourite hairdressing book – it'll give you ideas.'

'Ideas?'

'On my *hair*,' Rosemary said, as if it was the most obvious thing in the world. 'For tonight. For my conditioning treatment. See, this page,' she frantically tore through the book, 'somewhere here it gives you ideas on dealing with long hair like mine.' Finding the page, she thrust it under Jane's nose. 'Dealing with long hair,' she read out. 'See.'

'Is there nothing called "Dealing with disgusting hair?"' Miranda asked laconically.

Rosemary stopped, looking puzzled. 'But your hair *isn't* disgusting, Mir, it's *lovely*.'

'I wasn't—'

'Now, now,' Patrick cut in, 'I think it's time for you to man the ship, Rosemary, isn't it?'

'Woman the shop,' Rosemary giggled.

'Ha. Ha.' Patrick managed a passable laugh before saying

briskly, 'So off you trot, we've a customer due in any second now, give me a shout when she arrives.'

'OK. No problem.' Rosemary handed the book to Jane. 'Now, you study that and we'll have a chat about my hair later, OK?' She gave herself a sort of hug. 'Ohhhh, I just can't wait.' She danced out of the door, letting it slam behind her.

'Thank God for that,' Miranda gave a sigh of relief. 'Bloody headache tablets should use her to boost sales.'

Patrick laughed.

'She's a good kid.' Jane found herself sticking up for Rosemary. 'Yez should give her a break.'

'Yeah – break her arm,' Mir chortled.

Again Patrick laughed. 'Well,' he defended himself as Jane glared at him, 'I know it wasn't nice, but it *was* funny.'

That evening, after the salon closed, Jane gave Rosemary her first conditioning treatment. She pretended that she'd read the book Rosemary had given her, just to make the girl less apprehensive.

'Now,' she began as she tested the water and motioned for Rosemary to put her head back, 'I'll do this after work at least three times a week from now on. The idea is to make your hair shine and stop it from getting frizzy.'

'And you won't cut it?'

Jane didn't bother to answer. She'd jump that fence when she came to it.

Rosemary, sensing that she'd somehow offended Jane, babbled, 'I mean, I wouldn't mind you cutting it if I knew how it'd turn out.' She paused, 'I mean, all I ever see you three do is bouncy hair for old women and, well, I don't—'

'Bouncy hair for old women!' Patrick said aghast, as he wrapped his scarf around him. 'We don't do that!'

Rosemary's eyes widened as she realised what she'd said. 'Well, maybe not,' she amended hastily. 'Not quite, like. But, well, this place is not exactly Cutting Edge, is it?'

'No. No, it's not and . . . and thank God!' Patrick spluttered as he flounced away.

'Ohhh, he's mad at me now, isn't he?' Rosemary said mournfully. 'I didn't mean to annoy him.'

'He'll get over it,' Jane muttered, wondering how on earth she was ever going to get the kid to trust her. 'But Rosemary, we are all as good as Cutting Edge in here, you know.'

Rosemary remained schtum.

She began rinsing Rosemary's hair, running her fingers through it, massaging the scalp.

'Ohhh,' Rosemary closed her eyes. 'That's lovely.' Then she asked, 'How come all you get in here are the wrinklies?'

'We do get some young people coming in,' Jane said, trying to recall when she'd last seen one inside the salon. She remembered the guy from Cutting Edge saying that he thought they were an OAP joint. And they weren't. At least that wasn't the intention. 'Would you not normally come to a place like this to get a haircut?' she asked.

Rosemary shrugged. 'Well . . .' she hesitated. 'Maybe.'

'Cutting Edge or here?' Jane asked, more firmly.

'Ohhhh.' Rosemary giggled. 'Ohhhhh.'

'Well?'

'Cutting Edge is dead cool though, isn't it?' Seeing Jane's face, she said unconvincingly, 'But here is good too.'

She meant 'Cutting Edge is better'. Jane decided to say nothing more. It'd only stress her out and you couldn't be stressed doing hair. She concentrated instead on rubbing in the conditioner, running it through the hair from root to tip. Working with hair relaxed her. She loved it. As she massaged Rosemary's head once more, she wondered why Mir never got either her or Patrick to style her hair. Maybe Mir also thought that they just weren't up to scratch. It sent a chill right through her.

Rosemary was delighted with her shiny hair. 'Wow.' She turned her head from side to side in front of the mirror. 'Wow.'

Jane smiled, feeling vindicated.

'And it's free?' Rosemary asked.

'Yep.'

'That's brill.' Rosemary beamed at her reflection.

'It still needs some work.' Jane picked up a ragged-looking section. 'I'll trim it soon, but for now we'll just condition it. And here,' she rummaged around in her bag and took out some fancy scrunchies that she'd bought for Rosemary that lunchtime. 'No more elastic bands, right? From now on, if you want to tie your hair up, use these.'

'For me?' Rosemary hesitated.

'Yep. All of them.'

Slowly Rosemary took the proffered bands. BT's best. She stared at them wonderingly. 'These are *lovely*. Aw, thanks Jane.'

'Naw,' Jane waved her away. 'Thank *you*.'

## 13

'DI,' JANE YELLED, 'I've your lunch made.'
'All this shouting,' Sheila moaned. 'Is it really necessary?' She took a shaky sup of tea.

'WILL I PUT IT IN YOUR BAG?' Jane yelled even more loudly, amused at the way her mother shuddered violently. Without waiting for Di to answer, she opened her daughter's schoolbag and was just about to put the lunch box and an apple in, when a bright-pink envelope caught her eye.

Di came galloping down the stairs just as she pulled the envelope from the bag.

'Hey, you've no right to go poking in my bag!' Di hurtled into the kitchen, grabbed the envelope from her mother and furiously zipped up her schoolbag. 'I don't like being spied on!'

'I wasn't spying.' Jane looked at her mother for support. Sheila turned away. Jane turned back to Di who was scowling, her hands on her hips. As calmly as she could, she explained, 'I was just putting your lunch in your bag for you.'

'Yeah, well, you've no right to go taking out my *private* things.'

'Oh for God's sake!' Jane rolled her eyes. 'It's only a valentine's card. I thought it was a note from school. It's not as if I read it or anything.'

'Oh thanks,' Di drawled. 'Thanks for not reading my *private* things.'

'Don't talk to me like that!' Jane snapped. 'Don't you dare. I'll ground you tonight if you keep it up.'

Di stuffed the envelope back into her bag and began stomping around the kitchen.

Jane ignored her. She set Owen's place at the table and vowed that if he wasn't down in two minutes she was going to brain him. He was the world's worst kid for getting up. But at least with Owen that was about as bad as he got. She'd have gone mental if she had two of them like Di.

'So you've a boyfriend, have you, dahling?' Sheila asked, sounding interested. 'What's he like?'

Jane paused in what she was doing. How her mother had the nerve to ask that question she didn't know. She wouldn't have dared. Di had the uncanny knack of making a person feel about two feet high. She began to hum, making it appear that she wasn't listening.

'He's dead nice,' Di said nonchalantly. 'A good kisser, knows how to Frenchie really well.'

'Ugh!' Sheila sounded as if she was going to be sick.

'For God's sake,' Jane hissed. 'Your nana only asked you a question. One more cheeky remark and that's it.'

Di picked up her schoolbag. 'I was only *answering* Nana,' she said innocently, her big brown eyes open wide. 'Sorry if I *offended* you Nana.'

'You disgusted me, dahling, that's what you did.'

Di nodded, unconcerned. 'Aw, well, at least one person in the house will have a valentine's card.' She swanned out of the door.

'Oh,' Sheila sniffed. 'Now *that* hurt. That was deliberately aimed at me, dahling. She knows Declan wouldn't even think of it.'

Jane didn't bother to disagree with her. She didn't tell her mother that it was her sixteenth wedding anniversary that day. She didn't tell her mother that Jim, in the good days, had made a huge fuss of her on Valentine's Day. It was their day. Always had been. She tried to ignore the empty feeling Di's words had given her and went to haul Owen from his bed.

\* \* \*

88

Valentine's Day – his sixteenth wedding anniversary, Jim thought despondently as he crawled out of bed.

'Good morning,' Fred boomed, as he emerged, clean-shaven, from the bathroom. He gawked at Jim. 'Jaysus, you look like shit!'

'Thanks.' Jim flicked on the kettle. 'And you just smell like shit.'

Fred chortled good-naturedly. 'I'll have you know, this after-shave is dead expensive. The last mot I had bought it for me.'

'Trying to put the rest of humanity off you, was she?'

'Aw, you can be very fuckin' funny in the morning, can't ya?' Fred rooted around in the press and, taking a packet of corn-flakes out, began to eat them from the box. With his free hand, he flicked on the radio.

'. . . the question is – how many valentines will you get?' the DJ asked. 'It's lurve all the way today folks!'

'Fucking asshole,' Fred fiddled with the dial. 'Love me arse.'

'So, you going anywhere tonight?' Jim asked.

'What?' Fred found a station that he liked and sat down.

'Are you taking Gillian out somewhere tonight?'

Fred guffawed. 'Are you joking? I hate all that crap. It's a bloody money-spinner, that's all.'

Jim shrugged. 'Yeah, I'd say Gillian will really understand all those moral sentiments, Fred,' he deadpanned.

'And what does that mean?'

'Have you even got her a card?' It was a stupid question. He knew bloody well that Fred hadn't. Fred hadn't even given it a thought.

Jim felt that he had to say something because Gillian had told him that she had a huge surprise lined up for Fred. She'd tapped her nose, giggled and said, 'I want you to be there, Jimmy, I want everyone to see his wee-action.'

'A card?' Fred rolled his eyes. 'No way. Anyhow, she'll be cool about it. Gillian is a cool girl.'

'She'll freeze you out, she'll be that cool,' Jim said.

'Oh yeah,' Fred sneered, 'and what makes you the expert on women, all of a sudden?'

Jim flinched. 'I'm not an expert,' he muttered. He paused, then continued, 'It's just, women like that shit. A bunch of flowers, a card, it doesn't cost much.'

'It's not the cost, it's the principle.'

'Well, once a year is a weird time for you to have principles. They've never mattered before.'

'Fuck off.' Fred slammed down the flakes and glared at him.

Jim returned the glare. 'She's got something for you – it's a surprise.' He felt like a heel for ruining Gillian's thunder, but what else could he do?

Fred flushed. Gulped. 'Well then . . .' His voice trailed off. 'I guess I'd better . . .' He looked at Jim. 'Thanks.'

Jim turned his back and pretended that he was busy making a cuppa. Jesus, he hated Fred sometimes. The guy didn't deserve any girl, let alone one who was mad about him.

'Sooo,' Patrick waltzed into the salon with a grin the size of America on his face. 'Anyone get any valentine's cards?'

Mir narrowed her eyes. 'Yeah. I got one,' she snapped. 'From fucking Harry.'

Harry was Mir's fall guy, the one she used when there was no one else available. He gave her lifts to and from work, got drunk with her when she was mourning the break-up of a relationship and was generally a nice guy. He was also crazy about Mir and a complete doormat. This year, he'd obviously decided to declare his feelings and take the plunge, thus committing the ultimate insult in Miranda's book – a card from a friend.

'As if I wouldn't know it was him!' she sneered.

'Well, I think it was nice of him,' Patrick said sweetly, still smiling. 'Wasn't it nice of him, Jane?'

'Uh-huh,' Jane nodded. Attempting a grin, she added casually, 'Look at me, no cards at all.'

'You've had them for the last, I dunno, fifteen years, haven't you?' Miranda spat. 'It's about time I got my turn in the sun.'

'You will.' Patrick reached out to pat her on the arm.

Miranda pulled away. 'I don't need your sympathy, Patrick. And I don't need sympathy cards. If I wanted a sympathy card, I'd, I dunno, kill my mother or something.'

Patrick tut-tutted. 'Rosemary?' he asked.

'One,' she giggled. 'From Jaz.' She blushed. 'Me fella.'

Patrick and Jane made 'ooohh' sounds which had Rosemary giggling frantically while Mir looked on sourly.

'And moi,' Patrick beamed. 'Did I get a card?'

'A wild guess – I'd say you did,' Jane smirked.

'How did you know?' Patrick feigned surprise. Then, reaching into his bag, he drew out a box of chocolates. 'Well, to be honest and if I'm not going to depress Mir over there too much, I got a card *and* a box of chocolates this morning.' He offered the box to Mir. 'Want one?'

'That's right, make me feel miserable.' Miranda dug her hand into the box and pulled out a handful.

'Who from?' Jane asked.

Patrick grinned and tapped the side of his nose. 'Oh, I'm not sure, but I've got my hopes up.'

'Not the only thing that's going to be up, is it?' Miranda gave a dirty laugh and Patrick and Jane joined in.

Jesus, Declan D'arcy was a great laugh. Jim grinned as he pulled into a space in front of the Incredible Crisps' offices. His special Valentine's Day show was based on love – though what Declan knew about love could probably be written on the back of a postage stamp – and he'd got people to phone in and tell him their experiences of love. Jim wondered if there were really that many weirdos out there. Some people were so completely mental. The show should have had an 'X' rating. But it had been compulsive listening, as horribly irresistible as looking at a car crash.

91

It hadn't been too bad a day at all, Jim thought. OK, so it was crap that it was Valentine's Day and anyone with a partner was grinning from ear to ear – but it had been liveable. He'd coped the only way he knew how, by working his butt off. He was going to fill Philip Logan in on the latest details and he knew that Philip would be impressed with what he'd done. The Chains Bond crisps idea was a good one. Most people at work had filled out the form for him and it seemed that their kids had loved them. He was feeling the way he'd felt when he'd started marketing Incredible Crisps at the beginning. A bubbly excitement was beginning to build. He knew that with careful marketing, his idea could be big. Bloody big.

Di's card had pride of place on the mantelpiece. She'd moved the picture of Matt to one side so that her card took centre stage. Jane took Matt's picture and straightened it. She wanted everyone who came into the room to see that happy picture. Jane reached out and let her finger trace the face of her youngest son. He'd been such a happy kid. It had been the only consolation left when he'd gone.

She gulped, drawing her finger away, and stared determinedly at Di's card. It was small and completely unromantic. She hoped her daughter wasn't about to make a fool out of herself. *Darling*, the card said, *seven days spent with you makes one week*. Inside, the fella had scrawled, *To Di, loads of kisses on V day*. He'd signed it *Guy*.

Guy was a nice name, Jane thought. Sort of film star-ish.

She wondered where Di was now. She'd said she was heading to Libby's house but on Valentine's night it was highly unlikely that she was going to stick with Libby all night. God, it was a worry. She guessed she'd just have to trust her daughter, but trust and Di didn't seem to go together in the same sentence. She tried to reposition the card on the mantelpiece so that Di wouldn't know it had been disturbed.

'Here Ma.' Owen made her jump as he shoved a video under

her nose. 'It was the only decent film they'd left. I dunno what it's about though. Something about a hairdressers, I thought you might like it.'

Why couldn't Di just be the teeniest bit like Owen? She smiled at her son and took the video from him. 'Ta. *Steel Magnolias*,' she read, 'I've heard of that.'

'Great.'

'You going to watch it with me?'

Owen shrugged. 'Seeing as Da's not here, I guess I'd better.' He gave her a tentative grin.

'You're great.' She hugged him and he pushed her off, embarrassed.

God, she loved that kid.

Jim wished he could fall asleep, but the sound of his flatmate moaning and urging Gillian to 'Do it to me' made it impossible.

'Asshole,' he whispered.

'Asshole!' the parrot screeched.

Jim put a pillow over his head and tried humming.

It was no use.

He tried to think of something else besides what was going on in the bedroom.

That didn't work either.

How come Fred could get a woman to love him as much as Gillian obviously did? Fred with his dying bunches of flowers and his cheap tacky card. Still, it had been a good laugh when Gillian had presented Fred with a voucher for a parachute jump.

'I did try to get the sky-diving thing,' she said, 'but, nah, it was impossible.'

Fred should have got an Oscar for his mock-delight.

'He hates it, doesn't he?' Debbie had whispered.

'He's shitting himself,' he'd whispered back.

They hadn't been able to stop laughing all night.

Fred was now hoping to screw Gillian's brains out to put her in good form so that he could exchange the parachute jump for something else.

*Steel Magnolias* was too emotional. Owen left to get a coffee halfway through it and didn't come back. Jane wasn't surprised. She heard him playing his PlayStation in his room. She stuck out most of it, but eventually couldn't take it any more. Flicking the telly off, she went to bed.

She lay awake for a while until Di came home. She heard her daughter whispering to someone outside. It had to be *him* as the voice was too deep to be a girl's. She resisted the urge to peek out the window. Di would probably never talk to her again if she saw her. After a while she heard the sound of a key in the lock and Di whispering 'goodnight'.

Jane closed her eyes, willing herself to fall asleep now that her kids were safely home. Well, now that two of her kids were safely home.

'Night Matt,' she whispered to the silent room.

# 14

'HELLO, MAY I speak to Mrs Jane McCarthy, please?' Jane didn't recognise the voice. Long ago, she had grown wary of voices she couldn't identify. Sometimes journalists phoned up looking for quotes about her father. And with every tabloid in the land writing snippets of gossip about her parents each week, there was no way she was adding fuel to the speculation. A bookie had even started taking bets on when they'd get back together again. Apparently the odds on Declan having a new woman by the end of the year were two-to-one.

'Who's speaking?' She made her voice gruff to put any would-be hack off.

'Eh, it's Deirdre Mulvey – your son's tutor?'

'Sorry?'

'Owen's tutor. You *are* Jane McCarthy?'

'Yes. Yes I am.' God, what must the woman think of her? 'Sorry about that. I thought you were someone else.' The woman at the other end made no reply, so Jane continued meekly, 'What can I do for you?'

'It's about Owen – I was wondering if we'd see him in school this week?'

'Sorry?'

'He's been out sick rather a lot this term – this year in fact,' the woman amended. 'Frankly, Mrs McCarthy, it's a bit worrying, seeing as it's exam year next year.'

Owen? Out sick? She must have the wrong Owen.

'I'm sorry, Miss Mulvey,' Jane said pleasantly. 'Owen hasn't been sick at all. Are you sure you've the right Owen?'

'Yes.'

'Owen McCarthy. He's in second year?'

'That's right.'

There was a pause while she tried to digest what it meant. 'Are you saying that Owen—'

Miss Mulvey's voice, when it came, was sympathetic. 'He hasn't been showing up for school,' she said gently. 'He's missed about six weeks at least this year.'

*Six weeks!*

She wondered if she was dreaming. Owen went out every morning. He took his lunch, his bag, everything. He wasn't the sort of kid to bunk off.

'Owen's not the sort—'

'Well, he hasn't been in school.'

'He's a good kid,' Jane stammered. 'I-I can't believe he would deliberately miss school – there must be some mistake.'

'There's no mistake, Mrs McCarthy. Maybe you could have a word with him about it?'

She sounded quite firm. Jane gulped, her head reeling. 'I'll try,' she muttered, 'but I can't believe—'

'Now, I know that you and your husband have separated recently,' Miss Mulvey went on delicately, 'and that certainly would be a factor. Children react in different ways to these things. But Owen—'

'Owen is a good kid,' she repeated.

'Owen is very quiet, he never says much in class, maybe he needs to talk to someone?'

She didn't need advice on how to mind her kids. She tried to recall a picture of Miss Mulvey and she remembered a twenty-something with cropped dark hair and trendy clothes. The woman was only a kid herself! 'I'll talk to him,' she said. 'He'll be in school tomorrow.'

'Well, if he needs to talk, we've a social worker in the school.'

Owen didn't need a social worker. 'OK. Fine.'

'Thank you Mrs McCarthy. I'll be in touch.'

'Bye. Thanks.' She put the phone down and stared at it for ages. There had to be some sort of a mistake. There just had to be.

She was so preoccupied with what to say to Owen that after dinner she almost let Diane out of the house in a black hand-kerchief. A black handkerchief masquerading as a skirt.

It was the happy tone in her daughter's voice that caught Jane's attention. The skirt or lack thereof was the next thing to get her attention. Short and tiny and way too tight, it had been teamed with a pair of thigh-length boots. If she'd been touting for business she'd have made a fortune. 'Off,' was all she could manage.

Diane turned to protest and Jane nearly died. Her skirt had been bad enough but her *top*. Well, that's all it was. It certainly hadn't a middle or an end.

'You are not going anywhere in that,' Jane spluttered. 'Go upstairs and change.'

'What?' Diane gawped and put her hands on her hips. 'What do you mean?'

'I mean that you look ridiculous. You are not leaving this house half-dressed.'

'I look fine,' Diane said, her voice quivering. 'Libby said it was gorgeous.'

'Libby?' Jane rolled her eyes. 'Well, I don't think it's Libby who you're meeting, Miss, and believe me, you are not going to meet any fella looking like that.'

'Well a fella gave me the money for it,' Di said indignantly. 'Dad gave me and Owen money last week and told us to buy what we liked – didn't he Owen?'

Owen nodded.

'So I got this and he didn't see any problem with it.'

'Your dad is not one for acknowledging problems.' The words

97

were out before she could stop them. She hated the way Di flinched. 'Look,' she said, in a gentler tone, 'just change.'

'Yes, dear,' Sheila spoke up. 'Put on something a bit more flattering. That top does nothing for your chest.'

'Does it not?' Diane narrowed her eyes and wiggled her minute chest about. 'Just 'cause your generation was sexually repressed. I'll have you know, Gran, I'm very proud of my 36C bust.'

'It's Nana,' Sheila corrected. 'And dahling, if you're a 36C then my eyesight is worse than I thought. I really can't see very much there at all.'

Jane snorted a laugh and then pretended to cough.

Diane's eyes widened at the put-down. She opened her mouth to say something but no words came out.

Her mother was improving, Jane thought, amused. A few weeks ago she'd never have been able to come out with something like that. 'Upstairs, Diane,' she said.

'You wouldn't know what fashion was if it hit you over the head,' Diane said sulkily.

'Up.'

Bestowing a final glower, Diane stomped out, her skirt riding higher and higher up her backside with every step she took.

'I'll tell you,' Sheila cackled after her granddaughter, 'that new boyfriend of yours is going to be blind before long, the get-up of you will make the eyes pop out of his head.'

'I wish I could pop the tongue out of your mouth,' Di yelled back.

Sheila laughed good-humouredly.

Jane stood up to clear the table. Her mother had obviously decided to play Di at her own game, trading insult for insult.

'Ahh,' Sheila said fondly, dabbing her mouth with some kitchen paper. 'Di reminds me so much of Declan.'

Jane laughed.

Owen began helping Jane clear the table. He scraped the left-over food from the dinner plates into the bin and stacked the plates neatly for her.

'Thanks,' she smiled at him.

He shrugged and kept his head down.

He did that a lot, she suddenly realised, shrugging and not looking her in the eye. He'd always been quiet, but he used to laugh and talk with her. She tried to remember when he'd become so withdrawn, but couldn't. It had happened gradually. Maybe it was his hormones. Or maybe it was just guilt over bunking school that made him unable to meet her gaze?

But he'd been like that for years, another voice told her.

She studied him as he went about clearing up. He looked pale, she thought. But he was so dark that his skin had always seemed pale, especially in winter. She wondered if it was normal for a fourteen-year-old lad to help around the kitchen without being asked, to never go out, to have no friends that she could see. A sort of dread crawled into her stomach.

'How was school, Owen?' she asked suddenly.

He dropped the plate he'd been holding and it clattered on to the table.

'Mind my dress!' Sheila barked.

'Look, Mother, if you're not going to help, get out!'

Her mother made some comments that Jane only half heard, before self-righteously exiting.

Owen stood, head bent, still staring at the table.

'Well?' Jane asked again. She knew it was true, sure as anything. The way he'd dropped the plate told her everything. 'Owen?'

He shrugged, then picked up the plate. 'OK,' he muttered. He still didn't meet her gaze.

'OK?' Worry made her grab the plate from him and crash it down on to the draining board. 'How would you know it was OK? Well?'

His silence seemed to go on forever.

'Well?' she demanded again.

'Who told you?' he asked.

'Who the hell do you think? Your tutor told me! Can you

imagine how I felt being told that my son is not turning up for school? Can you imagine?'

'No.'

The way he answered her and his anxious, flickering glance stopped her dead. There was something there . . . she couldn't get a handle on it. He wasn't brash or cocky about it. He wasn't upset. He was just . . . nothing. 'So why, Owen?' she asked uncertainly, her annoyance evaporating. 'What's wrong?'

More shrugging. This time his head sank even lower, he tapped the toe of his trainer off the tiles on the floor.

'Is something wrong? Are you being bullied? What?' God, don't let anything be wrong, she prayed. She thought of what Miss Mulvey had said. 'Is it because of your dad leaving? Is that it?'

'Sort of. Kind of.' His voice caught. 'I just . . . I dunno, Ma. I can't face it – school and stuff.'

'What? You can't face school because your dad has gone?'

'Well . . .' He shrugged. Seemed to struggle with the words. 'I just feel it's stupid, Ma. A waste.'

'A waste?' Jesus, she was like a parrot. But she just couldn't get her head around it. 'A waste?'

'Uh-huh.' Owen gulped. He rubbed his face. 'Since . . . since Matt—'

She flinched. 'Matt?' she asked.

'I'm going out now!' Diane screeched from the hallway. 'And don't try to stop me this time.'

Jane hardly heard her. Instead she waved her away and studied Owen some more. She couldn't make herself get annoyed with him, though she knew she should. There just didn't seem to be a point to it. For the first time in four years he'd actually mentioned his brother and surely that was progress. She didn't want to make too big a deal of it though. Instead she refocused on his truancy. 'Nothing is a waste,' she said gently. 'Tell me, how much school have you missed?' She closed the kitchen door so that her mother wouldn't walk in on them. 'A lot?'

'A few weeks.'

'Owen!'

'Sorry Ma.'

He sounded genuinely sorry. She didn't know quite what to do. Maybe lads did this sort of thing all the time. She knew Jim had. Maybe it was nothing. 'And what did you do?' she asked. 'Where did you go?'

'Nowhere much. Just around the place. Playgrounds. Parks.' He looked at her. 'Sometimes I even climbed the tree in the field at the top of the road and just sat there watching people come and go.'

'The tree at the top of the road?' Jane rubbed her hands over her face. This just got worse and worse. 'That's thirty foot high – at least.'

'It's easy to climb.' His eyes grew sullen. 'It's not a big deal.'

'It's too dangerous!' She surprised both of them by yelling into his face. 'You never, ever climb that tree again, do you hear me? Never, ever!' She poked him hard in the chest. 'You do, Owen McCarthy, and I will, I will . . .' her voice broke. She bit her lip and fought to regain control.

'Ma—'

'Just, just don't climb it. OK?'

A second or two elapsed before he answered. 'OK.'

'Promise me?'

'Yeah.' He touched her arm briefly.

'OK.' She caught his hand in hers. Said fervently, 'And you'll go into school tomorrow, won't you?'

His shoulders slumped. 'Yeah.'

'And it's not a waste. Nothing is ever a waste. It'll only be a waste if you let it. Don't you know that?'

'Yeah.' He didn't sound convinced.

'I'll be checking up on you, you know. I just can't believe . . .' She didn't finish. What else could she say? 'It's not a waste,' she said again.

He didn't answer.

101

'And if you want to talk to me, Owen, you can. You know that, don't you?'

'Aw, Ma . . .' Owen rolled his eyes, mortified.

'About Matt, about anything – OK?'

He stared at the floor.

Jane tossed his hair. 'Now, start showing up at school and we won't mention it to Dad – all right?'

'All right.'

Jim would have done nothing anyway. He was too soft with the kids.

'Go on now, go and get your books for tomorrow.'

'OK.'

She watched him leave. Even though she believed he would go into school, she was sure she'd handled the situation all wrong. She felt she'd missed something, but she wasn't sure exactly what.

It came to her, just as he was climbing the stairs – it had almost been too easy.

## 15

Philip Logan was smiling. His team were smiling. Dave was even managing a grin of sorts.

Jim tried not to look too relieved as he pressed the remote control for the DVD. 'This is the ad campaign we've come up with,' he explained. 'We've a series of ads that'll run over the next few months. Slightly off-the-wall humour that kids go for.'

'I smell expensive,' Philip half-grumbled.

'Good sense of smell there, Phil,' Jim grinned.

Dave gave a cough and glared at him. Jim ignored the glare and continued, 'It's a great concept. Worth every penny.'

The screen lit up and Jim pulled down the blackouts on the windows. 'Make him like it,' he prayed silently. He'd spent ages with the ad people throwing about ideas until they'd all found something they could work with. It had taken him two solid weeks of sleepless nights and crazy days to get the thing exactly the way he'd envisioned it.

'Bitch!' Mir hissed as she put the telephone down. 'Another cancellation,' she called down the salon. 'Julie Edwards can't come today.'

'Why?' Jane asked.

'Dunno, she was dead evasive,' Mir reached under the desk and took out her nail file. 'What's the bet she's heading up the road – huh?'

Jane gritted her teeth and looked around the empty salon. Her business was coming apart at the seams and she was powerless to stop it. For the past couple of weeks, the amount of customers had dwindled to almost half. God, if she'd Pete Jordan in front of her she'd give him a piece of her mind, so she would. She could only hope that the novelty of Cutting Edge would wear off. And soon.

'Where is Patrick?' she asked, suddenly aware that he'd been missing all morning.

'Doing something important somewhere,' Mir answered and then cursed quietly as a nail broke. 'It's just not my fuckin' week,' she hissed.

It hadn't been the salon's week either.

'That's it folks, one hundred per cent of all kids prefer Chains Bond crisps to any other.'

The voice over: 'Chains Bond, the crisps with a twist.'

There was a spatter of applause and laughter. Jim grinned.

The follow up ads were equally bizarre.

When the DVD had finished, there was silence. Jim flicked it off and looked expectantly at Philip.

Philip shook his head and grinned. 'Fucking brilliant.'

'It is, isn't it?'

'You're not going to be able to make enough Chains Bond to meet demand,' Dave said. 'We'll see to that.'

There was more loud laughter.

Philip shook Dave's hand. 'You, gentlemen, have got yourselves a deal. I want all that stuff out mid-May.' He turned to Jim. 'And you – well done.'

Jim smiled. 'It's what you pay me for.'

'Yeah, I guess so.' Philip gave a final grin and a nod before being ushered out of the door by Dave.

'Now, Jane, have you missed me?' Patrick swaggered into the coffee room around four holding a box. He glanced around. 'Not much going on here, eh?'

Jane put down the phone on Owen's school. At least he'd

shown up. That was two weeks on the trot now. She felt she'd been stupid to worry so much. All lads bunked off.

'Sorry, Patrick, what?'

'I said,' Patrick dumped his box on the coffee table, 'not much going on here.'

'We'd only three customers in this afternoon,' Jane replied glumly. 'I let Mir go early, she's got some kind of hot date tonight. And Rosemary is down at the launderette. I'm doing her hair later. She's heading to the cinema so I told her I'd do a conditioning treatment. I might try and trim it as well if she'll let me.'

'Aw, well, maybe I have something here that might just boost things up a bit.' Patrick located a knife and sliced open the tape at the top of the box. Taking out a sheaf of papers, he handed Jane one of them. 'My flyers.'

'Oh good.' Jane had heard about nothing else all week. 'Let's have a read.'

Patrick smiled proudly. 'It's dynamite,' he grinned.

Patrick Costelloe's was written in red across the top. *Hair to have affairs with* was the cringe-making slogan.

'Hair to have affairs with?' Jane said faintly.

'Three days it took me to think up that one,' Patrick said smugly. 'Now, keep reading. It's a touch of genius if I say so myself.'

The leaflet went on to say that Patrick Costelloe's used far superior hair products compared to their chain-store rivals. At the end was printed, *You pay half the price – you'll get double the hairstyle.*

'Well?' Patrick asked.

Jane bit her lip. 'I dunno if we should use this Patrick.'

'And why not?' He sounded seriously offended.

'Well, for starters,' Jane began, 'we'll be sued. I mean, it is Cutting Edge you're talking about, isn't it?'

Patrick took the leaflet from her and made a big deal of examining it. 'Is it?' he smirked. 'Where does it say that?'

105

'Well, it doesn't but—'

'But nothing!' Patrick rubbed his hands together gleefully. 'I've consulted with a friend of mine, he's a brilliant solicitor and there isn't a thing they can do.' He jabbed the leaflet. 'Everything there is fact. No names are mentioned. It's all above board.'

Jane wasn't exactly sure that this was the right way to go about things, but as she hadn't an alternative to offer she didn't think it was right to criticise too much.

'I mean,' Patrick continued, 'if you'd still been with Jim, maybe we could have come up with a better idea, but I really, really think this is a winner. People are bound to take notice. Everyone likes good hair, don't they?'

'I suppose so.' Jane jabbed the leaflet, still trying to figure out what bothered her so much about it. 'It'll make us enemies,' she said eventually.

'And Pete Jordan is our friend?' Patrick opened his eyes wide in mock surprise. 'Oh, pardon me. Stealing all our business is a *friendly* thing to do? Robbing our customers is doing us a *favour*?'

'You know what I mean.'

'Stabbing us in the back is *nice*?'

'OK, you've got a point.'

'So,' Patrick waved a leaflet about. 'Are you in or are you in? We're going to be distributing them in the next couple of weeks.'

'Well, I guess I'm in.'

'Atta girl!' Patrick winked at her.

## 16

FRED WAS BRICKING it. 'It's all your fault,' he snapped at Jim. 'No it's not.' Jim unlocked his car door and Fred climbed in beside him. 'If you'd told Gillian from the start that you hate all this outdoor stuff, she wouldn't have bought you a parachute jump.'

'She bought me a parachute jump because you told her I liked abseiling or some crap like that.'

'Sky diving,' Jim corrected, grinning. He was driving Fred to the aerodrome as Fred didn't think his nerves would stand it. Gillian and her mates were going to meet them there to cheer him on.

'For fuck's sake.' Fred buried his head in his hands. 'What am I going to do?'

'Tell her the truth – that you're terrified.'

'The truth?' Fred guffawed. 'Jaysus, that's mad. I can't do that.'

'Well then, it's the high jump for you.'

'You're fucking enjoying this, aren't you?' Fred spat.

'Me? Naw!' Jim laughed.

'Well, I'm glad something can make you laugh. You've been so bloody miserable these last few months that I was beginning to get depressed meself.'

'As long as you don't get compressed, eh?'

'Fuck off!'

They arrived at the aerodrome at eleven. Fred was due to jump at eleven-thirty.

'Oh fuck,' he kept saying over and over.

'Look, Fred, you've trained for the past couple of weeks, it can't be that bad.'

'Oh yeah, say the parachute fails or I get it caught in the engine of the plane or something?'

'You could sue them.'

'Ha. Ha.'

'Here's the fan club,' Jim said, spotting Gillian across the tarmac.

Gillian saw them at the same time and began a sort of skipping run towards the car.

'Hiya boys.' She poked her head through the open window. 'All set, Freddie?'

'Oh yeah.' Fred gave a confident grin. 'Just have to, you know, get kitted up and have a chat with the instructor.'

'Well, you wanna hurry honey, aren't you gonna jump at eleven-thirty?'

'That's right.' Fred gave Jim a shaky grin as he climbed out of the car. 'Not likely to forget that, am I?'

'Naw. Come on. I'll go with you.' Gillian linked her arm through his and beamed up at him.

He smiled back down at her.

'Hi yez.' Debbie knocked on Jim's window. 'Hey, is this it? The "See Freddie Meet His Maker" fan club.'

'Just the four of us?' Jim queried. 'I thought—'

'Way too busy,' Gillian said. She pulled on Fred's arm. 'Come on, hon. Get your kit on.'

'That makes a change, I'll bet,' Debbie remarked.

Both of them laughed. Jim managed a grin. Jesus, it'd be just him and Debbie watching Fred jump. Well, Gillian too, only she didn't count. It felt suspiciously like a set-up.

Debbie went around to the passenger's side of the car and climbed in. 'Just the two of us, huh?' she remarked drily.

'Looks like it.' Jim gave her a brief smile and turned away. He'd met Debbie a few times since that night in the pub and

Fred was always slagging about how much she fancied him. It made him uneasy.

'Gillian's all excited about this,' Debbie went on. 'She hasn't talked about anything else for ages.'

'Fred hasn't talked about anything else either,' Jim grinned. 'For an entirely different reason of course.' He was aware of Debbie crossing her slender legs. She was wearing an ankle-length skirt, split at the side, and as she crossed one leg over the other, the split opened and revealed long tanned limbs. Jim stared out of his window with a forced intensity. He didn't want to look. He wasn't interested. And even if he was, he wouldn't know what to do about it.

'Nice car,' Debbie remarked. She pushed a switch and a little door overhead opened, revealing a pair of sunglasses. 'Hey, cool.'

Despite his jangling nerves, he laughed. 'Jane,' he winced a bit at saying his wife's name, 'used to call me "Gadget Man". The more gadgets in a car, the better I'd like it. Here, look at this.' He pushed another button and a little tray popped out between them. 'For McDonald's takeaways or whatever.'

Debbie gave a delighted laugh. 'And this one?'

'Heats up the seats in winter.'

'No way. Like an electric blanket for your arse?'

Jim grinned. 'Uh-huh.'

They caught one another's eyes and he gulped. He kept the smile fixed on his face, but a scary, uncomfortable feeling seemed to be creeping across him.

'Hey, hey, you guys.' Gillian broke the moment by hammering on the window. 'Come on, he's almost ready to jump. They'll let us watch it from that building over there.' She indicated a grey, small building with a tower. 'Hurry.'

Jim and Debbie climbed out of the car and followed behind her. She kept up an endless stream of chat the whole way across. 'Freddie's plane is going up any second now. He'll be number two to jump.'

109

'Number two,' Debbie whispered. 'How appropriate for a shithead.'

Jim pretended not to hear. Fred wasn't *that* bad.

They gathered with a small group of people who must have been there for other parachute jumpers.

Further down the strip a little plane was revving up. 'There it goes,' Gillian announced in a high-pitched, excited squeal.

The plane lifted off and began to gain altitude.

Jim winced at the small size of it. Jesus, Fred was some man to go up in that. He didn't know if he'd have the nerve. It looked a bit shaky too. Soon it was just a dot above them.

'*I think someone has just jumped!*' Gillian shattered the silence with her shriek. Everyone craned towards the window. Sure enough, a tiny dot could be seen floating downwards. And then another.

'*There's my Freddie!*'

Fred's parachute could be seen opening and, after an initial hurtling upwards, he began to float towards the ground. Jim realised he'd been holding his breath and clenching his fists.

'Isn't he wonderful?' Gillian breathed, turning adoring eyes on both Jim and Debbie. 'Such a man, such a nerve.'

'Such a nerd?' Debbie asked. But she was laughing as Gillian hit her.

The drive home had been celebratory. Fred was puffed up. 'Parachute jumping is like drinking a pint,' he declared. 'Second nature to me.'

'You are a wonderful human being,' Gillian breathed. 'Wonderful. Grabbing life by the throat like that. Me, I'd never have the guts to jump out of a plane.'

'Aw, well, that's probably because you're the nervous type.' Fred ruffled her hair fondly and ignored the guffaw of laughter from Jim. 'So, let's go grab a drink.' He talked loudly, just in

110

case Jim was planning on laughing too much. 'Are yez on, folks?'

They were standing outside Fred's flat. Jim jangled his car keys and shook his head. 'I've to pick up the kids in an hour, so I'll pass.'

Fred gave Gillian a squeeze. 'And you?'

'I'm for a drink,' she said. 'Debs?'

Debbie smirked. 'And play gooseberry? Naw, I'll head home.'

'You won't be a gooseberry,' Gillian cuffed her. 'And anyways, how'll you get home? I'm driving.'

'Walk? Catch a bus? Taxi?' Debbie answered.

'I'll drive you.' Jim felt he had to offer. He could hardly leave her to go home on her own when he had a car.

'A better offer you won't get,' Fred gave Jim a meaningful wink.

Both of them ignored him.

'Well?' Jim indicated his car.

'But your kids?'

'I'll have plenty of time.'

Debbie shrugged. 'OK, if you're sure.'

'Oh,' Fred chortled, 'he's sure, aren't you, Jimbo?'

Gillian giggled.

'Asshole,' Debbie muttered.

This time Jim didn't disagree.

As he drove Debbie back to the flat she shared with Gillian he couldn't think of a thing to say. He was completely useless at making conversation with beautiful women. Well, with any woman that wasn't Jane, actually. Being away from her was getting harder instead of easier.

When he pulled up outside she invited him in for a coffee. 'Kill some time before you see your kids?'

'Naw, thanks. It's cool, I'll, eh, just, you know . . .' his voice trailed off and he began studying his hands.

'Suit yourself.' Debbie pulled the door handle and made to leave.

111

'Thanks for the company today,' he found himself saying before he could stop it. 'The other two would have driven me mental otherwise.'

A smile lit up her face. 'And thank you for yours,' she said back.

Silence.

'Well,' she muttered. 'See you again.'

'Sure.'

'Maybe next Saturday? We're all heading out that night. It should be a blast.'

He let himself give a non-committal sort of a nod. She climbed out of the car and walked up the driveway to her apartment.

A sigh of relief escaped him. It was as if he could breathe again.


'I think you could do with a night out.'

Jane looked up from her hairdressing magazine. So far Patrick's flyers had failed to produce any more customers. If anything, numbers had continued to dwindle. The only thing she could do to stop herself from worrying too much, was to read the latest hairdressing mags. At least that way she'd be prepared for the young trendies when they eventually came.

'You need a night out,' Mir said again, as she leant against the reception desk. She took one look at what Jane was reading and grabbed it from her. 'That's boring!' she declared. 'Come on, Jane. How about a night out? My treat?'

There was no way she was going out with Miranda. Their conceptions of a night out were wildly different. 'Aw, I—'

'You can come back and stay at my flat, so you won't have to drive home and Sheila's in your house, so she can keep an eye on the kids.'

'My mother only has eyes for herself.' Jane snatched the magazine back and folded it up. 'Naw, thanks anyway Miranda.'

'Oh, go on. Don't be such a dry shite. D'you remember you,

me and Patrick used to always go out every Saturday? We haven't done it in ages – not since . . .' Mir trailed off.

'Not since Matt died,' Jane finished for her, her voice quiet.

'Yeah,' Mir said. 'So come on – we'll ask Patrick too.'

If Patrick went, she could be tempted. 'Well . . .'

'Oh, go on.' Miranda, sensing victory, gave her a poke. 'It'll just be the three of us, the way it used to be. Please – come out with us?'

'Are you going out?' Rosemary bustled up, all business. 'Like as in a staff outing? Can I come?'

'You have as much chance of coming as I have of liking you,' Miranda scoffed.

'Jesus, Mir—'

'Oh thanks,' Rosemary beamed. 'That means "yes" – right? That means I can go? Ooooh brilliant. I'm dying to go out with you, Mir. I'll bet you go to the coolest places. D'you go to that place – the Kitchen place? I've never been there. I bet you go there. Oooh great.' She looked at Jane. 'And will you do my hair for it? Jaz loves the way you do it.' She did a dance of some sort before waltzing back down the salon with some conditioner.

'What a complete loser,' Miranda said, sounding bewildered.

Jane giggled.

'You *have* to come now Jane. I mean, if you don't I'll end up killing her.' Her voice rose. 'Patrick isn't man enough to stop me.'

'Are you having a go at my sexuality again?' Patrick chided. 'Honestly, if I wasn't the boss, I'd sue you.'

'I'm trying to persuade Jane to go out with us one Saturday,' Miranda explained.

'Like we used to?' Patrick's face lit up.

'Only instead of convincing her, I've bloody well got Rosemary coming.'

'Aw well,' Patrick rolled his eyes. 'Enjoy yourself, sweet cakes.'

'What?' Miranda paled. 'No way am I going out with her on my own. No bloody way. Yez have to come.'

113

'I'll go if Jane goes.' Patrick looked at her questioningly.

Jane smiled. Talk about being railroaded into something. But still, the idea of a night out with Patrick and Mir appealed to her. 'OK,' she nodded. 'That'd be great.'

'Good girl,' Patrick grinned. He turned to Miranda. 'The three hairdressers ride again.'

'Ride being the operative word, I hope,' Miranda giggled.

Patrick gave her a clout. 'You bad bitch.'

'I'm a very bad bitch,' Miranda nodded. 'Thank you for noticing.'

## 17

IT WAS AS if she'd just told them she was going to bare all for *Playboy*.

'You're going out?' Diane glared at her. 'When?'

'Saturday night.'

'With who?'

'Patrick and Miranda,' Jane answered patiently.

'Oh.' Di seemed happy enough with that. Then she said, '*Where* are you going?'

'Diane,' Jane leaned towards her daughter. 'Do I ask you to fill in a questionnaire every time you sneak off to see your boyfriend?' At Diane's sullen look, she nodded. 'Well, then, mind your own business. I'm going out. Your nana will be here to see that nobody gets up to anything.'

'Who?' At the mention of her name, Sheila stopped studying her reflection in the teapot. 'What did you just say, dahling?'

'I said that you're going to be keeping an eye on Owen and Di for me on Saturday.'

'Me?' Sheila was horrified. 'Me? Keep an eye on those two?'

'Yes, Mother. Your grandchildren.'

'I don't need *her* to keep an eye on me,' Diane said scornfully. 'I'm fifteen.'

'That's right, dahling, you are.' Sheila gave her a beatific smile. 'Far too old to have Nana minding you.' She turned to Owen. 'And you're a big boy, too.'

'That's what all the girls say, isn't it, Owen?' Diane smirked.

Owen smirked back but didn't reply.

Sheila tut-tutted at their crudeness and turned to Jane. 'Now, dahling, you've heard them. They don't need me.'

Jane gave a tight smile. 'You'll be here on Saturday so you can keep an eye on the place. I'm going out and that is that.'

'I might need to go out myself—'

'Well, if Dad rings, I'll cancel my plans, OK?'

Sheila pursed her lips. 'There's no need for that sarcasm,' she quivered. 'No need at all.'

But there was, Jane realised. Her dad hadn't been in contact once since Sheila had left him and, despite Sheila saying that she'd handle it, she didn't seem to have done anything. There was nothing else for it, Jane realised, but to do what she'd spent her life doing. She had to go and sort it out herself. It might also be an opportunity to ask her dad to put in a word for the salon on his show. Desperate times called for desperate measures.

As Patrick said, business was business and the way things were going they needed all the perverts and loonies they could get.

## 18

'AND JAZ, HE jumped on the lad that was jumping on the other lad.'

'Did he?' Jane, combing conditioner through Nash's hair, tried her best to sound interested.

Nash was a friend of Rosemary's who'd decided to pay her a visit and at the same time get her hair washed and blow-dried and be waited on hand and foot by her mate. She thought it was a great laugh to have Rosemary scurrying to and fro making her cups of tea. Rosemary was throwing poisonous looks in her direction.

Nash nodded. 'He did. Flattened him with a magic right hook, nearly took his head off.'

Jane wondered if it would be possible to take Nash's head off. The girl never stopped talking and Jaz, Rosemary's fella, featured prominently in every story. He was like some kind of malevolent Superman, always around when fights broke out.

'The cops arrived soon after and we all had to scatter. Hey, hey Rose,' Nash bellowed across the salon, 'were you around when Jaz got carted away by the cops?'

'No,' Rosemary answered sourly. 'I had work to do at home.'

'Last Sunday night?' Nash scoffed. 'Hate that.'

It was just as well there were no other customers in the salon that afternoon, Jane thought. Nash wasn't exactly good for business. OK, she was young and she was a customer, but she'd spent the last visit describing in lurid detail how Jaz had lost his index finger. Eileen Simms, who had come back after her initial defection, had made a big deal of fanning herself and declaring that she felt sick.

'Now, Nash, lie back and relax.' Jane put the comb down and tucked a towel in around Nash's shoulders. 'I'll wash the conditioner out in about five minutes, all right?'

'Yeah, yeah, no problem. Hey Rose, get us a cuppa would you?'

Rosemary bristled. 'I'm a trainee, I've other stuff to do, haven't I, Jane?'

'It's all right Rosemary, I'll make it,' Jane said.

Immediately Rosemary scuttled over to the office. 'No, no, it's OK, I'll do it. I mean, I don't mind making tea I just don't like,' she paused, 'people – taking – advantage.' She scowled over at her friend. In a lower voice, she hissed to Jane, 'She's already got me to make her two cups. I just don't think it's fair that she comes in here, getting hairdos and ordering me about.'

'Well, it's not as if you're exactly busy, are you?' Nash cackled over. She had ears like a bat. 'Jane says that your hair reflects your inner health – isn't that right, Jane?'

'Yes.' Jane smiled ruefully at Rosemary who was giving her friend the fingers.

'In which case,' Nash went on, grinning broadly, 'Rose must be about to drop dead!'

'You bitch!' Rosemary tore across the salon and belted her friend.

Nash screamed with laughter.

'Girls!' Jane bellowed. 'Stop—'

She was halted mid-sentence as the door slammed closed. It would be bloody typical for a potential customer to see her trainee trying to strangle a regular. She was relieved to see Rosemary hastily drop a fistful of Nash's hair and instead pretend that she was doing something with the towels. The kid was learning.

'Hello,' a male voice said, sounding slightly annoyed. 'Can I speak to the manager?'

His voice was familiar though she couldn't place it. Turning around, she came face to face with Pete Jordan. Shit. Double shit. She assumed a vacant expression and wondered if she could get away with pretending that she was a customer.

'Hey.' Pete's irritated expression vanished and he crossed to meet her. 'We meet again. Jane something or other, isn't it?'

'Pardon?' She hoped her puzzled expression would put him off, make him think he'd made a mistake.

'Jane,' he said instead, more confidently. 'The woman that hates my light fittings.'

'Ooh, I'd say your fittings are heavy enough,' Nash called over.

Pete looked mildly disgusted as Jane started to laugh.

Rosemary belted her friend, hissing, 'That's rude. You don't talk rude to customers.'

'So,' Pete said, smiling patronisingly at Jane. 'I see you haven't defected from your local.'

'Er, no, ha.' God, how was she going to get out of this?

'So, where is he – the manager?' Pete asked. 'I need to see him.' He paused. 'Urgently, in fact.'

'But sure, Jane owns the place,' Rosemary said as if Pete Jordan was a complete idiot. 'She's the manager!' She gazed proudly at a mortified Jane, 'Aren't you?'

'Rosemary, will you wash Nash's hair, please?' Jane strove to sound normal, even though curling up and dying would have suited her better. 'Lukewarm water, OK?'

'Yeah, Rose, wash me hair,' Nash said, throwing her head back into the basin. 'Nice and gentle. Jane says that you can destroy it if—ooooh!'

Rosemary had turned on the water full force and squirted it into her mate's mouth. Her voice dripping with false concern, she said sweetly, 'Sorry 'bout that, Nash. You OK?'

'Bitch.'

Jane gave a nervous laugh. 'Mad,' she tittered.

119

'Just like you, eh?' Pete lifted an eyebrow. Not sounding quite as friendly as he had initially, he continued, 'Imagine forgetting that you owned this place when I talked to you last.'

'Imagine,' Jane said briskly, hating the fact that he'd caught her out.

'You taking tablets for it?'

She was not going to have him sneering at her. 'So, what is it you wanted?' She kept her voice neutral. For some reason, she felt embarrassed to be seen looking the way she was. Hair neglected, face make-up free, she was wearing old jeans and a sweatshirt with the words *Boston Chick* scrawled diagonally across it. He, on the other hand, looked quite the successful businessman. His clothes casual, yet madly expensive. No fear of getting hair dye on them, she thought. He was probably one of those owners that did no work yet took all the glory.

'What I want to talk about is this.' He pulled a folded-up piece of paper from his pocket. 'Your salon's back-stabbing advertising campaign.' He thrust the paper towards her. 'One of my stylists was handed it yesterday.'

*Oh wonderful.*

She folded her arms, realised it was a defensive gesture and immediately unfolded them. 'What's the problem?'

He raised his eyebrows. 'Do I have to spell it out?'

'That'd be an unusual way of doing it, all right,' Jane said.

Behind her, Rosemary started to giggle.

'The problem is, *Jane*,' Pete stressed her name, 'that in this leaflet you are basically having a go at us. At Cutting Edge. At our credibility.'

She took the leaflet from him. 'We are?' She was proud of her surprised expression. For some reason the fact that he was annoyed gave her a bit of a buzz. 'And where does it say that?' She arched her eyebrows and made a big deal of perusing the flyer. Looking up at him she shook her head. Copying Patrick, she said in a baffled tone, 'I can't see your name on it anywhere.'

Pete's eyes narrowed. 'Well, if it was we could sue you, couldn't we?'

Jane shrugged.

'Yeah. Yeah, yez could,' Rosemary piped up. 'Patrick told me we have to skid a very narrow line.'

'Rosemary, please keep out of this,' Jane said icily.

'I'm just putting him in the limelight.'

'Well don't!' Jane turned back to Pete. 'So, if all you have to go on is your own suspicious mind, I suggest you leave now.'

'I'm not going anywhere.'

'Well there's no reason why you should stay.' Jane indicated the salon. 'There are no more of our customers that you can actually steal.'

'Competition, dear girl,' Pete snapped, 'if you can't stand the heat, then get out of the kitchen.'

'I prefer to turn the heat off myself,' Jane said calmly, relishing his annoyance. 'Saves a lot of energy.'

The front door slammed and Mir struggled in with some leaflets of her own. 'Only came back to do Bridie Doyle's hair. I've her booked in for two. The leaflets are going a bomb. Jane wait until . . .' Her voice trailed off and her eyes lit up. 'Hiya,' she said, grinning at Pete. 'Hey – great hair.'

'Got it done in the overpriced place up the road.' Peter eyeballed Jane.

'Aw, well, we all have our crosses to bear.' Mir chortled.

'He owns Cutting Edge,' Rosemary, busy towel-drying Nash's hair, said. 'He's Eddie Jordan.'

Mir's mouth dropped so far open that she could have swallowed him whole. 'You own Cutting Edge?' she gasped. She made an unsuccessful attempt to hide the leaflets behind her back. A pile of them tumbled from her hands on to the floor where they lay face up.

Jane winced.

'Uh-huh.' Pete looked pointedly at the leaflets.

'You own it?'

'Uh-huh.'

'And Jane and Pat have let you live?' Mir said, recovering her composure. 'Well, things are looking up.'

Jane stifled a laugh.

Pete looked from one to the other. 'I'm leaving.'

'Just you or your actual hairdressers?' Jane asked, making Mir giggle.

'I won't dignify that with a response.' He glared at the two of them and then turned to Nash. 'And obviously your prices in this place are as low as your standards – your trainee just messed up towel-drying that lady's hair. It'll take the shine from it. It's no wonder you've lost all your business.' He gave a mock-pleasant smile and added, 'I can swat you like flies from a cow.' So saying, he strode from the salon and let the door slam after him.

'Asshole,' Jane, Mir and Rosemary said together.

IT WAS STRANGE to be going out, Jane thought. She hadn't really gone clubbing in years. And any time she'd gone for a drink in recent years, it was usually with Jim. They'd sit in a pub, trying to make conversation and failing miserably. She wondered why they'd bothered. Tonight was going to be different. Miranda and Patrick were a great double act and even though Rosemary was coming along, it should still be a good laugh.

She pulled a brush through her hair before heading downstairs. The kids had just come in from being with Jim and she wanted to chat to them before leaving. They were in the sitting room watching telly while her mother sat in state on the sofa with her nails soaking in some putrid-smelling liquid.

'Hi yez,' Jane smiled, 'Good day?' She tried to make it sound as if she hoped they'd had a good time.

'Brilliant,' Diane answered. 'Dad's great fun to be with.'

'People are always fun when you don't see them that much,' Sheila said smartly.

Jane was oddly touched by the comment. Her mother flashed her a sympathetic smile and Jane smiled back.

'True,' Diane surprised them by agreeing. 'Maybe you should remember that, Gran.'

'It's Nana,' Sheila corrected, stiffly. 'And I—'

'Oh God,' Diane talked loudly over Sheila's reprimand, '*What* are you *like*, Mam?'

'What?' Jane looked down at herself. 'What's wrong?'

'You. In bootlegs. Jesus.' Diane gave a snigger.

Her daughter's laughter fazed her. OK, so she'd expected Diane to be like this, Di didn't want her to go out, after all, but maybe she did look stupid. Maybe her new clothes *were* a bit on the young side for her. Maybe she should go and—

'I think you look great,' Owen said quietly. 'Really, you know, nice and all.'

Relief flooded through her. But Owen had been bunking school and it was probably his way of making it up to her. He'd say anything, she reckoned.

'You do,' Sheila agreed. 'You look lovely, dahling. Don't mind that sourpuss over there.'

Di glowered at her nana.

'Thank you,' Jane said, pleased. 'Now, Mam, I'm staying at Mir's tonight, I've left her number in the kitchen in case of any problems.' She picked up her bag from the chair and grabbed her fleece.

'And Di, if you're heading out, be in by midnight.'

'Oh,' Di smiled sweetly, 'I don't think I'll be going anywhere tonight.'

'Really? Why? Is it—'

The doorbell rang.

She had been going to ask Di if it was all off with the mysterious Guy, but she appeared to be in good humour so that didn't seem a possibility. Maybe they were cooling things, which would be nice. After all, Di did have her exams later in the year, it wouldn't do her any harm to study a bit more.

The doorbell rang again.

'You might as well answer that, Mam, seeing as you're on your way out,' Di remarked.

'I will. Bye now.'

They mumbled their goodbyes.

Pulling on her fleece, she opened the front door.

Outside, standing on the step, was an unshaven, ear-ringed, nose-ringed youth. He wore a long black coat and baggy black jeans. His eyes, which could have been nice, were outlined in thick black eyeliner. Long dreadlocks hung down to his shoulders like pieces of frayed rope.

'Sorry,' Jane tried to inject some sympathy into her voice, 'I've no money.'

The guy looked surprised and then drawled out a sympathetic, 'That's shitty.'

'Yes, it is, so would you mind—'

'Gooey!' Diane pushed past and to Jane's horror enfolded the youth in a bear hug – the kind of hug she'd recently started using on Jim. Turning to her, she announced proudly, 'Mam, this is Gooey.' Dragging him into the hall, she dismayed Jane further by saying, 'He's my boyfriend.'

Whoever she had imagined as her daughter's boyfriend, it certainly hadn't been *this*. The lad looked like an abused animal or something.

Gooey shoved his hand towards her. 'Hiya, Mrs D'arcy.'

'McCarthy,' Jane corrected faintly. He was some boyfriend if he didn't even know Di's second name. 'And you are – again?'

'Gooey.'

She watched, in a kind of frozen stupor, as Di beamed from her to him and back again. Where was Guy, the film star she'd imagined for her beautiful daughter?

'Interesting nickname,' she said pathetically.

'It's his real name,' Diane said. She gave Gooey a shove. 'Go on, tell my mam how you got it.'

Gooey looked mortified. He coughed and shuffled and mumbled away to himself.

'His mother was looking through a magazine when she was expecting him,' Di said, cutting Gooey off mid-sentence, 'and she saw a gorgeous fella in a magazine and she said that if she had a boy she'd name him after this fella.'

'A fella called Gooey?' Jane found that hard to swallow.

'She wasn't good at reading,' Gooey spoke. 'Me name – it's spelt G-U-Y.'

'Oh, right.' Jane didn't know if she should sympathise, laugh or cry.

'Gooey is heaps nicer than Guy,' Di smiled at him. 'Heaps better.' She turned to Jane and raised her eyebrows. 'So, you're going out, aren't you Mam? See you.'

She bloody well wished she wasn't going out now. What would those two get up to in her absence? Satanic rituals sprang to mind.

Di pulled Gooey by the arm, giggling into his face. 'Now, Goo,' she said, 'see, meeting my family wasn't so bad. You can meet my brother later and just ignore my nana. So, will we head upstairs? We can talk privately there.'

'There'll be no private talk in any bedrooms in this house,' Jane managed to splutter out. Then, knowing that Di would hate her for saying that, she conceded, 'If you want, there's always the kitchen.'

'Oh, brilliant!' Di said, her face contorting to convey how square her mother was.

Jane ignored her. She watched them head into the kitchen before going back into the sitting room. 'Mam,' she whispered, hoping Di wouldn't hear, 'Diane has,' she lowered her voice, 'a boyfriend outside. I wouldn't trust him with me let alone with her. You're not to let them go upstairs. I've told them they can use the kitchen. It's up to you to try and get rid of him, soon.'

Sheila looked stricken. 'Dahling, how do I do that? You know she won't listen to me. Maybe you'd better stay—'

'Are you joking?' Jane suddenly understood. 'That's the only reason I'm getting an eyeful of him.' She bit her lip. 'Now, Mam, please, will you keep an eye on her?'

'I was never much good at that sort of thing,' Sheila said mournfully. 'But I'll do my best.'

'It's okay Nana, I'll help you.' Owen grinned. 'I'll keep an eye on them, drive Di mad.'

'Oh, now, I don't want any fighting. Your mother never fought when she was a child.'

126

'I was an *only* child Mam.'

'So?'

Jane stared at her in exasperation. She was so tempted to ring and cancel, but she knew she couldn't. Di would have her trapped in the house for ever if she did that. 'Now just keep an eye on them, Mother. It's no big deal. Keep going into the kitchen to make tea or something. Do anything – I don't care.'

Sheila moaned slightly.

Poking her head into the kitchen, Jane noted that Diane had poured Gooey a cuppa and that he was eating the nicest biscuits. It all seemed innocent enough. 'Bye.' She managed a smile at Gooey who looked even more unattractive under the light. 'Nice to meet you, Gooey.'

'Enjoy yourself,' Diane said sweetly. 'Don't think of us *too* much.'

'Oh, I'll enjoy myself all right,' Jane smiled back. 'Thank you, Di.'

Her daughter's sour look almost made her laugh.

Jim showered and shaved. He hadn't wanted to go out with Fred and his mates, but the alternative – staying in with a laptop and a heap of figures – had decided him. Running his fingers through his short hair, he let it dry naturally. Now, he wondered, what did he wear? He'd never been much of a clothes man, Jane had bought most of his stuff for him. He tried to remember what she'd liked. There was a black shirt that she'd bought him once, so he put it on. He'd a black pair of jeans that would match it. Dressed, he sat down and flicked on the telly. Fred wouldn't be ready for ages. He was worse than a woman the length of time he took. Everything was tried on and discarded until he was looking the best he could. Which, Jim grudgingly admitted, was always pretty good.

'Bless me father, for I have sinned,' Fred chortled when he did eventually emerge.

'What?'

'You.' Fred gestured to Jim's clothes, 'You're like a priest.'

'What?'

'You don't want to be giving out the wrong signals to Debs now. A priest is definitely *not* what that lady wants.'

Jim scowled. He'd had enough of Fred's comments about Debbie. 'Fred, get lost. I don't give a toss what Debbie or anyone else thinks, right?'

'Oh yeah, right,' Fred drawled, in such a way that Jim knew he didn't believe him.

'Leave it, Fred.'

'It was just a joke.'

'Jokes are funny.' Jim tossed the remote control on to the sofa. 'You're not.'

There was an edgy silence until Fred muttered, 'I'm fucking sorry, all right? Jaysus, you're as narky as an auld wan. It's worse than having a woman in the place.'

Jim gave a reluctant grin.

'Comes from the lack of a sex life, Jimbo.'

MIRANDA WAS WAITING for her outside the salon. The minute Jane saw what Miranda was wearing, her new clothes seemed frumpy and old. Miranda was dressed for clubbing in a tiny white mini-skirt, impossible heels and a backless white top. Over her shoulders she wore a diminutive red-denim jacket. Her make-up was subtle except for the crimson lipstick which gave her a Marilyn Monroe pout.

'Hiya.' She gave Jane the once over. 'You look great.'

'Not as great as you though,' Jane said enviously.

Miranda shrugged modestly. 'Well,' she said, 'I just wish Patrick would hurry up or I'll freeze the arse off myself. At least you'll be warm.' She shivered slightly.

Wouldn't she just? Jane thought glumly. She wondered what had possessed her to bring her navy fleece. The lack of any other coat, maybe? She'd no fancy little bits of jackets to wear on a night out. Everything was sensible and warm. She wanted to kick herself.

'Hi yez,' Rosemary called, tottering up the road towards them. 'Is Pat not here yet?'

'Naw, just the cow pat,' Miranda mumbled.

Jane elbowed her to shut her up. Honestly, Miranda could be awful cruel sometimes.

'What on earth is she wearing?' Miranda whispered. 'Jesus tonight, what *is* that?'

'It's a skirt,' Jane whispered back. 'Will you stop?'

'Would you let your Di out in it?' Miranda asked.

Jane didn't answer.

Rosemary came towards them. Her legs were lathered in fake tan. The bits that she'd missed stood out as white streaks. She wore a huge pair of platform heels that made her legs look slightly deformed. Her skirt was a short wrap-around that didn't quite wrap. She sported a top which proclaimed to the world that her other job was as a porn star. Her hair, which Jane had washed for her that evening, stood up in massive peaks on the top of her head. She wore no glasses and, as a result, was squinting madly. And her neck, wrists and fingers dripped in bright, fake gold. However bad Di could be, Rosemary was worse.

Rosemary stopped a few feet from them and gazed at Miranda in awe. 'Wow! Great minds think alike – huh?' She indicated their short skirts.

'Wha—!' Miranda spluttered before beginning to cough as Jane gave her another dig in the ribs.

'I'm not mad into white myself,' Rosemary confided, standing close to Miranda, as if they were best friends, 'but on you it looks great. And your top!' Reverently, she fingered it.

To Jane's relief, Patrick chose that moment to arrive.

'Hi!' He waved at them from his Celica. 'Climb aboard you beauties.'

Rosemary giggled frantically. 'Aw, stop. Go away.' Then she asked, 'Can I sit in the front?'

'You can indeed, madam.' Patrick opened the door for her. 'In you come.'

Rosemary looked at Jane and Miranda. 'Yez don't mind, do yez? I mean, if one of you wants to sit in the front . . . ?'

'Go ahead,' Jane grinned.

'Mir?'

'Yeah. Yeah.' Miranda gave a bored sigh.

Looking as if she'd just won the lottery, Rosemary scuttled into the passenger seat. 'Oooh,' she squealed, 'this is like being important.' She gazed around in wonder. 'This is a *lovely* car, Pat. Ohhh, I hope someone sees me sitting in it.'

Miranda yawned widely as Jane grinned.

'Where will you be driving?' Rosemary asked. 'Will you be going by St Anne's Park?'

Patrick shrugged. 'If you want.' He gave the dash an affectionate pat. 'I'll drive this little goer anywhere.' He started the car and pulled out.

'Oh *please*, let's go there,' Rosemary begged, looking at them all with shining eyes. 'My friends live around there, I'd just love them to see me.' She giggled a bit, 'I told them I was going out with my boss from work and that he drove a cool car and none of them believed me. Of course,' she added seriously, 'I never told them you were, you know,' she flapped her hand about a bit, 'sort of gay.' She shrugged. 'That would have spoilt the story a bit.'

'And why spoil a good story with the truth, eh, Rosemary?' Miranda said drily.

'Yep. True enough,' Rosemary agreed. 'So,' she turned to Patrick, 'can we go around there?'

'Only if you promise to snuggle up to me if they're around. No point in letting the whole world in on my shameful life, huh?' Patrick grinned and winked at Jane and Miranda.

'It's not shameful,' Rosemary said. 'Just, like, really really *weird*.'

Miranda exploded in a laugh and Rosemary gave her a puzzled look, before giving a fake laugh herself.

'St Anne's Park detour, here we come,' Patrick said.

'Oooh.' Rosemary almost wet herself with excitement. 'The last time I was in a car this big was for my mother's funeral. Ooooh.'

Jane settled back into her seat, smiling. She was glad she'd come. Still, a call home wouldn't hurt. She took her mobile out and began to dial.

Gillian drove Fred and Jim to the pub. There was no way Fred was driving. 'I'm having a few jars, doll,' he said, patting his belly. 'A man like me needs his drink.'

''Course you do.' Gillian patted his belly too. 'I'll drive.' She fished her keys from her bag. 'I don't wanna drink anyhow. There's this psychotherapist back home who says that drink is bad—'

'That's all there is in your country,' Fred said knowledgeably, 'loonies with qualifications telling the rest of the world how to live. I'd have none of that meself now.'

'I dunno that loonies—'

'Would you, Jimbo? Would you let some looney tell you how to face your fear and all that crap?'

Gillian looked offended. 'It's not crap.'

Jim shrugged. 'Facing me fear, I don't mind. But someone telling me it's bad to drink, now that's a looney.'

Both Gillian and Fred laughed.


After half an hour looking for Rosemary's mates Patrick decided that the night out had better start. Rosemary reluctantly agreed, while peering desperately out the window.

'It's like the Wild West around here,' Miranda whispered to Jane as they drove back up Rosemary's street, which was a sad affair of boarded-up houses and burnt-out cars. 'No wonder no one's around; probably all out joyriding.'

Jane shot Miranda a warning look. It wasn't a bit funny. No wonder poor Rosemary never looked well, the poor kid probably did her best with what she had. Her affection for Rosemary grew. She was glad the kid was working for them. Maybe it'd give her a chance.

'So, where to?' Patrick asked. 'Pub first and then a club?'

'Fine by me.' Miranda crossed one perfect leg over the other. 'Let's go to The Orange Tree and then hit,' she frowned, 'The Kitchen maybe?'

'The Kitchen?' Rosemary said the words reverently. 'As in *The Kitchen*?'

'Naw, as in The Dining Room,' Miranda deadpanned.

'As in The Kitchen,' Jane smiled.

'Wow.' Rosemary was seriously impressed. 'That's brill. The last time I tried to get in there, they wouldn't let me.'

'Well, they'll let you in tonight.' Patrick gave her a fond smile. 'You're with us.'

Rosemary's eyes widened. A slow smile broke over her face. 'Yeah,' she said, as if hardly daring to believe it. 'Yeah, I am, amn't I?'

'Hey, competition alert,' Patrick called.

A Cutting Edge salon came into view.

They rolled down the windows and, to the amazement of passers-by, gave the building two fingers while Patrick shouted out 'crap styles' at the top of his voice.

Debbie wasn't there when they arrived at the pub and Jim, to his surprise, felt slightly let down. It wasn't as if he was interested or anything, but she was good company. Talking to her was better than hearing about Fred and his parachute exploits for the millionth time.

'Some of the other guys were shitting themselves,' Fred said to an agog table. 'But I wasn't. Naw, if I died, I died, but yez know, there's no point in dying if you haven't lived – is there now?'

Jim had had enough. He excused himself and went to the bar to get in a last round. The barmen were rushing about like mad things.

'Yo?' one of them said.

'Two Guinness, one Carlsberg, Heineken, Southern and white.'

'And a vodka and lemon,' a voice from behind said. 'Get you later.'

Jim turned around to find Debbie smiling at him. He grinned back before confirming the order with the barman. 'You're late,' he commented.

'Yeah.' Debbie shrugged off her jacket, revealing a tight top with plenty of cleavage. 'Work was a bitch today so I went home and took it easy. There was no way I was coming straight in and heading straight back out. I'd a nice Chinese,' she grinned slightly, 'dinner, that is. Then a big bubbly bath and, 'cause I'd the flat to myself, I spent ages just mooching about in my dressing gown before I got ready. It was brill.'

Jim tried to push the image of her in a bath out of his head. Jesus, what was he like? 'Well, it's good to see you,' he said awkwardly. Then, smiling, added, 'I'd no one to talk to in the Snigger-at-Fred part of the night. It was awful hard trying to smile and look impressed along with everyone else.'

Debbie laughed her husky laugh. 'Spineless git.' She gave him a puck on the arm and suddenly looked embarrassed. There was a small silence before she said brightly, 'Here's your drinks. I'll give you a hand to carry them over.'

The barman began placing the pints along the bar top. Debbie picked up two pints and the Southern Comfort and told him that she'd see him at the table. Jim pointed out where they were sitting and watched her shapely form disappear into the crowd.

Two pints of Guinness and the vodka were banged down in front of him and absently he handed over some notes. His head was a mess. Here he was barely separated, yet thinking of someone else. Rebound city here I come, he thought morosely.

To hell with it, he thought, as he got his change back from the barman, Jane didn't want him any more, so what did it matter what he did?

# 21

AFTER THE PUB they headed to a club. They had no problem getting into The Kitchen. Patrick put his arm around Rosemary, making it look as if they were a couple and they were waved in. Garage music pumped out of speakers and the place was beginning to fill up.

'You've a nerve trying that.' Miranda rolled her eyes at Patrick. 'The dogs in the street know you drive on the wrong side of the road.'

'Well, he didn't on the way here,' Rosemary said, confused. She looked even more confused as the other three started laughing. 'What's the joke?'

'Nothing,' Patrick said as he headed to the bar.

Coming back laden with drinks, he said, 'Mir, you're going to freak. Guess who I just spotted on the other side of the room?'

Miranda froze with her pint of Guinness halfway to her mouth. 'Who?' There were about a million people who would cause her to freak if she met them when out. All of them male.

'Harry.'

'Aw, Jesus! Aw no!'

'What's wrong with him?' Jane asked. 'It's not as if he ever, you know . . .'

'He never what?' Miranda snapped.

Jane tried to think of a tactful way to say that Miranda hadn't ever been dumped by him. 'Well,' she eventually muttered, 'you've never been in a relationship with him, have you? He's your friend.'

'And who the fuck wants a male friend hanging around them when they're on the prowl?'

'Well, Patrick is our friend,' Rosemary piped up. 'We don't mind him being here.'

'Patrick is one of us,' Miranda snapped. 'He's looking for a man too. Here,' she stood up and pushed Rosemary off her seat, 'let me sit there, with my back to the room. You take my place.'

Rosemary was only too delighted to be of help. 'Oooh,' she said as she was about to sit down in Miranda's seat, 'there's a fine thing on his way over. He's definitely coming this way. Ooooh, I wonder who he wants.'

The 'fine thing' slapped Miranda on the back, making her drink splash on to her brilliant white skirt.

'Oy! Watch it.'

'Sorry,' the guy grinned. He turned to Patrick. 'I *thought* it was you at the bar. How's it going, folks? Hey, Jane, long time no see!'

'Hiya, Harry.' Jane smiled at the tall, dark, good-looking guy that had plonked himself right next to a scowling Miranda.

'You'll pay for this to be cleaned,' Miranda grouched, furiously trying to wipe the stain out of her skirt.

'Sure. No probs. Take it off and I'll take it away with me now.'

Rosemary giggled in near hysteria.

'And who's this?' Harry asked, turning great brown eyes in Rosemary's direction.

'Rosemary,' she said, her eyes big with awe. 'Hiya.'

'You've ruined my skirt!' Miranda gave him a puck. 'Don't mind Rosemary.'

'I told you I'd get it cleaned,' Harry said mildly. He held out his hand. 'Hiya, Rosemary. How's it going?'

'Great. Brill. Thanks for asking. Hiya.'

'D'you work with this shower then?'

'Yeah. Just started a few months ago.'

'Well don't let this one boss you about.' He jerked his head towards Miranda. 'She can be a right bitch. Tries it on with me sometimes too.'

Rosemary tittered violently.

'Are you here with friends?' Jane asked swiftly. Miranda was going to brain Rosemary if she didn't stop hyperventilating.

'Yeah, a few of the lads from work. One of them is getting hitched on Monday, so we're getting him plastered at the moment.'

'Well, don't let us keep you,' Miranda snapped. 'You go and enjoy yourself.'

'And it was great seeing you too, Mir. Listen, making any sweet music lately with musician man?' He winked at the others as he said it.

'Making a symphony actually,' Miranda said, flicking him a disdainful glance. 'Now, go on and toddle off to your friends. We don't want to keep you, they need someone with your dazzling wit to entertain them.'

'Save a dance for me, huh?' Harry caressed her shoulder briefly before she shrugged him off.

Jane gave him a sympathetic smile but he didn't return it. Instead, he nodded briefly and sloped off.

'You're horrible to him,' Jane chastised. 'He was only being friendly.'

'If I want him to be friendly, I'll call him. That's our arrangement.'

'Bloody stupid if you ask me,' Patrick said mildly. 'I wouldn't throw him out of bed for eating crisps.'

'Well, with your performance record, that's all he would be doing, isn't it?'

'Mia-ow.' Patrick made scratching motions with his hands.

Miranda picked up her little bag, 'I'm going out for a smoke. I hope the record will be changed by the time I get back.' A guy passing the table threw her an admiring glance. 'Hiya,' she smiled at him, her face one high-voltage beam.

The guy grinned back and a conversation ensued.

'That's him for the sack tonight,' Patrick observed wryly.

Jane winced. Now where would she sleep?

He was at the stage where he was aware he was drunk. He knew what he was doing, but he didn't care that much. He was conscious of laughing a lot and making other people laugh. He was also aware of Debbie hanging on to his arm and snuggling into him and he liked it. Damn it, he was a free man. He had nothing to feel guilty about.

When the others said that they were heading off to a club however, the guilt set in. 'I'll, eh, give it a miss,' he mumbled.

'Aw, come on.' Fred looked devastated. 'Don't be a fucking . . .' he frowned, searching for a word to describe guys that didn't go to nightclubs, '. . . a fucking *tissue*,' he finished.

Gillian squealed with laughter. 'You!' she belted him. 'Whatta word. Don't be a tissue! Gweat!'

'Well,' Fred asked Jim, 'coming?'

'Nope.' Jim stared into his pint glass. 'I'll, eh, just hang on here and finish my pint.' He wished Debbie would let his arm go.

'I'll hang on too,' she said, startling him.

'Oh,' Fred winked lewdly, 'hey, hey, hey.'

'Yeah, make hay while the sun shines, isn't dat wight, Debs?' Gillian hooted.

Fred guffawed at his girlfriend's wit. 'See yez,' he said, injecting a wealth of meaning into his words.

'You don't have to—' Jim turned to Debbie, but she was watching the others leave.

'Fred is as bad as Gillian,' she said when they'd all disappeared.

'Naw, Fred's definitely worse,' Jim grinned. Debbie didn't grin back. 'You didn't have to stay,' he said quietly, 'there was no need.'

The long, appraising look that Debbie gave him made him squirm. He busied himself draining his pint glass.

'I stayed because I wanted to ask you something,' Debbie said coolly.

He was aware of the heady scent of her perfume and his heart began to speed up.

'Don't you want to know what it is?' she asked.

'Sure.'

Debbie coloured slightly. She glanced at her perfect nails, rubbed her hands together and looked back up at him. 'I like you, Jim, I really do.' As he made to interrupt, she held up her hand and talked over him. 'I've gone out with you a few times in the past couple of months and we always end up chatting together—'

'You're good company.'

She went on as if he hadn't spoken. 'Tonight, I hang on to your arm, I brush off your leg and you enjoy it. Then you say you're not going to the nightclub. The other week we had a blast at the parachute jump and you drive me home but wouldn't even come up for a coffee. Every time we go out it's the same, you're blowing hot and cold on me. I guess,' she swallowed, 'I just want to know where I stand.'

Jim stared at her. Jesus, she was honest. *And* she liked him. 'Debs,' he began, 'I'm thirty-five, I've two teenage kids and I'm barely separated. It's all wrong for you.'

'Let me decide that.' She turned from him and said quietly. 'I hope you don't think I come on like this to every guy—'

'You're not coming on to me. I understand what you're saying.'

'And?' She paused. 'Where do I stand? Am I wasting my time? 'Cause I really like you Jim.'

Jim could not believe it. She really liked him. This beautiful woman with the gorgeous body and great personality was into him. 'I like you too,' he said quietly. His heart twisted as Jane's face flashed into his head. 'But, like, I'm all over the place at the moment. And, well, I don't want to hurt you.'

'What makes you think you will?'

'I dunno. I just want to be fair to you . . .'

'Forget about me,' Debbie said, 'what do *you* want?'

He wanted his wife and kids back, that's what he wanted. But that was never going to happen. 'I guess if I hadn't so much baggage and well . . .' The drink was making it hard to say what he wanted to say. He wasn't much good at saying things anyway, preferring to do things instead. So he cut to the end. 'I'd want you,' he said simply. 'Any guy would.'

'We can work on the baggage.' Debbie's eyes were shining. 'Can we not just go for it? The way you feel, the way I feel. Isn't it worth a try?' She moved nearer him on the seat.

The proximity of the woman was making it difficult to think. He was alone. She was available, desirable and he liked her a lot. Everything seemed so simple. 'You sure you want to?'

'I've never been more sure of anything in my life.'

*Jesus.*

'OK,' he said slowly. 'Why not?'


Jane ended up at Patrick's flat. Miranda had left with the guy she'd picked up and there was no way Jane was heading back with them. Patrick had eventually persuaded her against getting a taxi home in favour of staying the night at his place.

He drove Rosemary back to her house first. She insisted on being let off at the top of her road.

'It's best if you don't come to the door,' she said.

Patrick didn't argue. Rosemary's estate was frightening enough during daylight, at night it looked even more terrifying.

Once Rosemary had left, a silence descended on the car. Jane spent the time staring out at the darkened streets, amazed that so many people should still be wandering about at this late hour.

Eventually Patrick spoke. 'She does it all the time,' he muttered.

'What?'

'Mir. Every time I go out with her, she leaves with some horror.'

140

'Jealous, are you?' Jane teased.

Patrick shrugged, slowed the car down. 'Naw. It's just that she never seems to learn. He'll be gone by Monday and we'll have tears everywhere. Did you see the way he was groping her when she was telling us that she was leaving with him?'

Jane nodded. She'd wondered how on earth Miranda could put up with it. 'And she's so good-looking too – she could have anyone.'

'She *does* have anyone,' Patrick said, causing Jane to smile briefly. 'She's a bloody idiot.'

'You've changed your tune.' She gave him a puck. 'Normally you're all over her, getting the juicy gossip.'

'I know, I haven't the heart to slate her,' Patrick sighed. 'The tears are real.' He stopped talking until he had negotiated his way on to the motorway.

'I dunno why she does it,' he muttered. 'It's like she thinks that's all she's good for. When I try to have a serious talk with her, she loses the head. I don't bother any more.'

'Harry's mad about her.'

'Harry's mad full stop.'

They laughed quietly and said nothing more until they were safely ensconced in Patrick's apartment. It was a shrine to minimalism, Jane marvelled at his good taste. 'Well, if the salon fails, you could always become an interior designer.'

'You think so?' Patrick looked chuffed as he handed her a glass of wine. 'Barney says it's cold. No personal things around.'

He dropped the name Barney into the conversation so casually that Jane wondered if she should know who he was. A brief search of names and she couldn't put a face to him. 'Barney?' she asked, looking at Patrick over the rim of the John Rocha wine glass.

Patrick smiled. 'The valentine's card and chocolate box man.'

'Get lost!'

'He made himself known to me a few weeks ago.' Patrick sounded as if he'd been waiting all night to divulge the details.

141

He leaned towards her, his eyes bright and a big stupid smile on his face. 'And I did have an idea that it was him – well, hoped actually. Only I couldn't be sure. He's a guy I met last year and we'd kept in touch.'

'*And?*' Jane asked. It was nice to see Patrick so happy, he'd been let down badly in the past. It gave her a sort of pang though, to see the way his eyes lit up just talking about Barney. She used to be like that. Ages ago.

'Well, we're taking it slowly – you know – best thing really. But he's lovely.'

There was a small silence before Jane said softly, 'Good. I'm glad. It's important to be happy.'

Another silence descended, punctuated only by the clock ticking.

'And you?' Patrick asked cautiously, 'are you happy, Jane?'

'We're not talking about me.' She forced a bright smile on to her face.

'We are now.'

He expected an answer, but she didn't have one. Was she happy? She never much thought about it. Sometimes it was better not to analyse stuff too much. There was a time she'd been sad, devastated, angry, guilty, but was she happy? Not as much as before, she had to admit. But then again, she could never hope to be as happy as before. 'Happy enough,' she said without conviction. 'I mean, things have changed for me. I've just got to make the best of it. I reckon if Mam wasn't living with me, things might quieten down. Her and Di knock sparks off each other.'

'So she's still with you?'

'Yeah, and there's no sign of her leaving,' Jane muttered. She refilled her wine glass. Talking about home could only be done when well plastered. 'I'm going to have to go and see Dad in the next little while. Mam told me not to, but I'm beginning to think she was only saying it for show.'

'Mmmm.' Patrick studied his best mate. He'd known her for

ages. She'd been the quietest, most unassuming woman he'd ever met. Yet she'd known what she wanted and had gone for it. Why she'd chosen him to go into business with, he could never figure out, but she did and they'd had a blast together. It was Jane's organisational skills that had kept their heads above water in the early days. 'And how's Jim?' he asked, wondering if she'd snap his head off. 'Do you see much of him?'

'Only when he picks the kids up.'

She was *definitely* sounding snappy. He took a risk and said, 'And that's it? Yez don't talk any more?'

She shrugged, saying nothing, about to tell Patrick to leave it. But he looked so concerned that she couldn't. Instead she said softly, 'I dunno Patrick. It was after Matt . . . things changed . . . he blamed me.'

'He'd never do that,' Patrick said with quiet conviction.

Jane shrugged again. A sort of sadness washed over her. She clamped it back. 'Sure,' she muttered.

'That man loves you, Jane.'

'Loved me,' she corrected.

'D'you remember when he first met you and he couldn't screw up the courage to ask you out?'

She didn't want to remember.

'Three months solid he came into the salon looking for a wash and blow dry – d'you remember?'

'Patrick—'

'Mir thought he fancied me,' Patrick chuckled. 'Of course *I* knew he was straight, but I kept serving him anyway, hoping for a road to Damascus type conversion.'

'He was a bit scared of you, all right,' Jane grinned.

'But he kept coming back,' Patrick said. 'And then one day you served him because I was busy with someone else, and he asked for a wash and blow job by mistake! Poor Eileen Simms nearly died.'

Jane smiled. 'So did Jim,' she said softly. 'He was mortified. He started stammering and apologising and everything.' She had fallen in love with him then, she remembered. His shyness, his awkwardness. Later, she'd loved his laugh and the passion he had for his work. All the stuff that had annoyed her more recently.

'He'd never blame you.' Patrick touched her arm.

She didn't bother to answer.

'And anyway, there's nothing to blame you for.'

She wished he'd stop. 'Any more wine?'

'Yeah. Sure.' Patrick took her glass and padded across to the drinks cabinet. He uncorked another bottle of red and poured her some. 'Here. The best stuff in the flat for my wonderful partner.'

Jane smiled and took it from him.

They clinked glasses and sat in silence for a while.

Jane wondered why Patrick was staring at her. She gulped down half the glass and liked the way her head swam.

Patrick reached out and tipped some more wine into his own glass before saying, 'Sometimes . . . I dunno, Jane . . . life is shit hard.'

'Tell me about it.'

'And there is nothing you can do about it.'

'Huh.' Jane closed her eyes. She didn't want to think like that. She let Patrick's words wash over her.

'I remember when I was about twelve, suddenly realising that I was different to all the guys I knew. At fifteen, I had a massive crush on the captain of the rugby team. I fantasised incessantly about him, tried to stop, but couldn't. I went out with piles of girls to make the thoughts stop.'

Jane heard Patrick laugh a bit, but it wasn't a humorous type of laugh. It was sad. She opened her eyes. Patrick was swirling his wine around as he talked.

'It was no good, I couldn't shake it. I became the biggest stud in school instead. And underneath, I knew I was a complete weirdo.'

'You're not weird, don't mind Rosemary,' Jane smiled sleepily.

'Naw, that's not what I'm saying,' Patrick said intently. 'I mean, I sort of knew what I was inside, only I denied it to myself. Couldn't face it. Couldn't even look at myself in the mirror. I spent my life running from my life, you know?'

'Did you?' Jane, her thoughts fuzzy, wondered why on earth Patrick was telling her this.

'Eventually I cracked up. Got counselling. And I remember the day I told the counsellor that I thought I was gay, he just looked at me. I think he knew it anyway, but I had to say it. I guess by saying it I accepted it.'

'Well, I'm glad you're you.' Jane gave another sleepy smile.

'I am too, now,' Patrick said. He laid his glass down on the glass coffee table and said, 'I learnt, Jane, that accepting stuff is the best freedom there is. You know, it stops you fighting things you can't change.'

'And we wouldn't change you, not for the whole world.' Jane squeezed his arm. 'You're the best mate there is.' Her head was spinning. 'I'm glad you told me that, Patrick.'

'You are?' He smiled at her.

'Yeah, I love bedtime stories with a happy ending,' she grinned and then wondered why he looked sort of disappointed.

He lifted himself off the sofa. 'I'll get you a few blankets.'

'Ta.' She sprawled out, too lazy to undress.

Patrick gave a small smile. '*And* maybe a bucket.'

Jane giggled. It was ages since she'd been drunk and it felt great. 'I won't be sick, I'm not that bad.'

'You're not bad at all.' He tousled her hair.

Debbie didn't come up to the flat and Jim didn't ask her. Instead he accompanied her back to her flat and kissed her outside her gate.

'I feel like a teenager,' she giggled.

'Do you?' Jim asked, smiling. 'Well, I hope I'll do instead.'

'You'll do nicely, so you will.'

She wrapped her arms around his neck and he could feel the

145

softness of her breasts pushing against him. It turned him on so much. They kissed again, his tongue probing her mouth. He felt he was going to explode if he did it any more. Breaking apart, he cupped her face in his hands, 'Call you tomorrow – OK?'

If she was disappointed, she didn't let on. 'Great.'

He waited until she was safely inside and then turned and began the long walk back to Fred's flat. Part of him was singing, but the other part was dead confused.

'Night!' She'd opened her flat window and was yelling at him.

He grinned and lifted a hand in salute. 'Night yourself.'

The dead confused part wondered what the hell he was doing. The singing part told him that he was moving on.

# 22

JANE TOOK A deep breath as she pulled up in front of a big square house set well back from the road. This was it. The claiming back of her life. Of her house. She tried to block out the fact that she was only doing what she'd done from infancy, sorting out her parents' lives yet again. It had been four months now, the longest split ever, and she was becoming slightly concerned that her mother would be a permanent fixture in her bed. And, after avoiding Matt's room for so long, sleeping in it every night now was hard. Sometimes hugging his teddies comforted her, other times she cried herself to sleep. She didn't know if she could stand it much longer. But it was better than letting her mother sleep in it. Sheila wouldn't hug Keano, wouldn't say goodnight to Matt.

Jane climbed the five large stone steps that led to the front door of the house. The door was a huge oak affair, complete with stained-glass windows on either side. The sound of the bell echoed inside the hall and she soon heard footsteps. The door was answered by a small, narrow, dude-ish looking man. His voice, when he spoke, was all cigars and whiskey.

'Yo, Jane.' He pulled the door open wider. 'How's things? Long time no see!'

'Dad.' Jane gave a nod and, pushing past him, entered the hall. 'Is there somewhere we can talk – in private?'

Declan D'arcy shut the door. 'Hey Dad! How ya doin'? Gee, it's great to see you. How's things?'

'Can we talk?' Jane asked again. She was not going to be sidetracked by her father's trendy jargon and funny jibes.

'Straight to the point – that's my Janey,' Declan grinned. 'Ever consider a career in radio?'

'Dad, I didn't come here to be entertained. I want to talk.'

'Nothing I like better than talkin'!' There was a pause as he awaited her laughter. When none was forthcoming, he continued, 'It's gonna be difficult. I've a few lads here from the station. We're having a big confab on the direction the show is gonna take in the next few months. I dunno. You're lucky you caught me here, normally I'm down the station.'

'So, can you talk or not?'

'In about an hour,' Declan said. 'You can make yourself a cuppa if you want.' He followed her into the kitchen. 'You're wasting your time if it's about Sheila,' he warned.

Jane froze for a second, before choosing to ignore the comment. How many times had she heard that in the past? 'Go back to your important meeting, Dad,' she said airily.

When she turned back, he'd gone.

Typical.


The meeting finished up exactly an hour later. It ended with much laughter and backslapping. Her dad insisted on dragging a pile of men into the kitchen to say 'hello'.

'This, fellas, is my daughter, Jane,' he bellowed. He did a big flourishy thing with his hand. 'She owns a hairdressing place on Yellow Halls Road.'

'Cutting Edge?' someone asked, impressed.

'No,' Jane answered a little too brightly. 'The other one. Patrick Costelloe's.'

'Don't know that one,' the guy replied, sounding puzzled. 'My wife now, she went to Cutting Edge the other day. Dead expensive it was. I dunno how they can justify those kinds of prices.'

'Send her to us next time,' Jane said. 'We're reasonable and the products we use are of a higher quality.'

The guy shook his head. 'Naw, she thinks if she pays a lot,

148

she'll look good. Jaysus, all I keep telling her is that plastic bags are cheaper.' He slapped his thigh at his wittiness and some of the others laughed along.

'My wife Sheila takes out a mortgage whenever she goes anywhere,' Declan guffawed. 'I'm telling yez, if we spent as much on property as she does on her hair, we'd own New York City by now!'

'Hair-raising or what?' some other guy said.

Her dad's show was going to go down the tubes if this was the sort of stuff they thought was funny, Jane thought.

'I cut me own hair,' a completely bald guy said.

There was more laughter.

'My wife sued me when she found out I had a hairpiece. She thought it was one of those sexually transmitted diseases!'

Hand-clapping and knee-slapping this time.

'Hey, maybe we should do a section on hair and hair tales on the show,' Declan said.

They all agreed that this was a fabulous idea. It got scribbled down in the bald guy's notebook and, after saying goodbye to Jane, they all trudged off. Declan saw them to the door, laughing every inch of the way. When he got back into the kitchen, he still had a grin on his face. 'Mad bastards or what?' he said.

'Definitely mad and most definitely bastards,' Jane couldn't resist answering.

'Aw, now, Janey,' Declan placated.

She hated it when he called her that.

He flicked on the kettle. 'Tea?'

'I've had about five cups in the last hour,' she said. 'So, no thanks.'

'Five?' Declan gave her a look of mock horror. 'I only said "a cuppa". Jesus, women, yez all take advantage of my good nature.'

She smiled despite herself. 'Yeah, right.'

There was a silence while Declan made himself tea and a sandwich. For the first time Jane took in what he was wearing.

149

He was dressed like a guy in his twenties as usual. Jeans with turn-ups, Doc Martens, a sweatshirt saying: *DJs do it on air.* His hair was closely cropped and he sported a gold stud in one ear. The stuff of teenage mortification.

'So, what's this chat you want to have?' Declan sat across from her. The grin was gone from his face and he looked uneasy. Not for the first time, Jane became aware of a weird role-reversal taking place.

'It's about Mam.'

'I fucking knew it.'

'She can't stay with me for much longer.'

Declan took a bite from his sandwich. He munched it for a while, before saying matter-of-factly, 'So, throw her out.'

'Dad!'

'Well, why not? If I know her, she's monopolising the bath-room, the shower and the hairspray. She's eating her rabbit food all the time and refusing to do any cleaning – yeah?'

Jane squirmed. 'It's not that bad—'

Declan gave a snort of laughter. 'Neither was Boyzone.'

'I want you to ask her back.'

There was more laughter. 'You have *got* to be joking!'

'Dad—'

'No way. And Janey,' he reached across and tugged her hair affectionately. 'You know I'd do anything for you – but I sure as hell won't do that.'

Jane was confused. Normally, to get her dad to make it up with her mam, all it took was a bit of grovelling on her part. OK, so she hadn't done that much grovelling. 'Please, Dad, tell her you miss her. Beg her to come home. It'd make her so happy.' She paused. 'And me too.'

'Has she sent you?'

'No, she doesn't even know I'm here.'

'Well, at least she has some pride.' He stood up and shoved his plate and cup into the dishwasher. 'But there is no way I'd have her back. Getting rid of her has been the best thing I ever did.'

'You didn't get rid of her.' Jane felt some sympathy for her mam. 'She left you.'

To her surprise, her dad chuckled. 'So that's what she told you – is it? She left me. Well, I guess she *would* say that.'

'What do you mean?' Jane tried to keep her voice angry, but she couldn't help feeling uneasy at his laughter.

'I just got fed up with her,' Declan said, as if he was talking about some piece of furniture. 'She was always moaning on about something – when she wasn't *leaving* me that is. So that day, when she rang up the radio station and gave me major earache for telling everyone about our sex life, I just told her to go. "Piss off," I said. And when I got home, she'd pissed off. Best thing ever.'

This was new territory for her. Her dad had never done that before. Delicate handling was called for. 'You were wrong to tell everyone about your sex life,' she said, forcing her voice to be gentle. 'That sort of stuff is private.'

'I said that we'd had sex ten times in one night,' Declan explained, his mouth curving up in yet another smile. 'Jaysus, sex ten times in one century would be more like it. I'm a showman, Jane, an entertainer. I tell great big fat ones.'

'Yeah, well, no one else knew it was a lie. It was horrible.'

'It made your mother out to be every guy's dream date – will you get a grip, babe!'

'Not every woman wants to be perceived like that, Dad.'

'Oh, yeah. Sure.'

He really didn't get it. He never had. He'd done the same to her when she was a kid. Her love life had been the nation's favourite topic and the break-up of a relationship was greeted with cards from every corner of the country with people telling her how sorry they were. He'd never understood the meaning of the word 'private'. 'So,' Jane said eventually, 'you're not going to ask her back?'

'No, I am not.'

A major grovel was called for. 'Dad, please—'

151

'Jane,' Declan interrupted, 'it's about time you let your mother stand on her own two feet. She doesn't need a babysitter. You're a grown woman now, you've your own life. Butt out of ours.'

Butt out!

*Butt out!*

She was only the one who'd kept their lives together for the past thirty-odd years. And now she was being told to 'butt out'. It hurt. She picked up her bag and coat. 'Don't worry, Dad, you've made your point. You don't need me. Fine.'

'Aw, now I didn't mean—'

'Get your listeners to advise you instead. After all, they've plenty of opinions.'

'Aw, Jane—'

But she was hurrying towards the door and refusing to listen to him. Why had she bothered?

'Jane, please,' her dad was saying.

'I'm going, Dad. And,' she whirled around to face him, 'don't even think of apologising on your pathetic show, because I never listen to it anyhow.'

'So *you're* the one person who doesn't,' he joked feebly.

'I'm out of your life.' She slammed the door in his face and revved up her car so hard that she was surprised the engine didn't explode.

Well, that was it. If he wanted her to butt out, she would.

And JESUS, she was going to *kill* her mother when she got home.

'How come you didn't tell me that Dad had thrown you out?'

'Pardon, dahling?' Sheila took the cucumber from her eyes and sat up gingerly. 'What's that you said?'

'I said,' Jane flung her coat across a chair and advanced on her mother, 'why didn't you tell me that Dad had told you to leave?'

Sheila paled. 'Have you been to see him?' she demanded.

'Have you been to see him after I expressly told you not to? Have you?'

'Yes, yes I have, Mother.' Jane stood over her mother and glared at her. Sheila seemed to wilt before her eyes. 'And it's just as well too, or you would have gone on making a huge fool out of me for God knows how long!'

'I'd never make a fool out of you, dahling, you know that.' Sheila pursed her lips. 'I mean, I didn't technically lie to you – I was going to leave him anyway. I told him I was leaving and he said fine.'

'He said, "piss off"!'

'Oh, now really dahling, there's no need for that type of language.'

'Isn't there? *Isn't there?*'

'Well, no. Not that I can see,' Sheila said primly. She swallowed hard and continued, 'I *told* you not to go and see him. I knew he'd only upset you.'

'You lying to me upset me, Mother,' Jane gulped. 'How dare you not tell me the truth? I went around to sort it all out and I made a right eejit out of myself.'

'Well, whose fault is that?' Sheila asked sharply. 'I told you not to go and you went. It's about time you realised, dahling, that you cannot control our marriage.'

'I'm not trying to control—'

'Yes you are dahling,' Sheila said, sounding quite cross. 'You always thought you could sort us out, but we would have sorted ourselves out anyway. You know your father, he only does what he wants, when he wants.'

Jane gawped at her mother. She had never spoken to her like this before.

'And really, dahling, what happens in everyone's marriage is private, isn't it? I mean, you've told me to mind my own business over you and Jim plenty of times.'

'That's different!'

'How?' Sheila demanded. 'How is it any different?'

'Well . . .' Jane bit her lip. 'Well, I dunno. It *seems* different.'

'Well it's not. It's the same. And I could be interfering and say to you that maybe you and Jim should talk to each other more, but I don't, because it's not my business. If you *asked* me my opinion, I would give it, but you haven't, so I won't. Because it's – not – my – business.'

Jane stared, stunned, at her.

'So, to finish,' Sheila said, 'I am sorry that I didn't tell you Declan had asked me to leave.' She made a big deal of examining her nails. 'I suppose,' she said, with difficulty, 'I suppose, I just wanted to save face, in front of my daughter and grand-children.'

There was a silence.

Jane studied the top of her mother's bent head. Saving face was so important to this woman and she had ruined it for her. And of course, she was right. She shouldn't have gone around to her dad when she'd been told not to. 'I'm sorry, Mam,' she said, half-choking on the words. 'You're right.'

Sheila gave her a watery smile.

'And I won't interfere any more.' Jane sat down beside her. 'What's your business is your business. And Di and Owen won't find out.' She took the risk of touching her mother on the shoulder. 'We'll let them go on thinking that Granddad Deco is suffering big-time.'

'Thank you, dahling.' Sheila patted Jane on the arm. 'I think I'd like that.'

They smiled hesitantly at each other.

'And,' Jane bit her lip, 'what you said about Jim and me . . .'

'Not my business.'

'I know. But, it's just that we tried to talk and, well, we, we physically couldn't do it. He'd end up walking out all the time or I'd cry. That's all there was to it.'

Sheila said nothing, just squeezed Jane's hand.

'So it was the best thing for both of us, for him to leave. The silence wasn't good for the kids.'

'No, it couldn't have been,' Sheila said. 'And if there's anything I can do to help, dahling, you only have to ask. I mean, the time you went out and I minded the two kids wasn't bad at all. I managed perfectly well, so if you need me to do it again – I'm here.'

'Thanks.'

Sheila squeezed her hand again. 'Anything at all.'

She felt happy as she waited for Jim. The talk with her mother had done her good. Maybe now that they'd come to an understanding, it'd be nice to have her around. At least it'd be another adult to talk to in the evenings when the kids had gone to bed. And Sheila had offered to watch the kids, which meant that she could get out for a drink after work with Patrick some time.

The future was looking decidedly upbeat.

At half past eight Jim pulled up in front of the house and let the two kids out.

'Tell your father I want to see him,' she said to Owen as he came up the driveway.

'If it's about Gooey, don't bother,' Di said, 'I've already told him.'

'It's none of your business what it's about, miss,' Jane said. She gave Owen a gentle push. 'Owen, go now, before he drives off.'

'Will I tell him to come in, like?'

'Yes.'

'Are you going to take him back?' Di startled her with the question. She was looking at her mother with eyes that barely concealed her hope and delight.

Jane touched Di on the shoulder. God, the poor kid, thinking like that. 'No baby, I'm not. I just—'

'Yeah. Yeah. Right.' Diane stomped upstairs, taking her frustration and embarrassment out on every step.

Owen was coming up the drive with Jim. Jim was wearing the black shirt she'd bought him ages ago and a pair of black Levi's. A bit priestly, but he got away with it.

'You wanted to see me?' he asked, grinning in the way she remembered from back when he'd first asked her out.

'Uh-huh. Just for a chat,' she clarified. She turned to Owen. 'We'll be in the sitting room, you can get yourself something to eat in the kitchen.'

Owen sloped off.

Jane ushered Jim into the sitting room. 'Tea?' she asked.

'Naw. Thanks.' Jim shoved his hands into his jeans pockets. 'I'm heading out later, so I need to get back.'

'Heading out?' She hated the lonely sound of her voice.

Jim gulped. Scuffed his shoes on the carpet. Brought his dark eyes up to hers. 'Yeah, just like you last week. Di said you didn't come home.'

'No. I stayed with a friend.' She deliberately didn't mention Patrick and was glad to see the slight wince he gave.

There was a silence.

'So, what do you want to talk about?'

'Our daughter.'

'If it's about her boyfriend, she told me.'

'Did she now?' Jane quirked her eyebrows. 'And what exactly did she tell you?'

'That she's seeing a guy called . . . I dunno . . . something weird, and that she's very happy.'

'A guy called Gooey,' Jane said slowly. 'An eighteen-year-old guy called Gooey who looks like a cross between a down-and-out and a dog with mange.'

'Right.' Jim nodded.

'Right?' Jane couldn't believe this. 'Is that all you can say?'

'OK, so he's not good-looking – big deal.'

'Di also told me that he's unemployed and left school at fifteen. Jim, he's a bad influence. And God, the last thing she needs is a bad influence. She's difficult enough as it is.'

'Well, if he's wrong for her, I'm sure she'll find out herself. She's an intelligent girl.'

'More intelligent than her father, that much I can see.'

156

'Well, what do you want me to do?'

'Tell her not to see him.'

'Oh for Christ's sake, I can't do that! I don't even know the lad.'

'I know him.'

'So you tell her, if it bugs you so much!'

Jane bit her lip and turned away. 'She won't listen to me,' she muttered.

''Course she will,' Jim said, softer now. 'She's always talking about you when I take her out. She keeps tabs on all the stuff you do.'

She didn't need his sympathy. This, this fecker who was heading out for the night. 'It's not the same.'

Jim flinched. 'Well, there's nothing I can do, Jane. I'll have to wait until I meet him.'

'Well, if it takes as long as it took me to meet him you'll have some wait!'

Jim shrugged helplessly. 'What do you want me to do? I can't force her to let me meet him, can I? Be reasonable.'

God, she hated being told to be reasonable, especially by Jim, Mr Rational himself. Oh, he could put everything into neat little boxes and only open the ones he wanted to. No matter what happened, he went out to work, he came home, he went to work. His bloody life could fall apart and he could still go out. She glared at him, feeling tears of frustration well up inside her.

'Hey.' Jim had reached out to her and she pulled away as his hand brushed her shoulder.

'Get out! Just . . . just get out and come back when there *is* something you can do!'

Startled, he gazed at her. 'Jane—'

'Out!' More in control now, she walked to the sitting room door and held it open for him. 'Bye now.'

He looked steadily at her for a few seconds before walking past her. At the door he turned. 'I'll talk to her about it,' he muttered.

157

'I won't hold my breath.' She couldn't help herself. 'You were never much good at talking.'

He bowed his head and shrugged. 'Sometimes words are just too fucking hard.'

He caught her off balance. 'No words at all are even worse,' she said back softly. 'Sometimes—'

'I'll talk to Di, OK?' Jim interrupted her. 'That's all I can do.'

'Ohhh,' Jane nodded furiously. 'I agree with that.'

Jim looked hopelessly at her before walking out through the front door and off down the driveway.

He drove until he reached a little lay-by. Pulling in, he cut the engine of the car. He stared out of the window for a long time.

It was the first time Jane had been angry with him in years. He didn't know if it was a good sign or not. Maybe he should have stayed and rowed with her. Maybe he should have just stood on his front step and shouted at her and let her shout back at him. Maybe it was just what they needed.

He laid his head on the steering wheel and wondered what would happen if he went back and told her that she was being unfair, that talking to Di was not the only thing he could do, that he could do so much more if he had the chance.

But he'd had the chance, he thought.

Four years ago he'd had a chance to stand by her and he'd messed it up.

He started his car and knew that he'd never go back and say those words to her. Never.

## 23

IT COULDN'T BE right, Jane thought, staring hard at her bank statement. Surely there had to be a mistake. She ran down the list of standing orders and checked it off against her bills – yep, everything had been paid, nothing had been done on the double. Her half of the mortgage had gone through and her wages had been lodged.

Her *pathetic* wages.

She and Patrick were now earning less than Mir. Business was falling off rapidly, despite days upon days of handing out Patrick's leaflets. He'd printed thousands of them and so far they'd had about three extra customers. But lost about fifty to the salon up the road. If things continued like this, there'd soon be no business left and then what would she do?

A small flutter of fear began in her belly. She couldn't ask Jim for more money, he was giving more than his share as it was. Despite the fact that he was no longer living with them, he still paid half the mortgage. And the money he gave for the kids was more than enough. Well, it had been until she'd started to earn peanuts.

And of course there was her mother. Cast adrift without a penny from her father, she was now an extra drain on the household. Especially as she kept forgetting to turn off the immersion and spent all day huddled beside the fan heater, saying that she was cold. The electricity bill had gone through the roof since she'd arrived.

There was nothing for it, Jane decided, if her mother had

pledged to do anything to help, well then, she'd just have to prove herself.

She found Sheila and Di sitting together on the sofa. For once they weren't sniping at each other. In fact, they looked quite cosy.

'Now, dahling,' Sheila was saying, 'you only file in one direction. That way you'll have lovely strong nails.'

'Like this?'

'It's not a sander you know,' Sheila laughed, taking the nail file away from her granddaughter. 'It's a delicate piece of board and you must treat it as such.'

Jane smiled, before noticing that Sheila had again raided the kitchen press as a bowl of hot olive oil was on the floor. Expensive olive oil. Obviously they'd both been soaking their nails.

'Mam,' she said, trying to keep the irritation from her voice, 'I need a word.'

'Just a minute, dahling, I'm doing your daughter's nails. Honestly, what are you teaching the child about grooming? – she hasn't a clue.'

'Will you French polish them too?' Di asked.

'I'll put a coat of strengthener on them,' Sheila said. 'They're too short for French polishing just yet.' Seeing Di's disappointed look, she added, 'I'll see if I've some falsies in my room later.'

'Great. Thanks.'

Jane waited as Sheila filed Di's nails for her and applied some varnish. Di was in her element and Jane smiled to see the happy expression on her face. Sheila, too, was happy. There was nothing she liked better than talking about hands or toes or hair.

Finally, Di held up her fingers and grinned. 'Libby will be raging when she sees these. She's not able to file her nails properly at all. They're all chipped and broken.'

'Bring her over some evening,' Sheila said. 'I'll do them for her if she wants. Honestly, the world is in a terrible state when girls can't look after their appearances properly.'

Di danced out of the room. 'Hey, Mam, aren't they nice?' She fluttered them under Jane's nose.

'Gorgeous,' Jane grinned. 'You'll have every fella after you with nails like that.'

'Don't want every fella, just one.'

Jane tried to keep the smile plastered on her face as Di left.

'Well, dahling,' Sheila began tidying up her nail-care products, 'what is it you wanted?'

'You're not going to like it, Mother.'

'Well, it can't shock me as much as Di not being able to file her nails properly.'

Jane smiled at her mother's naïveté. 'OK, well, that's re-assuring because I'm stuck for cash and I've no way of sup-porting two kids, a mortgage and you.'

'Oh.' Sheila froze in the act of putting her emery board away. 'Well, I have no money to lend you, dahling, and I can't go asking Declan for money.'

'I know.' Jane nodded. 'So that leaves just one option.'

'You want me to go!' Sheila's hands fluttered to her throat. 'Oh, dahling, where will I go?'

'No, Mother, I don't want you to go,' Jane said softly. 'But you will have to start paying your way.'

'But I've no money!'

'Yes, which is why you'll have to get a job.'

'A job?' Sheila mouthed, barely whispering. Then she gave a brittle laugh. 'Oh, dahling, I couldn't possibly get a job.'

'Why not?'

'Well,' Sheila licked her lips. 'I'm Sheila D'arcy, aren't I? Wife of the most popular entertainer in the country.'

'Who is not supporting you,' Jane put in gently.

Sheila looked aghast. 'But,' she stuttered, 'but what will I *do*?'

'I don't know,' Jane said. 'Anything. Mam, I wouldn't be asking if I wasn't strapped. The salon is doing badly at the minute and I can't afford . . .'

'Ask Jim for more money.'

161

'To support you? You want my ex-husband to pay for you?'

'Ohhh,' she curled her lip disdainfully. 'I never thought of it like that. Yes, I wouldn't take money from a wife-deserter. But, dahling, I can't get a job. There has to be another way.'

'Well, unless you're any good at robbing banks.'

'That is just not funny.' Sheila stood up shakily from the sofa. 'Oh my, I've a headache coming on. I'm going for a lie down.'

'You said you'd do anything to help me, Mother,' Jane said as Sheila began to climb the stairs. 'I believed you.'

Sheila turned stricken eyes on her daughter. 'Dahling, I meant it. I truly did. But this . . .' She swallowed hard. 'Oooh, my head.'

## 24

JANE AND ROSEMARY spent the morning handing out the last of the flyers to uninterested passers-by. The whole thing was made worse because it was lashing with rain. And, after going to the effort of handing leaflets to people, it was disheartening to see them crumple them up and shove them in their pockets without even glancing at them.

'I think this is worse than being a billboard,' Rosemary remarked as the rain streaked down her face, making tracks through her heavily applied false tan. 'At least if you're a billboard, you've wood protecting your clothes. My skirt is soaking now. And look at me legs!'

Her legs were purple with cold. Purple and brown.

Jane wondered if she looked as bedraggled as her trainee. If she did, she'd be in no fit state to cut anyone's hair that afternoon. 'Come on,' she said, taking the leaflets from Rosemary. 'Let's head back. I think we're wasting our time with these anyway. We handed out loads last week and no one has come in because of them.'

'No, they haven't.' Rosemary clumped alongside her, pulling her jacket over her hair. 'Just the granny brigade and they come in every week anyway.'

'Rosemary, don't call our customers that.'

'I don't. Nash does.' She giggled a bit. 'Nash says you'll probably blue rinse me for this IHF competition, but I said that you won't.'

Jane resisted the urge to brain the kid. Confidence-boosting she was not.

'You won't, sure you won't?'

'Rosemary, please stop saying stuff like that. If you don't want to do it, just say so – right?'

'Aw Jane—' Rosemary looked contrite. 'Sorry. It was a joke.'

Jane couldn't bring herself to smile. 'I won't blue rinse you, but you'll just have to trust me and let me get on with it. Otherwise there is no point in agreeing to be my model.'

'OK.' She looked at the ground.

'OK,' Jane said.

Silence descended as the rain got heavier.

'What is this IHF thing anyway?' Rosemary broke the silence. 'All me mates want to know – they don't believe that I'm going to be a model. Is it an important thing?'

'Yeah.' Jane nodded. 'It's sort of like the Oscars of Irish hair-dressing.'

'The Oscars?' Rosemary let out a little squeal of delight.

'Basically, what happens is that the hairdresser styles the hair, then the model gets her make-up and clothes done, and later there's a reception where the models parade their hairstyles in front of the judges.'

'Oooh.' Rosemary hugged herself. 'And can anyone go?'

'Anyone with a ticket. Everyone dresses up and has a bit of craic. It's good fun.'

'And have you ever won before?'

'Once. Years ago.' Jane smiled at the memory. 'I won Trainee of the Year.'

'Trainee?' Rosemary looked impressed. 'Ooooh, that was good. Maybe I'll enter one year.'

'Maybe you will.' Jane smiled at her.

'My dad wouldn't laugh then,' Rosemary said cheerfully. 'He thinks I'm mental, see. He thinks I want too much. He says that aiming high is only for people with bad shots. He says we should always aim level with what we're given. That's crap, isn't it, Jane?'

'Oh, I don't want—'

'I mean, you didn't aim as high as you could have, did you? I mean, what with you winning that competition, you could have done much better. But you didn't.'

'Sorry?'

'You're happy styling oldies' hair in a small place.' She paused. 'Though,' she amended, 'you can do young hair too.'

Jane nodded approvingly. 'Yep, I can.'

'So that means, me, well, I can aim as high as I want. There's no law says I have to stay where I am, is there?'

'No.' Jane wished she'd stop. It was really great to think that an eighteen-year-old kid with nothing behind her thought she was a failure.

'I like your salon,' Rosemary said. 'But—'

'I have kids,' Jane said suddenly. 'Kids curb your ambitions, you know?'

'Mir said your fella had a big job. It didn't curb his.'

And it hadn't, Jane thought bitterly.

'No man is going to stop me,' Rosemary smiled brightly. 'Especially not me da.' She paused again. 'Or Jaz for that matter.'

She'd been like that once, Jane thought. All she'd wanted was to be a hairdresser. A top stylist with a chain of stores named after her. But it hadn't happened.

She wondered what exactly *had* happened.

It was turning into a wonderful day. First getting soaked in the rain, then two of her customers cancelled and to top all that, because she'd left the house in such a hurry that morning, she had forgotten her lunch. It was probably sitting in its foil wrapper on the counter top at home. She'd made her favourite too, egg, cucumber and tomato. Now Sheila would probably eat it, after taking out the egg, of course. And scraping off all the butter. And the mayo. So far, Sheila hadn't succeeded in getting any interviews and was lolling around at home, plucking her eyebrows and saying how useless she felt.

Jane searched her purse to see if she had any change to get a sandwich at the local shop. She had three euros. It was so long since she'd bought a sandwich that she didn't know how much one would cost. 'How much for a sambo at Lisa's?' she asked.

'Too bloody much,' Miranda muttered. 'They're meaner than a gang of Rottweilers.'

'Pack,' Patrick corrected absently. 'Dogs are pack animals.'

'Why don't you pack it in?' Miranda suggested as she towel-dried some poor victim's hair.

Rosemary giggled, then stopped suddenly and scurried away to the other end of the salon.

She was copping on, Jane thought, getting to know when to steer clear of Miranda. 'Three euro be enough?' she asked.

No one answered her. 'Anyone else want anything?'

'Yeah, the guy from Saturday night cut to ribbons and salt poured into his open wounds,' Miranda snapped.

'I feel like that about my husband sometimes,' Miranda's customer ventured.

'Well, at least he stayed around long enough to marry you,' Miranda said. 'At least he didn't treat you like a cow on the first date.'

'What?'

'Hit the hay and milk you for all he could. And then shit all over you.'

'He does that now . . .'

Jane left before she heard any more. It was a typical Monday with Miranda. She passed Cutting Edge on her way to the shop. The place was hopping, which was a bit depressing. They'd only had three customers in so far that day. And they'd only come because Cutting Edge was booked solid.

Lisa's was packed too. They made up fresh sandwiches and there seemed to be crowds waiting to be served. It seemed every business on the street was doing well, except them. Jane joined the end of the queue and again cursed herself for leaving her lunch behind. It wasn't like her, she was normally so organised. And now her mother would find it and . . . She concentrated hard on the menu on the wall, wondering what she'd have.

'Yeah?' a woman asked. 'Whaddya want?'

'I'll have—'

'Hurry up now, we've not got all day!'

'A white sandwich with—'

'No white bread.'

'A brown sand—'

'No brown.'

'A white roll? Have you got that?'

'Are you being smart? I've no time for smart-arses. Now, what do you want?'

'A white roll with ham, cheese, spicy chicken, crisps and tomato.'

The woman began flinging food everywhere as she made up the roll.

Suddenly, a bright orange sign on the wall behind the woman caught Jane's attention. *Staff wanted. Apply within.*

'Is that job gone by any chance?' she asked.

The woman paused in her shovelling of food. 'Is dat job gone, she asks?' She flung back her head and let out a bellow of a laugh. 'D'you think there'd be a queue a mile long waiting to be served if the job was filled?'

God, she was horrible, Jane thought. So rude. It was no wonder people weren't queuing up to work for her. But maybe . . . naw, she couldn't. But maybe . . .

'Two euro seventy.' The woman peeled off her glove and held out her hand for the money.

'I might have someone who'd be interested,' Jane said as she paid. 'Can she come for an interview tomorrow morning?'

'An interview.' Again the woman laughed. 'And where would I get time to give an interview? Look,' she said as she handed Jane her roll, 'if this person can speak English, make rolls up and take money, she can have the job.'

'Really?'

'You think I've time for joking?'

Jane shook her head. 'No. No, of course not. Well, I'll, eh, let this person know.' God, it had been so easy. Now her mother was set. 'Keep the job open, won't you?'

'Luv, it's been open for the past month.'

A man behind Jane banged on the counter. 'Oy! Anyone serving here?'

'I'll have her here tomorrow,' Jane promised, but the woman wasn't listening. Angry words were being bandied about between her and her customer.

Jane grinned. Patrick's words came to mind. Business was business and a job was a job. If her mother could work here, she'd work anywhere.


'Serving sandwiches?' Sheila could barely get the words out. 'Dahling, I can't serve sandwiches.'

'It's easy. People tell you what they want and you shove it between two slices of bread.'

'No. I don't mean it like that. *I mean,*' Sheila took a deep breath, 'I'm Sheila D'arcy. I just don't "do" serving sandwiches. I mean, what will my public say?'

'Dad's public,' Jane corrected briskly. 'And Mam, I don't care. You will do this job until you can find another that suits your needs better.'

'I'm quite capable of finding my own job, thank you,' Sheila said crossly. 'I was hoping at worst to be a sales assistant in somewhere like BT's, not—'

'They don't take credit card scammers, Nana,' Di, who had just entered the room, piped up in a mock-helpful voice.

'Right, for that, I'm not plucking your eyebrows,' Sheila said smartly.

'Awww,' Di looked devastated. 'Please, Nana.'

'No.'

'Mam, I mean it.' Jane decided to finish the conversation

168

before Di and her mother went for each other. As her mother went to protest further, she added, 'And I am not having this conversation again. I'll drive you to work tomorrow and after the shop closes you can call in on me at the salon and we'll go home together.'

Sheila moaned despairingly. 'You're a hard woman, Jane,' she sniffed. 'You never used to be like this.'

'Like what? Anxious about money? Well, sorry, Mam, but my business has never been in trouble before – all right?'

'Oh, dahling, you're so dramatic!'

'Tomorrow,' Jane nodded. 'You'll start work tomorrow.'

As she left, she heard Di promising to show her nana how to butter bread with hard butter if only her nana would do her eyebrows.

'I'll do one eyebrow,' Sheila replied.

'Cool!'

## 25

J IM FLICKED OFF his mobile phone and frowned.

'So, who was that?' Fred asked as he leaned over Jim's dinner. 'The gorgeous Debbie?'

'Nope. Just Di.'

'Oh.' Fred looked disappointed. 'So, what is the story with Debbie? Have you two, you know . . . ?'

'Have we two, what?' Jim asked flatly as he bit into a slice of pizza. Jesus, he'd really have to start eating properly. Most days it was pizzas or chips or, if he felt like cooking, waffles and sausages. It was all getting a bit monotonous. A bit like Fred actually.

'You and cat-woman – have yez shagged each other yet?'

'Her name is Debbie and it's none of your business.'

'So you haven't.' Fred pulled back with a look of bitter disappointment on his face. 'I dunno what the hold-up is.' He paused. 'Or,' he said slyly, 'maybe *that* is the problem? *A hold-up.*' He chortled loudly.

'Is Gillian around?' Jim asked. ''Cause like, she's the only one who ever laughs at your jokes – don't go wasting them on me.'

'You are so narky since you left yer woman,' Fred muttered. 'I dunno, she's managed to turn you into a right ballet shoe.'

'I'd rather be a ballet shoe than someone who walks around with their foot permanently in their mouth.'

Fred laughed. 'Good one, Jimbo.' He nicked a piece of pizza from Jim's plate and, munching on it, asked, 'D'you fancy heading out somewhere mad later?'

'Nope.'

'Aw, come on, I sold three cars today.'

'Nope.'

'Seeing Debs are you?'

'Nope.'

'Then why not?'

''Cause I've a busy schedule. The Chains Bond crisps are being launched tomorrow and there are a couple of other promotions that I've to handle as well.'

Fred yawned in pretend boredom.

'Is Gillian not around?'

'Naw, she's a bit narky this week, so I said I'd stay well clear. I asked her if it was her time of the month, you know, trying to be understanding, and Jaysus, she belted me.' He touched his face gingerly. 'So, like, I'm letting her sweat. I'll give her a bell in a day or so.'

'Aw, Fred, you know how to treat a woman, that's for sure.'

'There's only one woman in my life,' Fred said, as he went towards the parrot cage. 'And it's Parrot here.' He shoved his nose in and the parrot rubbed her beak on it. 'Who's a lovely girl?' he crooned. 'Say, "Gillian is a narky bitch" for me.'

'Bitch,' Parrot squawked.

Fred laughed. 'And say, "Jimbo is a wanker."'

'Takes one to know one,' Jim grinned.

He was rewarded with a piece of parrot food right smack in the middle of his pizza.

'Seriously though,' Fred sat down beside Jim on the sofa. 'Is it hot and heavy with Debbie?'

Jim glared at him in exasperation. 'Fred, you're sitting on my projections.'

'Ouch! Painful!' Fred smirked and, removing a pile of paperwork from under him, he handed it to Jim. 'I just want to tell you, right, and it's not my business, right, but that Debbie is big into you. Gillian says she's mad about you.'

171

Jim continued to gaze at his laptop. He was sure Fred was just fishing for information.

'Now,' Fred moved nearer to him. 'You don't want to be getting too involved with her, you know. Women let you down, Jimbo. Look at Jane and what happened there.'

'Jane didn't let me down.' Jim started to type.

'She got pregnant and trapped you.'

'Fred—'

'And your mother let you down.'

'My mother let me down?' Jim stopped typing and gazed incredulously at his mate.

'Well, she died, didn't she? How permanent is that?'

Jim couldn't speak. He simply couldn't say a thing. The guy was unbelievable. After staring at Fred for a while, he turned back to his computer.

'And your grandmother – what a ball-buster!'

'Fred – leave it!'

'Women let you down. It's their nature. They want you and when they have you, they don't want you any more. That's why,' Fred jabbed him, 'you can't fall for any tricks she might pull on you.'

'Fred—'

'It's time to enjoy life now. You and me and the lost years – eh?' Fred gave him a friendly thump on the arm.

Jim managed to smile. 'I will enjoy life when I get about a million people to buy a million bags of crisps.'

'All work and no play makes Jim a dull boy.'

'And all play and no work makes Jim an unemployed boy.'

He was glad to see Fred sigh deeply, as if something pained him very much. Shaking his head, Fred got up from the sofa and left the room.

## 26

SHEILA WAS BARELY recognisable as the groomed, sophisticated woman that had left with Jane earlier that morning. She staggered into the salon at six, breathing heavily. Clenching the back of a chair, she lowered herself into it with the air of one who has seen too much. 'Oh my God,' she half-heartedly fanned her face. 'I just want to die, right now, this second.'

'Good day?' Jane asked, ignoring the hysterics.

Patrick laughed and tried to turn it into a cough. 'Would you like a cuppa, Sheila?' he asked solicitously.

'Patrick, dahling, I would kill for a cuppa. Strong, no sugar, skimmed milk.' Sheila closed her eyes. 'Oh, I just want to die, this second,' she said again.

'So, you won't be looking for a lift home then?' Jane began putting her combs and brushes into the steriliser. 'Has Rosemary gone with the towels?' she asked Miranda.

'Gone with the bloody fairies, if you ask me,' Miranda snapped.

Jane didn't reply. Miranda still hadn't been coaxed out of her bad mood. It'd take another worthless fella to do that.

'I had such a dreadful day, dahling,' Sheila moaned loudly. 'That woman, Lisa, is as hard as nails. And talking about nails, she bawled me out when one of mine fell into the coleslaw.'

'Your nail went into the coleslaw?' Jane said in disbelief. It'd be typical of her mother to get fired on her first day. Well, not typical, as she'd never *actually* had a job before, but still . . .

'And she wouldn't even let me look for it. Thank you,

dahling.' Sheila blew a small, weary kiss as Patrick laid a cup of tea before her. 'It would only have taken a minute or so, I mean, how many bright red things can one find in a tub of 'slaw? But no, she dumped it all into a big bin and told me to file my nails and dress more appropriately.' Sheila looked down at herself.

'"This is Louise Kennedy," I said to her. And she said she didn't care if it was the Pope.' Sheila lowered her voice, 'She used the "F" word, no less. She didn't care if it was Pope eff John Paul, I shouldn't wear it in her shop in future. Vulgar. That's all she is – no breeding.'

The door of the hairdresser's burst open and a red-faced Rosemary ran in. 'Hi yez. I dropped the towels off and I'm just . . .' She stopped mid-sentence, then blushed and smiled delightedly. 'Oh, oh, oh, are you Mrs D'arcy? Declan D'arcy's wife?'

Sheila preened herself. 'I am indeed.'

'A famous person.' Rosemary's jaw almost hit the ground as she turned and looked at the other three. 'A famous person right here in our salon.'

'She's my mother,' Jane said, rolling her eyes. 'She was working up the road today.'

'Declan D'arcy is your father?' Rosemary looked at Jane with new respect. 'Wow, Jaz loves Declan.'

'Unlike myself,' Sheila said, causing Patrick and Mir to laugh.

'You look fab,' Rosemary said, awestruck. She touched Sheila's cardigan reverently, 'Your cardigan is the biz. I saw something like that in Dunnes. Is that where you got it?'

Miranda laughed and so did Jane. Sheila narrowed her eyes. 'Was that a joke?'

'No.' Rosemary gulped. 'Twenty-five ninety-nine, Dunnes, last Saturday.'

'Well, it most certainly is *not* Dunnes,' Sheila hissed. She pursed her lips and looked with deep disdain at Rosemary. 'So, Jane,' she said imperiously, 'are we leaving now?'

'Eh, yeah.' Jane fetched her coat and came out in time to hear Sheila whispering to Patrick that if he didn't hire people with a bit more class the place would go down the tubes.

'Are you volunteering your services?' Patrick asked smartly. 'A more mature trainee is just what we need. A floor-sweeper, cleaner-upper, head washer—'

'No, no Patrick, I don't think so,' Sheila said, not amused. 'And that's in *very* poor taste if you don't mind me saying. It's no fun to be working at my time of life.'

'It's no fun to be working at any time of life,' Jane said.

A rap on the door stopped the conversation.

'That'll be Harry,' Miranda said, 'let him in Rosemary.'

Patrick raised a quizzical eyebrow at Jane, who shrugged.

'He's only picking me up,' Miranda shouted over at them.

'Ohhh,' Patrick grinned. 'Picking you up, very nice.'

'I've to go to my mother's tonight.' Miranda stalked by him. 'It saves me getting two buses. So yez can put yer dirty thoughts away.'

'Did I hear dirty thoughts being mentioned?' Harry poked his head through the door. 'Are you having dirty thoughts about me, Mir? Are you?' He jabbed her in the arm as she stalked by him. 'Bye fucks, eh folks!' A quick wave and he was gone.

'Isn't he funny?' Rosemary smiled. 'Dead nice too. Dead good-looking.'

'Dead stupid,' Patrick muttered.

Jane tugged Sheila's arm. 'Let's head, Mother. That's if you're not going to drop dead on me.'

Sheila threw an anguished, look-how-badly-I'm-treated grimace at Patrick before sighing, 'Coming, dahling.'

Di and Owen were plonked in front of the TV when she got in. There was a smell of burning coming from somewhere. Both the kids seemed oblivious to it. 'What's burning?'

'Oh shit.' Owen pushed past her and ran into the kitchen. Jane was in time to see him grab the grill pan and run over to the sink with it. He turned on the tap and the meat for dinner turned from a burning inferno to charred blackness.

'Sorry, Ma,' he muttered.

Sorry? Now, on top of having to listen to her mother moaning about her day, there was no dinner. Jane dropped her bag on to the table and glared at him. 'Sorry!' she mimicked. 'Sorry! The one thing I ask you and your sister to do and you mess it up. Is it too much to ask that you at least keep an eye on the dinner for me?'

Owen gulped, his eyes downcast. 'It was just, well, Dad's—'

Dad! 'Oh God, well, if it was Dad who asked you to do it, you'd do it, wouldn't you? Huh?'

'Naw, it's just—'

'But me, I don't count, do I?' She stalked over to the meat and glared at it. She opened the kitchen window to let the smoke out. Turning back to her son, she said in a big mock-sarcastic voice, 'I mean, I only wash, iron, clean and clothe yez, don't I?'

'Aw Ma—'

'Well, d'yez know something? You can make your own dinner. I'm not doing it.'

'Dahling, don't you think, you're maybe overreacting . . . ?' Sheila said hesitantly from the doorway. 'It's only a little meat.'

'A little meat that I paid for,' Jane whirled on her mother. 'Me! Me! D'you hear that?' She poked her face into Di's, who'd come out of the sitting room and was standing, pale-faced, at the door. 'I paid for that meat you've just incinerated. My business is struggling and the last thing I need to see is burnt bloody meat!'

'Dad's ad is on tonight and we wanted to see it,' Di said quietly.

'And I wanted dinner when I came home. But, oh no, that didn't matter to you, did it? Well, yez can make your own.'

'Oh dahling, now . . .'

'Don't "darling", me, Mother!' She stomped up the stairs. God, it felt good.

She couldn't stop shaking as she sat down on Matt's bed. Huh, they wanted to see Jim's ad. He was obviously more important than her. It was typical, Jim took them out at the weekend, showed them a good time and they thought he was wonderful. Easy now he didn't have them all week. And now there was no dinner for her and she'd been out working for the lot of them. Well, to hell with it. She stood up from the bed and brushed herself down. She was going out herself, to a nice restaurant to have a nice meal. The other three could go and starve for all she cared.

'Mam?'

She jumped, startled. 'What?'

It was Owen. 'We're sorry, OK?'

'It was a mistake, Ma,' Diane said, as she pushed her way into the room, 'it was Dad's ad, see—' She stopped. She bit her lip, then shrugged. 'Well, sorry anyway,' she muttered.

It was as if she was a balloon that someone had just deflated. There she was, all ready to head out and now . . . well, there was no way she could *now*. In fact, she didn't know what to do. It was hard to do anything. It touched her more than she cared to admit that Diane had apologised. Owen was a pet, he'd do it no problem, but Di – she swallowed, blinked rapidly and looked at her two kids; one brazen-looking, despite the apology, the other gaping at the room he probably hadn't entered in four years. 'OK,' she said, hoping she didn't sound too humbled. 'Thanks.'

'I'll find something else and put it on,' Owen mumbled. 'Maybe some sausages?'

'Thanks pet,' Jane smiled at him. 'And I'll send out for chips.'

All three stood there exchanging awkward smiles.

'Go, go on,' she said gently to Owen, breaking the silence. 'Get those sausages on.'

'Yeah. OK.' He hesitated for a second, stared around the room and then backing out, he pounded down the stairs.

She was alone with Di. 'Go on down and see your father's ad.' She gave her a hesitant smile.

177

Her daughter didn't seem to hear her. Instead, she reached out and touched a red and white scarf that was hanging from the shelf. 'He was mad into United, wasn't he?'

'Sorry?'

'Matt,' Di whispered. 'He loved United.'

'Yeah.' Jane gulped at the mention of her baby. 'Yeah, he did.'

'I got him this for his birthday.' Di smiled suddenly as she ran her fingers down the length of the scarf. 'He was thrilled with it. D'you remember?'

How could she not remember? Every little thing that had made that child happy was etched into her mind in technicolor. 'Yeah.'

'He was such a funny little guy.'

Jane said nothing. She couldn't. She just watched Di stroke the scarf until the physical pain of it was too much for her. 'Just, just, let's just go and get some dinner,' she said. Her voice, sounding so normal and assertive, made her feel good again. 'Come on.' She put her arm around Di's shoulder.

Di put her arm around her too. 'We really are sorry Mam. Nana told us how hard you work and how worried you are and we really are sorry.'

Jane felt a lump in her throat. 'I'm not that worried,' she soothed. 'And don't you worry either – we'll get through this – OK?'

'The ad for the crisps is on,' Sheila shouted wearily. 'It looks stupid.'

'Ohmigod!' Without waiting for her, Di legged it out of the room.

'Well, I'm not watching a wife deserter's ad,' Sheila's voice came from downstairs. It rose quite substantially as she added, 'My daughter might shout at me, but I'm still loyal to her. Go on Owen, you watch it, I'll do the sausages.'

Jane smiled. Absently she readjusted the scarf so that it was centre shelf. A sudden, bright picture of Matt dancing around the kitchen in the scarf flashed before her. He was five and laughing. Jim was picking him up and holding him upside down, while she begged Jim to stop. Jim saying fine and grabbing her instead. Tickling her hard. Matt almost getting sick with laughing so much. Jane squeezed her eyes tight shut. The pain seemed to lodge in the hollow space right inside her. Sometimes, like now, it was as if she could feel Matt beside her, sense him standing, looking at her with his big eyes. But of course, he never was and her arms ached so badly to cuddle him and hug him that it was easier not to acknowledge it. She took deep breaths, opened her eyes and, with an effort of will, smoothed the duvet down. Then she exited the room, closing the door behind her.

She met Sheila in the kitchen. 'Just minding the sausages, dahling, making sure they don't burn.'

Jane smiled. 'Sorry for snapping at you.'

'Oh snap away. I feel I'll get used to it in my new job.' She turned a sausage over, wincing as some fat landed on her blouse.

'Thanks, Mam.'

'No problem, sausages I can do.'

'No, I mean for having a word with the kids, for making them apologise.'

'I didn't make them do anything. They know when they've done wrong. Despite being so weird, they are nice children, dahling.' She paused. 'You've done well.'

And sometimes, like now, despite everything, she felt that she actually had.

## 27

'EMERGENCY STAFF MEETING,' Patrick announced the first Monday in May. 'Very important.'

All three of them looked up. Mir was plucking her eyebrows in the salon mirror, Jane was reading the paper and Rosemary was reading aloud her horoscope.

'Someone is going to enter my life,' she proclaimed breathlessly. 'Someone will be a force of change for the better.'

'Yes,' Patrick said, tapping her on the shoulder, 'me.'

Rosemary looked devastated. Then unsure. And finally she erupted in semi-hysterical giggles. 'Ohhh, that's a joke, right? You don't really mean that, sure you don't?'

'Staff meeting?' Patrick gently took her magazine away from her. 'Emergency staff meeting?'

'Oh, right. Yes. Of course. Of course.' She jumped up from her chair and knocked her knee against the counter. 'Ooooh.' Hobbling behind Patrick, she babbled, 'Gee, thanks for including me on this. Emergency staff meeting. Wow.'

She followed Patrick into the staff room. She stood by the door while Patrick took the swivel chair and Jane and Mir shared the sofa.

Patrick waited until there was silence before he began. 'Well,' he licked his lips. 'As you can see from the lack of clients, the flyers didn't really help things a whole lot.'

'They made things worse,' Jane pointed out. 'No offence Patrick, but please don't say you've spent money on anything else.'

'No, I haven't.' Patrick sounded offended. 'In fact,' he went on, 'what I'm about to say will actually *make* us money.'

'Do I have to sit in on this?' Mir asked. 'Like, it's your business and—'

'Yes, you do,' Patrick snapped. 'I need everyone's opinion on this.'

Jane resisted the urge to tell him that it was her business too. But there was no point in getting his back up. Time enough for that when he came up with another hair-brained scheme. 'So, what's this idea?' She strove to make her voice sound interested.

'Well,' Patrick smiled smugly. 'I was trying to figure out, over the weekend, what it is that makes people go to Cutting Edge instead of coming here.' He nodded encouragingly at them.

'So, what does?'

Silence descended.

Jane hoped this wasn't going to go on too long. Thinking about stuff like that was enough to start a major depression.

Patrick clucked. 'OK,' he said, turning to Rosemary, 'let's start with their number one fan over there.'

'Where?' Rosemary asked.

'You,' Patrick said patiently. 'Why would you go to Cutting Edge?'

Rosemary blushed and squirmed. 'Well, I'd come here,' she said. 'Like *now* I would. Now that I know you all.'

'Why would you go to Cutting Edge?' Patrick was striving to sound patient. 'Come on,' he cajoled, 'tell the others what you said to me the day we handed out the flyers.'

'Ooooh, I couldn't.' Rosemary looked as if she wanted to blend into the wall. 'You got all annoyed and offended and wouldn't talk to me.'

'She'd go to Cutting Edge,' Patrick stated, 'because they're better than us.'

'Aw, thanks,' Mir glared at her.

181

'But *why* are they better than us?' Patrick was now standing over an embarrassed Rosemary. 'Tell them, Rose.' Turning to Mir and Jane, he added, 'You won't believe this.'

'Then why bother telling them,' Rosemary asked sullenly.

'Why?' Patrick asked again.

He really was composed, Jane thought. Normally Patrick would be hopping about in semi-hysteria if things were going wrong.

'Well?' he asked Rosemary again.

''Cause they charge more.' Rosemary looked defiantly at all three. 'They charge more so they should be better.'

There was a silence.

Patrick looked triumphantly at Jane and Mir. 'And therein lies our next plan of campaign.'

'You're going to up the prices?' Mir asked incredulously. 'You can't do that, we just slashed them last month.'

'Don't you see,' Patrick looked at them as if it was obvious. 'By not valuing ourselves, no one else did either. Like Rosemary, people do think that paying more means a better service. For instance,' he nodded at Mir, 'why don't you ever let Jane cut your hair?'

Mir squirmed.

'You also go about in designer clothes when you can buy the same stuff in Dunnes.'

'Designer gear is better,' Mir spat. 'Everyone knows that.'

'And so is,' Patrick clapped his hands, 'designer hair!' He looked at Jane and Mir. 'Well?'

It was true, Jane realised. Even that mate of her father's had said that his wife went to Cutting Edge because it was expensive. Maybe it would be worth a try, it couldn't make things much worse. Fair play to Patrick for thinking that one up. 'I agree,' she nodded slowly. 'Sure, when you think of it, my mother is a prime example of that sort of thinking.'

'Isn't she just,' Patrick smiled delightedly.

'OK,' Jane grinned. 'Let's hike up the prices. Only, well—'

It was as if Patrick knew what she was going to say. 'Don't worry, the granny brigade will still get a special OAP rate.'

'Don't call them that,' Jane glared at him and indicated Rosemary. 'For God's sake!'

'So basically we're all now working in a high-class place as opposed to the low-class place of last week,' Mir said laconically.

'And it's all thanks to me!' Rosemary looked as if she couldn't believe it. 'I'm helping to save the salon. Imagine!'

'Yep. You did your bit,' Patrick smiled at her. 'Now scoot. You too Mir. There's a gran – a senior citizen due in for ten. Gimme a shout when she arrives, OK?' He turned to Jane and giggled. 'Come on partner, let's decide how much to charge.' He pulled a piece of paper from his pocket and waved it about. 'I took the liberty of writing down a list of Cutting Edge's prices.'

They spent much of the morning talking. Well, there wasn't a whole lot else to do. Three customers in three hours. They agreed to charge two euros more than Cutting Edge for all their cuts. 'After all,' Jane said, 'the stuff we use is better quality.'

Patrick rang the printers and asked if they could get a list of charges run up. He e-mailed the information over and when that was done, he turned back to Jane.

'I've a few more ideas to run past you.'

'Well, if they make as much sense as the last one, I'm all ears.'

'OK, first one, and don't get offended, is that you, me and Mir should do a few advanced styling courses. If we're to compete we need to know what's going on. I think we've grown lazy because we've never had competition before.'

'Fair enough,' Jane nodded. 'Makes sense.' She smiled brightly at Patrick. 'God, you've been a busy little beaver, haven't you? Thinking up all these wonderful ideas.'

'Well,' Patrick blushed, 'to be honest, that was the only idea of mine he did agree with.'

'He?'

'Barney,' Patrick said. 'I ran my ideas past him at the weekend.'

'Oh.'

'You're going on the first course,' Patrick went on, 'seeing as you'll be in the IHFs. As soon as we see the right one, I'll book you on to it. That Julian Waters one you were on about should be good.'

Jane bit her lip. 'I was on about it before we started losing money. I dunno if we can afford to go to him now.'

'We can't afford not to,' Patrick said sternly.

Jane liked that he'd said that. Making a mock-glum face, she said, 'OK, I'll *force* myself.'

Patrick grinned. 'Now, for the next idea, I had a think about what it is that Cutting Edge is doing and how we can do it better.'

'We are not having a light fitting like theirs.'

Patrick laughed and flapped her away. 'No. Nothing like that. Cutting Edge salons are big, quite anonymous really, aren't they?'

'Uh-huh.'

'And we are small and intimate. So let's go for that. Let's make that our selling point if you will. We'll chat to the customers, find out about them and keep the information on the computer. That way, when they come in again, it's like we remember them.'

'But we remember them anyway.'

'But when we get more business we won't.'

Jane made a face. 'I dunno, it sounds a bit mercenary.'

'OK, forget that for the moment.' Patrick was impatient to get on. 'Still on the intimate theme, let's give them some cakes and nice biscuits with their cup of coffee. Cutting Edge,' he rolled his eyes, 'only offer coffee. We can do better than them on that.'

'Patrick, it's a hairdressers, not a restaurant. And what happens if hair gets into the cakes?'

184

'Mmm.'

'Maybe some kind of packaged biscuits instead?' Jane suggested.

'Yeah. Yeah. Sounds good. Now, Barney said to give the ideas a month's trial. That way we can see what's working and what's not.' He bounced up off the sofa. 'Oh, I can't wait. Declaring war on Cutting Edge has to be about the most exciting thing to happen to us in decades.'

He was seriously mental, Jane thought, grinning.

## 28

O N THE FIRST day of June, Jane took a day off work, bought a bunch of carnations at the florist's and drove to the graveyard. It was a beautiful day, the sky was baby blue and the sun seemed to bounce off the streets. All around her, people flaunted acres of flesh, tanned or otherwise, as they strutted about in shorts and T-shirts, or thigh-high skirts and belly tops that exposed flabby stomachs. Jane wore a pair of wide black hipsters and a white cotton shirt. A white scarf held her hair back in a ponytail.

She didn't want to dress too summery – visiting a graveyard didn't merit the bright greens and yellows that fashion seemed to favour this year. She wasn't a big believer in graves, but twice a year, on Matt's anniversary and birthday, she came to say hello and tidy it up a bit. She liked to come on her own, without the kids, so that she could talk to Matt without upsetting them. She'd bring Di and Owen some other evening, though she knew that Owen in particular hated coming.

As she neared the plot, she saw that someone was already there. Down on bended knees, this person was throwing weeds into a black sack.

Jim.

Damn! Why had she come so early? She should have known he'd be here, and there was no way she wanted to talk to him. But now that she was here, it couldn't be avoided.

Hearing her footsteps, Jim turned around. 'Hiya.'

He looked tired, she thought. 'Hi.' She gave him a brief smile and, crouching down with her back to him, she set about arranging the flowers in the little jar that always stood in front of the headstone. Firstly, she took out the dead carnations from her last visit.

'Throw them in here.' Jim offered her his plastic bag.

'Ta.' Without looking at him, she tossed them into the bag. Then she concentrated on her flowers. She didn't hurry herself, hoping that he'd take the hint and go. He didn't, instead resuming his cleaning of the grave.

'Surprising how many weeds gather,' he muttered.

'Yeah.' She made a big deal of arranging the flowers. She took the yellow carnation from the middle of the bunch and put it at the front.

'There's a freshly dug grave backing this,' Jim said conversationally. 'It must have been a child – see all the teddies?'

Jane looked and immediately wished she hadn't. It was a child all right. A smaller child than their Matt. Seeing all the flowers and toys resting on top of the clay brought a lump to her throat. 'Poor parents,' she muttered.

'Yep.'

They didn't speak as they worked on. Jane had nothing else to do so she sat hunched over her flowers, not willing to do anything else that might involve interaction with Jim. From behind her, Jim pulled and smoothed and cut. She wished he'd go so that she could just be on her own. He'd never been so attentive when they were together, preferring to walk around the graveyard rather than listen to her talking to Matt. Not that Matt was there or anything, but—

'Is Di all set?'

His voice broke into her thoughts. 'Sorry?'

'Her exams. The Junior Cert is starting Wednesday, isn't it?'

'Yep.'

'Betcha she's swotting away today, isn't she?' Jim asked.

Jane shrugged. 'That's Di, everything at the last minute. Having a school dropout for a boyfriend can't help matters, mind you.' The barb just popped out of her mouth and it wasn't the right place for it. 'Sorry,' she muttered.

'I've spoken to her, if you must know.' Jim put down the scissors he had been chopping the grass with. 'And I don't know what else I can do.'

'You can meet him,' Jane said. 'You wouldn't be so bloody complacent then.'

He shook his head helplessly. 'Let's just stop this. Just for today – OK?'

The way he said it hurt her, though she didn't know why. Quickly turning away again, she tried to look as if she'd suddenly become interested in something. A plane flew overhead just in time. As she gazed at it, she could sense Jim looking at her and the fine hairs on her arms seemed to be standing to attention. Why couldn't he just go?

'When you're finished there,' his voice was hesitant, 'd'you want to go for a coffee?'

No, she did not bloody want to go for a coffee! Why the hell did he think she'd want a coffee?

'It's just, you know, well, it's . . .' Jim didn't finish his sentence. Instead, he gazed into the middle distance and muttered, 'Mattie would've been ten today and like, well, we're his parents and no one understands like us, do they?'

He'd never understood, that was for sure. But he wouldn't even understand *that* if she said it to him. She was about to refuse, but the sight of him putting the weeds into a plastic bag that he must have brought with him touched her. 'No,' she said. 'They don't.'

'So – a quick coffee?'

'Just a quick one,' she agreed.

'Fine,' Jim nodded. 'I've got to head back to work this afternoon anyhow. How about you?'

'I took the day off,' Jane said, then wished she hadn't said it in quite such an I'm-better-than-you-for-doing-that manner as hurt flashed across Jim's face. Instead of apologising she stood up and dusted herself down. Jesus, why the hell had she agreed to go for a coffee with him? Chit-chat with her estranged hubby hadn't exactly been on her agenda.

Jim stood back from the grave and observed his handiwork. 'Looks great – huh?'

She didn't even bother to answer that. Instead, she walked ahead of him, away from the grave and once outside had a mad urge to jump into her car and drive off. Instead, she waited while he dumped his gear into the boot of his car and wiped his hands clean down his jeans. Thank God she wasn't doing his washing any more.

'There's a coffee shop over there that I sometimes go to,' Jim said, pointing at a small dingy place across the road. 'They do nice stuff. How about that?'

'Fine.'

She followed him across the road, not wanting to walk beside him in case they looked too cosy. It was childish, but necessary.

Once inside, he told her to grab a table. 'Coffee and a danish?'

'I don't eat them any more.' Why was she saying these things? She only ate about two a day. 'Just a coffee.'

'Fine.' He joined the queue and she sat down. It was a typical Jim place, she thought absently. She used to find it cute and endearing, the fact that Jim always sought out the crummiest places to eat and drink. It was almost as if he felt sorry for the people running them or something. Still, when he arrived back at the table she was sorry that she had been so pig-headed about the pastry. His looked lovely.

The coffee wasn't bad either.

'Want some?' He moved his cake towards her.

'No. I told you, I don't eat them any more.'

'Why not?'

'I saw a programme on telly where a guy said that they can cause cancer.' Actually, it had been barbecued sausages, but she wasn't telling him that.

Jim looked at the cake doubtfully before taking a huge bite. 'Good way to go.'

189

Jane didn't answer. No way was a good way to go.

'How are you?' Jim asked. 'You know, with it being his birthday and all?'

Too late for all this, Jimbo, she wanted to say. 'I'm fine,' she answered instead. Her voice was a little too bright. 'You?'

He shrugged and sipped some coffee.

'I saw your ad the other night.' Jane felt desperate to change the subject. 'It's good. Funny. The kids love it.'

'Thanks.' Jim grinned and the flash of his white teeth made her heart flip over. 'The crisps have taken off in a big way. We weren't expecting it to be so successful. It's like a craze.'

'And it was your campaign?'

'Uh-huh.'

'Great.'

'Your dad gave them a great plug on his show last week.'

'My dad always liked you.'

'Yeah.' Jim fell silent again.

'I—'

'Listen, Jane—'

They stopped.

'You first,' he said.

'I was going to say that I have to go now.'

'Oh . . . right.'

'You?'

'What?'

'What were you going to say?'

Jim peeled a piece of pastry from his cake and flaked it between his fingers. 'Doesn't matter,' he said flatly. 'See you.'

'Yeah.' Jane stood up. 'And, er, thanks for the coffee.'

'No probs. Wish Di luck for me.'

'Sorry?'

'In the exams?'

'Oh, right. Sure. But maybe you should ring her yourself.'

Jim nodded. 'OK.'

It was painful, this conversation making. Every time she talked

190

to him, she was reminded of the gulf between them. She brushed a stray hair from her face. 'Bye now.' She didn't wait to see if he'd reply or not, she just made a bolt for the door.

Di and Owen were waiting for her when she arrived home.

'Are you not studying, Di?' Jane asked as she flicked the kettle on. 'It's maths tomorrow, isn't it?'

'English,' Di said. From behind her back she produced a bunch of flowers. 'I was just going to put these in water. They're for you.'

'Me?' Jane said, surprised. 'Why?'

'They're from me and Owen,' Di said, handing them to her. Then gulping slightly, she said awkwardly, 'Because it's a hard day for you, today.'

'Oh guys.' Jane thought she was going to cry. 'Come here.'

They crossed to her and she wrapped her arms around them. 'Owen wanted to get you a box of chocolates but Nana said that it would ruin your skin and your figure.'

Jane half-laughed, half-sobbed.

'So we got them instead,' Owen said.

Jane closed her eyes. 'You could have got me anything and I'd have loved it,' she whispered. She hugged her kids hard. 'Thank you so much.'

29

J IM WAS AT work by five-thirty. He badly needed to get some sleep and a quiet office seemed the ideal place. There wasn't a hope back at the flat between Fred and Gillian and the bloody bird.

Fred had told him to spend the night with Debbie. 'Or maybe you'd get even less sleep then, huh, boyo?'

'Ha. Funny.'

Only it hadn't been that funny. It had been quite tempting actually. But staying the night with Debbie was taking their relationship into deeper waters and he didn't know if he wanted that just yet. She was a great girl, loads of fun, dead gorgeous and when they were together he could forget about Jane for a while. But a while wasn't enough. He needed to be sure he was doing the right thing.

He unlocked the front door of the building, punched in the access code and strode towards his office. Posters of Chains Bond were everywhere. The crisps had been the firm's greatest success story to date. Philip was due in that day for an update, hence the posters. It made it look as if the whole firm was behind his snacks. Though Jim felt pretty sure that Philip wasn't stupid enough to believe it.

He sat down at his desk and flicked on his computer. At least if someone did come by, it'd look like he was working. He laid his head down and closed his eyes.

Jane wrote a card for Di and left it on the table. *Good Luck in your exams* she wrote. She signed it *Mammy* and *Owen*. It looked

192

sort of lonely with just the two names there, so she added Jim's in too.

Beside Owen's.

He felt as if he'd just drifted off to sleep when the ringing of a phone woke him.

'Sleeping beauty, there's a call on line one for you.' Maud was waving at him through the glass door.

Jim grinned sheepishly at her and, yawning widely, picked up his phone. 'Jim McCarthy here.'

'Jim, it's Dave. My office, now.'

The phone was put down at the other end. Jim rubbed his face and yawned again. Glancing at his watch, he saw that it had just gone nine. Jesus, he'd slept for hours. He wondered what Dave wanted. He couldn't figure out if he'd sounded pissed off or excited. Still, he'd know soon enough.

'You want to get a tonic.' Maud poked her head in the door. 'You look wretched. An iron one would do the trick. Will I get it for you at lunchtime?'

'Nope,' Jim said firmly, 'just tell Dave I'm on my way if he rings again. I have to have a shave and tidy meself up.'

'Aw, you're gorgeous anyway,' Maud said, as if talking to a five-year-old. 'Wrecked-looking, but lovely.'

'Just tell Dave – yeah?' Jim tried not to grin too much as he walked out past her.

'That woman,' her mother always referred to Lisa as 'that woman', 'asked my advice yesterday on what to wear.'

'Did she?' Jane was only half-listening. The traffic was totally gridlocked and she was wondering if she should cut down Merrion Square or just keep going.

'Of course, I told her that nothing I'd seen on her to date would do her any justice. I mean, she's a big woman, Jane, and big women do not wear small prints.'

'That's right.'

'So she asked me what she should wear to make her look good and I was tempted to say that even I wasn't able to solve that problem for her, but instead I told her that if she let me have the afternoon off, I'd have a look around the shops and come back with a list of recommendations. Now, wasn't that a brainwave?'

'That's right.'

'It must be important – I thought at first it might be a man, but what sort of a man would inflict someone like her on himself? So I really don't know. What do you think Jane?'

'That's right.'

The punch her mother gave her made the car swerve into the wrong lane and from behind someone beeped long and hard. 'Mother, do you mind? I'm trying to drive!'

'You weren't listening to me.'

'I was. You were talking about the woman you work with.'

'Yes, and?'

'Mother, I'm trying to concentrate on the road here!'

Sheila glared at her and Jane glared back. The traffic began to move again and Jane turned away.

'Well, I've a half-day today, dahling, when you'll be working, so I suppose I can't complain.' With that, Sheila took out her nail case and began to clip her nails on to the floor of the car.

To Jim's surprise, Philip was in Dave's office. 'I thought we had a meeting scheduled for two?'

'We did, but I've taken the liberty of rescheduling it,' Philip boomed. He crossed to Jim and pulled him towards a seat. 'Sit down while I tell you my news.'

Jim looked at Dave, who gave a grimace of a smile.

'These bloody crisps have exploded,' Philip said loudly, 'and it's all thanks to you, wonder boy.' With that he clapped Jim on the back.

Jim shrugged. 'Aw, well now, everybody did—'

'Rubbish,' Philip said expansively, 'if you hadn't come up with the chain angle we'd all be trying to market them as sophisticated snacks. Oh no, you are the man of the moment.'

'Yeah?'

'Absolutely!' Philip turned to Dave. 'Isn't this fella a bloody genius, Dave? Isn't he?'

Dave had difficulty answering with a smile on his face. 'He does what he's paid to do,' he eventually choked out.

'He bloody does,' Philip agreed. 'So that's why,' he paused dramatically, 'that's why I want him to come on the show with me.'

'Show?' Jim glanced at them both, trying not to sound alarmed. 'What show?'

'The business type thing,' Philip gestured with his hand, as if that'd make it clear. 'You know, the yoke on Tuesday nights!'

'*The Angle is All*,' Dave put in. 'Prime-time TV.'

'I've been asked to go on,' Philip nodded proudly, 'seeing as Chains Bond are now the biggest-selling snack in the country! And,' he crossed to Jim and put his huge hand on Jim's shoulder, 'they want my marketing people there too. Brilliant publicity for this firm.'

'So let Dave go,' Jim said, trying not to panic. 'He's the boss.'

'I don't bloody want Dave,' Philip said. 'Sure I don't, Dave?'

'No. You've made that *very* clear, Mr Logan.' Dave began to tap his pen on his desk as he said to Jim, 'He wants you, wonder boy.'

'Well he can want all he likes,' Jim stood up. 'There is no way I'm going on television.' Turning to Philip, he said, 'It's not in my brief to do TV appearances.'

Philip looked taken aback. Jim heard Dave's sharp intake of breath.

'Well it is now,' Philip said sternly. 'You've marketed my crisps brilliantly from the outset and now you are going to take the credit for it.'

'I get paid for it. If you want, pay me more, Philip, but I am not going on telly.'

'Now hang on Jim—' Dave was up out of his seat.

'How much more?' Philip asked. 'Say it and I'll do it, but only if you go on telly.'

'He'll do it anyway,' Dave said, trying to sound calm. 'It's not our business to go ripping off our clients.'

'It's not our business to go on telly either,' Jim stated. Jesus, there was no way he was doing it. No way. He'd make a bloody eejit out of himself. The thought of everyone gawking at him as he sweated under TV lights in a shirt and tie was nightmare territory.

'Mr Logan,' Dave said smoothly, 'could you excuse us for a minute please?'

Philip, looking disgruntled, stomped out of the room. He was a man used to having his own way.

'What?' Jim said once the door had closed. 'You gonna tell me off?'

Dave came around his desk and glared at the younger man. They were nose to nose. 'If Philip Logan wants you to shovel his shite up, it's your job to do it,' he said evenly. 'If he wants you to turn cartwheels, you bloody take lessons. Have you got that, Jim?'

'No, actually, I haven't,' Jim said calmly. 'I market his crisps. That is all I do. I do not make TV appearances. If I wanted to do that I would have done a communications course instead of a marketing course. Now, Dave, while you're shovelling shite up and turning cartwheels, maybe you can shove that up your tight arse as well. OK?'

Dave went white, then red and finally purple. 'I will ignore that,' he said, his whole body trembling. 'But only because Philip Logan seems to have taken a shine to you.' Pushing his face nearer Jim's he went on, deliberately slowly, 'It is in your contract that you will do whatever the firm deems *necessary* and *reasonable* in order to promote a customer's products. This, Jim, is *necessary* and *reasonable*. You will get yourself a new suit and new shoes, and you *will* be available next Tuesday week for recording, or else you'll be in breach of contract – understand?'

The implication was only too clear. Breach of contract meant he'd be out on the street with no bloody job and he couldn't afford that. He was beaten. Swallowing hard, he pushed past Dave and out of the office. From behind, he heard Dave say, 'He's doing it, Philip.'

Oh, good Christ.

Four customers were in the salon at the same time. Patrick was orgasmic with delight. 'Two trendy twenties,' he said excitedly to Jane as he escorted her into the office. 'And two bouncy hair beauties.'

'Patrick, don't—'

'Rosemary came up with that name. It's better than the Granny brigade. Really that girl is quite bright when she's not being so irritating.' He held the door to the office open for her and when she was sitting comfortably, he handed her a leaflet. 'I was wondering what you'd think about this?'

'A course in advanced styling,' Jane read. 'Yeah, great. Is this the one I'll be going on?'

Patrick beamed. 'Yep. Two weeks from now in Killarney, for a whole weekend.'

'Killarney?'

'Uh-huh. It's with Julian Waters too.'

'But Killarney? I can't. I've the kids, and here and—'

'You've Sheila. She'll keep an eye on them.'

'For a whole weekend? She'd run a mile!'

'So much the better.'

Jane chuckled slightly. 'Look, Patrick, I'd love to go, but I can't, I really can't.'

'Two nights in The Abbey Hotel?'

'Don't!'

'A massage and hairdo thrown in?' Patrick looked at her beseechingly. 'Please?'

'No.' Jane stood up. 'No, I can't. Sorry.'

'Well,' Patrick tittered nervously, 'you'll have to find a way. I've booked it already.'

197

For a second, she was dumbfounded. He'd booked it without consulting her – that was going a bit too far. Drawing herself up to her five foot two she glared at him. 'Patrick, you seem to forget that I own half of this place too. You can't go booking courses and spending money without telling me.'

'But we agreed that you were going on a course!'

'Yeah, but not for a weekend! Jesus!'

'Oh for God's sake, Jane! Don't be so negative! Where's the fighter in you? If you want to win this competition you need to learn from the master. You are going. And anyway,' he paused, 'you need a bit of a break, you know.'

Jane opened her mouth to protest, but all that came out was an indignantly spluttered, 'Break?'

'You've had a hard time lately,' Patrick muttered. 'I just thought, well, Killarney and all . . .' his voice trailed off.

'When I feel I need a break, I can pay for it myself,' Jane said with dignity. 'I don't need charity.'

'You do need a break though, honey chicks,' Patrick said gently. 'You look tired.' He paused. '*And*, you'd be doing yourself a favour – learning from a master so that you stand a shot in the competition come October.'

'I thought you said I'd win?' Jane retorted. 'I thought you had great confidence in me.'

'Oh I do. I do,' he placated. 'But a weekend away can't do any harm. And to be honest, until business picks up a bit more, we can afford to be a stylist down. And Jane, how can you turn down Julian Waters?'

'Seeing as he's gay, I don't think it'd be a problem.'

'Oh, very witty.'

Jane smirked at him.

'Come on, Jane. In your heart you know this has to be done. You need this course just to get a few hints. He's one of the judges this year, you know.'

He had a point, Jane reluctantly admitted. If she stood any chance at all . . .

198

'Do you want to win this thing or not?' Patrick dangled the tickets in front of her. 'Do you want to save our business?'

'Don't be so melodramatic.'

'I don't care if you don't want to sleep in the hotel – get yourself a cardboard box on the side of the road if you want – but do the bloody course.'

He was right. These days it seemed that Patrick was always right. 'OK then.'

'Now don't pretend you're not delighted. You'd cut your arm off to do a course with this guy normally.'

'If I cut my arm off, I wouldn't be able to do it at all, would I?'

He grinned. 'Smart bitch.'

'That's me.' Jane grinned back.

'Oh yeah,' he gave another nervous laugh, 'I booked Rosemary in as well. She can be your model for the weekend. You don't have to hang around with her or anything.'

He left before she could react.

'I am *so* excited.' Rosemary sat herself down on the chair as Jane got out her brushes. 'A *real* hotel. And being with other real models. It's like a dream or something.'

'It's a nice hotel too,' Jane found herself smiling. 'The food is lovely and they have a swimming pool and a jacuzzi.'

'*No!*'

'Uh-huh.' Jane began to brush Rosemary's hair. It had grown terribly bushy in the last while. It badly needed a cut. There was an enormous knot that wouldn't come out.

'And will there be servants and everything?'

'Waiters at dinner time to serve you your meals.'

'Get away!'

'And anything you like for breakfast – you can even have it in bed.'

Rosemary curled up her lip. 'Sure me dad has that all the time at home. That's not a big deal. Ouch!'

199

'Sorry. Sorry.' Jane braced herself to deliver the bad news. 'Rosemary, this hair has to be cut.'

'I know.' Rosemary seemed unperturbed. 'I've saved up and I'm booking myself into Cutting Edge next week.'

'You are not!' Jane almost laughed. 'You can't do that. You're our model.'

'But—'

'I'll do it for you now – remember our bargain – you have to trust me.' Without even waiting for Rosemary to say anything, Jane just chopped a piece of her hair off. It was slightly unprofessional, but there was no alternative. 'Now, relax.' She tried to ignore the big horrified eyes of the kid in front of her. 'Your Jaz will love it,' she said. 'Promise.'

Rosemary smiled nervously.

It was the most satisfying hairstyle she'd done in ages. All the little frizzy bits that had bugged her for months lay in a pile on the floor.

Rosemary was not looking too happy though. 'You're cutting loads off, aren't you?' she asked faintly.

'Just the dead ends,' Jane replied cheerfully.

When she'd finished, Rosemary had lost a third of her hair.

'Now,' Jane said, plugging in the dryer. 'Wait until you see what I've done – it's the same, but shorter.'

Rosemary couldn't speak. Her eyes were focused firmly on all the hair sitting in her lap.

Jane began to blow dry. Rosemary's hair was a pleasure to work with – its natural curl lent itself very well to scrunch drying. When she'd finished, the highlights in Rosemary's hair gleamed with good health. She'd cut it well, Jane thought proudly. OK, it was an easy style that wouldn't win any prizes, but Rosemary looked about a million times better.

'Jaz likes my hair long,' Rosemary whispered.

'It is long,' Jane said. 'See.' She held a mirror to the back of Rosemary's head.

'Oh, it sort of goes in a triangle at the back!'

'Yeah, I layered it like that so that it wouldn't frizz out so much. It stops your hair from getting too full.'

'Oh.' Rosemary looked as if she couldn't quite make up her mind about it. 'It looks, well, young-looking.'

'You are young.' Jane tweaked Rosemary's nose affectionately. 'Now, go on and ask Jaz what he thinks of it.'

'I will.' Rosemary paused. 'And, eh, thanks Jane. Thanks for doing my hair. I quite like it.'

# 30

JIM PICKED THE kids up on Saturday as usual. He was mortified, he'd left his wallet behind in the flat and his car was low on petrol. Unless he asked Jane for a loan there was no way there'd be any trip that afternoon. He cursed himself as he rang the doorbell.

'It's Dad.' He heard Di's cheerful voice coming from her bedroom. 'I'll get it.' Her feet pounded down the stairs and a second later the door was flung open. 'Hi. Stand in Da, won't be a second.'

Jim moved into the hall. 'Is your mother in?' he asked.

Di looked hopeful, then suspicious. 'Yeah. D'you want her?'

'Just for a sec.'

'Are you going to fight?'

Jim winced. Jesus, what did the kid think of him? 'No. Not unless she wants to.' He gave her a grin.

Di looked sceptical but called Jane. She stood sentinel beside him as Jane emerged from the kitchen. Jim's first thought was that Jane looked fantastic. She'd had her hair done differently and it really suited her. His next thought was why the bloody hell had she got it done? It had looked fine before, long and shiny. So he decided to say nothing about it. 'Eh, this is a bit awkward,' he began, 'but I've left me wallet in the flat and I've no money for petrol, so I was wondering—'

'If I could lend you some?' Jane finished for him.

'Bang on. Just until tonight.'

'Oh, a likely story,' Sheila called out her tuppence worth. 'Neither a borrower nor a lender be.'

202

No, Jim thought, just a bloody sponger be.

'So, how much?' Jane interrupted his malevolent thoughts. 'All I have is a tenner.'

'That'll do.'

She disappeared in search of her purse and Di ran up the stairs to hurry Owen along. Jim waited in the hall, praying that Sheila would be content to call out insults rather than appear in person.

Jane came back a second later. 'Here.' She held out the money towards him.

As he reached out to take it, their eyes locked. The words popped out before he had a chance to stop them, 'Your hair is beautiful. You look . . . beautiful.'

Jane flushed.

'Oh, it's amazing what ten euros will buy these days,' Sheila shouted.

'Don't mind her,' Jane whispered. 'She's just tired. She's to go into work today and she's taking it out on everyone.'

'Work?'

'Yep. Making sandwiches.'

He couldn't help the laughter that bubbled up. 'Feck off.'

Jane smiled at him and it felt good.


They stopped at a petrol station and he half-filled his tank. Then, driving Northside, he said, 'I've just to get my cash from the flat and we'll head off somewhere. Anywhere you want to go?'

Owen shrugged as Di's brow furrowed in thought. 'What about the beach at Malahide? We always used to go there as kids.'

'It'll be freezing,' Jim said.

'I don't care.' Di tossed her head. 'We always had such a laugh there. You used to chase Mam with fistfuls of sand, d'you remember?'

Jim wished that his daughter wouldn't do this. She was about as subtle as a neutron bomb. Every time she came up with a suggestion for somewhere to go, happy families always played a part. 'The beach will be too cold,' he said firmly. 'How about a movie?'

Di nodded. 'Suppose.'

'Owen?'

Owen shrugged. 'Don't care.'

Jim wondered if Owen cared about anything. Not for the first time he felt uneasy as he studied the sombre set of his son's face. He wondered if he should mention it to Jane. He decided to wait and see how the day went.

Di wanted to see his flat. So far, he'd avoided having to show them the place, but now it couldn't be helped. 'It's a bit small,' he explained as he ushered them into the flat itself. 'I'll be getting a place of my own soon, but for now I'm stuck here.' As he drew near the door, he heard voices. He hoped to Christ that Fred and Gillian were decent. That would be all he needed to nail his coffin with Sheila.

'Does Fred live here too?' Di asked.

'Well, it's Fred's place, he lets me kip on his sofa bed, but like I said, I'll get somewhere myself soon.' Jim pushed open the door, striding ahead of his children in order to shove Fred and Gillian out of the way if he had to.

To his horror, Debbie was there. She was perched on the edge of the kitchen table, drinking coffee.

'Eh, hi guys.' Jim strove for a normal tone. 'Forgot me wallet.'

'Men – huh?' Debbie, dressed in a denim miniskirt and tight top, crossed to the coffee table and tossed it at him. 'Still, when you're so gorgeous we can—' She stopped abruptly as Di and Owen filed in behind him.

'My kids,' Jim gulped, shoving his wallet into his back pocket. 'Di, Owen, this is Gillian, Fred's girlfriend, and this girl here is, eh, Debbie. She's eh—'

'I'm Gillian's friend,' Debbie said smoothly. 'Hi.'

Jim gave her a grateful smile.

Diane was staring in open admiration at Debbie. 'I like your skirt,' she said. 'D'you get it in TopShop?'

'Yeah, could have,' Debbie smiled. 'You look like your Dad you know. Both of you.' With that she winked at Jim.

Jim turned to the kids. 'So, will we head?' he asked hastily, wanting to get out of there before anything incriminating was said.

'Oy, Jimbo, have you got the sprogs?' Fred walked out of the bathroom, freshly washed and shaved. He smelt like a flower shop. 'How're yez?' He tossed Di's hair with his hand. 'How's things? Long time no see.'

Di hastily flattened her hair back into place and scowled at him.

The lack of response didn't bother Fred. 'So,' he asked, 'what do yez think of yer old man being on telly?'

Jim glared open-mouthed at him. The one bloody thing he'd told Fred not to say and the bloody eejit had just blurted it out.

'Telly?' Diane, Owen, Debbie and Gillian said in unison.

'When?'

'How?'

'Why didn't you say?'

'Sorry.' Fred did look sorry. 'I kept telling myself not to say anything and then it just came out.' He looked around at them all. 'Let's just try and forget it.'

'Forget it!' Gillian squealed, belting Fred. 'How can we when we've a celeb in our midst? Oh, Jim, tell us all!'

'Are you on telly, Dad?' Di asked. 'When?'

'Tuesday week at eight,' Jim said resignedly. 'I've to talk about the crisps.'

'Aw, that'll be a real cruncher.' Debbie pinched him affection-ately.

Everyone laughed. Jim moved slightly away from her, he didn't want his kids getting any idea about what was going on between them. Not that there was an awful lot. 'Anyway, we'd better go,' he said. 'A film to catch.'

'You must tell us later about you being on telly,' Gillian warned.

'Sure. Bye.' He was aware that Debbie was looking slightly hurt as they left. He felt like a heel.

Jane was in the garden when he dropped the kids off. As he handed her her money, he said, 'Is Owen OK, Jane? He seems a bit, I dunno, down.'

'Down?' Jane said sharply. 'What d'you mean?'

Jim shrugged. 'He's just really quiet or something.'

'That's Owen – he is quiet.' Jane stood up from where she had been weeding the flowerbed. 'He's like you, as you'll no doubt discover in a fortnight's time.' She pushed her hair from her face and shielded her eyes to look up at him. 'I'm going away for the weekend and I need you to keep an eye on them.'

'What? Here?'

'Yes. You can take the sofa or the, the other bed.' She shrugged. 'Matt's old bed.'

'Oh.'

'You *can* do it, can't you? I don't want to stand in the way of your social life.'

He couldn't figure out if she was being sarcastic or not. 'You know the kids come first with me,' he said. 'I'll get the days off work. So, where are you going?' He knew it was none of his business, but he couldn't help it.

'Just to Kerry.'

She was being evasive. 'With?'

'Someone I know.'

'Right.' He paused. 'Anyone I know?' He didn't think he imagined the smirk on her face as she shrugged.

'Nope. Bye now. See you next week.'

'Yeah. Sure.'

Ha! That showed him, Jane thought, as she went inside. She grinned. Maybe it was horrible of her, but if he could buy orange shirts and go out, well then, so could she. Difference was, he probably was really going places and she really wasn't, she thought ruefully. Still, he'd never know.

The kids were in the kitchen, eating as usual. 'So,' she smiled brightly at them, 'did you have a good time?'

Di declared that she'd had a brilliant time. 'We got to see a really sad film and it was great,' she said. 'And we had something to eat. And, oh yeah, we saw his flat.'

'Oh?' Jane tried not to sound too interested. She knew that he was living with Fred, he'd told her that much, but as to what the place was like, she didn't know. It was probably a pigsty knowing Fred. And Jim.

'It was gorgeous,' Di said. 'Wasn't it Owen?'

'Didn't really notice.'

'And we met Fred's girlfriend and her friend – didn't we Owen?'

'Uh-huh.'

'Gillian and Debbie,' Di said. 'And Debbie was so glamorous. She had this fab skirt on.'

'She fancied Dad,' Owen put in.

'What?' Jane and Di said together.

'She did,' Owen said matter-of-factly, 'she pinched him on the arm and he moved away. *And* she winked at him.'

Di rolled her eyes. 'She'd never be interested in Dad,' she scoffed. 'She's nice. Dad's too old for her. Debbie looked about the same age as Fred.'

'Fred's older than Jim,' Jane said, trying not to sound alarmed.

'Is he?' Di said mildly. 'Well, he looks younger and no way would an old person wear a skirt as short as Debbie's.'

'I think she liked him though,' Owen said.

The nerve of the girl, Jane thought. And pinching him. Huh, she hoped that Jim wasn't going to fall for it. After all, he did have two kids to consider.

'Dad must go out with them,' Di mused. 'They said they'd see him later.'

'Isn't it well for him going gallivanting,' Jane muttered. 'Easy now he doesn't have two kids to mind. And give me that!' She grabbed a packet of biscuits from Di. 'They have to last all week you know.'

'They'll be stale by then,' Di pouted.

Jane ignored her and put the biscuits back in the press. She longed to ask more about this girl, but knew she'd sound too anxious if she did. And besides, there was probably nothing in it. After all, Di, the big romantic, hadn't noticed anything. Owen was the one who'd made the comment and he hadn't even noticed what the flat was like, for God's sake. Not that it mattered if someone fancied Jim. It didn't matter at all, really. She just didn't want him to forget about his kids.

'Don't you have study to do?' she asked Di.

'In a bit.' Di poured herself some juice. 'I've to go and wash my hair now.'

'D'you want me to style it for you?' Jane asked suddenly. It'd give her a bit of practice before this course. 'I can do something really nice with it if you like?'

'Mam!' Di rolled her eyes. 'Nice? God, no. Who needs "nice" hair?'


'You never told us you were going to be on telly,' Debbie said, as he walked her up to the door of her flat. 'How come?'

Jim grinned. 'If I'm going to make a right eejit out of meself it's not something I want witnessed by all my friends.'

'You won't.' Debbie put her hands lightly on his shoulders and moved towards him. 'You'll be brill. You look the part anyhow – sexy and interesting. I'd watch the telly just to look at you.'

Jim laughed. 'Better turn the sound down then.'

They kissed briefly before Jim said quietly, 'Look, Debs, I owe you an apology. About today, when my kids were there—'

She put her finger to his lips. 'No you don't. I know you have to take it slow with them. I'm happy to be Gillian's mate.'

Jim nodded. 'Thanks.'

'Coming in for a coffee?' She turned to unlock the door. 'It's just us. Gillian is going back with Fred. Well?'

He wondered if she just meant a coffee. 'Aw, I dunno. I'm pretty wrecked. And I've some work to catch up on.'

'A coffee won't take long. Well,' she amended, 'not if you don't want it to.' He followed her inside.

Jane sneaked a peek through the crack of the kitchen door. Di and Gooey were sitting on opposite sides of the table. Di had done her hair so that it stuck out all over the place. It looked completely awful. Gooey was much the same. Reluctantly, Jane had to admit that in this respect anyhow, they were well matched.

'Hi Ma,' Di called loudly, making her jump.

Jane flushed, then stood up and tried with some dignity to walk into her own kitchen. 'Hello,' she said, making an attempt to smile at Gooey. 'How are you?'

Gooey mumbled something incoherent.

'Great,' Jane beamed. She indicated the kettle. 'Mind if I make some tea?'

'Well, it *is* your tea and your house,' Di said nonchalantly. There was silence as Jane filled the kettle. Silence as she waited for it to boil. Then, just as she was carrying her cup out the door, Di said, 'Oh yeah, I forgot earlier, Dad's going to be on the telly.'

She almost dropped her cup. 'What?'

'I said,' Di repeated, 'that Dad is going to be on the telly.'

'Really?' Jane walked back to the table and sat down, ignoring the glare Di gave her. She could stay now until Gooey went. 'When?' she asked. She smiled brightly at the two of them.

Gooey stared hard at the table and bits of his biscuit seemed to explode all over the place as he bit into it.

'Next week on some business show or other.'

'When did he tell you this?'

209

'Today.' Di had on her bored voice. The voice that was really saying, go away, Mam.

It made Jane more determined to stay.

'He didn't mention it to me.'

Di sighed but didn't reply.

It was amazing how her daughter could make her feel like the class nerd, Jane thought. She took a sip of her tea and wondered what to say next. 'Why is he on the telly?'

''Cause he's going to dance naked in St Peter's square.'

Gooey gave a strangled laugh and bits of biscuit landed on the table.

'Why is your father going to be on the telly?' Jane asked again, keeping her voice even and ignoring Gooey as he surreptitiously tried to rescue his mashed biscuits.

Di rolled her eyes and gave a martyred sigh. ''Cause of his crisps.'

'Thank you, Di.'

'You are most welcome, Mother.'

Jane gritted her teeth at Di's fiercely polite tone. That kid was heading for big trouble if she kept—

'Gotta go.' Gooey stood up. In his haste he banged against the table and knocked over his cup. His tea went everywhere. 'Aw, shit!' He attempted to stem the flow with his hands. Di grabbed a cloth from the sink and began a mopping up operation. Gooey muttered an apology and announced again that he had to go.

'Aw, Goo, hang on. It's only ten.'

'Naw, better go. Bye.' His eyes barely met Jane's as he muttered, 'Bye Mrs D'arcy.'

He still didn't know her surname, Jane thought.

'*Now* see what you've done,' Di whispered furiously, flinging down her cloth and flouncing out of the room after her boyfriend.

Lovely. If she hadn't talked to him, Di would accuse her of being a snob and because she did, it was somehow her fault that the guy had spilt his tea all over the place and then legged it out the door. Typical!

## 31

IT WAS THE click of a kettle that woke him. Opening his eyes, Jim noticed that he was in a strange room. Well, not strange, 'cause he'd been there before, but what the hell *was* he doing in Deb's flat? On Deb's sofa? Still, his head felt less stuffy than it had in weeks. He must've had a good night's kip.

'Morning, sleepyhead.'

Deb's teasing voice, coming from behind, forced him upright. Peering over the rim of the sofa he saw Debs coming towards him, holding a cuppa.

'You were great company last night, I must say,' she grinned. She perched herself on the arm of the sofa and handed him his tea.

'Ta.' Looking down at himself, Jim noted that he was still fully clothed except that someone – Debbie probably – had taken off his trainers. 'Jesus, did I fall—?'

'Yep. You conked out while I was making you a coffee last night. I didn't have the heart to wake you. You looked so . . .' Debbie screwed up her face and rubbed her nose against his, '. . . so *cute*.'

'Jesus, sorry about that.'

'Naw, I don't mind.' Debbie laughed, 'It'll give Fred and Gillian something to talk about over breakfast.'

Jim grimaced, thinking of the slagging he was going to get. And it'd be no use protesting that nothing had happened, Fred thought everyone operated the same way he did.

'Toast?' Debbie asked as the toaster popped.

'Yeah. Great.' Jim stood up and stretched. He felt great. Amazing what a good night's sleep could do. He couldn't remember the last time he'd had eight hours. Following Debs out, he sat down at the table and watched her potter her way about the kitchen. The white dressing gown she wore accentuated her dark hair. The dressing gown ended at her knees and Jim found himself wondering just what she was wearing underneath.

'Butter's on the table.' A plate of toast was shoved towards him.

Jim started, then gulped. 'Ta.'

He sensed her watching him as he buttered his toast. Glancing at her, he saw that she was looking thoughtfully at him, her chin cupped in the palm of her hand. 'What?'

'You talk in your sleep, d'you know that?' She sounded amused.

'So I've been told,' he muttered. Jane used to belt him whenever he woke her. And he always seemed to be saying . . .

'Who's Matt?' Debbie asked. 'You kept calling out that name. Jesus, I didn't know whether to wake you or not.'

The toast was like sandpaper in his mouth. He took a gulp of tea to help it down.

'Well?' Debbie asked, still grinning. 'Who is it? Some secret woman? Mathilda?'

Jim gulped. 'My son,' he said, wishing she'd stop grinning so much. 'He's, he's dead now.'

The grin left Debbie's face. 'Oh,' she said. 'Right.'

Jim suddenly wanted to get out of there. He'd no appetite for the toast now.

'How long ago?' Debbie asked, her voice gentle.

'Sorry?'

'How long ago did he die? Your son?'

'Four years.' Jim rubbed his hands through his hair and stood up. 'I better go now. It's, eh, late and I've to go into work before I pick up the kids.'

'But you haven't finished your breakfast,' Debbie exclaimed. 'There's no rush. It's only gone ten.'

'Yeah, well,' he attempted a smile as he searched for his trainers. 'You know Fred. If I don't get into the shower, he'll hog it all morning.'

'Under the sofa,' Debbie said, still staring at him. 'Look, Jim, did I say something wrong?'

'Nope.' He located his trainers and shoved his feet into them. He was all fingers as he tied his laces. 'I just have to wash and stuff. Get new gear. I'll call you.'

'OK. Sure.' She sounded slightly shell-shocked.

'I really will. See you tonight – OK?'

She just nodded.

Once outside in the sharp morning air, he cringed at his behaviour. Jesus, the girl probably thought he was mad. And maybe he was. Talking about Matt was never going to be on the agenda. It was too late for talking now, it was fine to remember him inside – Jesus, he couldn't seem to stop remembering – but the time for talking had come and gone.

## 32

FRED'S FLAT WAS full to bursting and Jim wondered despondently if there was anyone in Dublin that Fred didn't know.

'Good turnout, eh, Jimbo?' Fred boomed on his way to the kitchen to dump a pile of cans. 'And all in your honour.'

Since his gaffe with the kids – when he'd announced that Jim was to be on telly – Fred had decided that there was no point in crying over spilt milk. It wasn't every week that one of his best mates was on the telly and fuck it, he was going to throw a party. Unfortunately, it had been a surprise party and Jim hadn't been able to protest.

It was now seven-fifty, everyone was getting tanked up and Jim was due to be on in five minutes. *The Angle is All* was a highly successful business show where businessmen discussed their marketing ploys in an accessible way. For some reason, the show attracted audiences in the hundreds of thousands.

Jim wished that there was somewhere he could just die.

'Not your scene?' Debbie came across and linked her arm through his.

Jim grimaced slightly. 'The party's great, it's the entertainment I'm not going to enjoy. Jesus, Fred is a right bastard for doing this to me.'

'We can go off somewhere if you want?' Debbie suggested, taking his hand in hers and squeezing it.

'Aw, I dunno.'

'They won't notice you're gone,' Debbie whispered. 'Come on.'

It was tempting. He'd made such a bloody fool of himself at the recording. His sentences kept getting all twisted up and once he'd even forgotten the question he was asked.

'It'll be OK,' the producer had said, 'we'll edit all that out. Take your time.'

After that he guessed he hadn't been so bad, but still . . .

The signature tune came on and Fred stood up on the sofa and loudly told everyone to 'Shut the fuck up.'

Parrot started screeching and he yelled at her to stop.

Everyone began shushing each other.

'Let's head,' Jim grabbed Debbie's hand and she giggled as he pulled her out of the flat.

It was like watching an accident, Jane thought grimly as the signature tune of *The Angle is All* blared out of the telly. She didn't want to see Jim, yet she was drawn to watch it. Curiosity was a killer.

'Oh God, oh God,' Di began to mutter. 'Oh, he's on.'

Owen lolled back in the sofa, watching through slitted eyes.

Sheila haughtily exited the room. 'I'm surprised at you,' she said in an undertone to Jane. 'Encouraging this sort of thing. He left you, you know. I'd like to see him watching you if you were on the television.'

'Shut up, Nana,' Di hissed. 'We're trying to listen here.'

'Ohhh, don't let me stop you,' Sheila sniffed.

'Shush!' Di glared at her.

Sheila slammed the door.

The presenter introduced Jim and Philip.

'Ohhh, look at him,' Di shrieked excitedly. 'Look!' She began an ooh-aah session over Jim's clothes.

Where the hell had he got his new suit? Jane wondered. It had cost a bit. Dark grey with a dark grey shirt and tie. He'd had his hair butchered too, shaved close to his head. He looked like a holocaust victim. His hairdresser should be shot.

'Now,' the presenter said, 'Jim McCarthy is largely responsible

215

for Incredible Crisps' incredible success. Jim,' he swivelled to Jim, 'how so? Take us through it all step by step. Where did you succeed? What did you do that was so right?'

Jim's expression was one of a rabbit caught in headlights, Jane thought. She was just beginning to feel sorry for him when he began his answer. His voice and smile and sincere eyes coupled with his obvious enthusiasm for the marketing business made her heart twist up something rotten. The joyous look in his eyes as he described the search for the Chains Bond kid reminded her of when he'd talked about all the things they were going to do together. He hadn't looked like that in such a long time. It was like rediscovering all the things she'd fallen in love with as she watched him – the way he sat forward in his chair as he became animated about the ad campaign, the way he used his hands, the way he raked his meagre bit of hair, the half-embarrassed laugh he gave at the end of his answer. God, it hurt. She half-hated him for his enthusiasm. The show seemed endless with answer coming thick upon answer.

She was so busy feeling something akin to grief that she only registered that the programme was over when Di jumped to her feet.

'I'm going to ring him.'

'You can ring him tomorrow, it's too late now.' For some reason, she didn't want to have to talk to him. Or listen to the kids talking to him.

'It's only half nine,' Di said, sounding surprised. 'He'll be up.'

There was no arguing with that. 'Well, you can ring his flat, I'm not paying for mobile calls.' She glanced at Owen. 'D'you want to ring him?'

Owen shrugged. 'Well,' he answered, 'he was good, wasn't he?' He sounded as if he was looking for her permission to like his own dad.

Jane nodded and tried to inject some enthusiasm into her voice. 'He was,' she agreed, even managing a smile. 'And you

216

should tell him so. If I know your dad, he'll be worried about what you think.'

Diane was busy pressing buttons when Owen and Jane joined her. 'It's ringing,' she told them excitedly. Then, 'Hi, may I speak to Jim please? Jim McCarthy . . . he's what? Out? D'you know where?'

Jane watched the smile on her daughter's face suddenly disappear.

'Sorry. No, Jim *McCarthy*. No. No, he couldn't be. Are you sure?'

Di put the receiver down slowly and stood looking at it.

'Is he not there?' Owen asked.

Diane shook her head. Jane noticed that her eyes were glistening. 'Di, she began, 'what's—'

'He's gone out,' Diane said, looking at the two of them. 'Out with his girlfriend.'

'What?'

'The girl that answered the phone said that Dad had gone out with his *girlfriend* and they didn't know where he was and I said it was Jim McCarthy that I was looking for and she said that he had done a runner with, with, with Debbie. And she sounded a bit drunk and there seemed to be a party going on, so I didn't know if I believed her or not, but then in the background someone said that Jim had gone out with Debbie.' Her words were tumbling from her mouth and tears had begun to spill from her eyes. 'But, but maybe they made a mistake, I don't know.'

'Come here.' Jane pulled Di into an embrace, desperately hoping that her own shock didn't show.

When she looked around for Owen, he had gone.

Debbie wanted him. She was scrunched up beside him in the front seat of his car, her hand was fumbling with the zip on his jeans and her mouth was making mincemeat of his resolve.

His hands found their way under her blouse and up the front of her bra. As he rubbed her nipples, she moaned with pleasure.

217

His interview would be over by now.

Debbie slid her hand inside his boxers and began to rub him up and down.

'Aw, stop,' he whispered, not wanting her to.

'Why?' she asked, her brown eyes teasing. 'I've got you exactly where I want you.'

He pulled her on top of him and fumbled with the seat. Jesus, he hadn't had sex in a car in years. Not since Owen was conceived. Jim closed his eyes and gave himself up to the pleasure of being with Debs. There was no point in thinking of Owen and the rest. It was time to move on.

It was so long since a woman had loved him like Debs was doing.

Jane sat downstairs with a glass of wine and tried to block out the sound of Di sobbing upstairs. There was nothing she could do, nothing she could say to Di to make it all right. Because it *wasn't* all right. It didn't seem right. She'd tried ringing Jim but his phone was switched off. The bloody tomcat, she thought, gutted. Off with his latest fling. Debbie had probably bought that orange shirt for him too.

It was strange how hurt she was. OK, so they hadn't been happy, but to be replaced so easily by someone he probably hardly knew! It just showed what she meant to him. No wonder their marriage had fallen apart. She closed her eyes and took a sip of wine. She honestly thought he'd have more sense. He had two kids, a wife, and half a mortgage to pay. He had responsibilities. And this girl – well, she was bound to fall for him, wasn't she? Jim was shy, but when you got to know him, like she had, he was funny and quirky and romantic and mad. And Jim must like this girl.

And that hurt. More than she'd thought it would.

Well, she'd ring him tomorrow at work and ask him all about Debbie. She'd tell him how much he'd upset his kids. That should put a stop to his gallop.

In that moment she hated him. She really, really hated him.

## 33

JIM WATCHED APPREHENSIVELY as Jane slid into the seat opposite him. What should have been a brilliant day had suddenly turned sour. There he was, hero of the hour at work, everyone delighted with the interview he'd done and telling him jokingly that they were going to make him PR man for the firm.

The only person with any negative comments had been Dave. He'd sniggered and asked what had happened to his hair. 'Fall out with fright, did it?'

But he hadn't cared about that.

What he did care about was the scummy way his wife was looking at him across the table. Thoughts of the wonderful night with Debs faded as he studied Jane's face. Jesus, she was angry.

'Hi.' He gave her a smile. 'Want a coffee?'

'This is not a social meeting, Jim,' she said. She put her hands on the table and leant her head forward. 'Who the hell is Debbie?'

He was glad that he wasn't eating as he'd have choked. 'Debbie?' He attempted nonchalance and shrugged. 'Just, eh, a mate.'

'A mate?' Jane glared at him. 'In the physical sense of the word?'

'Aw, Jesus, Jane—'

'Well, that's what Di was told when she rang to congratulate you on the television thing last night.'

His stomach lurched. 'What?'

'Some girl in your flat told Di that you'd disappeared off with your girlfriend.'

Jim felt his world begin to flake. 'Di rang the flat?'

Jane nodded. 'So – is it true? 'Cause if it is, you've some explaining to do to the kids.'

He contemplated lying, but he could never bloody lie to Jane. She saw through everything. Slowly he nodded.

'You didn't waste much time, did you?' she asked. God, she wanted to kick herself as her voice broke.

He had to stop her. Reaching out he caught her hand, 'It's not like that, Jane. It just—'

'Save it for the kids.' She got up and left him.

She didn't want to go back to work but she couldn't face going home either. Maybe if she concentrated hard on her job, thoughts of Jim with some faceless female wouldn't bother her. And it did bother her. If she was honest, she'd say that she was jealous that he'd found someone so quickly. Not even her dad had done that. Jim, shy boy Jim, had actually scored. It was hard to believe really. Hard to take in.

Someone banged into her and glared at her. Jane hardly noticed.

'Hiya Jane,' Rosemary said brightly, when she arrived at work. 'I saw your mother in the shop at lunchtime. She was fighting with one of—'

'I'll be in the back.' She couldn't face anyone.

'— the customers. She was telling him that if he skipped the queue, she was going to skip over him and she wouldn't serve him and then . . .' Rosemary's voice trailed off as Jane pushed past her.

'You took a short break,' Patrick said from the doorway. He smiled, 'You're a glutton for punishment.'

'Patrick, can you just leave it – please?'

'What?'

'Just, just leave me for a second.'

'You all right?' Patrick ignored her, as he always did.

She couldn't bring herself to tell him. It would be too humiliating.

'You making a cuppa?'

'I, I dunno. Maybe . . .'

'I'll get it.'

She watched Patrick, through a sort of emotional fog, as he fussed with the teapot, humming tunelessly all the while. He poured some tea, got her two biscuits and, after neatly folding away the packet, crossed the room and handed her her mug.

She nodded her thanks. There was a small silence while she sipped some tea. She wished he'd leave.

He moved in beside her. 'Now, chicken,' he began, 'you tell me to mind my own business if you want—'

'Mind your own business.'

He gave a laugh that made her want to cry. 'What has Jim done?'

'What?' How did he know?

There was a hint of a smile on Patrick's face. Nudging her gently, he went on, 'You've been acting strangely all morning, chicken. Normally you're so in control it scares me. The only time the "in-control" mask ever slips, it's to do with Jim.' He tweaked her cheek gently. 'So, come on – spill.'

Was she really that obvious? Jane cringed.

'Well?'

He was going to sit there until she told him something. She didn't want to tell him, but if she lied, he'd know. It was hard to meet his eye as she muttered. 'He's, well, it looks like, as if, well . . .' It was hard to say it. She took a deep breath. 'He's seeing someone.'

'Seeing someone?' Patrick sounded confused. 'As in . . . ?'

'As in, you know, *seeing* someone.'

'No!' Patrick looked shocked. 'Well, he didn't waste much time, did he?'

'Nope.'

'And it's upset you?'

221

'Yeah. Yeah it has.' Jane bit her lip. 'I was married to the guy for almost sixteen years, Patrick. I just didn't think—'

'That it was as over as this?'

She shrugged, not trusting herself to speak. Last night, when he'd been on the telly, she'd seen him the way he used to be, but now . . .

'Do you want him back?'

'I don't know. I didn't think so. I don't *know*.'

'If you want him back, maybe you should talk.'

'Talk?' she laughed slightly. 'I've tried to talk. No. I guess I'm just, well . . . anyway,' she shook her head, 'I don't think I do want him. Not after everything.'

'Oh, right, I see.' Patrick looked confused. 'So, you don't want Jim any more – right?'

'Yeah.'

'Oh.' Silence. Then, 'Sooo, what is the problem?'

Men, even gay ones, could be so stupid sometimes, Jane thought. 'I'm not the problem!' She forgot she had a mug of tea in her hand and it slopped out all over the place. 'Oh *great*.'

'Here. Here, let me.' Patrick fetched a towel from the sink and handed it to her. He watched as she furiously wiped her clothes down. 'You're not the problem?' he probed gently.

Jane looked up. Auburn hair fell across her face and she brushed it away. 'No. I mean, it was a shock for me, yes. It was. But really, see, it's the kids. They're devastated. And it's me who has to pick up the pieces.'

'Why?'

'Oh, Patrick, don't go completely stupid on me.'

'I'm not.' Patrick took her cup and refilled it. Handing it to her, he said, 'It's not your problem. They're Jim's kids, it's his new relationship – it's up to him to talk to them.'

'Well, I'm the one who has to live with them.'

'Oh, I know, I know,' Patrick placated, patting her on the arm.

'Do you? Have you a wife and kids stashed away somewhere?'

'Now, don't *you* be stupid,' he admonished gently. 'But, look, you can't go about explaining Jim's actions to them. If he wants to go tom-catting and find sexy new women, it's his choice. You stay well clear.'

'I never said she was sexy.'

'No, no I know you didn't. She's probably *not*. In fact, she's probably a desperate hag whose biological clock is ticking away like some neutron bomb—'

'Patrick, you don't have to make me feel better.'

'But I have, yeah?'

His gentle smile was so concerned that tears pricked the back of her eyes. Blinking hard, she managed a watery smile, 'Yeah, I guess.'

He patted her head affectionately. 'So,' he said, 'let him explain – OK?'

Of course he was right. Jane wondered why she hadn't thought of it. 'What made you such a rock of good sense?' she asked, half-begrudgingly.

'Life, darling.'

They smiled at each other.

## 34

A s JIM THREW some gear into an overnight bag, he was aware that Debbie was watching him. She'd spent the night with him in the flat as Fred and Gillian had gone to Gillian and Debbie's place.

She sat cross-legged on the sofa, with a sleeping bag pulled over her. Dark hair spilled on to her shoulders and a rueful smile curled her mouth. 'I'll miss you,' she said, poking his leg with her foot.

Jim shrugged, 'You'll manage,' he muttered.

The last couple of days had been awful. Neither of his kids would talk to him. He'd called over the same night that Jane had confronted him in the café and it had been hell. Jane, to give her credit, had tried to make the kids see him, but they wouldn't.

Jane hadn't sneered as he thought she would. Instead, she'd been apologetic. 'I did try my best,' she said. 'But, well . . .' She'd shrugged and looked helplessly after her two offspring.

'It's fine,' he said, knowing that Jane knew it bloody well wasn't.

'Maybe Friday,' Jane said, 'you know, when you mind them, things will be different.'

He'd forgotten about it until that moment. And he was sick at the thought of it. Two kids and a mother-in-law from hell.

And even though he was tempted to call a halt to the whole thing with Debbie, he didn't think it was fair. It wasn't her fault and anyhow, she made him laugh and he hadn't laughed in what felt like years. She was dead nice and he felt good when he was around her. He turned to her now and smiled, 'I'll try and give you a ring when the kids are out,' he said. 'No point in rocking the boat.'

'Poor Jim,' she said softly. 'It's all my fault, isn't it?'

'Nah,' Jim shook his head. 'It's just a shock for them.' He shoved some aftershave into the front of his bag and zipped it up. 'Anyway, I'd better go. Jane said she's heading off early this morning.'

Debbie nodded. 'Take care,' she stood up and pinched his arm, 'Incredible Edible.' She planted a soft kiss to the side of his neck.


Jesus, where was he? Jane paced the hall from the front door to the kitchen and back again. She'd *told* him she was leaving early and that she wanted to be on the road by nine at least. Jim was always late for everything. The only time he'd ever been early was their wedding day and a fat lot of good that had done either of them. She wondered whether she should just go, but the fact that she was dressed in new clothes, with fab new auburn and red highlights running through her hair stopped her. It might be petty, but she wanted to show him just how gorgeous she could look. Plus, she hadn't told him where she was going; for all he knew, she could have a new relationship herself. She'd told the kids that she was going on a break for the weekend, so they couldn't spill the beans either. Not that they would. They still weren't talking to Jim though she sensed a thaw in Owen. He seemed unsure of what to do. She'd told him that Jim was still his dad and that it was OK to see him. 'I won't mind if you do,' she'd told him.

'But what about Dad's new girlfriend?' he'd asked. 'What about her?'

She had deliberately misunderstood the question and tried to make a joke of it. 'Well, I'm sure if you want him to bring her along, he will.'

Owen hadn't smiled back, just nodded.

Di was another matter. Jesus, the girl could do hysteria as an Olympic sport. Even the mention of Jim's name freaked her out. Jane couldn't understand it. 'But why won't you see him?' she'd asked, trying the same argument out on her that she'd used on Owen. 'He's still your dad and having a girlfriend doesn't change that.'

'Well,' Di had said, 'he's still your husband and the fact that he's moved out doesn't change that.'

Jane gulped. 'That's different.'

'Yeah?' Di had widened her dark eyes. 'Sure.'

That had finished the argument for Jane. There was no way she was going in any deeper. Anyway, Di would cool off. She always did.

The ringing of the bell broke into her thoughts. Jim's tall silhouette was framed in the glass doorway. Opening the door, she snapped, 'Well, you took your time. Out late last night, were you?'

Jim flinched. 'You wanted to be on the road by nine. It's nine now. Off you go.'

God, she hated herself for the barb. There she was, trying to pretend all was cool to the kids, but the minute he showed up in she went with the delicacy of a scud missile. 'I'm going now,' she replied, trying to keep her voice neutral. She'd already dragged her case to the car, so all she had to do was to don her newly acquired jacket, a little one like Mir had, and leave.

He had the nerve to close the door the minute she left the house.


Jane could be a right bitch, Jim thought. Jesus, asking him if he'd been up late. He'd killed himself to be on time – it wasn't his fault there'd been an accident on the motorway. Still, no point in explaining that to Jane. She knew everything. He found himself taking out his frustration on the cups and sugar and milk as he made himself a cup of strong tea.

He wondered if the kids were awake. Maybe he should do some toast as a kind of peace offering. He always used to do toast for them in the mornings. Well, the mornings when he was at home. He'd bring Jane a cuppa up too, to wake her up. He used to love looking at her first thing, all tousle-haired and sleepy-eyed. He sometimes thought he loved her more in the mornings than at any other time of day.

He smiled suddenly at the memory.

'I don't want any of your vomit toast,' Di said from the door. 'I'd rather die.'

His daughter was still in her nightclothes and her face was red and furious.

'I could help there,' he deadpanned, ''cause the way you're blanking me out makes me want to kill you.'

'You'd be up for murder then,' Di sneered, 'and you wouldn't be able to screw around.'

Jesus. He was sure no daughter should talk to her father like that. 'Don't talk to me like that!' He made his voice stern. 'I don't behave like that.'

'OK, I won't bother talking to you at all then,' Di said. 'So, have a happy weekend here – right, Dad?'

Rosemary was waiting, with an anxious look on her face. 'Hiya Jane, ooohh, isn't this great? I've never stayed in a hotel before. Jaz is dead jealous.'

'Is he?'

'Yeah. I had to promise him that I'd bring him some fancy soap and shampoo back. He said if I could get a shower cap and some polish that would be great too. He said they leave it in the rooms for you for free.'

'They do.'

'Wow!'

By three Jim was ready to surrender to depression. Di had gone out to meet Gooey and told him that she'd be back later. She

227

refused to say when later was. She told him that she didn't want a vomit dinner. Owen too, had left the house. He hadn't even said that he was leaving, he'd just sneaked out.

If things had been normal, it wouldn't have bothered him. But with everything in their young lives being turned upside-down, he didn't know what to do for the best. He flirted with the idea of ringing Jane to ask her if he should let Di out, or if she had any idea on where Owen could be, but chickened out. Jane would kill him. He wondered what the hell he'd say to Sheila if she asked where his kids were. She'd be sure to make a disparaging remark. Well, damn her, he thought viciously, she hadn't exactly clamoured to look after them, so he'd just tell her to mind her own business.

The hotel was gorgeous. Their room was spacious, with twin beds, a wardrobe, a dresser and a little table bearing a bowl of fruit. Munching on an apple, Jane inspected the bathroom. A shower, bath, toilet and washbasin in brilliant white. Black and white tiles gleamed on the floor and the walls were also deco-rated in black and white. This was going to be brill.

She was suddenly overcome with a sense of freedom. She could be anyone. She was away from home and God, it felt great.

'Gorgeous room,' Rosemary said, staring around, awestruck.

Jane grinned and plonked herself down on the bed. Picking up the phone, she ordered dinner for the two of them.

'I never believed in heaven until now,' Rosemary declared.

Jane laughed.

## 35

THE COURSE STARTED at nine sharp the next morning. As Jane showered, she found to her surprise that she was quite looking forward to it. It'd been years since she'd done one. There was a time when she'd known every trick in the book, every gel, every mousse, every type of roller. Her wish of opening a chain of salons had never materialised though. Jim kept trying to make her take the plunge, he'd even told her he'd do the marketing for her if she wanted, but having the kids made her wary about taking risks.

She pulled on a pair of white jeans and a bright pink T-shirt. Her hair shone thanks to Patrick's ministrations. He'd insisted, that as she was to be representing the salon, the least she could do was have decent hair.

Jane knew he'd only done it to cheer her up.

As she rubbed some bungee gum into the layers, she wondered how Jim was getting on. He hadn't phoned anyhow, so it must be a good sign. Maybe the kids were taking to him again.

Despite her bruised ego at his fickleness, she did hope they were.

'You are grounded,' Jim said. He kept his voice calm the way he'd promised himself and he looked Di straight in the eye.

'What?' There was a barely concealed sneer in her voice. The way her lip curled up as if she smelt something rotten hurt him.

'You heard.' He came around the table to face her full on.

'You weren't in until after two last night. You never phoned to say where you were or anything.'

'That would've been hard, seeing as I wasn't talking to you,' Di said, cool as a cucumber. 'What d'you want me to do, ring and then do some heavy breathing down the phone?'

'I expect you to ring at least. And anyhow, I'm sure your mother doesn't let you out that late. She never did when I lived here.'

'Well, you don't live here any more, do you? And things have changed.'

'Well, I'm living here this weekend and my rules stand. You are grounded for today.' Jim glared at her. He'd never before understood how Jane could get so annoyed at Di, but he did now. 'You can have the run of the house, but that's it. How dare you come home so late? What were you doing?'

'Want me to draw you a picture?'

'I want you to give me an answer.'

Di folded her arms and cocked her head to one side. 'Can't. I'm not talking to you.'

'Well, you'd better start. Otherwise you're grounded tomorrow too.'

'I did nothing much.' Di's eyes narrowed into slits. 'Just messing about with Gooey and a few mates.'

'Until two in the morning?'

'Yeah. It's no big deal. It's not like I stayed out all night, is it?'

'You're fifteen years old for God's sake.' Jim rubbed his hands across his face. 'Jesus, Di, talk to me, will you?'

Just for a split second, he thought he saw the old Di underneath the hard exterior. But it was brief. This new version of his daughter gave him another scum-of-the-earth look and shook her head. 'Ground me if you want, Dad, I don't care.'

She walked out.

Jim bit his lip. One down, one to go.

\* \* \*

230

The course was run in the hotel's salon, so Jane didn't have to hurry. She left Rosemary eating a full Irish breakfast in the restaurant and walked into the foyer where a receptionist directed her to a small room where coffee and biscuits were being served. She was asked her name and received a name badge.

'Grab a coffee, Jane,' the woman said, 'we'll be starting in about fifteen.'

As Jane made her way across to the coffee table, she was dismayed to see a tall figure chatting and laughing with a group of scantily clad hairdressers. What on earth was Pete Jordan doing here? she wondered. It wasn't as if he needed a course, he kept winning the bloody championship year after year anyway. You'd think, she fumed, that he'd let other people have a chance now and again.

She managed to get to the table without being spotted, but to her horror, as she took a coffee, Pete Jordan began to cross the room towards her.

'Hey,' he greeted her, patronising to the last, 'how's it going?'

Dressed in dark jeans and a bright blue T-shirt, he looked every inch the successful, happy businessman. And why wouldn't he be, after stealing all their clients? She shook her head, it was important to at least *appear* civilised.

'Are you on those tablets again?' Pete asked, eyebrows raised. 'Forgotten who I am?'

'How could I forget that?' Jane took a sip from her coffee cup and regarded him over its rim. 'Your business set up in direct competition to mine. It's a hard thing to forget.'

He nodded. 'And now your business happens to be the most expensive one in town.'

So he'd noticed. Jane allowed herself a smirk. He'd probably sent a little spy haring down the road to see how much they were now charging. 'Only because it deserves to be,' she said sweetly. 'After all, we use very high quality products.'

231

'And do OAPs appreciate that?' He actually sounded as if he wanted to know.

'Everybody appreciates that,' she said, gritting her teeth. 'As I'm sure you'll find out when all your business diverts to us.'

He threw his head back and laughed. 'Right,' he said, sounding amused.

Jane took a sip of her coffee. 'Now, if you'll excuse me, I've to drink my coffee and I'd like to do it without feeling sick.'

He didn't like that and she probably shouldn't have said it.

'Claustrophobic,' she said unconvincingly. 'I hate crowds.'

'Just as well you don't have to worry about that ever happening at work,' he said.

Bastard. 'Bye now.' She tried to say it pleasantly. 'See you on the course.'

'Yes. It'll be good. Joules is great.'

Joules! Pretending that he was well in. Was there no end to the man's arrogance? She didn't bother to reply, just smiled again and walked off, hoping to find a quiet corner where she could fume in private.

'You're grounded.'

'What?'

At least Owen didn't shout. He just looked a bit surprised and not too devastated.

'You heard.' Once again, Jim walked around the table and faced his other child. 'I said, you're grounded.'

Owen blinked. Once. Twice. 'OK.'

It took a second to register. There was to be no battle. 'Don't you want to know why?'

'I'm sure you've a good reason,' Owen said calmly. He picked up a slice of toast from the table. 'Eating this?'

Jim shook his head. 'No. And I'm surprised you can eat either. What the hell were you at coming home drunk last night?'

He saw his son gulp. Then shrug. 'I wasn't.'

232

'You were.' Jim took the toast out of Owen's hand. 'D'you think I'm stupid?'

'No, course not, Da.' Owen shrugged and admitted quietly, 'I was only a bit drunk. It won't happen again, OK?'

'Oh.' Taken aback, Jim was at a loss for words. 'OK, fine. But you're still grounded.'

'Uh-huh.'

'Where did you get the booze, anyway?'

Owen flinched. 'A few of the lads brought some cans.'

'And that girl?'

'What?'

'The girl that carried you home, did she bring drink?'

'Dunno. Could have.' Owen was shuffling from foot to foot. 'Can I go now? Is there anything else?'

'Yeah, as a matter of fact,' he said. Then as Owen showed no trace of emotion, he said in a stronger voice, 'Just 'cause your mother's away, don't think you can do what you like. I'm still your father.'

Owen gave a funny sort of a grin and nodded. 'Right.'

Jim watched Owen pick up the toast and leave the kitchen. He felt somehow as if he'd lost the battle with him. Maybe he should have asked him more about where he'd been. Owen going out was unusual enough in itself, Owen hanging around with a girl was even weirder. Still, maybe it was a sign that he was growing up. Most young lads drank at some stage and to be honest, he'd rather Owen out doing a few mad things than cooped up in his room the way he'd been the last few years. That had been unnatural.

The course was brilliant. Julian Waters talked about what styles suited what faces. With his model he demonstrated how to change a hairstyle simply by cutting into the guideline. Then there was a short break for coffee and after that, the models began to arrive.

There was no sign of Rosemary.

233

Jane waited and waited, her heart soaring and sinking every time a new model walked into the room. Eventually, trying to quell her rising panic, she walked out into the foyer to look for her. She stopped dead at the sight of Julian and Pete talking and laughing with one another. So Pete did know him. Typical. That's probably why he won every year, she thought, he probably knew all the judges. He'd enough money to bribe them anyway. He seemed to be in the middle of introducing Julian to a beautiful ethnic woman with glorious black hair. It looked very much as if this woman was going to be Pete's model. If so, she needed to find Rosemary quickly. There was no way she was being upstaged by him.

She crossed to reception. 'Excuse me,' she asked the receptionist, trying to keep her voice from spiralling upwards in panic, 'did a small auburn-haired girl pass by here by any chance?'

The receptionist looked blank and then said, 'Well, a girl had to go to the doctors with a burnt hand about half an hour ago. She left a message for a,' the woman consulted a card, 'Jane McCarthy.'

'That's me.' Frantically, Jane took the card. On it, Rosemary had scrawled: *Jane, have burnt my hand. Was eating breakfast and the coffee spilt all over me. Doc bringing me to his surgery to dress it. Will be back as soon as I can. Really, really sorry, but the bitch on reception,* Jane looked at the bitch, *wouldn't let me in to you.*

Jane closed her eyes and scrunched up the note. She hoped poor Rosemary was all right.

'Bad news?' the woman asked sympathetically.

Jane didn't bother to reply. Instead she stood looking resentfully at Julian and Pete and the beautiful woman. Eventually Pete and his model left Julian and returned to the room. Julian, after consulting some notes, made to follow them.

'Excuse me.' Jane rushed across to him as he looked at her impatiently. 'I'm Jane.' She tried a smile, which wasn't returned. Flustered, she babbled, 'And, eh, well, my model has had an accident, so, eh, I've no model.'

234

'No model?' Julian looked at her in disbelief. 'You come to *my* course with *no* model? I specifically said that everyone had to bring a model.'

'Well, she had to leave early, see, and well, I was wondering if you had a spare—'

'A spare model?' Julian quirked his eyebrows. 'Where? In the boot of my car?'

What a bastard. No wonder he and Pete got on. 'No. But I'm sure one would fit in your mouth,' Jane muttered.

'What?'

She flushed. What had possessed her? Still, he didn't seem to have heard or if he did, he obviously didn't seem to think he'd heard correctly. 'So the answer is "no" then, is it?' she asked sullenly, reminding herself of Di.

'The answer is "no".' Julian looked impassively at her. 'I do not bring extra models with me in case someone's gets lost. Now,' he said briskly, 'you may sit in and watch or alternatively, you can look for someone else, it's up to you. We start in five minutes.' He walked off.

Jane gave him two fingers. Well, she thought, no matter how good he was, she was never, ever going to spend her hard-earned cash on him ever again.

'Hello, hello,' the receptionist was waving at her.

What now, she wondered?

'I couldn't help overhearing,' the woman said, 'and, well, if you're really stuck, will I do?'

Jane winced. Marge Simpson was only in the halfpenny place. Still, beggars couldn't be choosers. 'That's very nice of you,' she smiled, 'but aren't you working?'

'I get off in five minutes,' the woman said. 'I'm June by the way. Now, I'll just wait for my replacement and I'm all yours. I'm glad I can help. That young lady wanted to go in to you and I wouldn't let her and now, well, I think it's all my fault.'

Jane smiled. 'Not at all.'

It was ten minutes before the second receptionist arrived and then June announced that she had to use the toilet.

Fifteen minutes late, they entered the room. Everyone looked up at them and she fancied that Pete Jordan was smirking at her. Ignoring Julian's grimaces, she quickly set up.

'Now,' June said, settling herself at the basin, 'I don't want anything really adventurous. I know what you hairdressers are like. Something nice and fluffy, I think.'

All through breakfast Jane had fantasised about the wonderful things she'd do with her scissors, but now, it just looked like being a straight curlers-and-hairnet job.

'Really, it's me who should be deciding,' she whispered. 'I won't make a mess, I promise.'

'No, I know you won't,' June said. 'Because I won't let you.'

Jane gritted her teeth and glanced across at Pete. He was deftly combing through his model's wet tresses. There was no way she'd even come close to him today.

'Now,' June said briskly, 'I don't want much off as I said, I like it fluffy – lots of body.'

Jane nodded, pretending to consider. Jesus, she thought, any more body and there'd be two of her. 'How about I layer it tight in at the back,' she suggested, 'and I even out the top? I think it'd look great on you.'

June shook her head. 'Nooo, I don't think so dear. That's the kind of thing my daughter has. I'm not into all that. I just want it fluffy.'

Jane wondered what on earth you did with someone who had definite ideas on what they wanted when what they wanted was completely wrong. She knew what she normally did. She gave it to them while trying to talk them out of it.

Diplomacy was called for.

She winced, thinking of Jim, Di and Owen. Diplomacy was not her strong suit.

An hour later and June's hair was a disaster. Jane had done her best to talk her out of her suicide style, but no way would that woman be deterred. She was delighted with the finished result, while Jane cringed. All she wanted to do was run out of the room before Julian caught sight of it. Pete had done a really radical style on his model's hair and while Jane wasn't mad on it, it was a damn sight better than what she'd done. More challenging too.

All around her fantastic styles were being invented and what had she done? Bloody 'fluffy'. Jane cursed her dowdy model who was singing her praises.

Julian came around and commented individually on everyone's work. It was amazing the hints he gave that could pull a style into a better shape. When he arrived at her, Jane blurted out, 'It's what she wanted.'

Julian nodded, frowning. Everyone was looking to see what he'd say.

Instead, he turned to June. 'And how about you, madam? Are you happy?' he asked.

'It's wonderful.' June patted and preened herself in front of the mirror. 'The nicest it's ever been.'

Julian patted Jane on the back. 'One happy customer who'll return again.'

'Yeah, but her friends won't when they see her hair,' she muttered in an undertone.

He gave a guffaw of laughter which transformed him from surly hairdresser into human being. 'Don't be so hard on yourself. The style is technically perfect. It's the best that could be done.' Giving her another grin he went on to the next student.

She hadn't looked at it like that, she thought. OK, it was a mess, but out of the mess, it was the best that could be done. She ought to be happy with that.

'Hey,' Pete came towards her, 'I see you've stuck to type.' He thumbed towards June.

'Absolutely,' Jane nodded, 'one happy customer, one technically perfect hairstyle.'

'That's not what I meant.'

'Is it not?' she said innocently. 'Why – what *did* you mean?'

He shook his head and stomped off. He even looked a bit rattled.

Later that night, when he was sure that the kids were asleep, he rang Debbie. She picked up and from the background noise, he deduced that she was in a pub. There seemed to be loads of loud laughter. Debbie said that she couldn't hear him properly, so he had to wait until she went somewhere quiet.

'Hi you,' she said. 'How're things going? Are they talking to you yet?'

'No.'

'Aw, poor Jim. Well, you've missed all the news while you've been away doing your domestic duties.'

'Yeah?' He found he was smiling as he listened to her bubbly voice.

'Liz and Edmond got a place of their own and they're having a housewarming right now, which is where I am. And, big news flash, Fred and Gillian have had a huge row and Gillian is at home bawling her eyes out, while Fred is here getting plastered and half-heartedly feeling up anything on legs.'

'Fred and Gill?' Jesus, he couldn't believe it. Still, it *was* Fred they were talking about – he'd probably just got bored.

'So, be prepared for a very sick flatmate tomorrow,' Debbie laughed.

'Great,' Jim muttered. 'Just what I need after this weekend.'

Debbie giggled.

That night, after Rosemary had fallen asleep, Jane picked up the phone to call Jim. She'd had such a wonderful weekend that she felt sort of guilty about him. He was bound to have had a terrible time. Besides, she wanted to check up on the kids. She couldn't help worrying whenever she left them.

His phone was engaged.

## 36

I T WAS WITH a heavy heart that Jane pulled into the driveway of her house. She felt even more depressed as Jim gave her the run-down on the weekend.

'I grounded both of them yesterday,' he said, as he helped her pull her bags out of the boot. 'Di was out until two the night before and Owen came home drunk. Of course, he tried to dodge upstairs on me but—'

'Drunk?' Jane laughed slightly. 'Don't be ridiculous, Owen wouldn't get drunk.'

'Well, he did on Friday. I thought grounding him would be a good idea.'

'How drunk was he?' she asked, wondering suddenly if it had any connection with Owen bunking off school.

'Well, I don't think he was really bad, but you know, he can't come home in that state.'

'Yeah. Right. Good.' She'd have to talk to Owen later – find out what had happened. 'Did he say why he was drinking?'

'Nah,' Jim shrugged. 'I reckon it's just a phase. All lads do it at some stage.'

He was probably right, but it was still worrying. 'I'll have a word.'

'Yeah. Good.' Jim nodded at her. He helped carry her case into the kitchen, then asked if she wanted it upstairs.

'I'll do it later. I'll just get a cuppa now. It's been a long drive.'

'Yeah, sure.' Jim moved out of her way. 'There are bars in the press you can have. I bought them for the kids only they

. . . well, apparently not talking to me means rejecting my grub as well.'

God, things must have been bad if Owen refused to eat chocolate, Jane thought as she fished them out of the press. They were his favourite too. 'So,' she asked Jim, 'where are the kids now?'

He shrugged. 'Dunno. They just went out. Wouldn't tell me. Another part of the not-talking-to-Dad clause, I guess.'

God, the man was hopeless. Couldn't he have just demanded that they tell him? Jane bit her lip so that she wouldn't say something stupid. That was Jim all over, come the heavy one minute and be completely walked on the next. 'And my mother?' she asked instead.

'Gone back to Hades in her burning chariot.'

The comment was so quick that Jane giggled. 'Stop!'

Jim grinned back at her. 'Sorry.' He shook his head. 'But Jesus, she's made my life a complete misery this weekend. Every time I walked into a room, she walked out. Then the kids started to copy her.' He paused. 'Anyhow, she's gone to work.'

'Oh, right.' Maybe this afternoon wouldn't be so bad, Jane thought. She'd have the house to herself. She could do a big clean-up and maybe read a book or something. Feeling more generous, she asked, 'D'you want a cuppa before you head off?'

He looked surprised, but pleased. 'Yeah, sure. If you want.'

She filled the kettle halfway and flicked it on. She was aware of him looking at her, but she couldn't turn around and meet his gaze, instead she got cups from the press and pretended she couldn't find the tea bags. The silence seemed to grow and grow.

Just as the kettle clicked off and she was pouring them both some tea, Jim asked, 'Did you have a good weekend?'

'Brilliant.' She sat down opposite him and pushed his mug across. 'I learnt loads.' She stopped. Decided not to be so childish. 'It was a hairdressing course.'

'Oh, right.' Jim didn't seem to know what to say to that. He sipped his tea and peeled open a bar of chocolate. 'It's a long time since you went on one of those – isn't it?'

'Years.'

'So, like, what did you do?'

It was weird at first, talking to him about the course. They hadn't really talked about small things in ages, but as she described Julian and saw him grin at her description of June, she grew more confident. 'She wanted "fluffy",' Jane said. 'I mean, can you *imagine* it? I might as well have just glued a cat to her head.'

Jim laughed and the sound of it was bittersweet.

'Julian thought it—'

The ringing of Jim's mobile cut her off. He looked at her apologetically.

'You better get it.'

'Yeah, right.' He seemed embarrassed as he fumbled it out of his pocket. He got even more embarrassed as he talked into it.

Jane knew it had to be Debbie and she cursed herself for being so nice to Jim. She was glad that he'd had a bad weekend, he deserved it. The bloody – she racked her brains to think of Mir's joke – the bloody koala bear that he was.

She noisily began to clear away the mugs.

Jim wished he'd turned his mobile off. Jesus, he'd completely forgotten that Debbie had said she'd ring him. He was meant to be back at the flat by now. He tried to talk to her as if she was just a mate, but he knew Jane wasn't fooled.

'Listen, talk later,' he eventually said. 'I'm not at the flat yet.' He flicked the phone off and turned to Jane.

'Well, you'd better go,' she said brittlely. 'You've got your orders.'

The moment was spoilt. She had her efficient face on, the one that completely closed him out. 'Yeah, right. I'll just get my bag from the sitting room.'

As he left the kitchen, he wished he didn't have to go.

\*   \*   \*

241

'I believe you were drinking on Friday,' Jane said.

Owen was watching TV, the remote in his hand, his feet up on the sofa. 'Yeah,' he muttered, without looking at her. 'I told Dad I was sorry about that.'

'He told me.' Jane pushed his feet off the sofa and sat beside him. He squirmed away, still looking at the telly. 'D'you want to tell me why you found it necessary to come home drunk?'

He grinned slightly. 'It wasn't like that. One of the lads had a few cans, that's all.'

'One of the lads – what lads?'

'From school. He bought them and we all just shared them. I only had a couple.'

'Owen, you're only thirteen – it's illegal!'

'Yeah, sorry.'

Jane took the remote from him and flicked the TV off.

'Hey!'

'Perhaps you'll look at me now?'

Owen stared at her with solemn brown eyes. 'I told Dad it won't happen again. What more can I do?'

'You can tell me.'

'It won't happen again.'

'And it's got nothing to do with bunking off school?'

'Ma!' He refocused on the telly. 'Gimme a break. I go in now, don't I?'

And he did. Perhaps it was just as Jim suggested, a lad thing. She decided to let it go. 'All right,' she tousled his hair. 'I forgive you.'

Owen shook his head and flicked the telly back on.

## 37

FRED BARELY GLANCED at him when he arrived back. Instead, nursing a can of lager, he kept his gaze on the telly.

'How goes it?' Jim dumped his sleeping bag on to a chair and grinned at his mate. 'I believe you had a wild night last night?'

Fred shrugged. He slugged some more lager. 'Goodfilmzis,' he muttered.

'What?'

'I *said*,' Fred repeated very deliberately, "Sagoodfilm.'

'Oh, yeah, right.' For the first time, Jim noticed the stench of beer, then he noticed that the normally immaculate Fred hadn't shaved and was dressed in a shirt that looked as if it had been puked on. 'Are you OK?' he asked cautiously. 'You look a bit rough.'

'Feel great!' Fred waved his can about and drink sloshed everywhere.

Jim tried not to wince as most of it went on to the sofa. Jesus, it'd smell like mad tonight. 'Good. How's Gill?'

'Don't talk to me about her.' Fred wiped his mouth and stood up. He jabbed his can towards Jim and swayed dangerously. 'I told her, I told her to go. I said I didn't want her. Women are all the same. Think they can pin you down. But not me. "Not me," I said to her. "I mean," I said, "look at Jimbo. Jimbo's wasted," zats what I said.'

'Thanks.'

'No, no, no, no,' Fred waved his arm expansively and yet more drink fizzed to the floor. "Snot an insult. Right. Right?'

'Yeah, whatever you say.' Jim studied Fred who was now

stumbling towards the fridge in search of more cans. 'So, what happened with Gillian?'

'It's over. That's all. Now where are the bloody cans?'

It was the first time Fred had ever taken a break-up so hard, Jim thought. Normally, after ruining some poor woman's dreams, Fred would be out enjoying himself for weeks afterwards. Still, it was not the time to say anything as the guy was going to pass out on the floor if he didn't shift him somewhere. He was just trying to coax him to sit back down again when the buzzer went.

'It's me!'

Jim buzzed to let Debbie up. Then he hauled Fred to his feet, saying, 'Come on – get your head down. Don't let Debs see you like this. She'll tell Gillian.'

'Couldn't give a shit,' Fred spat. 'Gillian fucking who? That's whad I want to know. Gillian who?'

'Yeah right.' Jim rolled his eyes and dragged Fred into his room. 'Just get some kip.'

'The fucking room is spinning.'

Jim closed the door on him. He'd be fine. From the look of him, he'd been up all night, so he was bound to conk out.

'Hi you,' Debbie, dressed in the catsuit he'd first seen her in, looked fantastic. 'Are you not going to let me in?'

'Well,' he shrugged apologetically, 'Fred is smashed. I should stay with him. Maybe you'd better—'

'Gillian is crying her eyes out at my place, but she doesn't *want* me to stay. So, come on, Jim, let me in – I've nowhere else to go. And besides, I haven't seen you in days.'

Reluctantly he let her past. Jesus, the way her bum looked in that tight black leather. And her hair . . .

'So,' Debbie crossed her legs and surveyed him, 'did you miss me?'

'I missed having someone to talk to,' he said ruefully.

'You look awful,' she said, sympathetically. 'Was it a bad weekend?'

'Bad doesn't even come close.'

'Aw, poor Jim,' Debbie said in mock-sympathy. She made a face and said, as if talking to a five-year-old, 'Come over here. I'll make sure no one else does anything bad to you.'

'Aw, pity about that.' Jim sat down beside her. Grinning, he added, 'And here was me thinking I'd just love someone to do bad stuff to me.'

'Yeah?' Debbie snuggled into him.

'Yeah. But seeing as there's no one around—'

'Come here, you.' Debbie pulled his face to hers and kissed him hard on the lips.

Jesus, she was gorgeous.

Just as she began unbuttoning his shirt, Fred stumbled out of his room and into the bathroom, where he was violently sick.

'Ugh, Jesus,' Debbie winced and pulled away.

'You all right, Fred?' Jim called.

'Fuck off!'

'Charming.' Debbie rolled her eyes. 'I dunno what's happened between the two of them, but whatever it is, Gill's better off.'

'He's cut-up over it.' Jim felt he had to defend Fred. 'Honest, I've never seen him like this. Normally he just gets on with life. He never gets in this kind of state.'

Fred re-emerged from the bathroom, wiping his mouth with his sleeve. Taking a look at Jim and Debbie he said, 'Can yez not go and fuck yourselves somewhere else?' He gave his bed-room door a hard slam.

'Fecker,' Debbie said. 'Come on, Jim, let's go.'

'Naw,' Jim shook his head. 'You go if you want. I'd better stay, just in case he does anything mental.'

'He won't,' Debbie said impatiently. 'Come on!'

'He's me mate, Deb, I can't.'

'Fine.' She didn't sound as if it was fine. 'Stay.'

'I'll call—'

But she was gone.

God, he was upsetting them all these days.

## 38

MONDAY MORNING. MIRANDA was stomping about the place as usual. Nothing ever changed, Jane thought as she pulled the appointments book from under the desk to check her clients for the day. It was funny, she'd been away for a weekend and somehow she was convinced that something had to have happened while she was gone. No such luck.

Still, at least something had changed, even if it was only slight. Ten customers were booked in, four of whom she didn't recognise. Business was on the up.

'Hey.' Patrick startled her, as he tweaked her hair. 'The wanderer returns.' Leaning over the appointments book so that she couldn't read it, he asked, 'Tell me, what did you think?'

'Oh, it was great,' Jane smiled. 'He was brilliant.'

'Yes, I know.' Patrick beamed delightedly. 'So, go on, tell me all about the weekend. What did you do?'

So Jane told him about Rosemary burning herself and the model that she had as a stand-in. 'And, yer man was there,' she added, 'Pete Jordan. He's not the smiley guy he once was. I think we've got him rattled.'

'Take a lot to rattle a guy like that,' Patrick said. 'Barney met him on a course once. Said everyone was eating out of his hand.'

'I wish one of them had *eaten* his hand,' Jane muttered.

Patrick giggled.

'Oy, Pat,' Mir held up the phone, 'For you. Some guy, says his name is Barney?'

246

Patrick scurried over to take the call and Mir stared grumpily at him before mooching over to Jane.

'That's the fourth time that fella has rung in the past week,' she grumped. 'And every time he rings he sounds different. He's as gay as Christmas now.'

'Probably because he is,' Jane grinned. 'He's Patrick's partner, I think. He's the guy who sent him the valentine's card.'

'Oh,' Mir's eyes narrowed. 'He never told me.'

'Told you what, Mir?' Rosemary looked at both of them. Her hand was wrapped in a big bandage.

'Well, someone obviously never told you to mind your own business.'

Rosemary's face dropped. 'Oh. I just thought, well, never mind . . .'

'Never mind what?' Patrick asked brightly.

'Oooh, don't ask,' Rosemary gulped. 'I think it's private.'

'Who is Barney?' Mir sounded annoyed. Patrick's grin only seemed to annoy her further. 'Well, go on tight knickers, tell me.' She poked him with her elbow. 'Who the hell is Barney?'

'Aw, he's that flippin' purple alley-gator that all the kids love,' Rosemary said, delighted to be of help and redeem herself for her nosiness. 'Yez know, he sings that sick song about everybody loving each other.'

'That's not the Barney we mean,' Patrick laughed indulgently. He'd grown quite fond of Rosemary in the past while. 'No,' he paused, then said half-shyly, 'Barney is my partner.'

'You've gone inta partnership, have ya?' Rosemary gawped.

'His *sexual* partner,' Miranda sniffed. 'God, Rosemary, you're awful thick.'

'Yer boyfriend like?' Rosemary's jaw nearly hit the ground as she stared wide-eyed at Patrick. 'Like, as in a *relationship*?'

'Yes,' Patrick nodded. 'He's the man who sent me the valentine's card and now, well . . .' he beamed happily, 'we're very close.'

'Awwww,' Rosemary smiled. 'That's lovely, so it is.'

'Well, I don't think it's fair,' Miranda snapped, not looking a bit pleased at Patrick's happiness. 'Jesus, straight guys far out-number gay guys in this poxy city. So how come you can get someone and I can't? How come?' She glared at Patrick as if it was all his fault.

'Give it a rest, Mir,' Patrick said, sounding irritated.

Rosemary tittered. 'It's not that hard to find someone. You'll *easily* do it. I mean, even I have a fella.'

Jesus, Jane thought, *why did Rosemary have to say that*? Miranda did not like people to be happy on a Monday morning.

'I met him last—'

'I'm not on the lookout for blind, brain-damaged specimens,' Miranda almost spat into Rosemary's face. 'So save it.'

There was an uneasy silence.

'He is not brain-damaged,' Rosemary said, her eyes filling up. 'He's—'

'Whatever he's like, I wouldn't want him.' Miranda turned to leave.

'No, Mir,' Patrick said quietly, 'you prefer the louts that use and abuse, don't you?'

Miranda froze.

Jane wished she could be somewhere else. A fight between Miranda and Patrick would be awful. 'Look guys, let's just—'

'What?' Miranda asked, '*What* did you say?'

'You heard.' Patrick's voice sounded harder than Jane had ever heard it before. His eyes seemed to bore into Miranda, who flinched.

'I don't go out with guys that . . . whatever the hell you said,' Miranda said defensively. 'The guys I go out with are fine.'

'Oh right,' Patrick said in pretend nonchalance. 'So *that's* why you were crying this morning, is it? That's why you waltz off with every deadbeat you find in every club we go to, is it? That's why *every* Monday, after these guys dump you, me and Jane have to try and coax you into semi-good form so that our customers won't get their heads bitten off – is it?'

'Piss off!'

'Well?' Patrick demanded. 'Is it?'

'Don't you dare! Don't you dare. That's – not – fair.'

'It's true though.'

Jane didn't know what to do. Jesus, they'd been mates for so long it'd be terrible if this fight ruined things between them.

'I, I, was wrong about you,' Miranda said to him. Her voice wobbled dangerously. Gulping hard, she said, 'You *are* a real man. A complete bastard.'

'And when in doubt, curse like a trooper, eh, Mir?'

Miranda jerked at his words. Blinking rapidly, her voice trembling, she said, 'I think I'm going home.' She looked Patrick up and down. 'I'll be *sick* if I stay here.'

'If you put as much effort into styling as you do into chasing hopeless losers, you'd have a bloody chain of salons of your own by this stage.'

'Aw, Patrick!' Jane interjected.

'Are you saying that I'm no good? That I'm lazy?' Mir shoved her face almost into Patrick's. 'Well?'

'Mir!' Jane said. 'Please. It was just said in the heat of the moment.' Desperately, she turned to Patrick. 'Wasn't it, Patrick?'

The silence seemed to last for ever. Eventually Patrick said gently, 'It was said as a friend, Mir. Look at what happened at the weekend—'

'I don't need your friendship!' Miranda grabbed her coat from the chair where she'd tossed it. 'And, seeing as I don't put any effort into my work, I don't need your poxy job, either.'

'Miranda!' But Miranda was storming to the door. Jane pushed Patrick. 'Jesus, Patrick, go after her!'

Patrick let the door swing shut behind Miranda. 'No,' he said, 'leave her. She's better off on her own.'

'I'm sorry,' Rosemary piped up. 'It was my fault. I shouldn't have said—'

'It was nothing to do with you,' Patrick patted her arm. He

249

glanced at Jane. 'Listen, Rosemary, hold the fort while I have a chat with Jane, will you?'

Rosemary, looking very pale and subdued, agreed.

Inside the coffee room, Jane tried to get him to go after Miranda. 'Jesus, she's left her—'

Patrick held up his hand. 'Jane, don't.' He shook his head. 'Don't give me grief. She had it coming.'

'No,' Jane shook her head. 'Not like that. What you said was awful.'

'Do you know what she did last weekend?'

'No, but Pat—'

'Well, I'll bloody tell you.' He paused for a second, as if willing himself to calm down. He closed his eyes and began slowly, 'We went out to a club. This band were playing and that musician fella, the one that dumped her ages ago, was playing. Well, Mir goes up and makes a complete fool out of herself. Laughing with him, flirting with him, she even kissed him. And when I tried to have a word in her ear, she turned around and told me to mind my own business and to get lost. So I did. I went home.'

'Yeah, well—'

'And then she rings me up on Sunday, crying her eyes out 'cause musician man had left with someone else and she had a go at me, *me*, for leaving her on her own.' He tossed his head. 'I mean, honestly!'

'She always does that.'

'Yeah, well, I've had enough. I'm tired of being good enough until something better comes along.'

He was very hurt over it, Jane realised. Hurt and furious. Patrick didn't get annoyed often, but when he did, he was immovable.

'She's, she's unhappy,' Jane said, understanding for the first time that Miranda probably was. 'She's just looking for love. OK, she gets it wrong but—'

'But why the hell is it our fault?' Patrick snapped. 'With her, it's always someone else's mistake. Yours, mine, Harry's. Never Miranda's. Never. And yet she goes about attacking kids like

250

Rosemary who – Jesus Christ – have absolutely nothing in their lives besides a fella and a two-bit training job.'

He walked to the door and just before he opened it, Jane said, 'Patrick, she's packed in her job. I mean, do you want your friendship to end because of it?'

'What friendship?' His desolate tone shocked her. 'It's all take, take, take with her. Harry will tell you the same. That man puts up with some crap. She's treated him far worse than she's ever treated me.'

'Yeah but—'

'No buts.' Patrick opened the door. 'Anyhow, she'll be back. I know she will. I mean,' he made a face, 'how else will she afford all her designer gear?' He gave a twisted sort of a smile and left.


Jim took out his organiser and keyed in 'Debbie'. Her home and work numbers flashed up on the small screen. He was about to reach for the phone to dial her work number when the phone rang.

'Philip Logan for you, honey pie,' Maud said cheerily. 'Your number one fan.'

Jim sighed. Philip would keep him for hours. Reluctantly he flicked his organiser off and prepared himself for the onslaught of orders from Philip.

'Philip,' he said in a tone that implied he was under pressure and couldn't talk for long. 'What can I do for you?'

'Ask not what you can do for me, but what I can do for you,' Philip chortled.

There was a brief silence. Jim took a deep breath, told himself to have patience and in a remarkably even voice, he asked, 'So, what can you do for me, Philip?'

'Atta boy!' Philip boomed so loudly that Jim had to take the phone away from his ear. 'You want to know, meet me in, mmmm, let's see . . .' He hummed and hawed and seemed to press a lot of buttons before he said, 'Meet me at Jury's at one.'

'I've got a lunch appointment at one,' Jim said firmly. Jesus, there was no way he was meeting Philip. Philip's idea of lunch was wine and food in that order. Dave would have jumped at it, but he didn't fancy sitting in a restaurant while Philip ordered the staff to jump through hoops for him.

'Cancel it,' Philip ordered.

'I can't,' Jim replied. 'My clients are important to me, as you know.'

'Fuck off with the bullshit and cancel,' Philip laughed. 'It'll be worth your while, I guarantee it.'

Jim sighed. Dave would go through him for a shortcut if he found out that he'd refused a potentially lucrative lunch with Philip Logan. 'Right. I'll rearrange my whole schedule to accommodate you,' Jim said with a bad grace. 'It won't be easy though.'

'Nothing worthwhile ever is, Jimbo. Did no one ever tell you that?' Philip gave another boom of a laugh and hung up.

The day had been a complete disaster, Jane thought as she pulled into her driveway. There had been an upturn in business, but because they were a stylist down, there were queues. It hadn't looked good, but it had felt great.

As Jane let herself in, Sheila drifted out of the dining room. Her mother was wearing a dressing gown, her head was swathed in a towel, her nails had been painted and the stink of them was all over the place.

'Hello, dahling,' Sheila smiled. 'Good day?'

'Terrible.' Jane brushed past her mother and had a look in the kitchen. Owen was standing over the cooker stirring a stew. He smiled at her and she smiled back. 'Where's Di?' she asked.

'In the shower,' Sheila answered. 'Honestly, that girl will have herself washed away – *if* we're lucky.'

Jane smiled despite herself and Sheila looked pleased. She sat down gingerly on a kitchen chair, being careful to keep her French-polished nails away from the furniture.

French polish and her mother usually meant only one thing. Her mother was going out somewhere.

'Are you going out, Mother?' Jane couldn't keep the surprise from her voice. Perhaps she was meeting her dad, Jane thought. They hadn't heard from him in weeks. Maybe tomorrow she'd tune into her dad's show and see what he was up to. There was no way she was ringing him, not after what he'd said.

'A woman doesn't have to be going anywhere to try and look her best,' Sheila said defensively.

'No, but she doesn't normally use expensive nail vanish unless she is,' Jane shot back. Her mother, much to her horror, had been forced to use cheap make-up in the last while as all her expensive stuff had run out. Bits and pieces of her former life's make-up had been hoarded away 'just in case'.

'Well, if you must know,' Sheila looked slightly embarrassed, 'I'm going to Lisa's.'

'Your boss's house?' Jane gawped. 'Why? Is she suddenly your best friend or something?' The last she heard, Lisa was as common as muck, with a mouth like a sewer and skin like barbed wire.

'A friend? *No.*' Sheila looked revolted at the thought. 'A woman interested in making the most of the little she's got? Yes.' She blew on her nails to hurry them up, before continuing, 'It was her idea. She was so delighted with the outfits I chose that she wants to learn more about looking well. Apparently, she's sep-arated and she wants to show hubby what he's missing. Now, I'm not a miracle worker, but I did say that I could give her a few hints on how to look after her nails and things. So she thought it'd be wonderful if I did a sort of,' Sheila screwed up her face as she tried to think of the right word, 'a sort of class in grooming, I suppose you could say. So I said fine.' Sheila smiled, 'And best of all, if I do this, she lets me off work for the next two days.'

'What? She's going to pay you two days' wages to file a few nails?'

'Apparently,' Sheila nodded. 'I mean, she's invited her friends to hear me talk and everything – wonderful, isn't it?'

Jane nodded. And what was more, her mother actually looked happy. Something like that would suit her down to the ground.

'And I'll tell you something else wonderful,' Sheila said, 'if this goes well, Lisa thinks there might be a business in it. People listening to me talking. Imagine!'

Jane winced. She didn't think it bore imagining. 'Eh, great.'

'She might *look* awful,' Sheila had her charitable voice on, the one she used for talking about travellers and refugees and ugly people, 'but she's very sharp. Always thinking of new businesses. She's more money than Jack Benny hoarded away. So, there we are.' She got up and went to the fridge. Taking out some natural yogurt and a grapefruit she proceeded to eat.

'Owen, is dinner ready?' Jane asked.

Owen peered into the pot. 'It's hot, I reckon so. Will I get the plates?'

'How can you eat that stuff?' Sheila shuddered. 'Nice fresh food, that's what keeps your skin intact.'

'Yeah, but your tongue keeps wondering what the hell it was invented for.' Di strolled into the kitchen. Staring down at Sheila's 'dinner' she made a face. 'Taste? Hello? Where are you?' she mocked.

'Well, dahling, I'd rather have bland food than a bland body.' Taking her food with her, Sheila exited.

Jane suppressed a smile. Sheila had really copped on to how to infuriate Di. 'What does she mean, "a bland body"?' Di whispered furiously. 'I'm thin. Amn't I thin, Mam?'

'Anorexic looking,' Jane soothed.

Pacified, Di sat down.

After dinner, Jane dialled Miranda. There was no answer, so she left a message on the machine asking Miranda to ring her.

Jim left the lunch with Philip at eight. He was locked and he knew he couldn't drive. He'd have to leave his car overnight and get a taxi home. Philip had offered to call him one of his cars, but Jim had refused. He needed to think. His head was spinning with Philip's proposal. It'd mean a complete change. Philip had told him he needed to know within the next couple of months. 'It's all a bit up in the air at the moment,' he'd said. 'But it'll definitely be happening, by the end of the year at least. I want you on board.'

It'd mean giving up everything he'd really wanted. But, Jim thought as he hailed a taxi, everything he'd ever wanted had given him up, so maybe . . .

## 39

I{\scriptsize T WAS LUNCHTIME} the following day before Jim realised that he still hadn't called Debbie. Between Philip's offer and Fred going on another bender, ringing Debbie had completely slipped his mind.

As Jim listened to Debbie's phone ringing, he half-hoped she wouldn't answer. He knew if she did, she'd probably be feeling a bit pissed at him.

'Hello?'

'Hiya, Debs, it's me. Jim.'

'Yes?'

She *was* angry. Jim gulped. 'Listen, sorry about the other night, Fred is in bits. He even got drunk again last night and he didn't go to work this morning.'

'Am I supposed to feel sorry for you both or something?'

'Aw, Debs, don't be like that. Listen, can I call around tonight? I promise I'll make it up to you.' Debbie said nothing. Jim took her silence as a good sign. 'Please?'

'Well,' she still sounded a bit annoyed, though not as much as before, 'don't come to the flat. Gillian is swearing vengeance on all things Fred at the moment – you included. I'll meet you after work, say around seven, outside Cleary's?'

Outside Cleary's. Jim felt his heart twist. He and Jane always used to meet there. Under the clock at Cleary's was the big meeting place. It was funny how stupid things like that could affect him. 'Sure,' he said. 'See you then.'

She hung up on him without even saying goodbye.

*   *   *

Miranda didn't show for work but Patrick wasn't too worried. 'Give her a week,' he said. 'She'll be back.'

'But what if she's not?' Jane asked. 'I think you should ring her and ask her if she's really left. Talk to her, tell her you didn't mean what you said.'

'But I did mean it.' Patrick wasn't going to budge. 'I meant every word. She *is* lazy, she *is* a tart.' With that, he asked Rosemary to get one of the customers a cuppa while he mixed a colour.

Jane took it that the subject was closed.

Sheila was relishing her lie-in. Getting up for work in the mornings was so tiring. It was now after three and she felt rested and refreshed. Maybe she would get up – after all, the sun was splitting the rocks outside and if she lashed on some suntan lotion, she might even get a bit of a colour. She tried not to think of the foreign holiday she would be on if she'd still been with Declan. Still, losing a foreign holiday and a tan was a small price to pay for not having to put up with Declan's fumblings in the bedroom. Sheila shuddered as she remembered. Don't even *go* there, she thought.

Instead, she let her mind wander to the previous night. It had been a screaming success and Lisa, who owned a lovely house – even if the interior designer had ballsed it up – had seemed pretty sure that more bookings would follow. It was the easiest thing to do, Sheila thought, hair and nails were so *interesting*. Talking about them to a room full of women was sheer heaven. And getting paid for doing it was the icing on the cake.

She stretched and savoured the silence in the house. The kids had gone out. Di had made her a cup of tea before leaving, in exchange for a lend of some pink nail polish. Sheila smiled. Di was a scream; moody as hell, but so quick-witted and smart. It was fun sparring with her. Owen, on the other hand, was the weirdest boy going. But then again, he had more of his father's genes than was good for him.

She turned on to her stomach and flicked on the bedside radio. It was nice to know what was happening in the world before getting out of bed. Although sometimes the news wasn't very interesting; all that political stuff could be mind-numbing. She didn't know why they bothered reporting it. Who would be interested in all that malarkey? Give her a good bit of gossip or scandal any time.

The news was as boring as ever. Sheila had virtually given up on it when the newscaster said, 'And finally, DJ Declan D'arcy's show has been voted the number one radio show in the country for the eighth year running. Declan says he's going to celebrate in style.' Then Declan's voice came on, 'No point in growing old unless you're going to do it disgracefully – huh?' There was the sound of loud laughter in the background before it cut to the studio again. The newsreader gave a giggle. 'Well, that's our Declan,' she tittered.

She went on to give the weather forecast but Sheila hardly heard it.

'That's my *pig* of a husband more like,' she muttered. 'I'll show him.'

She wasn't quite sure what she'd show him, but it'd be good.

# 40

JANE HAD DECIDED to go into town. There were a few things that she needed to buy. First on her list had been new trainers for Owen, but she'd crossed them out. He'd bought himself a pair last week out of some money he'd saved. They'd been in a sale, he said, and he just had to have them. Jane grinned. It was nice to see Owen getting enthusiastic about things for a change. He sort of coasted through life with no particular interest in anything much. Still, he'd started calling for some girl recently and Di had been slagging him about being in love with Charlotte the swot. It had caused a bit of friction at breakfast, with Owen sullenly denying that the girl was anything but a hanger-on.

Di had tapped her nose and giggled and waltzed out the door, leaving the usual trail of exasperation in her wake.

Jane kind of hoped Owen did have a girlfriend. Even though she had disputed Jim's comment the time he'd ventured his opinion on Owen being a bit down, it still bothered her. Maybe Owen was upset over the split? Maybe they'd handled things all wrong? Hadn't he bunked school? At least if he was socialising a bit more, it might mean that he was adjusting to things. She couldn't bear for her kids to be unhappy. They were the most precious things in her life and she didn't like to think that she and Jim had upset them.

She parked her car along the quay, shoved a pile of change into the parking meter and, hoisting her haversack on to her back, began the short walk into the city. She had just reached the beginning of O'Connell Street when a tap on her shoulder

259

startled her. She whirled around and found herself face to face with a small man with peroxide-blond hair and a stud in his ear. He was wearing jeans and Doc Martens.

'Dad,' she said, the tension leaving her. She gave him a sullen look. 'Hi.'

Her dad grinned. 'Thought it was you. Nearly didn't recognise you, it's been that long.'

Jane nodded. 'Well, you didn't exactly put a time limit on the "butt out" section of our last conversation.'

Declan laughed loudly, causing passers-by to stare at them. 'Amn't I always saying that you should be on the radio?' He slapped his denim-clad thigh. 'Honestly, you're so quick with the one-liners when you have to be.'

Jane folded her arms. 'Surprised you noticed, seeing as the only person you like listening to is yourself.'

Again he laughed, a big, hearty laugh, which boomed out across the street. He always laughed at stuff that made him uncomfortable. 'So,' he asked finally, 'how're things with you?'

'Pretty good.' Damned if she was telling him anything.

'Hiya, Declan,' a pretty blonde girl called out as she walked by. 'Love the show!'

'Thanks.' Declan blew her a kiss and she giggled and nudged her mate. He turned back to her. 'Fame is pretty good too, Jane,' he chortled.

Jane remained impassive.

'Have you time for a coffee?' There was a certain awkwardness about the invitation. An almost embarrassed shyness which wasn't like him.

'OK,' she shrugged reluctantly, 'why not?'

'Why not indeed!' Declan slapped her on the back – nearly crippling her – his reserve of a second ago forgotten. 'I know just the place.'

'It'll have to be quick,' Jane lied. 'I'm meeting someone later.'

'No problemo,' Declan began to lead her through the crowds. 'I know a cool place, does great coffees, juices, whatever. And no worries about a table, they've a special one for me. Jaysus, it's been so long since I've seen ya, we'll have loads to talk about.'

That'd be something all right, Jane thought sardonically. In her whole life she'd never had a proper conversation with her dad, unless you counted all the ones where she'd begged him to make it up with her mother.

Declan was as good as his word. Walking into the restaurant, he managed to attract everyone's attention by calling the head waiter's name at the top of his voice. In a cringe-inducing Italian accent, he yelled, 'Pablo, see Declan. Uno tablo par fuck-er.' Loads of gesturing followed and Jane, ready to die with shame, was ushered by her dad to a table in the very centre of the restaurant.

'Si?' the head waiter asked, pen poised.

'I'll, eh, have a coffee with the frothy bits and the spicy stuff,' Declan said with authority. 'Jane?'

'Just an ordinary coffee,' she mumbled. 'Thanks.'

The coffees arrived quickly, along with two small cream cakes. 'To congratulate you,' the waiter said.

Declan gave a self-deprecating bellow. 'Aw, thanks. Thanks.'

Some of the customers clapped politely and Declan stood up and took a bow. 'This is my daughter,' he said loudly, gesturing to Jane, 'in whom I am well pleased.'

Laughter was followed by more clapping. Jane had to smile like a performing seal. She wanted to die.

When the fuss had abated, Declan pushed one of the cakes towards her. 'Eat up there now, feed your face. Getting something for free always makes it taste better.'

'Why did he congratulate you?' Jane asked. The cake was nice though she'd have preferred a Danish.

'The best show on radio,' Declan said. 'I won it again.'

'Great.'

'Great indeed,' her dad said, totally missing the fact that she was being sarcastic. 'No one else can come close. My listener-ship figures are in orbit at this stage.' He beamed at her but there was a certain something missing from his eyes. It was the sort of smile she used sometimes when she didn't really feel like smiling.

'So, how's everyone?' he asked.

Jane shrugged. 'Fine.'

'Di?'

'She's just finished her Junior Cert and has managed somehow to latch on to an appalling boyfriend.'

'Yeah. How so?'

He actually sounded interested. But she didn't feel like elaborating. With her dad, he was liable to announce it over the airwaves. 'Dunno. But he's awful.'

'Aw, you're doing a Sheila on it. She never liked Jim. D'you remember?'

'I am doing nothing of the sort!' Honestly!

Realising that he'd put his foot in it, her dad changed tack, 'And how's my grandson?'

'Fine.'

'Good. Good.' Declan spooned sugar into his cappuccino. 'He still doing the skateboarding?'

That had been years ago. It just showed how much interest her dad had in her family.

'He stopped doing that,' she said icily. 'It was too dangerous.'

Declan chortled. 'And what lad stops doing something when it's too dangerous?'

'I *made* him stop.'

Silence.

'Oh, yeah. Right. Of course.' Her dad flushed. 'Very sensible too.'

And it had been. Even if Owen had been the best skateboarder around. Jane swallowed the last of her coffee and wondered how best to leave. This conversation-making was hopeless.

'And how are you?' Declan asked, 'since you and Jim . . .' his voice trailed off. Apologetically, he muttered, 'I met him a while ago – gave his crisps a plug on the show. He looked tired, I thought.'

All his socialising, Jane thought morosely.

'So,' he asked again, 'how are you?'

'Single.' She gave him a bright smile. Indicating her coffee cup, she said, 'I have to—'

'And Sheila?' He blurted the question out, his face flushing. 'Has she moved out yet? Set up in digs?'

The idea of her mother in digs brought a smile to her face. 'No, she's still with me. Why don't you ring and talk to her yourself?'

He ignored that. 'And I suppose she's helping out around the house, is she?' He looked cockily at her. 'Cleaning and dusting and hoovering to earn her keep.'

Jane felt sorry for her mother. 'Actually, Dad, she has a job.'

Coffee spluttered all over the table as Declan began to cough. 'A job? Sheila? My arse she has!'

'She makes sandwiches and rolls in a shop up the road from the salon.'

Declan gave a huge belt of a laugh. Coffee went everywhere. Jane was practically drowned.

'Sheila, a sandwich-maker? Jaysus!' He wiped his nose with his sleeve as coffee started to run down it, then, unable to stem the flow, he pulled his napkin out of his wine glass and began a mopping-up operation. 'That's a joke – right?'

'No,' Jane said weakly as she fished her own napkin out of her glass to wipe her face. She probably shouldn't have said anything. Her mother would kill her. But she was only sticking up for her when all was said and done. 'It's true,' she confirmed, remaining stony-faced. 'It's a good job. She works on her own in the shop on Sundays. And she's even started giving *nail* demonstrations.'

'And – makes – fucking – sandwiches!' Declan was coiled up laughing. His body shook trying to keep it in. 'The woman who has trouble buttering bread is making sandwiches for the good people of Dublin.'

263

Jane had to leave. To minimise the damage it was important to make a dignified exit. 'Thanks for the coffee,' she said briskly, refusing to be drawn into his laughter. 'Bye now.'

She didn't think her father even noticed. Well, there was a surprise.

# 41

IT HAD BEEN a good night, Jim thought, as he awoke in Debbie's bed. It hadn't started out too promising though, with Debbie being really narky at first. But when he'd told her of his seven-hour liquid lunch with Philip and his subsequent humongous hangover, she'd begun to thaw. A dinner and a few drinks later and he was feeling dead guilty as she radiated warmth and adoration for him once again. The night ended with her suggestion that they go back to her place.

'But what about Gillian?'

'She'll have gone to bed,' Debbie said.

So he'd followed her into her apartment and up to her bedroom. She'd flicked on the bedside lamp, which gave a dim yellow glow to the room. Taking his hand, she'd led him to the bed.

Sleeping after sex was a damn sight better than sleeping after downing a few cans, Jim thought.

It was five-thirty. Dawn light was just seeping into the bedroom and Jim knew he wouldn't sleep any more that night. He decided to get up, grab a coffee, and head back to his place to pick up some gear for work. He'd leave Debs a note or something.

He dressed silently, half-buttoning his shirt and shoving his socks into his trouser pockets. Carrying his shoes, he tiptoed towards the door. Debbie didn't stir. She looked great with all her black hair fanned out on the pillow. Jim opened the door and closing it silently behind him, made his way to the kitchen.

He jumped, startled, at the sight of Gillian nursing her own coffee.

'Hiya,' she mumbled.

Her eyes were red and her hair, normally so bushy and bouncy, was flat and uncared for. Snot was running from her nose and Jim, after staring horrified at her for a while, handed her a piece of kitchen tissue. 'Thanks,' she muttered, as she rubbed her face vigorously.

'Another coffee?' he asked. At least she was being civil to him.

'Yeah.'

They sat in silence as the kettle boiled: Gillian sniffing and blowing her nose, and Jim wishing he'd just done a runner when he'd woken up. Pouring the water into the coffee, he carried two mugs to the table. Shoving one of them across to her, he asked, trying not to sound too hopeful, 'D'you want me to go?'

'I thought he loved me, Jim,' Gillian said. A big fat tear rolled down her face and plopped into her mug. 'I really, really did.'

He was useless at this weepy stuff. Useless. Gulping hard, he wondered what to say. The truth maybe? 'I think he did,' he said. 'Does,' he amended.

Gillian looked up at him. 'Naw. He wouldn't have treated me so bad if he did.' More tears. More sniffing. More snot. More kitchen paper.

Jim wrapped his hands around his mug, gripping it as if it were some sort of lifeboat. 'He's been in a bad way since you broke up,' he consoled.

It was the wrong thing to say. She got hysterical. Hyperventilating and glaring at him, she said through her tears, 'And I'm not? Is that what ya saying?' Her bottom lip curled downwards and she sniffed loudly. Pointing to herself, she snuffled, '*I* am the injured party hee-a.'

'Naw,' Jim hastened to explain, 'I meant that I've never seen him so cut up about anything before. Like, he normally doesn't care if it's over, but he does this time. He's in bits.'

Gillian blinked her swollen eyes. 'Then why won't he ring me? What's stopping him?'

Jim shrugged. 'Dunno.'

'He's a shit, that's what.' A fresh batch of tears loomed.

'Why don't *you* ring *him*?' Jim asked.

Gillian looked at him as if he were mental. 'He's the one who told me to get lost! Are you joking? I do have some pride, ya know!'

Jim winced. Why couldn't he just keep his mouth shut? 'Look Gillian,' he said, trying to sound concerned yet not concerned, 'I dunno the ins and outs of the situation, so I can't comment. I don't want to say the wrong thing, OK? All I know is that Fred is more upset than I've ever seen him before – OK?'

'Do you wanna know the ins and outs?' Gillian virtually shrieked. 'Do you?'

Oh sweet Jesus. 'Naw,' he shook his head.

'What the hell is going on?' Debbie, white-faced, tore into the kitchen. Seeing Jim and Gillian there, she demanded, 'Well?'

There were more tears from Gillian. Jim stood by helplessly as Debbie put her arms around her friend and sat her back down on her chair. Jesus, give me Fred's binges any time, he thought.

Eventually Debbie calmed Gillian down. Getting her a fresh coffee, she made her sip it. 'Now, what's all this crying about, Gill?' she prompted. 'Come on. You'll have to tell me sooner or later. You can't keep things to yourself like this.'

'I'll, eh, just go . . .' Jim began to back out of the kitchen.

'No!' Gillian's sharp tone stopped his getaway cold. 'No, I want you both to hee-a what a swine Freddie is. He hasn't the nerve to tell you, so I'm gonna.' She sniffed, pulled herself upright in her chair and announced loudly, 'I'm pregnant!' Then she burst into more sobs.

Debbie looked at Jim. He looked at her.

'Aw, poor baby.' Debbie cradled Gillian's head in her arms.

'Don't mention babies,' Gillian wailed.

267

Jim was rooted to the spot. Gillian pregnant, he should have guessed. What else would send Fred into such a tailspin?

'How far gone?' Debbie asked, gently pushing Gillian's hair back from her face.

'Five months.' Gillian had begun to hiccup. 'And Freddie don't wanna know and I can't get rid of it, I can't.'

'Has he asked you to?' Debbie glared up at Jim as if it was all his fault.

'He just says he don't wanna know.' Gillian buried her head in Debbie's shoulder. 'And he says that . . . that . . .' She began to sniff again.

'It's OK,' Debbie soothed.

When Gillian got herself back under control, she continued, 'He says that I didn't really know him. That I nevea did. He says he hates sports and hiking and stuff and that we'd nothing in common and that it wouldn't work out and . . .' Her voice grew jumbled as she explained everything that Fred had said.

Jim was suddenly reminded of Matt, the way, if he fell, he'd cry and blubber and no one would have a clue what he was on about.

'What the hell are you smiling at?' Debbie snapped.

He hadn't been smiling, he didn't think. 'Nothing,' he mumbled. Images of his little boy disappeared and he was left with the heartbreak that was going on in front of him. 'Look, I'll go. I'll call you later, OK?'

Debbie barely nodded. She continued stroking Gillian's hair and telling her to 'let it all out'.

Jim, feeling as if somehow it was all his fault, let himself out of the flat. Jesus, he thought, Fred was a right bastard.

When he got back to the flat, Fred was sprawled out on the sofa, snoring loudly. He stank of beer and sweat and vomit. Jim's stomach did an involuntary roll as he surveyed his friend. There was a tiny part of him that actually felt sorry for Fred. It was no fun when your worst nightmares suddenly became reality.

Jim flicked on the switch for hot water and soon he was washed and shaved and ready to head off. Fred seemed to stir slightly at the sound of the electric razor so Jim moved closer to him and began to shave into his face.

'Uuuggh!' Fred moaned as he turned his head away. He put his hands over his ears and curled up in a foetal position on the sofa.

'How's Daddy today?' Jim asked, before he could stop himself. 'Enjoying drowning your responsibilities in drink?'

It was as if he'd put a bomb under him. Fred sat bolt upright, decided that it wasn't a good idea and sank back down again. White-faced he looked at Jim. 'She told you,' he said, sounding completely terrified. Then he groaned, 'Out of me way.' He stood up, pushed Jim away and staggered towards the bathroom.

Jim flicked off his shaver and waited for Fred to re-emerge.

'Sorry 'bout that,' Fred muttered sheepishly.

Jim said nothing, just continued to stare at him.

'Well how the hell do I know it's mine?' he snapped defensively.

'You said that to her, did you?'

'Damn right, I did.' Fred attempted to regain some dignity. He stood upright and walked in a straight line to the sofa. 'Women will all try and sucker you.'

'You know damn well it's yours,' Jim snapped. 'Unless it's a bloody immaculate conception. Yez were always together.'

Fred looked mutinously at him. 'It's none of your business – so keep out.'

'She's in bits you know. It's not good for her to be like that, not if she's pregnant.'

'Well, that's her fault, isn't it?' Fred stood up and faced him. 'Now, Jimbo, if you want to stay here, just keep that,' he jabbed at his nose, 'out!'

'You can't keep drinking and just hope it'll go away, you know,' Jim said.

Fred said nothing for a second. Then, a sneer curling his lips, he said calmly, 'So what? I should copy you, is that what you're saying?'

'What?' Jim was puzzled. 'Copy me?'

'Yeah.' Fred nodded. 'Work all the hours in the fucking day and hope things will go away that way.'

For a second, Jim was stunned. 'I bloody well don't,' he snapped. 'My job is a busy bloody job. I have to work, otherwise I go under.'

'Yeah, you'd go under all right, having to face things, wouldn't you, Jimbo?'

'Aw, Jesus.' Jim turned away from him, his heart hammering. 'You're still drunk. I'm going to work!' Hands fumbling, he zipped up his laptop.

'The solution to everything!' Fred called as he left. 'Work.'

'Naw, the solution to this is that I'm leaving.' Jim turned back to him. 'As soon as I get a decent place, I'm gone.'

'That's what you said to Jane too, was it?' Fred sneered.

Jim's answer was a slam of the door.

## 42

NERVOUSLY, JANE PRESSED the buzzer. A crackled voice answered. 'Who is it?'

'Me. Jane.'

There was a silence, then a very grumpy, 'What do you want?'

'Well, seeing as you've returned none of my calls, I thought it'd be nice to talk.' Jesus, she wondered, was she doing the right thing? Miranda was prickly enough, without her making things worse, but it had been two weeks now and she still hadn't come back to work. For some reason that she couldn't understand, she felt she needed Miranda to come back. Patrick was talking about advertising her job and Jane just couldn't let it happen without doing something.

The buzzer went to allow access to the building and as Jane climbed the stairs, admiring the wallpaper and carpets in the foyer, she thought that though Miranda might be stupid where guys were concerned, she was dead clever with money. The apartment block was beautiful.

Miranda was waiting for her at the door to her apartment. 'Come in,' she said, not sounding a bit pleased to see her, 'you'll have to excuse the state of me, I haven't had a chance to shower yet.'

She wore a long silk gown, patterned with large flowers. Her dark hair shone and even the fact that she looked as if she'd only just climbed out of bed couldn't obscure how good-looking she was.

'Tea?'

'Yeah, if you're making some.'

Without a word, Miranda padded out to the kitchen and reappeared a few minutes later with two mugs of tea. 'No sugar, loads of milk, right?'

'Ta.'

Sitting down in a chair opposite her, Miranda curled her feet under her and cupped her mug in both hands. She regarded Jane with cat-like eyes. She was a bit like a cat, Jane thought. Unapproachable and unreachable.

'Why didn't you return my calls?' Jane asked, trying not to sound hurt about it.

Miranda shrugged. 'And say what?' She arched her sculptured eyebrows. 'You only rang to ask me to go back, and until he apologises, I'm not setting foot in that place.' She took a sip of tea, all the while regarding Jane. '*Is* he going to apologise?'

Jane attempted a smile. 'Aw, Mir, just come back – he won't mention it. It'll be forgotten about.'

'Forgotten about?' The cool woman evaporated, to be replaced by the Mir Jane did know. Eyes blazing, she spat, 'Patrick called me a slapper—'

'He didn't!'

'Like hell he didn't – it's what he meant. He said I was stupid about fellas. Well,' she tossed her head defiantly, 'he can't go about saying stuff like that to his staff. I could sue him!'

'Don't be ridiculous. It was a fight. Said in the heat of the moment. I mean, look at what you said to Rosemary. That wasn't very nice either.'

'Rosemary is a twit. Full of big ideas and stupid dreams.'

'There's nothing wrong with having dreams.'

'There is if you're as thick as Rosemary.'

Jane left it. Arguing about Rosemary was not going to solve the situation. 'Look, forget about her, let's talk about you.' She attempted a smile. 'Will you come back?'

'He said I was lazy,' Miranda said next. She scowled at Jane, 'Am I lazy?'

272

'No.' Jane shook her head. 'No more than the rest of us anyway.'

'What?' Mir glared at her. 'So I *am* lazy?'

'He just meant that you'd grown complacent about cutting people's hair. We all have. It's important to keep up to date, branch out, attract younger customers. If there is one thing Cutting Edge has done for us, it's that.' She paused. 'You are not lazy, Mir.' Mir's softening expression made her say, 'If he'd been rowing with me, he would have said the same thing.'

It was the wrong thing to say. Mir's eyes darkened. 'Only thing is,' she said bitterly, 'you and Patrick never row, do you? He tells you all his little secrets and you tell him yours and I'm left out in the cold the whole time.'

'What?'

'I'm like a spare in that place. You and him are as thick as thieves.'

'He's my partner, Mir. We have to be.'

'He goes out with me at least once a week and does he tell me about his new fella? No.' She folded her arms and glared at Jane. 'But I bet he told you the first chance he got.'

'He told me the night we last went out together. You were too busy with a fella to bother.'

'Well, he had a chance to tell me after that.'

'When?' Jane found herself annoyed all of a sudden. This was petty. This was not what she'd come to talk about. 'You're too busy talking about your own disasters to listen to him.'

'Ooooh.' Mir stood up. 'So now you think I'm a slapper as well!'

'Oh, for God's sake—'

'If all you've come for is to have a go, then, then, then go!' Mir pointed to the door, her hand shaking.

Jane stood up. This was not meant to happen. She'd never rowed with Mir before, but then again, Mir had never shouted at her like this before. 'I didn't come to have a go.' Jane tried to keep her voice steady. This was awful. It was like her whole

273

life was crumbling down around her. First Jim, then her parents and now Mir. 'I just want you to come back to work. Please. We need you. Business is even picking up.'

'Well, bully for you and Patrick. But I don't let my employers call me a slapper and get away with it.'

'Mir, we're your friends.'

'Some friends.'

'Well, we care more about you than the ones you pick up on a Saturday night.'

Her words hit home. She was sorry she'd said them the minute they were out. Miranda looked as shocked by her as she had been by Patrick.

'Get out.'

'Mir, I'm sorry. I didn't—'

'OUT!'

'I'm sorry.'

'You can still get out.'

Jane stood her ground. There was no way her friendship was going to end like this. 'You can't keep letting people treat you like that,' she said.

Miranda began physically shoving her towards the door.

'That's all Patrick meant. You have to cop on Mir. You could have anyone, don't go for the dregs. You deserve—'

'Out!'

'—better!'

'What in the name of Jaysus is going on?'

The male voice froze both women in their tracks. Miranda glared at whoever was behind Jane. 'Fuck off and let me deal with this.'

'Hi, Jane, nice to see you.'

Jane turned around and saw Harry looking at them both in amusement. 'Did I miss something?'

She was flustered. What the hell had possessed her? Other tenants were looking at them from the safety of their doors. 'I, eh, was just going,' she mumbled.

'So I see,' Harry nodded. 'Mir was helping you. She's awful helpful is Mir.'

'Fuck off back to your cave, Harry!' Miranda made to slam the door.

Harry stuck his foot in the gap and got a right wallop for his troubles. He looked unperturbed by it. 'Jane, maybe you can enlighten me as to why she's lost her job? She won't tell me. I'm awful worried about her. I keep calling in to see how she's doing. Bringing her,' he fished out a naggon of vodka from his pocket, 'little treats to loosen her mouth, but she still won't tell me.'

'Loosen my legs more like,' Miranda said darkly.

Hurt flashed across Harry's face. 'You know that's not true,' he said quietly.

'Isn't it?' Miranda arched an eyebrow at him.

Harry flushed and shoved the vodka back into his pocket. 'See you around, Mir.'

His voice was cold and Jane saw that even Mir looked stunned by it. But she recovered. 'In your dreams,' she spat after him. When Harry carried on walking, Mir turned blazing eyes on Jane, 'Now, see what you've done! You made me say horrible things to him.'

'I didn't make you say anything,' Jane said, startled. 'You—'

'You put me in a bad mood. Now,' Mir said, 'go and sort someone else's life out. Your parents, how about them?'

The hurt started in her heart and spread into every part of her. How could Miranda drag her folks into this? What had her parents ever done to her?

'Thanks Mir.' Jane swallowed hard and forced herself to keep looking at her. Taking a breath, she said, 'Patrick was right. You bloody well blame everyone else, but your life is in this mess because of *you*! No one else. You were horrible to Rosemary, horrible to—'

The door was slammed in her face.

Patrick *was* right, she thought. With Mir, it was all take, take, take.

Trying to retain some dignity, she walked down the corridor. She didn't see Harry, who'd obviously been waiting for her.

'Jane,' he asked, 'what the hell is going on?'

In a pub in Rathmines, she told him the whole story. She was fair to everyone, she thought. When she'd finished, she looked at Harry. 'She won't talk to me or Patrick – maybe you can get her to come back to work?'

Harry shook his head. 'Naw, I'm finished with all that. The girl is more trouble than she's worth.' He took a gulp of his pint and smiled ruefully, 'Never too old to learn – huh?'

'Aw Harry—'

He held up his hand. 'That stuff she said to me today? Well, she can't think too much of me, can she?' His finger, long and slender, traced patterns on the cool of the glass as he continued, 'I've loved that girl since I first met her. But, I dunno, she's just not happy, is she? Not with anything she has.'

Jane nodded. 'She doesn't realise how bloody lucky she is,' she said, her bitter voice surprising them both. At Harry's sharp look, she said, 'You know, she's good-looking, she's got a nice apartment, a good job and, if she wants it,' she paused, 'a nice guy.'

Harry smiled. 'Thanks.'

She smiled back. 'Hang in there, Harry. Maybe one day she'll realise just what she's missing.'

His smile disappeared. 'I dunno if I can. Maybe it's time to move on. Maybe the best thing to do sometimes is to walk away.'

Jane thought of Jim. She thought of how he'd left. Slowly she nodded. 'But to move on,' she said, 'it's nice to know where you're going first, isn't it?'

'Suppose.'

Jane touched his hand. 'Hang in there, OK?'

# 43

A NOTHER SATURDAY MORNING. Jim climbed into his car, not sure how much more rejection he could take. It had been five weeks now and his kids still refused to see him. He did get the feeling, however, that Owen wasn't angry at him any more, but that only made it more confusing. Why the hell wouldn't the kid go out with him then?

Debbie had said to give them time, it'd work out she said. Then she announced that Gillian had asked her to be godmother to her baby. 'It'll be me and Gillian,' she'd told him, at the top of her voice one evening, in the hope that Fred would hear, 'two mothers is better than a whole *heap* of fathers.'

Jim had cringed, wondering if it was true. He felt like just about the worst dad in the world. And the laugh of it was that he'd been determined to be the best dad in order to make up for his own miserable excuse for a father. Maybe Gillian's baby *would* be better off without Fred to mess its life up.

Fred, of course, was refusing to talk about Gillian or the baby, denying the fact that the whole thing had anything to do with him. He'd come off the booze and was now working as if his life depended on it. 'I'm doing a Jim on it,' he kept sneering every time he left the flat.

Relations between the two had become so bad that Jim had announced that he was leaving. Fred had barely blinked at the news.

That was the effect his leaving seemed to have on most people, Jim thought ruefully.

\* \* \*

Jane was mortified. Well, part of her was mortified, the part of her that remembered the way Jim loved his kids. The other part of her, the nasty part, couldn't help feeling that it was his own fault. If he wanted to have a new woman, he had to pay the price.

'Sorry Jim,' she said. 'I'll kill Di when she gets back, I didn't even know she'd left and . . . well, Owen isn't feeling well.' She bit her lip. 'Or so he says.'

He nodded, blew air out through his lips. 'OK.' Then he said, 'Anyway, I guess I might as well tell you my bit of news now. I was going to let you know this evening but, well . . .' He looked questioningly at her. 'Can I come in?'

Caught off balance, she stammered out, 'Yeah, sure. Sure.' As she led the way to the kitchen, she wondered what the hell he was going to spring on her. Maybe he was dead serious over this Debbie? Jesus, her ego couldn't take that. She actually felt physically sick at the thought of it. Suddenly she wanted to shove her fingers in her ears and chant like she had when she was a kid to block out horrible stuff. Without even offering him a cup of tea, she stood in front of him with her arms folded. 'Well?' she demanded, 'what's the big news?'

'Two things.' Jim looked slightly intimidated by her aggressive stance. 'First is,' he fumbled about in his shirt pocket – a shirt she'd bought for him about five years ago, she noted. Pulling out a piece of paper, he handed it to her. 'It's my new address. I've, eh, moved out of Fred's place.'

His new address was in Rathgar. So he was moving in with this Debbie, was he? She was shocked at the sinking feeling in her stomach.

'I, eh, got a good bonus from work over the crisp thing,' Jim said as he pulled a wad of notes from his pocket. 'So I put a deposit on me own flat and here's some cash for you – well, for the kids really.'

His *own* flat. So he wasn't sharing it with Debbie or anyone. That was good, at least. Good for the kids, she thought.

'Here.' Jim held the money towards her.

Honestly, that was another bloody idiot thing he always did. No matter how much she'd badgered him, Jim had never bothered with a chequebook. He carried cash about everywhere. 'I don't need money,' she muttered, touched by his generosity. 'What we agreed on is enough.'

'It's not for you.' His voice grew intense and she saw his Adam's apple bob as he swallowed hard. 'It's for the kids. Save it for them or something.' He threw her a quick smile. 'Sure, I've probably saved as much by not taking them out on weekends.' Again, he shoved it towards her.

'The kids'll come round,' she said gently. She took the money from him and thrust it in a drawer. 'Thanks.'

'No probs.' He smiled briefly again before beginning a study of his hands. 'And, eh, another thing, eh,' his eyes met hers, 'I've been offered another job.'

'Yeah?'

He nodded. 'Uh-huh. It's marketing crisps full-time.'

Jane tried not to smile. Jim's job, though important and well paid, had always seemed funny to her. 'But isn't that what you do anyway?' she asked.

'Yeah, it is,' Jim agreed, 'but Incredible Crisps are going to do their own in-house marketing in future and they want me to head the team.'

'Oh, right.' Jane nodded. 'Well, that's great. Congratulations.'

'It'll be well paid, so that'll be good, but, well, I dunno. I dunno if I want to do it for ever.'

'Do you not?' What did he want, career advice?

'Like, if I turn the offer down, I'll get a chance to market other stuff 'cause I won't be doing the crisps any more.'

'Right.' She wondered why the hell he was telling her this.

'Plus, if I take the job,' Jim paused, 'it'll mean loads of travelling. Maybe even a move to England.'

The words hit her. 'A move?'

'Yep. It's a big job.' He looked into her face. 'Well?'

It was as if he was seeking permission from her. Well, damn

279

him, if he wanted to go, he could go. There was nothing stopping him. 'Well what?' she croaked out, her throat dry.

He looked taken aback. 'Well, d'you think the kids will mind? D'you think it'll work, me there, you lot here?'

'I don't know, do I?' She suddenly hated him. How could he even contemplate it, this move? How could he just up and leave them all? 'It's your choice. Why don't you ask the kids?'

'I will, but . . .' She was suddenly aware that there was only inches between them. 'What do you think? Do you want me to go?'

His brown eyes were so intense as they gazed at her, the smell of him was so familiar, she could even feel the heat from his body. Her heart flipped about in a weird way within her breast.

'What?' she stammered.

'Do you want me to go?' he asked softly.

She was aware that one word could change everything. One word and he'd probably kiss her. It was like being suspended in time, the way things seemed to slow down. 'Do *you* want to go?'

He moved closer to her. She could feel the back of his hand as it brushed hers. He didn't answer, just kept staring at her. She was vaguely aware that his hand was holding her wrist and that his thumb was caressing her palm. She wished he'd kiss her, just to feel his lips on hers.

'Well?' he asked, and there was a tremor in his voice.

She could almost taste his breath.

'Do you think I should go?'

His lips brushed hers as he asked the question. She delighted in the feel of them, the sensation of their closeness, the barest touch of them, the slight pressing of lip upon lip. His hand caressed the small of her back, his other hand creeping up to hold her head, entwine his long fingers through her hair. God, she loved that. He gave her a long, steady gaze before he kissed her, just long enough to turn her on. She arched her back and felt his body bearing down on hers as his kiss grew more passionate. She caressed the back of his neck, slipped her other

280

hand into the back pocket of his jeans and savoured the sensation of him being so close.

He was pressing harder against her. His breath was ragged and she could feel his erection through the denim. For one glorious second she wanted him. Wanted him to love her the way he used to. Wanted to love him the way she used to.

'Oh, God, Jane,' he whispered. 'Aw, Jesus, Jane.'

His voice broke the spell. 'Get away from me!' She turned her face away and pushed him off. She was aware that somehow the top button of her shirt had become undone and her bra had been unclasped. 'Just,' she held up her hands, as if to ward him off, 'just get out, OK?'

He stood uncertainly by, looking at her and then turning his gaze to his hands.

She wondered if he managed to sound so excited when kissing Debbie. She wondered if he ran his hands through *her* hair.

'You do what's best for you.' She moved away from him, towards the sink, trying to fasten her shirt. 'It's your choice. Have a word with the kids if you like.' Pulling a bag of spuds from the press, she said, 'Now, sorry to rush you, but I've to work this afternoon, so I'm a bit busy.'

What the hell had happened there? Jim wondered. One minute he was normal and the next . . . well he didn't know. His heart was pounding like mad and there was an unmistakable bulge in his jeans. Jesus, he'd really wanted her. Did really want her. In fact, just looking at her standing by the window turned him on all over again. He opened his mouth to say something, he wasn't sure what, when she said, 'Go on, go.'

'Oh, yeah . . . OK.' He bit his lip. 'I'll talk to them next week.'

'Fine.'

'And, eh, you have my number at the new flat and . . .' his fingers tapped the leg of his jeans, 'and well . . . bye,' he finished up. Jesus, he was pathetic.

281

'Bye.' She gave him a weird smile. 'See you next week.'

'Bye.' He didn't move. Couldn't move. 'I would have liked to kiss you some more,' he blurted out.

Her eyes hardened. 'Jim, you've got someone else now. You're not the two-timing sort, are you?'

He seemed to stand there for an age, just looking at her. Finally he bent his head. 'No.'

Once he'd left, she put down the potato peeler and sat down at the kitchen table. She touched her lips and closed her eyes. Part of her wished she'd kept kissing him.

## 44

Jim studied his two kids. Jane was working that morning and had given him the house so that he could tell the kids that he was taking the new job.

Neither of them would meet his eye. Owen was staring at the table as if he'd never seen it before and Di was alternately smiling nervously at him or else glaring in a very confrontational manner.

'Will this take long?' she asked in a pissed-off voice. 'I'm meeting Gooey in an hour.'

He didn't bother to say that he'd hoped they could go out later, he knew that would be the thing most likely to make her leave the room. 'I just want you both to know that I'm taking a new job from the beginning of December.'

No reaction.

'It'll be based in the UK so I'll probably be living over there from then on.'

Owen jerked his head up to look at him. He didn't say anything though.

Di gave a laugh. 'Oh, that's just great,' she said, in a voice that implied it was anything but.

'I'm glad you feel that way,' Jim said mildly. 'I just want—'

'Not only have you left us, not only have you found a bitch to shag—'

'Di, don't you dare—'

'—but now you're going to shirk your responsibilities as well. But I guess we shouldn't be surprised, should we Owen?'

Owen jumped as his sister barked out his name. 'Leave it, Di,' he said softly.

'No, no I won't.' Di stood up from the table. She blinked. Once. Twice. 'I hate you, Dad,' she said. 'I really hate you. How can you go and leave us?'

Her voice shook and Jim made a move towards her, but she backed away from him.

'But I haven't left you,' he said desperately. 'I'll be home every weekend if I can. You'll still see me just as often.'

'I don't want to see you. Can't you understand that?' She walked towards him then looked up at him. I – don't – want – to – see – you.'

'Look, I won't take the job if you don't want me to.'

'I don't care what you do.' Di turned on her heel and left.

'Di!' Jim made to go after her, but stopped when Owen said, 'Leave her, Dad. She's just upset.'

Jim paused, unsure.

'She thought,' Owen again stared at the table, 'well, she thought that you were going to get back with Ma, didn't she?'

'What?' Jim ran his hands through his hair. Jesus, this was a mess. Jane had asked him if he wanted her to be there, but he'd told her he'd handle it. Some job he was doing. 'Did Di tell you that?'

Owen shook his head. 'Naw, but like, it's what she always thinks. That's the way she is.'

Jim didn't know what to say. Owen was surprising like that. He was always dead wide where people were concerned. When he was a kid he'd stare at people for ages, as if he was figuring them out. It took a while before he'd ever speak to someone. 'Maybe you're right,' Jim conceded. 'And you,' he asked, as he slid into the seat opposite Owen, 'how do you feel about me taking this job?'

'It's your life.'

'Yeah, I know Owen, but you're my son.'

There was a long pause.

Owen, when he lifted his head up, had a funny look in his eyes. 'And so was Matt,' he barely whispered.

Jim felt as if he'd been hit.

'Take the job, Da, it's your life.'

With that, his son also left the kitchen.


Patrick arrived at the salon, rubbing his hands with glee. 'I talked to Barney yesterday,' he told Jane, 'and he's come up with more great ideas.'

'Yeah?' Barney was proving to be quite a powerhouse of ideas. 'What?'

Patrick glanced around the salon, which was fuller than it had been in months. 'It can wait,' he winked. 'Tell you after work. We can get a few jars and have a very interesting business discussion.'

Normally Jane would have jumped at the chance, but the last thing she wanted to be doing that night was talking business. Especially as Jim had phoned to say that it hadn't gone too well with the kids. When she'd phoned home, Di had answered, referred to Jim as a prick, told her she was glad to see the back of him and asked her did she want to speak to Owen. Owen had said that it was Jim's life.

'But how do you feel about it?' she'd pressed, wishing she could see the two of them.

'I dunno, Ma.'

And that's all he'd said on the matter.

There was so much more she felt she should say but couldn't. She knew he didn't want to hear it and it all sounded so trite anyway. I mean, she thought, as she put down the phone, were there words to apologise for messing up your kids' lives?


'So,' Debbie purred into the phone, 'how'd it go?'

'Rotten.' He didn't feel like talking to her. He didn't feel like doing anything much, except working and getting plastered, in that order.

'They'll come round,' Debbie was sympathetic, 'want company?'

'Naw,' he shook his head. 'I've a pile of work to get through. And I've to sort out the flat and stuff. Better if you stay away.'

'Sure you don't want to talk about it?'

'Positive.'

'Oh.' She sounded a bit hurt by his monosyllabic answer. 'Oh, OK then.'

'Bye now.' He ended the call and turned off his phone.

He just wanted to be on his own.

Patrick had ordered a cab for Sheila and waved her on her way. Looking distinctly put out, Sheila had muttered something about dinner and food.

'The kids will get their own,' Jane said, 'you just concentrate on mixing your yogurt into your stewed prunes.'

'Oh, OK, dahling.' Sheila air-kissed her and tottered off to her waiting cab. As she climbed in, she told the driver sternly to take her straight to her destination. 'No funny routes to up the price,' she said imperiously. 'And I don't want any opinions on politics or religion or racism discussed, please. I've done a hard day's work and I'm exhausted.'

'Can I put on deh radio?'

'As long as it's not Declan D'arcy, you may do as you please.'

'Hilarious, your mother,' Patrick commented once she was on her way. 'Highly irritating, but hilarious.'

'Highly *glamorous*,' Rosemary butted in. 'Even though she's old and all, she's an inspiration.'

'Really?' Jane glanced incredulously at Rosemary. She'd never much thought of her mother as an inspiration to anyone. 'How so?'

'Well,' Rosemary blushed, 'she's on her own and she hasn't let it get to her, has she?' She didn't wait for a reply. 'She's working in a crap job and she still does it. *And* despite all that, she always looks great, well, for an old person, I mean,' she clarified.

'Mmmm,' Jane smiled. 'I guess so. But you try living with her!'

'*And* she speaks really well, and she just looks classy. I mean, I could dress like her and stuff, but I'd never—'

'Excuse me,' Patrick tugged her sleeve. 'Jane, we've things to discuss now. Rose, you finish sweeping up the floor and you can go, all right? Don't bother to let us know, just leave.'

'Right.' Rosemary didn't like being interrupted by Patrick. She began to sweep up with bad grace.

Once in the office, Patrick outlined Barney's plans. He could barely contain the grin on his face. 'Well, you know the way Cutting Edge has all those posters in their window, showing all the winning hairstyles they've done?'

'Uh-huh – they've done the most damage to our business,' Jane said.

'Well, not any more,' Patrick almost sang. Then, as if imparting some magical secret to her, he whispered, 'He says to make out that we've won stuff too.' He sat back in his chair and observed her reaction.

'Make out we've won stuff too?' Jane couldn't believe she was hearing correctly. 'What do you mean "make out we've won stuff too"?'

'Just, you know, make out we've won things.'

'What things?'

'Hairdressing things, you fool.'

She really didn't get it. 'So, like, I go about telling everyone I've won competitions?'

'No!' Patrick chortled. 'Not exactly.'

She was smiling, but only because he seemed so hyper. 'So what the hell are you talking about?'

'This is what is so brilliant about it.' Patrick giggled slightly. 'Barney says that we can hang posters of our own models in the window and title the hairstyles. For instance, you do Rosemary's hair in a certain way and just call it "Winning Style". No one will know the difference.'

It took a second for Jane to absorb the news. 'Naw, I can't do that.' She paused. 'Can I?'

'You can!' Patrick was triumphant. 'You can call it "Championship" or "Prize-Winning" or pretty much whatever you want.'

'Jesus.' Jane was laughing. 'Are you serious?'

'As serious as cancer, darling lady.'

'And our prices – did he say anything about Cutting Edge upping their prices?'

'He said that Cutting Edge are now way overpriced. They'll have to come down at some stage.'

'Hopefully when they've lost all their business.'

'That's what he said too,' Patrick chortled.

'I like this guy,' Jane grinned. 'Can't wait to meet him.'

Patrick turned to the appointments book. 'Sooooo,' he tapped the pen against his teeth, considering, 'will I pen Rosemary in for a colour and cut next week? Can you do anything with her yet – will she allow you?'

'I won't cut,' Jane said, 'it won't have grown back in time for the IHFs. Get Nash in, Rosemary's friend, she's got good hair, I'll do some rolls and plaits and things and we'll shoot some photos. Call a few of the other models too, ones we've used before, I'll give them all a free haircut.'

'Marvellous.' Patrick rubbed his hands gleefully. 'And we'll say that you won the IHFs if anyone asks – OK?'

Jane nodded.

'Even if it was a lifetime ago,' Patrick chortled. He picked his coat up from the chair. 'So, will we celebrate with a drink or two?'

'Lead on.'

# 45

T<small>HANK GOD SHE</small> was driving, Jane thought grimly, otherwise she'd be up for – what was it called when you killed your mother? – matricide or something. Her mother had spent a good part of yesterday and all of this morning wittering on and on about her dad's radio show. Of course, it didn't matter to her mother that *she* was worried too. Worried about the kids – Owen had flunked his second year exams in spectacular style. She'd have to ask Jim to have a word with him and, thinking of Jim, she was worried about his new job and the effect it was going to have on all of them. She was worried *sick* about the bloody hairdressing competition because she couldn't make up her mind what way to style Rosemary's hair. But did any of that matter to her mother? Nope. With Sheila, her dramas had to take centre stage.

Her mother jabbed her in the arm.

'Mam, how many times do I have to tell you not to do that?' Jane glared at her.

Sheila sniffed disapprovingly. 'Well, maybe if you showed some respect and answered me once in a while, I wouldn't have to.' She paused, obviously waiting for something. When nothing happened, she demanded, 'Well?'

'Well, what?' Jane snapped.

'Oh, you're in a lovely mood today, dahling.' Sighing resignedly, Sheila fished some hairspray from her bag and sprayed it all over the place.

Jane started to cough as the stuff went up her nose. 'Mother! Will you open a window!'

'And have my hair ruined? You *are* joking, dahling.'

'Uggghhh!' In exasperation, Jane tried to keep the car straight as she rolled down her own window.

Sheila looked at her as if she was acting peculiarly. 'Now, I'm not being nasty, dahling, but if you bit Jim's head off like that, it's no wonder the alley cat walked out. Not that he should have. That man had nothing before he met you. Nothing.'

'Mam,' Jane said. 'Not your business?'

Sheila smirked slightly, before patting her hair and tucking stray strands back into place. 'Point taken. Now, all I asked you was whether you'd been in contact with your father or not, that's all. I don't expect to be attacked for a simple question.'

Count to ten. One. Two. Three. 'I wasn't attacking you and the answer is "no", I haven't.'

'No need to snap, dahling.'

Jane bit her tongue and remained silent. Maybe, if she let it go, that would be an end to the conversation.

And indeed, the subject was dropped for a few minutes. Her mother shifted about uneasily in the car seat and made a few doleful remarks about the way the passenger mirror always made her look awful. She then rubbed cream into her hands and plucked her eyebrows. Eventually, when she'd finished preening herself, she muttered, 'Well, someone – I don't know who – has been telling tales. Why else is Declan running the best made-to-order sandwich competition in Dublin – tell me that now?'

Jane almost swerved into the wrong lane. Someone behind blasted her out of it. 'What?' she asked faintly.

'You heard.' Sheila gave a martyred sigh. 'I am to be humiliated yet again. Your father is running a best sandwich competition. He knows where I work. He has to.'

'It could just be a coincidence,' Jane said, a sort of sick feeling invading her.

'Not at all,' Sheila said dismissively. 'He's running it because he knows I make sandwiches – that's why.'

Oh God.

'He's trying to humiliate me. He's doing a tour of Dublin sandwich bars and the best one is going to win some piece of stupid equipment. I mean, what will Lisa say when she finds out who I am?'

'I don't know.'

Her mother continued on and on until she got out of the car.

Jane wondered if she should ring her dad and ask him what the hell he was playing at? But maybe he'd tell her to butt out again. Yep, she thought, she'd been given her orders and there was no way she was going to interfere.

But a showdown on national radio between the two of them . . . It didn't bear thinking about.

She spent the morning working on one of the models that Patrick had got hold of. OK, it meant that they couldn't take as many appointments, but it would be worth it for the posters they'd shortly be hanging in their windows. She spent ages with the model, studying her face, working out what sort of a style would suit her best. Then she'd washed, conditioned and discussed with Patrick the best colours to use. He'd suggested a mixture of highlights and lowlights and she'd run with that. And then she'd begun to cut. At first she was slightly nervous, but then her creative instincts took over and she forgot that she was copying a style from a magazine and began to add in her own touches. As she cut and shaped, Jane blotted out everything else. That's what she loved about styling, all her worries disappeared. There was nothing more satisfying than creating a new look for someone. She and Jim had often thought how similar their jobs were – he marketed products while she marketed people. She was only vaguely aware of Rosemary watching agog from her corner of the salon.

Eventually, she finished up and, standing back from the model, she studied her. It was looking good. A sort of excitement began to build at the thought of blow-drying and seeing the finished result. God, she hadn't felt like this in ages.

'Not long now,' she told the girl who was looking doubtfully at herself in the mirror. 'Thanks a million for being so patient.'

The girl smiled.

'Photographer is due in half an hour,' Patrick said.

Jane nodded. She'd be well finished in half an hour. Out with her brushes and off she went, drying the roots, smoothing the hair down, getting it as shiny as it would go.

'Wow!' Rosemary said when she'd finished. 'Wow!'

'It looks great.' The model was overwhelmed. 'Jesus, it really suits me.'

Patrick came over. 'Looking good.' He put his arm about her. 'You haven't lost it, honey chicks, you haven't lost it.'

The haircut was a mid-length style with broken up layers. The ends were textured to give a soft but edgy feel and Patrick's colours made the whole thing look quite stunning.

'I think we'll call that one "Champions Hair".' Patrick kissed her on the cheek. 'Done by a champion.'

Jane smiled. Patrick was right. She really hadn't lost it. In fact, as she looked at it, she conceded that it was bloody brilliant. 'I reckon Cutting Edge will be 'edge cutting by the time we finish with them,' she joked.

'Stick to the hairdressing,' Patrick patted her on the head. 'Don't go it as a comedian.'

## 46

JIM TOOK A deep breath and tapped on Owen's bedroom door. It was the last thing he needed, a row with a son that he was barely on speaking terms with. If anything, the talk Jane wanted him to have with Owen would finish the relationship completely. On the other hand, if he didn't talk to him, Jane would be mega pissed off.

'I'm not asking you to row with him,' she'd said, 'just urge him to do better next year. I've already had a go at him over the results so I want you to give him some positive encouragement. We have to present a united front on this, Jim.'

Of course, she was right.

Just before he entered Owen's room, Jim glanced again at the results. How had the kid done it? One pass in English and an across the board fail in everything else. He didn't know whether to be angry or upset. 'Owen,' he called, 'can I come in?'

'Uh-huh.' Owen muted the television and sat up straight on his bed. His face was pale and wary-looking. 'Is this about me exam results?' he asked.

'Yep.' Jim sat down on the chair beside his bed. 'They're pretty appalling.'

'I know.' He paused. 'Sorry.'

'I want your promise that next year you'll do better. Or at least try to.'

'Yeah.'

This was going well, Jim thought. 'And if you've any problems that you'll talk to us and we'll try and sort them out. Get you extra tuition, whatever – OK?'

'Uh-huh.'

Jim wondered what else he should say. The whole thing had been very easy. And the fact that Owen was actually talking to him for the first time in weeks made him want to stay there and try to bridge the gap between them. 'It's not that we want you to be a genius, Owen,' he said, 'but you can do better, I know you can.'

Owen gave him a quick glance and shrugged.

'So,' Jim continued, 'what went wrong? Did you just go blank?'

'Nah,' Owen sighed, shot him a weary look. 'It was all the bunking off. I already told Mam this.'

'What?' Jim asked. 'What bunking off?'

Owen's face went even paler than normal. 'Nothing,' he stammered. 'Sorry.'

'What bunking off?' Jim asked, his voice rising. 'What are you on about? Did you bunk school?'

Owen looked at his hands and didn't answer.

'Answer me!'

'It was nothing. I don't—'

'Jesus Christ, Owen, why the hell did you bunk school?'

Owen seemed to flinch at his words. Jim attempted to touch him but he shrugged him off.

'D'you not like it? Do you not?' Owen still didn't respond and Jim looked at him despairingly. 'Well?'

'Is there something wrong?' Jane poked her head in the door. She looked ready to avert a fight. 'I thought I heard—'

'Did you know he bunked school?' Jim asked, turning to her. 'He's after telling me that—'

'I know,' Jane said, a bit too calmly, he thought.

'But sure, that's why he failed his exams,' Jim went on. He felt relieved that at least now he had a reason for the crap results. At least Owen wasn't completely stupid. 'How long has this been going on?'

294

Owen looked at him. 'I went in for the last couple of months.' He glanced quickly at his mother and then his gaze returned to his hands.

It was the gaze that did it. The silence that followed. The way Jane blushed furiously and averted her eyes from his. Jim looked in bewilderment from one to the other. Finally, he said, as he pointed at Owen, 'Am I getting this right – he's been bunking off and you never told me?'

'I think we should discuss this downstairs,' Jane said firmly.

'I'm his dad,' Jim stood up. He held the exam results towards her. His fist was clenched and the paper had crumpled. 'D'you not think I've a right to know that kind of stuff?'

'I sorted it,' Jane said. 'There was no need for you to know.'

'There was *every* need.' Jesus, he couldn't even shout at her and he wanted to, he really did, but the hurt seemed to have won out over the anger. 'I'm his dad,' he repeated despondently.

At least she had the decency to look ashamed. 'Yeah, maybe you're—'

'Maybe?' This was his wife, this was his son. His bloody family for Christ's sake. '*Maybe*?' he repeated. He felt as if he'd been hit with a sledgehammer.

'I'm sorry—' Jane began.

'Save it.' Jim threw the results at her as he walked out of the room. 'Draw me up a list of stuff I can be included in, OK? Gimme a call when it's done.'

From behind, he heard her go 'Aw, Jim' and he heard Owen stammer out an apology for landing her in it. After she'd told him not to worry, he heard her come out of the room after him.

He took the stairs two at a time and she'd only just managed to wrench the front door open as he drove off.

He knew Debbie was getting a bit pissed off with him, but he couldn't help it. She'd be in the middle of telling him something about work or a funny story and he'd come out with, 'I didn't think she'd exclude me like that. I never knew she could be so fucking horrible.'

This time, Debbie folded her arms and glared at him. 'Well, if you didn't think she could be so fucking horrible – why did you leave her?' she snapped.

'Sorry,' he apologised. 'I'm sorry – what's that, what were you saying?'

Debbie regarded him through narrowed eyes. He knew enough to know that that meant she was quite mad. 'Forget what *I* was saying,' she said. 'I'd much rather know why you left your wife.'

Jim turned from her and walked towards the window. Jesus, where had that come from? Tell her why he'd left Jane?

Debbie came to stand beside him. She too stood gazing out on to the back yard. Her voice softer now, she said, 'It's some-thing we've never discussed, Jim. In fact, you've discussed nothing with me about yourself. OK, I know what you do for a living, I know you like junk food and gadgets,' she gave a small laugh, 'I know *The Simpsons* is your favourite TV programme, but do I know anything else?' There was a pause. 'Nope.'

'There's not a lot else to know,' Jim said as casually as he could. 'It's not important.' His eyes stayed glued on a wheelie bin with a big smiley face stuck on to it. It was so naff, yet it touched him.

'It's not important that you spent almost sixteen years with a woman that Fred said you were so cracked over you practically kissed her knickers every night?'

'What?' Jim turned to face Debbie. 'You talked about me to Fred? Jesus,' he laughed crazily, 'I thought *he* was an asshole!'

Debbie flushed. 'Well, I got Gillian to ask him about you when I first met you. That's what she said that he said.'

'Oh yeah, and what else did he say?'

'Nothing.'

'What else?' Jim poked her with his finger. 'Go on.'

'Nothing!'

296

He began jabbing her with both fingers. That normally got Jane into fits of giggles. Instead, Debbie pushed him off and told him to grow up. 'So, you gonna tell me what happened between you and wonder wife or what?'

'Nothing happened,' he muttered, feeling a strange sense of loneliness. His hands dangled uselessly by his sides and he shoved them into the pockets of his jeans. 'We just, I dunno, drifted apart.'

'You drifted apart?' Debbie sounded as if she was either madly disappointed or completely disbelieving. 'Your marriage ended because you drifted apart?'

'Yep.' Thank God all that explaining was over. Jim wondered if she wanted to head out for a drink. He could do with a few to try and forget the hurt of earlier. 'Do you—'

'Did she drift or you drift?'

'Both. Eh, do you—'

'Where? Into someone else's arms or what?'

'Naw, nothing like that. We just . . .' Jim gulped. How did he explain? He'd never had to explain stuff before. 'It just ended.'

'But you loved her?' Debbie asked. 'At the end, did you love her?'

The way she asked the question was so intense that Jim knew it was important how he answered. It made him feel a bit trapped. 'Yeah,' he said simply. 'I did.'

Debbie gulped.

'But, and I swear to this,' he gave her a small grin and crossed his heart, 'I never spent me time kissing her knickers.'

Debbie smiled. She reached out and pulled him towards her. 'I'm crazy about you,' she whispered, entwining her arms around his neck. 'It makes me feel weird to think that there's another woman out there who had you first. I feel I have to compete, you know?'

He hadn't a bloody clue, but he nodded anyway.

'Come here, you.' She kissed him slowly on the mouth. Pulling away from him, she smiled suddenly. 'One day, Jim McCarthy, I'm going to figure you out. I swear I am.'

He gave a weak laugh. What was she on about?

The ringing of his phone shattered the moment. Jim was glad of the interruption, as he still couldn't get the fact of Jane not telling him about Owen out of his head. Even when Debbie was covering his neck with kisses, it wouldn't shift. Debbie was bound to notice his lack of interest if she carried on. 'Hang on a sec, Debs.' He moved away from her, ignoring her pout, and began his usual search for his mobile. He eventually found it under his jacket and flicked it on. 'Hi. Jim McCarthy.'

'Jim, it's Jane.'

Jim glanced at Debbie, mouthed, 'It's Jane', then watched Debbie flounce over to the table, fold her arms and glare across at him. 'What?' he said shortly.

'I'm sorry about earlier,' Jane muttered. 'I know I probably should have told you about Owen, but it all happened so quickly, it was all over so quickly that there didn't seem to be much need.'

'So, like, I'm not needed, is that it?' He didn't know whether he was being nasty to impress Debbie or to hurt Jane.

'No. That is not it.' Jane sounded hurt and he was glad. 'I'll tell you things in future.'

'OK.'

'But eh,' Jane hesitated slightly and Jim knew she was about to hammer him. She could always do it. Whenever she apologised and caught him off guard, she'd then land in with the big guns. It was something he'd slagged her over before, but now he knew it wasn't going to be funny.

'Well,' she began innocently, 'when I told you about Gooey and attempted to involve you, you said that there was nothing you could do.'

'And there wasn't.'

'Oh, yeah, like hell!' Jane scoffed. 'You just couldn't have been bothered. I mean, how am I supposed to know what you will be bothered to sort out and what you won't? Di is out every night with that waste of space. But can I do anything? No. Have I tried? Yes! Have you? No. Will you? Not bloody likely!'

298

Jim said nothing. Debbie shot him sympathetic looks across the room which he ignored. He kind of wished that Debbie wasn't there.

'Anyway,' Jane went on, not seeming to have noticed his lack of reply, 'I'll write down and inform you of all the comings and goings from now on. It'll be great to have some support at last.'

The last bit hurt. She would never forget, or let him forget, for that matter. 'I thought you rang to apologise,' he said steadily.

'Yes.' She sounded flustered.

'Well, you've done that. Thanks.' He flicked the phone off and immediately wished he hadn't. He stood staring at it for a couple of seconds and was startled when Debbie gave him a cheer.

'Way to go!' She giggled. 'Jesus, I'd hate to have a row with you. All that ranting and raving for nothing.'

Jim pocketed his mobile. He'd never rowed with Jane over the phone before. In fact, he'd never cut her off full rant in his whole life.

He'd never had to. He could always make her laugh instead.

As Debbie put her arms around him and buried her face in his neck, the sense of loneliness he'd felt earlier washed over him again.

## 47

WITH LONG, CONFIDENT strokes, Jane brushed Rosemary's hair until it fell like shiny springs down her back. All the conditioning treatments had made it gleam like something from a shampoo ad. With the right style, it could look fantastic. Jane still hadn't decided exactly what she was going to do, the shape of Rosemary's face would support quite a few styles well. Tonight she was just going to trim it to get rid of split ends and then cut it in a basic shape that could be manipulated without too much trouble.

She had just finished a section of Rosemary's hair when someone knocked on the front door.

'We're closed,' she shouted. 'Come back in the morning.'

'I want to talk now. We need to sort things out.' Pete Jordan was peering into the salon. 'This is getting ridiculous.'

Jane almost dropped her scissors in shock. For a second, she didn't quite know what to do. Then, after telling Rosemary not to move, she ran to fetch Patrick from the office. 'It's Pete Jordan and he wants to talk,' she whispered. 'What'll we do?'

'We let him talk,' Patrick said matter-of-factly. 'You open the door, we'll chat in here.'

'But I've Rosemary.'

'OK, we'll chat outside.' Patrick stood up. 'Now, just remember, concentrate on Rosemary's hair, don't go making mistakes at this stage. And for God's sake, honey pie, don't lose the head!'

Jane glanced quickly at him. *Don't lose the head.* He'd come a long way in a few months – Patrick used to lose his head on a regular basis.

She smiled and watched as he opened the door.

'Hello.' Pete Jordan nodded curtly at them before taking the seat that Patrick proffered. 'I thought it would be the best time to call, seeing as we've both shut up shop.'

'I've just this style to finish.' Jane brought Rosemary down to where Peter sat. 'I'll listen in.'

Pete hardly heard her. He was gazing in open admiration at Rosemary. 'Hey, great hair,' he said, impressed.

'Ooooh,' Rosemary giggled uncontrollably. 'Thank you very much. That's very nice of you. It's only really because Jane has been putting stuff into it every week.'

'Your model?' Pete asked.

'My model.' Jane tried not to sound too smug. Rosemary would be a match for his any day.

'And the girl in the posters?' Pete indicated the window.

'What about her?'

'Is she someone you used to use before?'

'Patrick.' Jane turned to him with a smile. 'Can you answer that?'

'I know,' Pete said, without giving Patrick time to answer, 'that this salon has never won a single thing. That shit,' he indicated the posters, 'is false advertising.'

'Oh,' Patrick managed to sound as if he'd never heard the word 'shit' before. 'Do we have to trade obscenities? Can we not just talk about things in a civilised manner?'

Pete made a sound very much as if he was choking.

'What exactly seems to be your problem, Pete?'

'Your signs. They're completely bogus. And I've also checked and no one from here has ever won an IHF award.'

Little feck, checking up on them, Jane thought. 'I've won it actually,' she said.

'Oh yeah, right,' Pete made a face. 'There is no record of a Jane McCarthy *ever* winning,' he folded his arms.

301

'That's because I registered under Jane D'arcy,' Jane said. 'I won Trainee of the Year.'

Pete looked taken aback. 'Sure, but that must have been years ago,' he spluttered.

'It was,' Jane nodded. 'But I don't like being called a liar, Mr Jordan, and if all you can do is sling insults, why don't you just leave? Right now.'

'I'm only here to try and sort things out,' Pete said.

'You're only here sorting things out because your pockets are feeling the pinch,' Jane retaliated.

Pete glared at her.

'Competition, Mr Jordan,' she continued, 'ever heard of it? If you can't stand the heat, then get out of the kitchen.'

Pete Jordan glared at her for a second. Flicking a glance at Rosemary, he nodded. 'See you in October at the IHFs. I'll turn your heat right off Miz McCarthy.'

'Hot or cold, it doesn't bother me.'

'Well,' Pete licked his lips. 'I can see calling down here was a waste of time. Maybe you and I will make more progress on our own, Patrick?'

God help him if he agreed, Jane thought. She'd brain him so she would.

'Ooooh,' Patrick hugged himself. Putting on a camp voice, he said, 'I'd love to make progress with you Pete. Come on, come on in here.'

All three burst out laughing as Pete rushed out the door.

'You know, I rang her this afternoon,' Patrick said as he came back from the bar with two pints. He sat down opposite Jane and looked expectantly at her.

They had decided to go for a drink to celebrate annoying Pete Jordan.

Jane took a sip of Carlsberg before putting the glass down. 'Who?' she asked. 'Who did you ring?'

'My old drinking buddy,' Patrick answered mildly. Before Jane could say anything, he held up his hand. 'It was a disaster.' He spread his arms wide and made a tragic face. 'I just told her that her job was open if she felt like coming back. I mean, it was nothing we hadn't said before.'

'And?'

'Oh, she said some dreadful things.' Patrick tut-tutted, making another face. 'I think she wanted me to grovel, but honestly Jane, what more could I do?'

With that question, his drama-queen mask slipped and Jane saw that he really did want to know. She reached out and patted him on the hand. 'Nothing,' she said. 'You've done your best. She knows she can come back.'

'She said some really quite horrible things,' Patrick said, sounding hurt.

'That's Mir though – isn't it?'

Patrick nodded morosely. 'Her own worst enemy.'

They drank in silence for a bit before Patrick asked hesitantly, 'And, dare I ask, how's your life going?'

'Awful.' Jane bit her lip. 'Jim is pissed at me, Di is in love, Owen failed his exams and my mother and father are about to launch World War Three live on radio.'

'What?' An amused smile danced across Patrick's face. 'Your mother and father what?'

So Jane told him, in clipped sentences, all about the sandwich competition.

Patrick cracked up. 'No way!' He tried to stop laughing and couldn't. 'Aw, God, no way! And he's going—'

'Next Tuesday,' Jane said through gritted teeth. 'And I don't know why you're laughing.'

'Because it's *funny*.' Patrick winked cheekily at her. 'And you should laugh too. Sure, your parents love it. Everybody knows that!'

'Well I don't. It's embarrassing.'

'Jane, honey.' Patrick reached across the table and took her hand. 'You have got to stop taking responsibility for everyone else. Stand back and look at the full picture. It's *hilarious*!'

His laughter was kind of infectious. 'And I thought you lot were supposed to be sensitive,' she tried to say grouchily. 'Can't you see I'm dying here?'

'Well, all the more reason to laugh.'

## 48

IT WAS ALMOST one o'clock. Jane glanced uneasily at her watch. Where on earth were the kids? Owen had told her he was heading to a friend's house and she hadn't been able to help the look of surprise on her face. She'd told him to be in by eleven thirty. Di had gone clubbing to celebrate her Junior Cert results. They hadn't been great, but compared to Owen's, they looked fantastic.

She knew she had to stop worrying about them, but the truth was, since Matt had died, she couldn't help it. Anytime they went out she dreaded getting an unexpected phone call or someone ringing the bell in the middle of the night. She knew she had to keep things normal for their sakes and not go all over-protective, but it was hard. She flicked on the telly to see if there was something she could watch to take her mind off things.

Nothing, as usual.

She went and got a coffee and carried it back into the front room. Sitting there, she'd be able to glance out the window from time to time. She was going to kill Owen when he came back.

It was two o'clock and she was wound up like a spring with worry, when she heard giggling. There was the sound of a key in the lock and to her relief, her two kids walked in the door. Owen came in first, then Di, with her hands on his shoulders.

'Where were you?' she demanded, trying to sound cross but just wanting to cuddle them. She glared at Owen first, 'Didn't I ask you to be in for twelve-thirty?'

'Uh-huh, but then I met Di and we walked around for a bit.'

Jane stared incredulously at him. 'You walked around for a bit with your *sister*?'

'Yeah.'

Behind him, Di giggled. Well, at least, Jane thought, there was a smile on her face for a change. 'And was the club good?' she asked, making a supreme effort to be nice.

Di looked blankly at her.

Owen poked his sister hard. 'Did you have a good night, Di?' he asked her. 'Ma wants to know.'

'Fanilliant,' Di slurred. 'Over early but.'

There was no mistaking her thick voice or the fumes that seemed to wash across the hall. Jane took a few steps towards her. 'Have you been drinking?' she asked, her nice voice gone.

'Me? No.' Owen said. 'Now, Di says she's knackered—'

'I was talking to your sister,' Jane snapped, pushing him out of the way. She stood in front of Di who'd begun to giggle help-lessly at her mother's expression. 'You have.' Jane was shocked. It wasn't that she thought Di wouldn't try a drink, but to end up in that sort of a state was a bit much. Christ, she must have had loads. She poked her face into Di's, knowing that it was no use confronting her in this state, but unable to help herself. 'Where the hell did you get the drink?'

'Chill out,' Di said between giggles, 'it's, it's Junior Cert, they all do it.'

'Yeah, they do, Ma,' Owen said helpfully.

'Am I asking your opinion? Am I?'

'No, but I'm just saying—'

'Well don't. Just keep quiet.'

'Aaahhh,' Di nodded sagely. 'The thing everyone is best at in this house, keeping veery, very quiet.' She bent forwards and made shushing noises.

Owen poked her again.

Jane closed her eyes and rubbed her hands over her face.

Di shoved Owen off and stood upright, swaying unsteadily.

'Where did you get served drink?' Jane asked.

Di bit her lip and gave an exaggerated shrug.

'You are not setting foot outside this house until you tell me.'

'So?' Di answered cockily.

'Di, stop it,' Owen said. 'Just stop it.'

'Awww, my brudder, the best boy.' Di put her arm around his shoulders and squeezed him. He smiled reluctantly at her. 'I love you, Ownie boy, do you know that? He walked and walked and walked me so that I could come home in a reasonable state. He's a lovely brudder. Just like Mattie was.' She gave him another squeeze. 'I love you Ownie.'

'Great.' Owen rolled his eyes at Jane and grinned.

It wasn't funny. Jane didn't smile back.

'You will not be able to see that boyfriend of yours unless you tell me,' Jane said again. 'Think about that now, Miss!'

'Poor Gooey, I got sick on his docs, didn't I Ownie?'

'So you said.'

God, she must have made a right show of herself. 'Where did you get the drink?'

Di righted herself. She shook her head defiantly and had to grab on to Owen to stay upright. 'I come from a dys . . . dys . . .' she stopped, started again, 'a fucked-up family, it's no wonder I drink.' The last part was said almost triumphantly.

Jane didn't know what happened then. All she knew was that she heard a crack and only then did she realise that she'd walloped Di right across the face.

Owen gasped.

A huge red slash instantly appeared on Di's cheek. Di put her hand to it and tears pooled in her eyes.

'Oh God, Di—' Jane stared at her hand, which was stinging, and then she stared at Di. 'Oh, I'm sorry,' she gulped, 'I'm sorry.' She held out her arms, 'Come here.'

Di backed away.

'Owen drinks,' Di said, her face screwed up to stop tears leaking all over her cheeks, 'and you don't say anything to him. Why do you give out to me all the time?'

307

'Thanks, Di,' Owen said, sounding annoyed. 'Thanks a bunch.'

'And he bunks school and I don't, but you don't give out to him, and then he fails his exams and you *still* don't give out.'

'None of that is dangerous,' Jane said, trying to make herself understood, but not knowing what she should be saying. 'Anything could have happened to you in that state. For God's sake, Di!'

'All you ever do these days is give out,' Di said, half-sobbing. Pushing past Owen, she stumbled awkwardly up the stairs.

Jane gazed after her.

There was a silence. Jane turned to Owen, who was also looking after his sister. 'Go to bed,' she said.

'Everyone drinks, Ma,' he said. 'It's just 'cause it's Junior Cert year, you know?'

'Yeah Owen – thanks for minding her.' She tousled his hair, wanting to hug him but knowing he'd only get embarrassed.

He smiled slightly before going upstairs.

## 49

JANE AWOKE BEFORE the alarm went off. The house was silent, sun sneaking in under the curtains. She lay still for a few blissful seconds in a cocoon of warmth under Matt's duvet before suddenly remembering the row of the night before.

Her heart sank and she groaned. After Matt had died, she hadn't slept for days. She'd been afraid to. Afraid to sleep and forget and then suddenly wake up and remember. It'd be like losing him all over again when she woke. Recalling that made her feel that she could cope with whatever the morning brought. OK, Di had been drunk, but she was home. She was safe. She was healthy and alive. They'd sort something out. She dragged herself from the bed and pulled on her dressing gown. Shoving her feet into tatty blue slippers she shuffled out of the room.

'Owen, school. Up. Now.' She gave his door a good hard thump. From behind it, she heard groaning noises, so at least he was awake.

She was about to tap on Di's door when she wondered if it would be better to go down and get her daughter a cuppa. She'd be feeling rotten this morning and maybe if she brought her up tea and a couple of Disprin, the gesture would help break the ice. Anything to help, Jane thought as she turned from Di's door and made for the stairs. The sound of a radio drifted up from the kitchen and Jane realised in shock that her mother was already up. In the whole history of their relationship, Jane could never remember Sheila being up before her. In fact, getting her mother up for work was harder than getting the kids out to school.

Her mother was eating a slice of thin, dry toast when Jane joined her. 'Hi, dahling,' she said, wiping her mouth daintily with some kitchen paper, 'I have the kettle on for you.'

'Ta.' Jane took a cup from the press and dropped a tea bag into it. Taking a couple of slices of bread, she shoved them into the toaster.

'What was all the fuss about last night?' Sheila asked. 'I heard shouting at around two which woke me.' She spoke in a faintly accusatory tone, which Jane ignored.

'Di came in drunk last night.' The kettle boiled and she made tea. 'We had a row.'

'Oh yes, teenagers do that, don't they?' Sheila gave a martyred sigh, as if she was used to handling drunken teens. 'Junior Cert results come out and they all get smashed.'

'And how would you know?' Jane asked. There were two Disprin in the press and she snapped them out of their foil.

'Your father's show, dahling. Every year, after the Junior Cert, he does a special on teen drinking. All those stupid parents ringing in baring their souls,' Sheila gave an affected laugh, 'they're wasting their time telling Declan about it. That man is only interested in hearing about one thing.' Jabbing her finger towards Jane, she spelt out, 'S-E-X. But you know what they say: what you can't have you always covet.'

Jane didn't bother to answer. Running down Declan had become routine by this stage. Her mother was definitely much stronger than she had been, especially now that Lisa was on side. When Sheila had revealed her 'true' identity to Lisa, a big bonding session had apparently taken place. Lisa had been dumped too and bore a chip the size of Everest about it. She'd told Sheila, who'd told Jane, that all her grooming was an effort to get hubby to notice her so that she could tell him to shag off. Lisa was the first friend Jane could remember Sheila ever having.

'A psychologist on your father's show said that teen drinking

310

could sometimes mask deeper feelings,' Sheila called out as Jane ascended the stairs. 'If that's any help, dahling.'

If she'd wanted to feel any worse, it would have helped all right, Jane thought.

'Di,' she called, tapping on the door, 'may I come in?'

There was no answer.

'Di!'

There were some groggy mumblings from within.

Owen appeared at his bedroom door. His uniform looked as if he'd dragged himself through a wringer, but Jane didn't bother to comment on it. 'There's toast downstairs,' she said. 'Go and get it.'

Owen gave her a shaky grin and, barefooted, he ran downstairs.

Owen's grin gave her confidence. At least he wasn't blaming her. And to be honest, it wasn't acceptable for a fifteen-year-old to be drunk. Feeling better, Jane pushed open Di's door.

Di, bedclothes pulled up to her chin, glared balefully at her. 'I never said you could come in,' she muttered.

Jane swallowed. Oh, how she longed to snap at her, but it wasn't the way. And what if Di told Jim that Jane had hit her? It'd make Jim hate her even more than he already seemed to and Jane didn't know if she could bear that. For the first time she was actually glad that the kid wasn't talking to him.

'I brought you up some tea,' she said softly, laying the cup beside Di's bed, 'and a couple of tablets for your head. They work well.'

Di looked suspiciously at her.

'It'll be hard to go to school with a hangover,' Jane said by way of explanation. 'And it's time you were up.'

Di winced. 'I don't feel well.'

'Most people don't when they drink too much,' Jane answered. Then, her heart hammering, she added, 'And I'm sorry I hit you last night. I shouldn't have.'

Di shrugged.

311

'But it hurt, you know, what you said about this family.'

Di looked up at her. 'Yeah. Sorry.' She gave her a big sullen look.

Jane decided that was the best she'd get out of her. 'Just don't do it again, eh? I was worried.'

She made her way to the door and was just opening it when Di said, 'Thanks for the tea, Mam. And the tablets.'

Jane smiled. 'No problem.'

Di smiled a little back. 'And sorry for making you worry.'

Jane's eyes filled with unexpected tears and she could only nod.


'Well, wish me luck,' Sheila said as she smoothed down the light green and pink skirt she was wearing. Picking up a baby-pink cardigan from the chair, she put it on. 'Your dad is coming to our shop today around four.'

Jane's toast felt dry in her mouth and her heart lurched. *How could she have forgotten?* 'Mam, do you have to?' she asked. 'I mean, do you want all the world to know your business?'

Sheila laughed tolerantly. 'Lisa says if she could tell the world what a faithless abuser she had for a husband, she would. She says I'm lucky to have such a platform. Anyway,' she tossed her head, 'he's the one doing the sandwich contest. He's out to humiliate me, well, the boot will be on the other foot.'

'Yeah, but Mam—' Jane didn't get to finish her sentence; Sheila left the table and went upstairs to get her bag.


Jim was on his way to Galway when the Declan D'arcy show came on. He almost crashed the car when he heard that his father-in-law was standing outside the sandwich shop his mother-in-law worked in. At least, Jim was pretty sure it was Sheila's shop.

'And now, folks,' Declan said, in his gravelly voice, 'we're outside Lisa's for today's sandwich challenge.' People cheered in the background. 'Now, let's give a description of the place for those of you listening in and not able to see it – which is all of yez, I guess.' He laughed at his wit and continued, 'Northside Dublin. Very salubrious lookin' indeed with its cool wood finishings, in keeping with the general up-your-arse poshness of the place. And speaking of posh, the Patrick Costelloe hairdressing salon is just down the road from here and it's brilliant. My daughter works there – she's the best hairdresser in the country.'

Jim grinned as he changed lanes. Patrick would be well pleased with that plug. From the radio came the sound of someone squealing. 'I work there too,' the squealer squealed, 'I'm Rosemary. I know Jane. We all work there. Yeahhhhh.'

Jim cringed. That bit wasn't so hot. He could picture the kid getting yanked by her hair all the way back down the street by Patrick.

'Yeah, rock on Rosemary,' Declan said, sounding mildly amused. 'I'm sure you do. Anyway, plugs aside, let's enter this emporium of sandwich-making and meet the staff.'

Oh shit, Jim thought.

There came the sound of footsteps and then Declan began describing what the place looked like inside – how they had adorned the walls with flags and how posters with funny sayings were scattered about. 'What about this one?' Declan read aloud, '"Give a man a fish and he'll eat for a day, teach him to fish and he'll destroy the world's oceans."' He chortled a bit and said, 'So, everyone, I'm now standing beside Lisa, who owns this place. Bit of an environmentalist are ya, Lisa?'

'Naw,' a woman replied, in a thick Dublin accent, 'just antiman. The rest of the poster should read, "teach a woman to fish and she'll do it properly".'

'Yeah, but only after she's put on her make-up, eh?' Declan bantered.

His comment was met with deafening silence from Lisa.

'Well, now,' Declan sounded a bit flustered, 'I'm told ya make great sambos, Lisa? Is this true?'

313

'Only after I put on my make-up, Declan,' Lisa answered smoothly.

There was a huge guffaw of laughter from the people gathered. Declan graciously laughed as well.

'And is it just you working here?' Declan asked. 'I was, eh, told by my researcher that there's two of yez?'

Jim, about to take off at a green light, held his breath. Jesus. This was great.

'Go Sheila!' someone yelled.

The customers broke into a 'Go Sheila' chant.

'I have my very valued assistant,' Lisa said. 'As you can see, she's popular with the punters and is a brilliant worker.'

'She is?' Declan sounded doubtful.

'She is?' Jim also asked.

'Come on out here, Sheila.'

There was a lot of clapping as Sheila appeared.

'It's your wife, Declan,' Lisa said. 'The one you dumped like a dose of the runs a few months back? Huh, I bet you knew she worked here. Out to humiliate her, you were!'

There were a lot of gasps and giggles from the shop floor. Declan made amazed spluttering sounds, but just from knowing him, Jim knew he was spoofing. Declan had known Sheila would be there.

'Hello, Declan.' Sheila sounded very composed.

'It's my wife everyone,' Declan announced.

People clapped. 'So, hey, how are you?' Declan asked, sounding as if they were best buddies. 'Long time no see. You're looking well. You've obviously been busy in the make-up department. Ha, ha.'

'Indeed,' Sheila replied drily. 'Well, when you've been kicked out of your home and not given any financial support, you do what you can to survive.'

In the background, people gasped.

Declan attempted to laugh it off. 'Aw, now, that's not true. You were well provided for. Anyway, we're here to taste the sandwich—'

314

'When your only daughter takes you in *despite* being left by her own cad of a husband, you try to make the best of things.'

'Bitch!' Jim shouted at the radio.

'Aw now—' Declan attempted to say.

'And if you want a sambo, it won't be free,' Lisa interrupted. Her voice turning to a holler, she shouted, 'You'll pay like everyone else. We do have a living to earn, you know, and no fecker of a man is getting it free from us any more!'

'Well said!' Sheila cheered.

Declan laughed along as if it was just a big joke, but there was an edge of panic to his voice as he asked, 'How much for a cheese salad with ham?'

'To you – three-fifty,' Lisa answered.

'Gimme one then.' Declan no longer sounded jovial or civil, just extremely pissed off. 'And just for the record, folks, this inter-view was not meant to go like this.'

'Lettuce?' Lisa barked.

'Yeah.' Declan said. Into the microphone, he announced, 'Service is not great. No smiles here at all.'

'Cucumber?'

'Yes.' Back to microphone he commented, 'She's only giving me two slices.'

'Oh, Declan, don't be so petty,' Sheila muttered. 'Judge the sandwich on its merits.'

'I have to judge the service too,' Declan said self-righteously. 'And just because you're my wife, I can't show favouritism.' Then, sounding frustrated, he added, 'And anyway, I don't care about the bloody sandwich, I only came here to see you.'

'To humiliate me, more like!' Sheila sniffed.

'*No*,' Declan stressed. 'To see you. I set this whole thing up.'

There were gasps from the spectators and someone groaned in the background.

'I mean,' Declan clarified, 'there *is* a real sandwich bar competition, but I wanted to see my wife because I missed

315

her and . . .' his voice stopped its upward swing and instead he muttered, 'I want her back.'

'Yeah, right.' Jim muttered. It was a typical D'arcy ratings booster.

'Yeah, right,' Sheila laughed.

'And don't do that don't-mess-with-my-knickers laugh,' Declan hissed. 'I bloody mean it. I'm sorry. I want you back.'

'Tomato?' Lisa barked.

'Eh, yeah.' Sounding distracted, Declan said, presumably to Sheila, 'Well?'

There was a long, long silence. Then Sheila said, 'Three-fifty for the sandwich, Declan, and to be honest, I wouldn't go back to you if you were a magnet and I a pin. Well, unless it was to stick myself into you very, very hard.'

'Sounds promising,' Declan joked.

There was more silence.

'I even got you this ring,' Declan said shakily, his voice unsure. There were more gasps from the audience as he produced something from his pocket.

'Why, thanks,' Sheila said. From what Jim could gather she took the ring and then said, 'Three-fifty please.'

It was a quiet and sober Declan that parted with his money. The shop seemed to have fallen silent.

In an effort to divert what was a highly embarrassing situation for the host, a drum roll was started up. 'And the verdict on the sandwich?' the speaker boomed.

'Not hungry,' Declan muttered.

They cut to a commercial break.

Jim let out a whoosh of air and wondered what the hell would happen now.


What happened was that Declan walked out of the shop and down the road to the hairdressers. Shoving open the doors, he strode past a chastened Rosemary, five agog customers and a wide-eyed Patrick. 'Tell her she has to come back to me,' he shouted at Jane who was busy cutting a client's hair.

Jane felt her stomach heave, especially as people had gathered outside the shop to have a gawk in the windows. Rosemary had filled her and Patrick in on all the details and Jane just wished she was dead. Years and years of humiliation welled up inside her.

'You tell her to come back to me,' Declan said again. 'I bought her a ring and she bloody took it off me and she still won't come back. Jesus!' He strode closer to Jane. 'You were the one who told me that she wanted me back!'

'That was months ago, Dad,' Jane hissed, trying to keep her voice down, but knowing it was futile. The whole story would be all over the place tomorrow. 'Things change. I mean, you didn't want her back then . . .'

'Well, I do now.'

'So tell her!'

'I bloody well did and she threw it back in my face.' He looked like a kid who hadn't been invited to a birthday party.

'Well, I can't do anything,' Jane said. 'It's not my business – you told me to butt out, remember?'

'Why do women never forget these things?' Declan shouted. 'You lot are descended from bloody elephants.'

From outside came the flash of cameras.

Jane gritted her teeth and turned to her customer. 'Just tilt your head a little please?' The customer obliged and muttered a 'Hiya' to Declan who ignored her.

'Well?' her dad demanded.

'I'm at work, Dad, I don't conduct my affairs in the glare of the public. OK?'

'Well, it wasn't meant to happen like that! She was meant to give me a sandwich and I was going to give her the ring. But she got all snotty on me.'

Jane said nothing, instead she stared pointedly at her customer's head and hoped that by ignoring her dad, he'd get the hint and go away.

'Hey, Deco.' A customer, arm outstretched, came towards him. 'Love the show.'

Declan glared at her, then he glared at Jane. He glared at everything around him and finally stomped out.

No one said much when he left.

Eventually after about ten minutes, the customer muttered, 'Someone told me he's dead nice to his fans. Some story that was.'

And that was when Jane realised that her dad probably did want her mother back. Her dad never snubbed fans. Even when things were bad, his fans always came first.

Only now, it looked like Sheila had.

She attempted to explain it to her mother when she got home. Sheila was having none of it. Drunk on victory, she kept admiring the ring he'd given her. 'My arse,' she kept saying, whenever Jane tried to get her to see things properly.

She'd recently started saying 'my arse' to everything she didn't agree with. It was a new expression, one she'd presumably learnt from her employer.

Jane was about to tell her mother that she couldn't stand much more of it when the phone rang.

'What?' she snapped into the receiver.

'It's just me.'

Hearing Jim's voice made her heart lurch. What was he going to have a go about now? 'Yeah?' she said warily.

'I was just wondering,' he paused, 'if you're OK? You know, with the stuff on the radio today? I know how much you hate all that.'

She couldn't speak for a second. It touched her that he'd rung. 'Thanks for calling,' she said, hoping her voice wouldn't tremble. 'It was nice of you.'

'No probs.' He sounded quite cheerful, not like the guy that had glowered at her last Saturday. 'Just remember what I always used to say – d'you remember?'

'Yeah.' She remembered how he'd wrap his big arms around her, kiss her head and tell her that although they were

318

her parents what they did was nothing to do with her. She was still Jane and she had her own life and they had theirs.

'Just thought I'd remind you.'

'Thanks,' she said softly. 'Patrick said the same.'

'He's right.'

Jane didn't want to let him go. Even if he didn't say another thing, she just wanted to know that he was on the other end of the line. 'I had a row with Di,' she confessed suddenly. 'She came home drunk after her Junior Cert results came out.'

'Oh . . . right.'

She knew he was wondering why she was telling him this, and what it had to do with anything. And it had nothing to do with anything, yet everything to do with it. 'I hit Di across the face,' she confessed.

'Jesus!' Jim sounded shocked. Then he said, 'And now, how're things?'

'Well, not too bad, but she's well hungover.'

He gave a splutter of a laugh.

His laughter warmed her.

He paused. 'Thanks for telling me.'

'You're her dad, you should know.'

'Right.' He sounded as if he was smiling and that made her smile. 'Listen, Jane, gotta go. I'm in Galway and I've to go to a business dinner in an hour. See you Saturday?'

'Sure. Bye.'

When he hung up, she felt lonelier than she'd felt since he'd left. But to feel anything other than angry with him was weird. In a nice way.

## 50

'PHILIP LOGAN HAS offered me a job,' Jim told Dave as they sat across from each other in Dave's office. 'I've accepted it provisionally, but I'll work until Christmas here and then I'll leave after that.'

Dave didn't congratulate him, instead he regarded him through narrowed eyes. 'So that's it. You're just going to up and leave us in order to market crisps?' There was a bit of mockery in his voice and Jim flinched. Normally he didn't care what the hell Dave said, but this time he felt the blow.

'You were always quick on the uptake, weren't ya, Dave?' Jim said, rising from his seat. 'There's no flies on you.'

Dave gave a bit of a chortle as Jim stomped out.

In the corridor, Jim laid his head back against the wall and closed his eyes. In his heart he knew that Dave was just jealous, but the slur hurt. Marketing crisps was not how he'd seen his life, he'd wanted to do so much more. There was the anti-drinking campaign that Dave was working on, he'd have loved to get that project, but Incredible Crisps was his baby and he supposed he should feel honoured that he was in charge of them.

But, Jesus, even the Chains Bond thing was boring him now.

He guessed it was because he'd no one to share it with. Not really.

It was all over the papers. 'End of the Road for Sexy Sheila and Deco D'arcy' was the banner headline in one of the tabloids. There were pictures of them on their wedding day, the infamous picture of them both in their sexy night attire, posing on their bed, and pictures of Jane as a baby.

'Awww, you were so *cute*,' Rosemary remarked.

Pictures of Patrick Costelloe's adorned the front page too. It was described as 'the place where a rejected, dejected D'arcy sought refuge from his humiliating show'.

Patrick was trying not to show his delight with the salon getting front-page publicity. He was all tea and sympathy, but every so often his face kept breaking into a huge grin.

And the customers had been pouring in all morning. Just like they'd been queuing up at Lisa's to get a sambo made by Sheila.

Jane felt like an animal in a circus.

Jim picked up the paper. He was bored out of his tree. Debs couldn't come over that night as Gillian had been advised by her doctor to rest. 'If I leave her, she'll start cleaning the flat,' Debbie giggled, 'so I'll see you another night – right?'

He was going to offer to go over, but he knew that the sight of him and his connection with Fred would only upset Gillian, and if Gillian got upset, Debbie would kill him.

Turning over the front page of his paper, Jim saw yet another spread on the D'arcy marriage. Declan was still declaring that he hadn't left Sheila destitute and she was keeping a noble silence on the matter. 'I've said all I can,' was her response.

My arse, she has, Jim thought in amusement.

A sudden longing for home seemed to wrench his heart. In a flash of clarity, he realised that this single man status wasn't him. Dating Debbie wasn't him. Living in this flat wasn't him. But the deafening silence at home wasn't him either.

Trouble was, Jim thought, he didn't know what *was* him any more.

Di wanted to take sixty euros out of her savings. She stood petulantly before Jane, ready to do battle if she had to.

'Why do you need it?' Jane asked.

'It's Gooey's birthday in a couple of weeks and I want to get him something nice.'

'OK.'

There was a moment of stunned silence.

'You mean I can take the money out?'

'Yeah, you can.' Jane turned from her. 'It's nice that you want to buy him a birthday present.'

'Can I take seventy instead?'

'Di, why do you always want more than—'

'OK, OK, I only asked.' Shoving her savings book into her pocket, she slouched from the kitchen.

Jim had just begun to type up a schedule for one of his projects when the buzzer went. It had the sound of a trapped bluebottle magnified by a million. Every time he heard it, it made him jump.

'Yep?'

'Hey, how's it going, my friend?' Fred's booming baritone almost took the intercom off the wall.

Jim winced, wondering what he wanted. They hadn't really been in contact since Jim had left, but enquiries had yielded information to the effect that Fred was still working furiously and had stopped the heavy boozing.

He buzzed Fred up and stood waiting for him at the door.

'Nice pad,' Fred said as he walked towards him. 'You must've been pretty well paid by your crispy friend.'

A girl from the flat opposite came out on to the landing. She gave Jim a shy smile as she locked her apartment door.

'No views like that at my place,' Fred said wistfully as he watched the girl's retreating back. 'You are one lucky man, Jimbo.'

'Shag off,' the girl hissed, turning back.

'You offering?' Fred called after her.

Jim smiled despite himself. He'd missed Fred's awful sexist remarks and his un-PC views of life. 'I suppose you want a can?' Jim asked as he led the way inside.

'On the ball, there, Jimbo,' Fred nodded, shutting the door behind them. He looked around and made more admiring remarks. Taking an opened can of Bud from Jim he drank thirstily. When he'd finished, both men stood staring at each other.

Fred broke the silence. 'Can we shove all the shit, you know, about Gill, behind us?' he asked. As Jim was about to interrupt, he held up a hand and continued, 'Look, I know you think I treated her badly, but fuck it, that's me, you know. I didn't judge you when you upped and married what's-her-face.'

'Jane,' Jim suggested.

'Yeah, her,' Fred said dismissively. 'I mean, right, you took one road and I'm just taking the other one.' He paused, then said quietly, 'But, like, it's got nothing to do with you and me, has it?'

Put like that, Jim still didn't agree. 'I think what you've done is crap,' he said.

'Yeah. Right.' Fred shuffled from foot to foot. He gulped, before saying haltingly, 'But, Jimbo, we've been mates a long time. I don't want to lose that.'

Neither did he, Jim thought. Fred had always been there, through everything, his dad leaving, his ma dying, everything. Through Matt.

He hadn't been a lot of help, but he'd been there.

'Yeah,' Jim agreed, wondering if he was doing the right thing, 'Me neither.'

Fred looked as if he'd been pricked with a pin. He grinned in relief. 'Knew that,' he said cockily.

Jim grinned back.

They clicked cans.

'Anyway, any news?' Fred asked.

Jim shrugged. 'Nothing much.'

'I had a bleedin' scare last week,' Fred made himself comfortable on Jim's sofa. 'All Parrot's feathers fell out. Had to take her to the vet. Cost me a fortune. She's fine now though.'

'Good.' Jim found it a bit bizarre to be talking about Fred's parrot when the subject of Gillian lay between them.

'She's as right as a good screw,' Fred nodded. 'The bleedin' vet said she was the cleverest bird he'd ever met.' He said it with the pride of a doting parent. 'I told him I'd taught her meself. Dead impressed he was.'

Jim smiled. Bloody vet wouldn't be impressed if he'd to listen to her every night, he thought. They talked about other things, Fred mostly leading the conversation. He wondered how Jane was putting up with her mental parents and Jim gave him a censored version of events.

Eventually, as midnight drew in, Fred got up to leave. 'Better head.' He pulled on his jacket and just as he turned to leave, he asked casually, 'How is Gillian, anyway? I haven't seen her in ages.'

Jim wondered if he really expected Gillian to call him with progress reports. He thought not, it was just Fred asking the question he'd bloody well come to ask four hours ago. 'She seems grand,' he answered, equally casually. 'Debs said her blood pressure is up and she's to take it easy, but other than that, she's fine.'

'So she's having the baby – yeah?'

'Well, unless they've invented some other way of doing things.'

Fred didn't smile. 'Righto, thanks for the drink. Maybe we'll head out somewhere one weekend?'

'Sure.' Jim agreed. 'Gimme a ring.'

Fred left and Jim polished off the last remaining can. He fell asleep on the sofa.

# 51

JANE AWOKE FEELING nervous. It was fifteen minutes before the alarm was due to go off and she lay staring at the ceiling, trying to quell the queasiness. This was it. Make or break time. It was funny how the competition had crept up on them all so quickly. All week she'd been having awful dreams about her colours going wrong, or cutting Rosemary's hair in a weird style, or Rosemary transforming into a different model with a funny-shaped face. Every time she woke, her heart was hammering like a drum, but the sense of relief was wonderful. She wondered if it would backfire completely on the salon if things did go wrong. Having been featured on the front pages of most of the nationals, the salon didn't need the publicity any more. They had plenty of customers and Patrick had reluctantly advertised Mir's job last week.

Still, Jane thought, entering this competition had given her focus for the first time in what felt like years. No longer was she just existing from day to day, no longer was she just putting in the hours at the salon, she was actually improving her skills and come what may, it was good for her, despite all the pressure and the nightmares. She was out to prove herself – to show that she was good and not some hick, OAP hairdresser.

And Patrick was fired up too. He seemed to love the backbiting that was going on between themselves and Cutting Edge. There was a great buzz around their salon that had never been there before.

Her alarm began to bleep and she hauled herself up in the bed. Time to get the kids up and out.

Di wanted to ask her something. It was so obvious. She was passing the butter, bread, and teapot without so much as a grumble. She had even given her a sunny smile and asked her if she was nervous.

'So Di,' Jane was determined not to be taken for a fool, 'what is it you want?'

Her daughter paused in the middle of lifting her teacup to her lips. She flushed, put down the cup and shrugged. 'Oh, that's typical,' she snorted. 'I try and be nice and I get accused of wanting something!'

'Which is?' Jane asked patiently.

There was a pause. 'Just, well, there's a party on tonight. Gooey's party. And I was wondering if I could go?' The last part of the request was muttered hurriedly.

'So you didn't want anything,' Jane said pleasantly and resumed eating her breakfast.

Di said nothing. Did nothing. Then, when the silence got too much for her, she snapped, 'Well, can I? Can I go?'

'Will there be drink there?'

She gave a mutinous shrug.

'More importantly, will you be drinking?' Jane asked.

'No, I won't. I promise, all right?'

It was said with very bad grace but Jane believed her. Di was many things, but she was not a liar. 'Be back by one,' Jane said.

'One?' Di rolled her eyes.

'Yes.'

'Fine.' Di muttered a 'dorky' under her breath and stomped off to get her coat for school.

'I can't *wait* for tonight.' Rosemary swung her legs back and forth in her chair. She'd been on a sunbed for the past few weeks and she glowed like a shiny brown penny. Her hair cascaded down her back and Jane, blow drying it, felt a little tremor of excitement at the thought of working on it that evening. It hit her like a small shock, the fluttering anxiety she felt. She found, quite unexpectedly, that she was looking forward to it.

Sheila was still in bed when the phone rang. Lisa had given her the day off after another successful 'ladies night' the evening before. She was going to get up, nibble on a grapefruit, make up a face pack and do her hair. After that, well, the day was hers to do with as she wanted. Only thing was, she didn't want anything much. There were only so many episodes of *Oprah* or *Ricki* one could take. And afternoon television was so bland. It wouldn't have been too bad to go to work really, mix with the outside world, share a bit of scandal. But, it was her day off and enjoy it she must.

The phone stopped ringing but started up again a few seconds later.

Honestly, Sheila thought, as she put her feet into her crocodile slippers, she just hated talking to people first thing out of bed, but maybe it was Lisa asking her to come in. She wouldn't want to let the woman down, not after she'd been so supportive of the 'Declan debacle' as they'd affectionately nicknamed it.

She lifted the receiver and put on her posh voice, 'Hello?'

'Aw, it's yourself!' Declan's unmistakable accent boomed down the line.

'Jane is not here.' Sheila was deliberately frosty. 'Bye now.'

'No, no,' Declan sounded flustered. 'No, it's you I want to talk to.'

'Oh, are you taping this for your show?'

'No!' he sounded annoyed. 'What do you take me for? I was just wondering if I could drop over tonight.'

'Drop over? Why?'

'To see you.'

'No,' Sheila said, relishing her power. 'I will not meet you tonight. I'm not a pushover – I'm not easily swayed.'

'So you still haven't had the operation then?'

327

'I beg your pardon?'

'You know, the one to remove the pole from up your arse.'

'Oh Declan, that's you all over. Can't get your own way and you immediately make crude jokes. Your adolescent humour may woo the public, but it does nothing for me.'

'Sorry.' He paused. 'Anyway, I'm going to come over.'

'I don't care what you do Declan. You can come or not, I don't care.'

'Fine.'

'Fine.'

He put down the phone.

Damn it, she thought. She should have done that first.

Jane couldn't concentrate at all. Patrick sent her home with strict instructions to relax. 'I'll pick you up at four and we'll drive over there. You get a bath or whatever and calm down.'

So she'd gone home, only her mother was ensconced in the bathroom and about an hour later, smelling like the entire contents of The Body Shop, she emerged, oblivious as usual to other people's needs.

'Oh, dahling,' her mother smiled pleasantly at her, 'will you style my hair? You see your—'

Jane made herself take deep breaths before she said crossly, 'I'm doing a competition tonight Mother. I'll see enough hair there, so I don't need to be looking at yours. And right now, I need a shower.'

'But your father said he might call around,' her mother said. 'I think he's going to ask me back.'

Jane rolled her eyes. 'He already has Mother. It's been all over the papers these last two weeks, now if you'll just get out of my way . . .' Saying this, she elbowed her mother aside and stalked into the shower.

Of course, her mother hadn't even cleaned it and the floor was sopping. So that took another ten minutes. By the time she emerged, she had just two hours to kill.

*   *   *

328

Jim wasn't in the mood for going out but Fred had rung him and he felt he had to. Of course, Debbie had flipped. 'Oh,' she said, 'that's lovely. He left my friend in the lurch and there *you* are going out with him.'

What was it with women? Jim wondered. Couldn't she see that his going out with Fred had nothing whatsoever to do with him and her? Or him and Gillian for that matter? So he'd listened to Debbie rant on with no idea of what to say to her.

Eventually, when she'd run out of steam, he said, 'I'll give you a bell tomorrow, OK?'

'It'll have to be, I suppose,' she'd said.

He didn't know why she was so huffy. She'd told him that she wouldn't be able to go out anyway as she was having a girls' night in with Gill. They were going to get videos and paint toenails and stuff, so he'd thought that it'd be fine. He'd squeeze Fred in and they'd all be happy.

Some hope.

## 52

IT WAS THREE-THIRTY. Jane couldn't stop pacing up and down the kitchen. If she'd had a packet of fags, she would gladly have smoked the lot.

*Oh God!* she thought.

'Will you sit down?' her mother said irritably. 'You're making me nervous.'

Through her own fug of nerves, Jane managed to register that her mother looked totally ridiculous sitting at the kitchen table in a six-hundred-euro, off-the-shoulder, sequinned black dress. Sheila had also tried to do an overly elaborate hairstyle which now sat like a squashed blonde cat on the top of her head.

'Here,' Jane reached for her bag and pulled out her comb, 'let me fix that for you.' She felt that if she was doing something with her hands, it might get rid of the nerves. She worked rapidly, the deft way her fingers parted, sectioned and styled giving her reassurance in her ability.

She'd already rung the salon to check on Rosemary's clothes and to double-check that Rosemary had actually made it to the beautician's without any mishaps.

Jane had just inserted the final pin into her mother's hair when the doorbell rang. Four on the button. Shoving her comb back into her bag, she took a deep breath. 'Wish me luck,' she said.

'You don't need luck, dahling,' Sheila kissed the air around her, 'you're a D'arcy – talented and wonderful.'

They smiled at each other, Jane basking in her mother's approval.

'Bye.'

'Bye, dahling.'

From upstairs came the shout, 'Good luck, Ma.' The two kids, who were on a half-day Friday, were smiling at her from the landing.

'Give it loads, Ma,' Owen smiled.

Di managed a fairly friendly, 'Do well,' before sauntering back into her room.

Her heart filled with trepidation, Jane opened the door to Patrick. 'Your carriage awaits.' He did a big bow for her and, taking her hand, led her outside.

The minute her mother left, Di scooped up Gooey's present from under her bed, shoved it into a plastic bag and went downstairs. 'I'm going out, Nana,' she said, 'I'll be back later.'

Her nana looked ridiculous in that black dress, she thought.

'What time, dahling?' her nana asked. 'I'll need to know in case your mother rings.'

So her mother hadn't told her nana what time she had to be in at. 'Four,' she said nonchalantly, chancing her arm.

'I'll take that as one-thirty, dahling and no later.' Sheila gave her a clipped smile.

One-thirty wasn't so bad, she conceded reluctantly. Without answering she left the house.

Fred called around at nine and together they headed for a local pub. For the first time in his life, Jim found it hard to talk to Fred. If the conversation became any more stilted, it'd keel over and die.

It was going to be a bloody long night.

At nine-thirty the doorbell rang and, peering through the curtains, Owen saw his Granddad Deco shuffling nervously from foot to foot. There was no way he was staying in the house

331

listening to the two of them squabbling. He legged it down the stairs, wrenched open the front door, yelled to his nana Sheila that she had a visitor and was gone.

Declan looked quite well, Sheila thought, as she walked towards him. Dressed in a shirt, tie, and a well-cut pair of Louis Copeland trousers, he almost looked like an adult.

'Oh,' she gave a sniff, 'so you decided to call, did you?'

Declan shrugged, quirked an eyebrow and said, 'Well, you look like you were expecting me.'

'Ha, ha, ha.' Even to her own ears, the laugh sounded false, so she stopped. 'I always wear this old thing about the house,' she said. 'It saves my good clothes getting destroyed.'

'The good stuff you wear for work – like?'

'I do beauty sessions,' Sheila answered scornfully. 'They're my *real* work, you know, since I—'

'Was flung out and left prostitute, yeah, I know.'

'*Destitute*, Declan,' Sheila corrected.

'It was a joke, oh fair one,' he grinned.

There was no way she was smiling back. After all he'd put her through, was still putting her through. Who on earth did he think he was? Did he *honestly* think he could snap his fingers and things would go back to normal? Did he really think that she was going to stand being slagged off regularly on the radio? And who was he to slag anyone anyway?

'So, what's the occasion, Declan?' Sheila folded her arms. He attempted to move inside the door and she asked again, 'What's the occasion?'

'Well, if you'd let me in, I might tell you. I don't want the world knowing what I'm gonna say.'

'Well,' she said in mock surprise, '*there's* a first.'

She was startled to see the shamed look on his face. So startled that she moved sideways to let him sidle by her. He carried on past her and into the kitchen.

'Is Janey not here tonight?'

'She's at a hairdressing competition with work.'

'Oh right.'

'And you're not having tea or anything else,' Sheila said imperiously. 'This is Jane's house, I can't go throwing about good food and drink. She's been left by Jim you know.'

Declan nodded. 'D'you know, Sheila, being poor suits you almost as well as being rich. You could get drama from a bleedin' roll of Sellotape.'

'Well, at least I got something out of nothing. I wish I could have got some money from my husband when I needed it.'

Another ashamed look. Really, Sheila thought, Declan wasn't arguing with his usual flair at all this evening. 'Well, what can I do for you?' she asked again.

Declan sat down. 'Come back,' he said.

It was the simple way he said it that touched her. But it was also extremely strange. 'Oh, come on, you can do better than that,' she scoffed. 'Come back?' She arched her eyebrows and thanked God that she'd plucked them earlier that day. 'You really expect me to drop everything and go back to you?' Her dress clung in all the right places as she walked towards where he sat. 'Declan, we hadn't made love in over four months and you told everyone you, you . . .' Sheila shuddered. 'Well, that we did it ten times or something like that. I can't remember.'

'Call it wishful thinking.'

'I call it lying. I call it making a laughing stock out of me. I call it the words of an impotent man.'

She knew she'd hurt him, but it was about time it was voiced. He couldn't perform and as a result he kept talking about it and making out he was some sort of sex god. The whole thing was killing them – this dancing around the subject, pretending it wasn't there. 'Declan,' she said, 'you've got to see someone.'

He looked at his hands for ages. Then he turned them over and looked at the backs. 'And what will the papers say to that?' he asked quietly.

Sheila knelt down. There was a tearing sound as the fabric

333

of her dress caught on the heel of her shoe. Still, if she got back with Declan, she could always get another one. 'We'll find out if it happens, dahling.'

He looked at her. 'We'll?'

'Yes. *If* you'll see someone.'

He sat there for a while then slowly nodded. 'I've missed you,' he whispered.

Sheila nodded. She'd known he would. She'd known when he kicked her out that he was going to regret it, so she'd bided her time.

'I thought, you know, it was cool at first,' Declan swallowed. 'Kicking you out saved me from, well, you know – I couldn't bear for you to . . .' he stopped, '. . . witness my failure all the time.'

'I know, dahling.' God, she'd have to stand up soon, her knees were killing her.

'But then, when I won that bloody award thing, it wasn't the same, not being able to share it with you or even Janey. And, Jaysus, I didn't know what to do. I didn't know how to get you back. I felt if I did a big public thing, you'd come back.'

Sheila nodded. Really, men felt they had to explain everything. *Of course* she knew.

'Why didn't you come back that time?' Declan asked. He reached out and touched her face.

Sheila spent a few seconds just enjoying his fingers as they trailed their way down her cheek before answering. 'I knew it would be no good, that you weren't ready, dahling.' She put her hand up to stop him from going any further. 'I stayed away because it was good for you. For us.'

'Oh Jaysus.' Declan wrapped his arms around her, totally ruining her hairstyle. His finger pierced itself on one of her hairgrips and cursing, he pulled away.

Sheila smiled at him as he sucked on his bruised finger. Thank God she could now go back home. How Jane and Jim had ever slept in that bed was beyond her. She looked at Declan and he looked at her at the same time.

He was so much nicer when he wasn't being a famous DJ. Their eyes locked and bending towards her, he kissed her. She'd missed that – the warmth of someone loving her.

'Tell you what,' Declan said, 'if things in this house aren't too tight, I'd kill for a cuppa.'

Sheila smiled at him. He smiled back. They were going to be OK again.

# 53

I T HAD BEEN a long night, Jim thought. He resisted the temptation to look at his watch and when he did, he almost groaned to see that it was barely ten o'clock.

'Another?' Fred stood up and put his hand into his pocket. 'My shout?'

'Yeah, go on.' Jim hoped that if he got drunk it would help the conversation flow better. It kinda made him sad that he and Fred should be scrounging around for something to talk about, but he was too aware of what a bastard Fred was for it to spur him on to try harder. Fred either didn't notice or was hell bent on ignoring the atmosphere. He filled in the gaps in the conversation with mad stories that made them both laugh. And while they were laughing, the world seemed to right itself for a few seconds.

It was while Fred was up at the bar getting the drinks that Jim's mobile rang. Who the hell would be ringing him so late? he wondered. He hated late calls, they always spelt bad news. He'd just answered the phone when Fred arrived back with two creamy pints of Guinness.

'Tell ya what, Jimbo, you're lucky with your local. They do a good pint.'

Jim barely heard him. It was Debbie on the other end, sounding as if she was about to have a breakdown. In the background, Gillian was telling her to calm down.

Gillian telling Debs to calm down – something must definitely be wrong.

Debbie blabbered something that Jim couldn't make out.

'Who is it?' Fred asked, taking a gulp of his drink.

'Debs, I can't make out what you're saying.' Jim tried to sound patient.

'He-a.' There was a bit of a tussle and Gillian came on the line. 'Jim, we decided to ring you 'cause you probably are dee expert.'

'On?'

'Childbirth.'

'Sorry?'

'What are dee symptoms? I've been in already this week with a false alarm and no way am I going in again.'

'She's going to have it on the floor,' Debbie, missing her usual sexy huskiness, shrieked down the line. 'She's been holding off these last couple of hours. And I just couldn't deliver a baby. Oh, God.'

Jim had to hold the phone away from his ear. Christ, he wouldn't want Debs on his team in a crisis. 'Have you a pain?' Jim asked, feeling like a total fraud. What the hell did he know about childbirth? His last kid was born ten years ago.

'Pains in my stomach,' Gillian said. And as if to demonstrate this fact, she let out a yowl and all he could hear was Debbie telling her to 'bloody breathe'.

'That sounds bad,' Jim said. 'Maybe—'

'Sounds bad,' Debbie shouted. '*Sounds* bad – you should *see* her. Oh God, I'm going to throw up.'

'She's a bit upset,' Gillian confided. 'I dunno. I didn't think she'd be like this.'

'I think you should go in.' Jim was not going to be responsible for her having the baby in the apartment. 'Even if it's a false alarm—'

'It's not a false alarm,' Debbie shrieked. 'Haven't I been telling her that for the last few hours?'

'Call a taxi,' Jim said. 'You're in no fit state to drive.'

'Have you ever tried to call a taxi on a Saturday night?' Debbie was hyperventilating. 'It'll be hours. Oh God!'

'An ambulance?'

'Yeah. Yeah, OK. And Jim—'

'Just get off the phone and call an ambulance,' Jim ordered. 'I'll meet you in there, OK?'

The line went dead.

Jim clicked his phone off and looked at Fred who'd turned as white as the line of foam on his upper lip.

'Was that Gillian?' he asked nervously.

'Yeah.' Jim pocketed his mobile. 'She's going in to have the baby.'

'Oh, yeah, right.' Fred turned from him and, lifting his pint up, drank thirstily.

The action infuriated Jim. 'Oh. Yeah. Right,' he said, copying Fred's laid-back voice. 'Is that all you can say?'

Fred looked up. 'Yeah. What else is there?'

'That girl,' Jim jabbed his finger towards his mate, 'has gone in to have your baby and all you can say is "oh, yeah, right"?'

'Yeah.' Fred glared at him. 'I didn't ask her to have it, did I? I don't want a bloody kid. It's her lookout.'

Jim had had enough. He stood up abruptly, almost upending the table. People from other tables glanced at him uneasily. 'You make me fucking sick – d'you know that? All you care about is you. *Hey,*' he yelled, '*this fucker's girlfriend is having his baby and he's dumped her.*'

'Shut up!' Fred jumped up too and poked his face into Jim's.

'Lads, lads,' the barman attempted to intervene.

'He has a parrot that he calls Parrot and he gives her more affection than he does to anyone else!'

'She bloody well deserves it. She doesn't hightail it out when things go wrong, does she?'

'She's in a fucking cage, how can she?'

'Lads – out.' The barman caught them both by the arm and attempted to push them towards the door.

Both guys shrugged him off.

Jim jabbed a finger into Fred's chest. 'You're a loser Fred. A fucking loser.'

'Oh yeah?' Fred's curled lip gave him an ugly look. 'And you're not? You don't even have a bloody home any more. You fight with your wife, your kids wouldn't talk to you for fucking ages, you work all the time and you shut everyone out. Don't call *me* a loser.'

Jim grabbed Fred by the shirt and Fred pushed against him. The barman gave up and went back behind the bar. Picking up a phone, he started dialling. 'Lads, I'm calling the cops.'

'But at least I had that,' Jim snarled, shaking Fred like a rat. 'At least I had all that, and d'you know what? I'd chop me right arm off to have it back. And you, you fucking wanker, you could have it all. A girl that loves you, a kid. Jesus,' he threw Fred from him and stalked from the pub, 'you make me sick.'

He didn't wait to see if Fred was all right. His head hammering, his heart racing, he stumbled out into the inky black night.


The mansion house was packed. The hairstyling had been done and the ramp and the lights had been set up for the various competitions. Entrants for the fantasy hair competition were receiving the most attention, with photographers fighting to take their picture. One girl was trying to balance what looked like a birdcage on her head. Inside, hanging from a loop of hair, was a perfect stuffed budgie.

Everyone was dressed in up-to-the-minute fashion, backless tops, tight trousers, short skirts. Jane, as usual, felt completely unhairdresserish in her black trousers and tight T-shirt.

Drinks were being served at the bar and loud music was pumping from the speakers.

It was ten minutes before the start of their competition and she was behind stage giving advice to Rosemary on how to walk. 'Modelling is just as important as the hairstyle,' she advised. 'Just

339

walk on, don't acknowledge the applause and be untouchable, unreachable, OK?'

'Yeah. Yeah.'

'A bit like the hairdresser herself, eh?'

Pete Jordan must have sneaked up behind her. Jane flushed. The man had been studiously avoiding their party all afternoon and now, when he could get a dig in, here he was, sniggering away.

'I'll give that comment the attention it deserves,' Jane muttered. 'None.'

'Not a bad job,' Pete nodded to Rosemary. 'Still, I'm told the judges this year favour the brunettes.' With that, he waltzed off.

'Bastard,' Jane hissed.

Sheila had located some sausages and an egg in the fridge and had decided to show Declan that she could now attempt a fry-up with the best of them. He was sitting down, looking at her in admiration.

'You look nice beside a cooker,' he told her seriously. 'It sort of suits you.'

'It's quite easy really.' Sheila brushed a tendril of hair from her face. 'Jane is marvellous at it. She can even get the eggs from the pan without breaking them.'

'Aw, she's a great girl, all right,' Declan mused. 'Turned out very well.'

'She did,' Sheila pricked a sausage and the grease spat back at her, burning her wrist. 'Oh, honestly,' she exclaimed, as more grease splattered on to her dress, 'this will be ruined.'

'So what?' Declan stood up and wrapped his arms around her waist. 'Can't you buy twelve of them now if you want?'

The words gave Sheila a nice warm glow inside.

They were both startled as the front door slammed open, crashed closed and pounding footsteps legged it up the stairs.

'Jaysus.' Declan looked at Sheila in concern.

'Di,' Sheila said wearily. Then, deciding to show Declan what else she'd learnt, she said, 'I'll go and have a word with her. See if she's all right. Honestly Declan, she's a very difficult child. You would not believe the hostility that emanates from her.'

She handed the frying pan to him and gingerly approached the bottom of the stairs. 'Di, dahling,' she called, 'is everything all right?'

There was no answer, though she fancied that she could hear the child sobbing. She walked up the rest of the stairs and commented, 'You're back very early.'

'Ten out of ten for observation,' Di replied in a hostile but shaky voice.

From downstairs she heard Declan give a guffaw of laughter.

'Are you all right?' She took the risk of tapping on her door. 'Are you crying?'

'No. Go away!'

'Di, dahling.' Sheila tapped the door again, praying that Di would stay inside. She'd have no idea what to do if the child appeared. But Jane would expect it. Jane would like to know what was wrong. 'Are you sure? Your mother will—'

'I'm fine!' Di shouted, her voice spiralling upwards and not sounding fine at all. 'Leave me alone!'

'OK.' Sheila couldn't help the relief she felt. But she'd done her duty. She was a concerned grandmother. 'If you're sure.'

Di didn't bother to reply.

Thank God, was all Sheila could think.

The hospital was packed when Jim arrived. He asked at reception and was told that Gillian was up in a labour ward. Following directions, he found himself outside the glass doors. A passing nurse located Debbie for him and she arrived out of the labour ward, pale but smiling.

'Oh Jim.' She crossed towards him and caught his hand in hers. 'Thanks for coming.' Squeezing his hand, she added glumly, 'Sorry about earlier, I think I got a bit nervous. Hot water and towels seemed to be on the agenda.'

Jim laughed. 'A *bit* nervous?' he teased.

Debbie punched him lightly. 'Will you hang around? D'you mind? They say it'll be born tonight sometime.'

'No probs. How's Gill?'

'She's great.' Debbie made a face. 'Better than I'd be anyway. I mean, the *pain* she must be in. She's high with the gas, but she won't have the, you know, injection thing?'

'Epidural?'

'See,' Debbie said, 'I *knew* you were an expert. Two kids qualifies you to know these things.'

'Three,' Jim corrected automatically.

Debbie blushed, 'Sorry. I didn't—'

'No, it's OK,' Jim said hastily, wishing he'd kept his mouth shut. Giving her a gentle push, he added, 'Maybe you'd better get back in there. You might miss all the action.'

'Yeah.' Debbie squeezed his hand. 'Thanks for coming.' She paused just before she pushed open the doors. 'Was Fred with you when I rang?'

Jim nodded. 'I told him, but he, eh, he didn't want to know.'

Debbie bowed her head. 'She keeps asking for him. I dunno if it's the gas or what, but it's like she thinks he's coming.'

'Well, he's not.'

'Bastard.'

Jim nodded slowly, 'Yeah.' He watched the doors swing shut behind her and saw her go into the first room on the right. Walking back down the corridor, he found a small waiting room with a telly in it and sat down. It was going to be a long night.

## 54

THE BELL RANG for the start of the competition and one by one the models and their stylists walked on to the ramp. The stylists stayed at the top of the ramp while their models walked down it, turning their heads left and right to show off their hair. The judges, one of whom was Julian Waters, were placed at tables on either side. As various salons appeared, huge cheers went up. Pete Jordan's model looked stunning in a tight, black velvet dress, with a plunging neckline and a thigh-high side split. Her hair, glossy and curly, fell to her shoulders and was a mixture of coffee, gold and caramel lowlights. It was simple, yet very effective, though not exactly a competition hairstyle, Jane thought.

'Cutting Edge of Yellow Halls Road,' was called out as they took to the ramp. Flash bulbs popped and Pete stood proudly by, acknowledging the applause and attention. He was the hot favourite to win and Jane couldn't help envying him his smooth composure. She was a wreck.

'And now, representing Patrick Costelloe's, Jane McCarthy and her model, Rosemary Dalton.' In the crowd, Patrick was giving her the thumbs up and beside him, a tall, peroxide-blond man, who must be Barney, was nodding in approval.

Rosemary looked like the princess Jane had promised. Her style was funkier than Pete Jordan's. More modern. And best of all, Rosemary loved her hair. The colour scheme that Jane had chosen for her was red and orange. Rosemary wore a retro orange and red sunburst top and red, figure-hugging jeans.

343

She had a lovely figure, they'd discovered, and tight things suited her. The hairstyle Jane had decided to go for was the look Di was so fond of – a bed-head. She'd done a mixture of highlights and lowlights and Rosemary's hair was now a glorious blend of reds and oranges and yellows. Then, freehand, Jane had texturised the hair and the result was pretty good.

Rosemary, after initially looking terrified, walked down the ramp with confidence. As the applause grew, so did her poise. Some guy in the crowd wolf-whistled her as she passed and Jane saw her face light up with pleasure. Once her walk was over, she took Jane's arm and together they left.

Backstage, she flung her arms around Jane and hugged her hard. 'I look so lovely,' she half-sobbed. 'And it's all thanks to you. I feel like a film star or something.'

Jane hugged her back. 'You look like a film star, Rosemary.'

'You and Pat,' Rosemary wiped her eyes, causing her mascara to run. 'You have made my year. I am the luckiest girl ever. I really am.'

She was the loveliest girl ever, Jane thought fondly, giving her another hug.

Back in the hall, Jane looked for Patrick and Barney. Patrick spotted her immediately and greeted her with a smile.

'Well?' Jane asked anxiously.

'It looked good, hard to tell though. Cutting Edge will be difficult to beat. And that other guy, what was his name?' He looked to Barney for support.

'Vernes or something, wasn't it?'

'Uh-huh,' Patrick nodded. 'Fantastic use of colour. Very original. They did the floodlights, did you manage to see it?'

Jane nodded, her high hopes disappearing. Maybe she'd flop completely.

'And where is our star?' Patrick shouted, spotting Rosemary hiding behind Jane. 'Where is she?'

Rosemary giggled.

'This, Barney,' he pulled Rosemary forward, 'is Rosemary. Isn't she lovely?'

'Beautiful.' Barney gravely took Rosemary's hand and kissed it.

'Aw, stop!' Rosemary flapped them away.

'And this is Jane.' Patrick introduced her to Barney.

Jane smiled. 'Patrick has told me so much about you.'

Barney smiled and clasped her hand firmly. 'Likewise, only he never said you were so talented.'

'Flattery will get you places I'm sure you've no desire to go,' Jane giggled.

Barney laughed.

'Hey, great job,' a guy with a huge scar on his face crossed to Jane. Nash trailed in his wake. 'Jaz,' he said, nodding to Jane.

'Aw, hi Jaz,' Jane nodded to him. He was worse-looking than Gooey, if that were possible. Thin and scrawny with hair like a badly peeled spud. 'So, d'you like what I did to your girlfriend then?'

'Aw, she's lovely any time.' Jaz winked at Rosemary who seemed to melt just looking at him.

Jane smiled. It was a nice thing for such a rough-looking lad to have said. 'She is, isn't she?' she agreed.

'How about we go and get a drink, eh?' Barney asked.

'Does that include me too?' Jaz asked, rubbing his hands together and looking hopefully at Barney.

'Sure.' Barney flashed Jane and Patrick a grin before disappearing with his new-found friends.

'And I thought Di's fella was bad,' Jane said in bewilderment. 'Jesus!'

Patrick laughed.


'Hey, hey, Jimbo.' Someone was shaking him. He felt stiff and sticky. Opening his eyes, he saw a lurid black and white print and his mind went into a tailspin.

345

'Jimbo!' Once again he heard the voice. The print disappeared and a face gawked at him. 'Hey, it's me.'

It was Fred. Jim sat up and rubbed his eyes. The last he remembered he'd fought with Fred or maybe he'd only dreamt it. But no, he was in a hospital, 'cause he felt hot and the smell of disinfectant in the air would kill most living things. 'Fred?' Jim said, swallowing hard as his mouth was dry. 'Is that you?'

'Yeah.' Fred hunkered down beside him. 'Is this where she is?'

'So you decided to come, did ya?' Jim was unable to help the smile that crept into his voice.

Fred gazed at his hands, the normally cocky look gone from his face. 'I tried not to but, well . . . I thought about the stuff you said and, well . . .' he paused, then coughed. 'Anyway, I'm here now and I can't get anyone to tell me where the fuck she is.'

'She was asking for you earlier.' Jim stood up. Jesus, his legs were stiff. He looked at his watch. It was only eleven-thirty, but it seemed much later than that. 'Debs is with her now.'

'Is she OK?'

'She's in the labour ward,' Jim said. 'The baby's due tonight.' He watched the terrified look that crept over Fred's face and decided not to say any more. Instead, he left the television room and walked Fred up the corridor. Pointing through the glass doors, he said, 'It's the first room on the right, that's where she is.'

Fred stared at the doors as if they were the gateway to hell. He looked at Jim in desperation. 'Will she want to see me?'

'Only one way to find out.' Jim opened the door slightly. 'Nothing ventured, nothing gained.'

'Yeah. Yeah, right.'

Taking huge whooshes of air, Fred readied himself. He squared his shoulders and had one foot inside the door when from down the corridor, someone called, 'Hey, hey you two, what are you doing?'

Jim turned and saw a woman in a green coat striding towards them. 'This is Fred,' he indicated Fred. 'He's going in to see Gillian Rodgers. She's in that room there.'

'Well, if she's in that room there,' the doctor said sharply, 'she's in labour and from what I can remember, she already has someone with her. Only one person allowed, I'm afraid.'

'Well, that's it.' Fred sounded relieved. 'Did me best.'

Jim glared at him. 'He's the baby's father,' he said to the doctor, 'and the girl with Gillian will let him in.'

'And will Gillian?'

'I dunno—'

'Yep.' Jim gave Fred a dig in the ribs. 'No probs. Just ask.'

At that moment, Debbie came hurtling out of the room, shouting at the top of her voice, 'Doctor, Doctor? God, is there a doctor?'

Pushing them aside, the doctor hurried towards Debbie.

'I think the baby's coming,' Debbie said, sounding as if she was going to cry. 'She says she wants to push. Isn't that a sign?'

The doctor nodded, closed the door firmly on Fred and Jim and bustled into the room. Debbie was about to go after her when she looked up and spotted Fred. Her eyes narrowed and tossing her head, she walked off.

'She can't do that,' Fred spluttered. 'I'm here now. She can't just go and ignore me like that.'

Jim resisted the temptation to tell Fred that he'd ignored Gillian for months, but he didn't. The fact that Fred had come to the hospital at all was a miracle, it couldn't go wrong now. 'Go in,' he said, decisively, 'go on.'

'It's my baby in there,' Fred said, as if he was psyching himself up.

'Yep, and you've more right than Debs to see it born.'

'Right. Yeah.'

'So, what are you waiting for?'

'Dunno.' After more deep breathing Fred pushed the door

aside and strode through it. Jim followed. If Fred hesitated again, he'd never go in, and Jim was damned if he was going to let that happen.

Fred stopped outside the door to the room and he almost turned and fled when he heard all the commotion from inside.

'Go on,' Jim urged, looking around desperately in case they'd be thrown out. 'This is it, Fred. Hurry up, would ya!'

'Right!' He shoved open the door and strode into the room. 'Gill,' he said loudly, 'I'm . . .' Whatever else he was going to say died on his lips as he took in the scene inside. '*Jaysus!*'

'What are you two doing?' The doctor turned furiously to them. 'Someone get them out. This girl is about to give birth.'

'Hey, I've something to say—' Fred protested, his hands in the air as a nurse made to shove them out.

'Is that, is that my Freddie?'

'Get them out!' the doctor shouted.

'Yeah – it's me.' Fred shoved the small nurse aside and stood, arms dangling, gazing at Gillian.

'I'm here, Gill – I came.'

Jim pushed him nearer the bed. If Gillian got another pain, Fred would do a runner. This had to be settled quickly, especially as the nurse was gawking indignantly at Fred and seemed about to summon help.

'Oh, Freddie.' Gillian sounded as if she was close to tears. 'Come he-a.'

'Jesus!' the doctor and Debbie said in unison.

'Out!' The nurse tried to ferry Jim towards the door.

'I missed you.' Fred stood beside Gillian but stopped short of taking her hand. Instead he wiped damp hair from her brow and said tenderly, 'I've been a fucking jerk.'

'Naw. You just got scared, it happens.'

'Jesus!' Debbie said on her own this time.

'Jim told me I was a lucky fucker to have you, said he'd cut his arm off to have his family back, he said—'

Gillian grasped his hand. 'I knew you'd come. Didn't I say he'd come, Debbie?'

Debbie nodded.

'Do you want this person at the birth?' the doctor demanded impatiently.

Gillian nodded and then let out a yell. 'Owwww.'

'Oh fuck – what's happening? Fred glanced around in terror. 'Jesus, someone help her.'

'Just hold her hand,' Debbie said to him as she kissed Gillian on the cheek. 'Come on, Jim, let's go,' she said as she pushed past him.

As Jim made to follow Debs, he saw Fred reaching for the gas mask and shoving it over his face. 'No, it's for her,' the doctor shouted.

It was going to be a rough night for Fred, Jim thought, grinning.


There was silence in the hall as the president of the hairdressing federation began to speak. Jane had just finished thanking Barney for all his help with the salon. He'd been dismissive of it, told her not to mention it. Then he'd shuffled away to get a few more drinks in.

The president was now talking about what they looked for in the winning styles. Jane felt Patrick reaching for her hand and squeezing it. Jane grinned at him and squeezed his hand back. It had been a brilliant night, the best she'd had in ages. Of course it would have been better if Mir had been there, but it couldn't be helped.

'And now to our decision,' the president continued. 'As you know, we mark under various categories . . .' Jane tuned out. It was the same speech as all the other years. The next thing he'd say was that the standard had been very high.

'Of course, this year's standard was exceptionally high . . .'

It was a difficult choice.

'. . . and the choice was very difficult.'

349

But in the end . . .

'. . . it came down to what I personally liked the best and in third place is . . .

The name of the winner was lost to her as her mobile rang.

Jane's heart went cold as she saw that it was her home phone number.

Debbie was in a funny mood, Jim thought. It wasn't that she was angry exactly, it was more that she was answering all his questions in monosyllables. Her arms were folded, her legs were crossed and she was sitting angled away from him, in the chair beside the telly.

'What's up?' he asked uncertainly. He couldn't figure her out. Surely she should be glad that he'd managed to get Fred to come, last minute and all as it was.

Debbie fixed him with a gaze that made him catch his breath. Her huge eyes were pooled with tears and she said quietly, 'Well, if you can't figure that out, then there's no hope for us, is there?'

Why did women always do that? Why did they always give a cryptic answer to a perfectly simple question?

'Is it because you wanted to see Gill's baby being born?' he asked. He moved nearer to her, but she flinched. 'I mean, I think it was great that Fred came—'

'So do I.' Her tone was clipped.

So it wasn't that. Jim sighed. He tried again. 'Look, Debs, either tell me what's wrong or else I'll probably say something else to annoy you.'

'You couldn't do any worse than you already have.' Deb's voice shook and she sniffed.

What had he said? Mentally, Jim ran over everything that had happened that night and he still—

'You'd "chop your right arm off to have your family back", would you?' Debbie asked, her voice shaking. 'That's what you told Fred, wasn't it?' She jabbed her chest. 'What does that make me feel like? Huh?'

350

Oh Jesus. Jim winced at the look of hurt on her face. He reached out to touch her, but again she moved away. 'I only said it to make Fred realise what he'd be giving up,' he explained. 'It's nothing to do with you. And I value me arm, I really do.'

'Sure.' A tear rolled down her face.

'Debs—'

'You've never told me anything about yourself, Jim, never confided in me why you and your wife split—'

'I did so,' Jim raked his hand through his hair. 'I told you we drifted—'

'Wonderful,' Debbie sneered. 'You never talk about your son that died—'

'That's . . . that's . . .' Jim shook his head. 'That shouldn't affect us.'

'You are *going out* with me.' Debbie stood up. More tears had spilled out and were running down over her nose and plopping on to the floor. She came towards him and held her hands in front of her as she said fiercely, 'I tell you everything. I get nothing back.'

'You do. I tell you stuff.'

'Nothing – that – matters.' Debbie brushed her face with her hand, smearing her lipstick all over the place. She shook her head. 'You and Fred are the same. Neither of you gave me or Gill anything concrete. You even took a job without thinking about me.'

'Aw, now—'

'Is that why it ended with your wife?' she asked suddenly. 'Did you shut her out too?'

'Does it matter?'

'Yeah, if you still love her. I mean, you don't love me, do you?'

'I—'

'You love your wife, Jim. You should go back to her.'

'It's over,' he said desperately. 'Jesus, Debs—'

'Either you leave this hospital, or I will,' Debbie said, ignoring

351

him. 'And I think that since I've been with her all evening, I deserve to be here.'

'There's no need for this,' Jim said, knowing he was only saying it for the sake of it. He'd hurt her and he knew there was no going back. And what he'd said to Fred *was* true. He *would* chop his arm off to have his family back and maybe while he felt like that, he shouldn't be seeing Debs. He'd thought he was moving on, but maybe in order to move on he had to have somewhere he wanted to go. 'Debs—'

'Stop.'

They stared at one another. Jim was the first to drop his gaze.

'So, will you go, Jim? Please?'

'How'll you get home?'

She gave him a weary look. 'Just go.'

He nodded and picked up his jacket from the chair. When he looked at her again, she was facing the other way, pretending to look out the window. 'I'm sorry,' he said quietly. He didn't know if she heard.

He had just unlocked the car door when his mobile rang.

It was Jane and she was crying.

## 55

J IM DROVE LIKE a maniac to the hospital. This could not be happening again, he thought. Please, God, not again. It became a sort of prayer in his brain as he drove through the Dublin streets on the way to the Mater. He hadn't been able to get much out of Jane until his mother-in-law came on and told him that there'd been an accident and to get to the Mater as quickly as he could.

When he got there, he parked his car assways and ran up the steps. Jane met him in the hallway. Sheila had her arm around her. Jim stared at the tableau the two made and, his voice contracting with fear, asked, 'What's happened?' Jane covered her face, so he looked to Sheila. 'Jesus, tell me!'

'It's Owen,' Sheila said, as Jane let out a moan, 'he's been knocked down.'

The words hit him like blows. No way, not again.

Jim covered his face and sat down on a hospital chair. Jane and Sheila sat beside him. Almost out of instinct, he put his arm around Jane's shoulder.

He knew she was remembering that awful night too.

*Matt danced by her out of the house, saying that he was getting his bike out of the garage. She meant to tell him to put his helmet on, but for some reason decided not to. Maybe it was because Matt lost everything and if she asked him to put on his helmet, they'd be looking for it for hours, and by the time they found it, he'd have decided not to bother going out. And she wanted him out. He had been watching telly all day; it was about time he got a bit of exercise. Five minutes later, she heard a scream. And she knew it was Matt. But she hadn't moved, just stood in the kitchen with her eyes closed, until one of the neighbours had come running up her driveway. And she'd been so afraid to go outside, because she'd known . . .*

*He'd died that night.*

*Jim had made it to the hospital just as Matt died. He'd been away on business and the minute he walked into the little room and held his son's hand and said, 'Hi, Matt, it's me, Dad,' Matt had just gone.*

*Like a light being put out.*

*The nurse said that often happened. 'It's like they hang on until everyone important has come,' she'd said.*

*Jim had spent months wondering what would have happened if he'd never arrived.*

'Excuse me.' A doctor tapped Jim on the shoulder. 'Are you the McCarthy boy's parents?'

At his question, Jane wrenched herself free from his embrace and stared wildly at the doctor. 'Yes, yes, we are. What's happened? Is he OK?' Grasping his arm, she said, 'Please, don't say any fancy words, just tell us.' Her voice broke, 'We lost another boy, you see and—'

'Jane, dahling,' Sheila smiled uneasily at the doctor and put her arm around her once more. Softly, she said, 'Come on now, just listen to the doctor.'

'Yeah.' Jane nodded and blinked rapidly. 'Yeah,' she said again.

The doctor smiled sympathetically at her and indicated the chairs. 'Would you like to sit down again?'

'No.' Jane shook her head frantically. 'We just want to know – don't we, Jim?'

Jim nodded. He had to swallow hard. He looked at the doctor, a young guy with a chart. He probably didn't even have kids himself . . .

'Your son has been in a serious accident,' the doctor began.

Jane moaned and covered her face. Sheila pulled her close. Jim felt himself drifting.

'We've done all we can to make him comfortable.' The doctor looked at the three of them. 'He had some internal injuries and we've done a scan and, well, at the moment he's stable. Other than that, it's hard to say, at the moment.'

'He's alive.' Jane mouthed the words cautiously. 'He's alive and might get better?'

'It's early days,' the doctor said. 'But, yes, he's alive.'

'Can I see him?' Jane asked.

The doctor nodded. 'Don't get upset by the machines,' he said, as he led the way to ICU. 'They're the things keeping him alive. It might be frightening at first.'

The ICU was scary and the sight of Owen, looking so small and pale, did shock her. Jane went towards the bed and touched her son's face. He didn't react. Beside him, machines bleeped and whirred.

'Owen, it's Mam,' she said softly. *Mam.* She wanted to cry at the sound of the word. She caressed his cheek and kissed his face. She rubbed her finger up and down his hand. His skin was so soft, so vulnerable. Never had he seemed more precious than he did in those moments.

He could die.

It was too enormous to take in. Too much to think about.

She felt her mother rubbing her back, trying to calm her. She turned to the doctor, 'How did it happen?'

'There was a girl with him,' the doctor said, 'she's being treated for shock. I can take you to see her when she's ready, but maybe it's too much—'

'No,' Jane shook her head. 'I need to know.'

Jim didn't want to touch Owen. He didn't want to acknowledge the fact that the horribly bruised body in the bed was his son. It was like his whole existence had frozen over. He was in a little pocket of air and all about him was ice. It'd been

355

like that after Matt had died too. It'd been like that a lot in his life.

The doctor led them towards a cubicle where a young girl lay on a bed. Her name was Charlotte, the doctor had said, and she was a friend of Owen's.

Jane's first thought was that the child was stick-thin and earnest-looking. Black bushy hair fell to her shoulders and pale blue eyes, swollen with tears, gazed fearfully at them as they entered. On either side of her were her parents.

They smiled awkwardly at each other and then Charlotte's mother said softly, 'I'm sorry about your boy. How is he?'

Jane opened her mouth to answer, but nothing came out.

Jim stared hard at the wall.

'Not good,' Sheila said softly. She put her arm around Jane and forced her to sit down.

'Is it all right if we talk to Charlotte?' Jane asked, gulping. 'It's just, well, I just need to know what happened.'

'Charlie?' her mother asked.

Charlotte nodded.

'Will we stay with you?' her dad asked, ruffling her hair.

'No. No, it's OK,' Charlotte spoke. She had a light, nervous voice. 'I'll be fine.'

Her mother opted to stay anyway, while her dad went to get them all some tea.

Jane licked her lips nervously. It had all happened so fast. She wondered if she was in some sort of horrible nightmare. She was upset, but it hadn't got right in yet. Not right in, under her bones. 'Hiya,' she managed. 'I'm glad you're all right.'

'Thanks.' Charlotte bit her lip.

'So, can you tell me what happened?' Jane asked.

Charlotte sniffed and a tear plopped from her eye on to her bedcovers. She took the tissue her mother offered. 'He was running,' she said, in a barely audible voice. 'And he didn't see the car.'

356

'Running from what?' she asked. 'Was someone chasing him?'

Charlotte nodded.

'From who?'

Charlotte looked at her mother.

'Go on, Charlie,' her mother coaxed. She looked at Jane. 'It might upset you both, the way it happened.'

Jane didn't feel she could be any more upset. 'Just tell me the truth, Charlotte, *please*.' She touched the girl gently on the hand. 'I need to know.'

Just as Charlotte was about to begin, Jim stood up and walked out.

'Jim—' Jane said, but stopped. Refocusing on Charlotte, she said gently, 'Please go on.'

Charlotte nodded. 'OK,' she said softly. 'Owen, well, he was running away from the guy in the off-licence.'

'The off-licence?'

'Yeah. He'd gone in to nick some whiskey.'

Nick? 'Steal?' Jane whispered.

'Yeah.'

Owen stealing? No. No, it couldn't be true. She stared blankly at the girl, unable to say anything.

'He only does it now and again,' Charlotte went on. 'For a buzz, he says. He normally takes crisps and once he took a pair of trainers, but he's not bad. He only does it for the buzz and tonight he wanted a buzz.'

'Buzz?'

Charlotte nodded. 'Yeah. To get a buzz he does mad stuff like climb really high trees and nick things.'

It seemed to Jane that she was about to fold in on herself. 'And he stole the whiskey?' she whispered.

Charlotte nodded. 'Yeah, but you see, the guy in there had chased Owen before, over some crisps, and, I guess he must have spotted him tonight, because when Owen took the whiskey, the guy chased him and then . . .' Charlotte gulped, 'and then . . .' she couldn't say it. Her voice wouldn't let her.

357

'It's OK.' Jane reached out and patted her hand. 'It's OK.'

Charlotte began to cry. Her mother pulled her into an embrace and she cried harder. 'He was my friend,' she sobbed. 'My friend.'

'He *is* your friend,' Jane said firmly. 'Is.'

Sheila left the room. There was no need for her to be there. There *was* a need for Jim, however, and there was no way he was going to leave her daughter to do all the worrying alone.

It was hard, traipsing the slippery corridors in high heels and a tight velvet dress which was ripped at the seams. Her hair was coming undone too, and wisps of it hung like cheap thread down the sides of her face. But that paled in comparison to the rage she felt building inside her. From the moment she'd set eyes on Jim McCarthy, Sheila had disliked him. She'd been right then and she was going to be right again. Well, to hell with it, things had gone far enough.

She spotted Jim, his forehead pressed against the cool wall tiles. He was standing beside the coffee machine though Sheila didn't think he'd even got himself a drink. 'So this is where you've got to, is it?' she asked archly. 'You've abandoned my daughter yet again to press your head against the wall.'

'Sheila, don't start.'

'I haven't. Yet.' Sheila gave him a poke. 'What do you think you're playing at? My Jane is up there, devastated, and what do you do? Walk off as if it's no concern of yours.'

'I said, don't bloody start!'

'Well, you did it to her before and there's no way you are doing it again. Pull yourself together and be a man for a change.'

Jim turned around. The bleak look in his eyes made her half-sorry she'd been so harsh.

'You let her down over Matt—'

'Don't talk about Matt, *please.*'

Sheila paused. 'Sorry,' she said softly. 'I know it hurts.'

Jim squeezed his eyes tight shut and turned away.

358

'But Jim, Jane needs you now. You have to be there for her.'

Jim said nothing for ages. He rubbed his hands over his face and Sheila felt like shaking him. However bad Declan was, he certainly knew how to cope in a crisis. He'd driven her and Di to the hospital and then he'd taken Di home because she was so upset.

'Jim?' she said again.

'I dunno what to do,' he said dazedly. 'I dunno what she wants of me.'

Sheila was tempted to tell him to do the opposite of what he'd done the last time, but she held it back. 'Just be there. Don't leave her on her own.'

'But she wants to know things and I don't.'

'Jim,' Sheila said, 'you don't have to listen, you don't have to talk. All you have to do is *be there*.' She waited for a reaction. 'Now, I'm going back to the house to see if Di is feeling strong enough to come in now. For your own good, Jim, go to Jane.'

'And she'd want that?'

She'd known he was stupid from the minute she'd met him. A crisp man, how are you? '*Yes*, she'd want that.'

Jane thought it was her mother returning and she didn't even look as the person walked into the room. It was only after Charlotte was taken home by her parents that she turned around and saw Jim sitting beside her.

So he'd come back.

She wondered how long it would last.

# 56

JANE DIDN'T THINK she'd ever been so aware of time as on that night. It had the slow, sluggish quality of a nightmare. Everything she did seemed steeped in a million moves, a million little details and throughout it all, there was a sickness in her heart and a granite-faced stranger by her side. Jim hadn't said much at all. He'd asked her if she wanted coffee and she'd wanted to tell him that no, she wanted her son to be bloody all right, but instead she'd nodded and he'd got up and taken ages to come back. The coffee had now grown cold and she spent her time staring into it.

Jim walked to the window, walked back. Walked to the window, walked back. If he didn't stop soon, she was going to scream. All that fucking endless movement and the loneliness of him being there. It would have been better if he'd done what he'd done before – just bloody fucked off for a week.

He began to walk to the window again and Jane gritted her teeth, it was not the time for an argument. As he walked back towards her, she surprised both of them by flinging her cup of cold coffee at him. It hit his shirt and dripped down the front of his jeans.

God, it had felt good.

Jim stared at the stain as it spread over the crotch of his jeans. 'What did you do that for?' He sounded more bewildered than annoyed.

'I did it because you are fucking pissing me off.' The words forced themselves from her. She could hardly talk, she was clenching her teeth so tight. 'All you can fucking do is walk and bloody walk and meanwhile our son, our son—'

'And what the hell am I meant to do?' Again he sounded bewildered, though at the mention of Owen, she noticed him flinch.

'Forget it.' Jane turned away and picked up the coffee cup from the floor.

'No. No, I mean it,' Jim said savagely. 'What *would* you like me to do? Make him better? I can't do that! In fact, I can't seem to do anything right, can I?'

'Oh, bring out the violins!'

It was as if she'd slapped him. He seemed to snap out of whatever mood he'd been in. Making a grab for his jacket, he haphazardly started shoving his arms into the sleeves.

'Jaysus, I'm going. I can't take this any more.'

'Yeah, go on. Leave me like you did when Matt died.'

'Don't say that – I didn't leave you.' He poked his face nearer hers, 'I *didn't* leave you.'

'You just couldn't bear to be with me, could you?'

'That's not—'

'You went away for a week after the funeral. What do you call that – huh?'

'But I came back,' he said. 'I came back.'

'No you didn't,' Jane said bitterly, the hurt of that time filling her up. 'You never came back.'

Jim opened his mouth to say something then, defeated, he turned away from her and left.

He walked and walked and walked. Clear of the hospital, he kept going. Somehow, he thought that if he walked far enough, he could leave his thoughts behind. But it didn't work. His whole rotten life paraded itself in his head. The dazzling, shining, eleven years of bliss with Jane outdone by the early stuff and the later stuff.

Eventually, Jim stopped. He didn't know where he was exactly, but he knew it wasn't where he should be. The only problem was, he didn't know where he should be. With Matt, he hadn't been able to handle anything, not the way Jane cried, or the way the kids had been, or the way he'd felt himself.

But what he'd done then hadn't worked.

He thought that no matter what he did, things couldn't get much worse.

'Now, here you are.' Sheila placed a cup of tea in front of Di.

'How is he?' Declan asked. 'Did you see him?'

Sheila glanced at Di, then, knowing that the child wasn't stupid, said, 'He's . . . he's comfortable.'

Di sniffed.

'And Jane?' Declan asked. 'How's she bearing up? Is Jim with her?'

Sheila nodded. 'For the moment,' she muttered disapprovingly. 'However long that lasts.'

Di glanced at Sheila. She didn't want to hear her giving out about her dad like that. But maybe if her dad hadn't done what he did, things might have been different. After Matt's funeral he'd left for a week and no one had known where he was. When he came back things had changed, no one talked to anyone any more and no one mentioned Matt. She wondered if Owen died would they just forget about him too? Would she have to remember him all on her own again? She'd be the only kid left and she'd be on her own. There'd be no Owen to tease and—

'Hey, hey,' a warm arm was wrapped around her. The smell of smoke enveloped her. 'Don't cry.' Her granddad shook her affectionately. 'Your Owen, he'll be fine, he's a fighter, so he is. He bleedin' takes after his granddad, so he does.'

Di wiped her face. She didn't want to cry in front of them. A lace handkerchief was pushed towards her. Her nana's. Di thought of all the times Sheila had blown her nose in it and it took every ounce of courage she had to dab it on her eyes.

'Owen's far *better* than your granddad, dahling,' Sheila said smartly. 'Don't let him scare you – it's bad enough that he has his arm around you.'

Di managed a smile. The two of them were getting on famously, bitching and backbiting. 'I don't mind his arm – it's fine,' she said.

'And your brother will be fine too.' Her granddad cuddled her. 'Jesus, it's nice to have a young wan to cuddle,' he said. 'Your mother would never let me near her. Like a porcupine, she was – all spikes and bristles. Born with a pole up her arse, just like her mother.'

'I'll shove a pole up your arse if you don't stop it,' Sheila bantered back. She poured more tea into Di's cup. 'Now, I've put sugar in it, don't worry – it won't ruin your skin or any-thing – but it's good for shock. I know you want to look well for that creature you're seeing.' She turned to Declan. 'He's an unusual boy. His name is Gooey. Jane isn't keen on him at all.'

'Neither am I, any more.' Di wiped her eyes again. She was not going to cry over Gooey, not when Owen was so sick in hospital. 'It's . . .' she blinked rapidly. 'It's off.'

'Oh.' Sheila didn't know what to say to that. 'Oh dear.'

'And I'm not upset over it.' Di tossed her head. Her voice was a bit wobbly as she added, 'Not a bit.'

'That's the spirit, dahling.' Sheila smiled proudly at her. 'No man matters enough to cry over. Like the worms they are, they all come crawling back in the end.'

'Yeah. Look at me,' Declan said, without a trace of embar-rassment. 'Didn't I come crawling back? And your mother can vouch for how many times I've done it in the past. He'll come back or else he's a fool.'

'You stay strong, my girl,' Sheila went on, 'keep yourself looking well and don't show him you care. That's the secret for a contented life.'

'Really?' Di asked.

Sheila nodded. 'Now, if your mother would only take some

of that advice, Jim would have come back long ago. But that's Jane all over – never tries to impress anyone. Slobs about—'

The shrill ringing of the phone shattered whatever else she had to say.

'He's still stable, the doctor's just finished letting me know,' Jane said. 'It means that he hasn't got any worse, which apparently is a good sign.'

The reaction to the news was celebratory. They couldn't have been more excited if they'd won the lotto. Jane hadn't meant to get their hopes up like that and when a tearful Di came on the phone, she felt that she had to bring things back down to earth.

'There's a long way to go,' she said.

'Can I come in?' Di asked, ignoring her. 'I promise I won't get upset. I'd like to see him.'

There was no way Di could come, Jane thought, not with Jim missing. Jesus, she hated Jim for this. 'Tomorrow Di,' she said. 'It's not as if you can see him now anyway.' Then before Di could say any more, she said, 'I'll have to go. I'll ring later on.'

Putting down the receiver, she walked back up to ICU and stared in at Owen, still as frozen snow. If anything happened to him, it'd be her fault. He'd been too quiet, she should have known, but because it suited her, she'd ignored all the signs. What kid bunked school unless there was something up? And Jim had told her he was drunk. He'd even asked her if Owen was a bit down. As for the things that Charlotte said he'd done . . .

She was a hopeless mother. If only she could turn the clock back . . . if she could borrow back some time. If she could just have another chance. Just one more chance. She wouldn't mess it up this time. When Matt had been in this position, she'd wondered how it could have happened to her. How could her lovely life be ruined so much? Why had it happened to her and Jim?

Worst of all was the irreversible nature of it. The suddenness. The shock. It was like being told by a very stern parent, 'that's that, now get on with it'. And getting on with things after her precious child had disappeared out of her life had been so hard. Too hard to explain with words, with tears, though she had cried, but she could have cried twenty-four hours every day for the rest of her life and it still wouldn't have filled the empty space inside her.

Now, looking at Owen, she knew that even with Matt gone, she *had* been lucky. So bloody lucky. She had two kids that she loved. If only she'd seen it like that . . . Please, she grovelled with any God that existed, I won't mess up this time. Just another chance . . .

She was vaguely aware of someone standing beside her.

The someone said, 'I was looking all over the place for you. How is he?'

Even when he'd first asked her out in the sunshine days of her youth, it didn't compare with her relief at having him with her at that moment.

'I'm glad you came back,' she said simply.

He managed a half-smile and together they turned to look at their son.

## 57

SHEILA FOUND THEM together in the waiting room the next morning. Jane, her head on Jim's shoulder, was fast asleep. Jim was trying to drink a coffee without waking her.

Unable to help the sarcasm, Sheila asked, 'So you stayed, did you?'

Jim just flicked her a look that said he wasn't going to get involved in her pettiness.

Sheila tried not to flinch. He was right of course, it wasn't the time for any of that. She tried again, 'Any news?'

'He's stable,' Jim answered. 'The doc said that he had a good night and it's a case of wait and see. We can go in to him in a while.' He looked at Jane and the tenderness in his face caught Sheila by surprise. 'She's only just fallen asleep,' he said. 'She was pacing the floor all night. The minute she sat down, she conked out.'

'Poor dahling.' Sheila patted Jane on the wrist and she sat bolt upright.

'What's wrong? Any news?'

'Jesus!' Jim glared at Sheila. 'What did I just say? She'd only just fallen—'

'I'm sorry. I didn't know I wasn't allowed to *touch* my own daughter.' She turned to Jane, ignoring another 'Jesus' from her son-in-law. 'I patted your wrist, dahling, and you woke up.'

Jane rubbed her eyes and yawned. 'I didn't want to sleep anyhow.' She shot Jim an accusatory look. 'I told you that!'

'What harm is a bit of sleep?'

'I told you I didn't want to.'

'Men, they never do what they're told.' Sheila smiled up at Jim who'd stood up and was now scowling at them. 'Any chance of a coffee Jim? I want to talk to Jane.' Dismissing him, she added a 'thanks'.

'Jane?' Jim asked sourly, 'do you want a coffee?'

'Yeah. A strong one.'

Jim dumped his coffee cup down and left the room.

Sheila embraced Jane awkwardly. She wasn't into hugging or holding, mainly because it tended to crease linen suits, but in these circumstances she knew that Jane needed all the hugs she could get. 'How are you, dahling?'

'OK.'

Sheila glanced at Jim's retreating back. 'Is he,' she said the 'he' as if Jim were something that had just evolved from the swamp, 'minding you all right?'

Jane nodded. There was no point in giving her mother more ammunition. 'A bit shaky at first, but he's doing his best. He finds it hard, Mam.'

'And you don't?' Sheila scoffed.

'Yes, but that's just Jim, it's the way he is.'

'Abnormal,' Sheila confirmed. 'What man runs away from his own son's funeral?'

Not this again. Jane sighed wearily, the last thing she needed, today of all days, was her mother bitching about Jim. 'He was devastated, Mam. You saw the way he was. I don't think he was thinking straight.'

Sheila felt like saying that in her opinion, Jim had never thought straight, except of course when he'd married Jane. But she didn't. Instead she changed the subject. 'Your father wants me to move back,' she said. 'I told him I'd think about it.'

In ordinary circumstances, Jane would have been ecstatic, but now it didn't seem to matter that much. 'Good,' she nodded. She wondered when the doctor was going to come. He'd said last night that he'd be around first thing. Well 'first thing' had been and gone. She glanced quickly down the corridor.

'And I'm keeping my job,' Sheila went on, studying her nails and tut-tutting at one that had chipped. 'I quite like work actually.'

There was a doctor coming towards them.

Sheila fell silent, but the doctor walked on, obviously on his way to someone else.

'Jesus,' Jane muttered.

Sheila patted her hand.

After a second or two, she said, 'By the way, just to warn you, Di is coming in later. She insisted.'

'OK.'

'And she's a bit delicate. Neanderthal man is off the scene.'

'Oh?' Well at least that was some good news.

'She's very upset, though she's being very brave about it. Won't tell anyone what's happened, but I'd say she's the one that got dumped.'

Poor Di. Jane wished she was there so she could comfort her. It was no fun being dumped.

Her two beautiful kids, one in hospital, the other at home crying her heart out, and where had she been? Out enjoying herself.

She felt terrible.

She didn't deserve a second chance.

But God . . . didn't that mean she needed it even more?

They were let in to see Owen that afternoon. 'Two people only,' the doctor said.

Jim looked at Di, who'd just arrived. 'You go in,' he said. 'I was in last night.'

Jane said nothing. Jim was drinking coffee constantly and had become edgy. The hospital was slowly driving him mad. The strain of waiting for news was killing him. He was coping, but only just. And the only just was for her sake. She didn't want to push him any further.

'Come on, Di,' she said. 'It's not as scary as it looks.'

To her surprise, Di took her hand and together they walked into the room. Owen looked exactly the same as he had done the previous night, he was still pale, though Jane didn't know if it was wishful thinking or not, but his face didn't look quite as white.

'Can I touch him?' Di asked.

'Yeah, take his hand,' Jane whispered. 'The doctor said we can talk to him. Just say "hi" or something.'

'Hi, Ownie.' Di pressed her brother's hand and told herself not to start crying. 'It's me – Di.' She felt a bit weird talking to him like this, but she'd seen a programme where a girl had talked to her brother and her brother had woken up.

'I just want to tell you that what I said that night, the night I was drunk, well, it was true.' She hoped he knew it was when she'd told him she loved him. 'And also, Ownie, please don't leave me on my own – sure you won't?' The last part came out in a sob.

The next thing she knew, her mother's arms were around her shoulders. It felt nice. 'My poor baby,' her mother rubbed her back. 'Don't say that.'

'Oh, Mam,' Di sniffed and knew snot was going to run out of her nose and go everywhere. 'Oh, Mam.'

Holding each other tight, they walked out of ICU and past Jim, Sheila and Declan.

'What's the matter?' Jim caught up with them as they reached the empty coffee room. He looked at Jane over the top of Di's head. 'Did she get upset?'

What an idiotic question; Jane glared in exasperation at her husband. Jesus, if he'd been man enough to go into the room and see his son, this would never have happened.

'Sit down Di,' she said gently, prying the sobbing teenager away from her. 'I'll get you a coffee.'

'I'll get it,' Jim offered, digging in his pockets for some change.

'You stay with Di.' He went across to the machine and began shoving coins into it.

Jane continued to rub Di's back as Jim crossed towards them with the coffees. He placed Di's on the table beside her. Looking uncomfortable, he muttered, 'Di, there's a drink there for you if you want it.'

'No. No, I'm fine.'

'You're not fine,' he said gently. 'You're upset. But it looks worse than it is. Maybe you shouldn't have gone in to see him.'

'And who *told* her to go in?' Jane asked, before she could help herself. At least that was one thing he couldn't blame her for.

'Yeah, I know,' Jim said ruefully, seemingly unaware of her anger. He ruffled Di's hair. 'But I thought she was able to cope with it.'

'Like you are, you mean?' Jesus, she couldn't help it. There was a slow rage building up inside and if she didn't let it out, she was going to explode. The stunned look on Jim's face only infuriated her further. 'You'd rather subject Di to it than go in yourself. You really are hopeless, do you know that?'

Jim slapped his styrofoam cup down and hot coffee slopped out over his hand, burning his fingers. 'And you are such an expert in reminding me, aren't you? You and your stuck arse mother.'

'A stuck arse? Wow! A new word!'

'STOP IT!' Di stood up, tears running down all over her face and plopping from her chin on to the floor. 'Just stop! You both make me sick! Sick!'

'Di—' Jane attempted to touch her, but she pulled away.

'You are always angry at Dad, Mam. And you,' she shot a look at Jim, 'are just useless. Owen is sick and all you can do is fight. Huh, if he dies, you'll probably forget about him the way you did with Matt.'

'What?' Jim paled.

'You won't talk about Matt. *You*,' she turned venomous eyes on Jim, who visibly flinched, 'you didn't even *cry* when he died.

370

And now it's Owen's turn and I'm not going to forget about him. You can fight all you like, but I'll remember him.'

'Aw, Jesus, Di—' Jim looked helplessly at Jane.

'And I'm sorry that you had to get married because of me, I know you both probably hate me for ruining your lives.'

'Di!' Jane stared at her, appalled.

'Gooey was right, you know,' Di sniffed. 'He said I only went out with him to annoy you, and it's true, I did. You only notice things that annoy you, Mam.'

*Which was why she'd never noticed anything wrong with Owen.*

Jane closed her eyes. What Di said was true.

'You two are so wrapped up in being miserable that you don't care about me or Owen.'

'That's not true,' Jane gulped. 'We care so much. We do. Honestly.'

Di said nothing. She just gulped and scrubbed her eyes with her hand.

'I always worry about you,' Jane whispered. 'Always. When you're out late, I worry. When we fight, I worry. Wasn't I worried when you came home drunk? And I'm worried now.'

'Gooey used to tell me he loved me,' Di cut across her, 'and it was nice.'

'But *we* love you too,' Jane said desperately, making a move towards her. 'Don't we Jim?'

He blinked hard, then gulped. 'Yeah. Of course.'

Di backed away from both of them.

'You and Owen and Matt were the best things to happen to us,' Jane said. She stood in front of Di, not knowing whether to touch her. 'Me and your dad,' she said softly, 'we loved you all so much. If we didn't, we wouldn't be so upset now.'

'And it's because we're upset, we're fighting,' Jim said. 'Isn't that right?' He looked to Jane for support.

'Yep.'

Di's body sagged as she looked from one to the other. 'So why don't we ever talk about Matt?' she asked.

371

Jim gazed at his shoes and bit his lip.

Jane wanted to shake him. Why couldn't he just say how he felt? As usual he was leaving it up to her. Oh, she'd wanted to talk about Matt – wanted to talk about him to anyone who'd listen. But the person who'd mattered most to her, the person who she'd wanted to talk to the most about him hadn't been able to handle the memories. So she'd choked it all back.

'When he died,' Jane began, 'it broke our hearts. And when things break, it's hard to mend them again, Di. Things like this leave you changed, because the bits get rearranged in a different way.' Jim slowly brought his eyes to meet hers and she turned to Di. 'But if it upsets you so much – I'll try. Honestly I will.'

'We'll both try,' Jim promised softly.

It hurt her heart to hear him say that.

His words seemed to do the trick. Di gave a watery smile.

Maybe a better relationship with her daughter was what she'd have to settle for out of this whole mess, Jane thought. She held out her arms. 'Come here.'

Di fell into them and Jane thought of how good it was to hold her daughter so close. She gave Jim a half-hearted, apologetic smile and he returned it despondently.

# 58

PATRICK ARRIVED ON the third day. He handed her a huge 'get well' card and a basket of fruit. Seeing him was so comforting. He enfolded her in a tight hug. 'You poor, poor thing,' he kept muttering as he rubbed her back. 'You poor, poor thing.'

She hadn't been able to cry. It was as if all her emotions were frozen. It was better that way, because she couldn't have kept going otherwise.

Jim, after some polite conversation, wandered off and left them on their own. He wasn't into talking to visitors. Even when some of his mates from work had arrived, he'd been unable to say very much. Jane took Patrick down to the canteen and bought him a coffee. It seemed that she'd done nothing but drink the bloody stuff for the past few days. Patrick looked great, full of the joys of life. He was like some kind of exotic bird in the general gloom of the hospital canteen.

'So,' he leant across the table, giving her the full benefit of his acrid aftershave, 'how are you coping?'

Jane shrugged. 'We're coping. Just doing what has to be done, you know?'

There was silence.

She didn't want to talk about it, didn't want to voice her fears. Instead, she sought for another subject. 'Hey, how'd we do in the IHFs?'

Patrick waved his arm around. 'Oh, you don't want to talk about that now,' he said dismissively.

373

'I guess that means we didn't win?'

'Second.'

Second was good. Well, it would have been good if they hadn't so desperately wanted to beat Cutting Edge. 'Second?' She tried to look pleased.

Patrick had a grin the size of America on his face. With a sort of squeal, he said, 'And Cutting Edge got *third*!'

'*No!*' She laughed for the first time in days. 'No!'

'Pete Jordan was disgusted. He was disgusted!' Patrick chanted loudly, making people look at him. 'He came over to us at the end and said that we'd only come second because Rosemary had good hair to begin with. He tried to make it sound like a compliment, but d'you know what Rosemary said?'

'What?' She found it hard not to smile at his enthusiasm.

'She said, right.' Patrick straightened up in his chair and squinted his eyes in the way Rosemary did, causing Jane to giggle. 'She said, "I suppose your model had good hair to begin with too, Mr Jordan. It's kind of hard to tell now!"'

'No!'

'Uh-huh. Then he stomped off, after saying that we were the most ignorant crowd he's ever come across.'

'Great.'

Patrick grinned, pleased to have made her smile. 'So,' he continued, 'we got loads of photos of Rosemary for the window and, eh, well, Barney said that it might be nice to do a few bill-boards.' Before Jane could protest, he held up his hand, 'It won't be expensive and besides, we're doing so well now. You wouldn't believe it Jane, the posters and the fact that your dad was in has them flocking to the place. We need to keep the ball rolling. Cutting Edge has been the best thing to ever happen to us.' He beamed delightedly at her. 'There's always a silver lining.'

She wished she could believe that.

'Oh, by the way,' Patrick reached into a plastic bag and pulled

374

out a pile of envelopes. 'A lot of our regulars have dropped in cards for you.' He pushed them across the table to her.

Jane stared at the pile and touched them. 'Tell them thanks very much,' she said softly.

'I already did.' Patrick reached out and clasped her hand.

Jane laid her free hand on top of his and never wanted him to let go.

Jim arrived back at five. He'd showered and shaved and still didn't look any better for it. 'Sorry I was so long,' he said, 'but there was stuff I had to take care of.'

Bloody work.

Jane made no comment.

'You can head home if you like. I'll be here. I'll ring you if anything happens.'

There was no way she was going home. And his assumption that she would angered her. 'You only want me to go because your fancy piece is probably coming in,' she said, glaring at him. 'I know the way your mind works, Jim.'

He looked hurt and she knew she'd been way off the mark.

'I want you to go home because you need a break, Jane.' He raked his hands through his hair. 'You've been here three days now, you need a decent wash and a sleep. Your mother wants you to go with her. She's waiting in reception for you.'

Jane bowed her head. 'Sorry.'

'Don't be.' He poked her with his finger, then stopped suddenly. 'And it's off with Debbie, if you must know, so she won't be calling in.'

'Oh.'

There was a pause.

'Sorry.'

'Don't be.' His eyes met hers. 'Don't be,' he said again, softly. He held her gaze for a few seconds and then indicated his mobile. 'I'll ring you, OK?'

'OK.'

Jane didn't know who initiated it first, but suddenly she was in his arms and he was holding her fiercely.

There was no need to say anything.

# 59

THERE WERE NOISES coming from somewhere, weird noises that seemed vaguely familiar and yet hard to place. They sounded like . . . it flitted away again before he could catch it. There was a lot of darkness around him, and pain. A kind of deep pain, like an army marching on his brain. He felt the pain seep down into him, like water on sand. Through the pain he felt his neck and shoulders and hands. His stomach and hips and legs. It was as if he was sliding slowly into his body, visiting it after a long time, and he couldn't quite fit any more.

Light seemed to be filtering into his head, filling the darkness and frightening it away. The sounds seemed to be getting louder.

There was a pressure on his hand.

A voice.

He tried to catch what the voice was saying – he could make out words, but there were too many. It was hard to make sense of them. He just let the words pour over him like light rain. Refreshing him. The voice was lilting and soft. His hand was pressed again.

Slowly, he moved his head towards the sweetness of the voice and a buzzing sound, coupled with shouts, disorientated him.

It might be safer to stay where he was.

'He moved his head!' Jane said to the doctor. 'I was telling him about work and he moved his head.' She watched anxiously as the doctor peered at read-outs and stuff that she couldn't understand.

'Are you sure?' he asked. He flipped open his chart, wrote notes, then replaced the chart at the end of the bed.

'Of course I'm sure.' Jane didn't know whether to celebrate or kick herself. 'He moved it very slightly, but it was a movement.'

'Well, he does seem to have settled down a lot.' The doctor kept his voice cautious. 'Just keep talking to him, if he did it once, he'll do it again.' He touched Jane. 'It's a good sign, the earlier he responds, the more chance he's got of making a full recovery.'

As he left the room, Jane felt her heart sink. Somehow, she'd expected more. She'd hoped that this was it, that Owen would be fine. But they never told you anything.

Once more, she took Owen's hand and began talking.

Jim, coming back from the canteen, met the doctor in the corridor.

'Your wife thinks Owen might have moved his head,' the doctor told him.

'Yeah?' He was too numb to take it in. If he didn't get out of here, he'd crack up.

The doctor put a hand on his shoulder. Very gently, he pulled him aside. 'If I were you,' he advised, 'I'd get into that room while I still have the chance. If that boy wakes up and you're not there, well . . .' He shrugged. 'Women find it hard, things like that. Take it from me, I've seen it happen a lot.'

Jim looked after the doctor. How the hell did he know what their relationship was like? But maybe he was right, maybe he should go in and just sit there.

The thought terrified him.

Jane looked up as Jim came in. He sort of edged around the door and walked towards the bed as if there were needles on the floor.

'His head moved,' she said.

Jim nodded. He took a seat on the opposite side of the bed.

'Talk to him,' Jane said. 'He might want to hear your voice.'

Jim shook his head. What could he say?

'*Please* Jim,' she said. 'Just a "hi" or something? He might be waiting to hear your voice.'

Yeah, like the way Matt had been. But they knew Matt was dying that time. There had been no hope, but Owen was alive. He'd moved his head. Jane was looking at him and Jim knew that if he was to salvage anything out of this, he had better talk to his son.

Slowly he took Owen's thin hand. It was lukewarm and felt soft. His heart lunging about in his chest, he whispered, 'Owen, it's me. It's Dad.'

The figure in the bed didn't move.

He remembered holding his mother's hand when she'd died and talking to her just like this. But he'd been a kid then and hadn't really known what death was. He felt sick.

'Owen, I dunno what to say. Just get better.'

Jane started to talk to him then, while Jim continued to hold Owen's hand and listen to his wife talking on and on and on. She told Owen about all the happy things they'd done together. The time they'd gone to the beach and the five of them had gone swimming and lost their way back to their towels. How they had searched for hours for their gear and they'd been freezing. How Matt had stolen someone's towel to wrap around himself and they'd come after him. Jim found himself smiling at the memory, smiling at Jane as she recounted the tale.

He could make out what the voice was saying now. The words had meaning and shape and form. Putting them together built up pictures in his head. Funny pictures that made him smile and want to see the voice. It was as if he was pulling at himself from the centre, from some dark place deep inside. Rising up towards the surface of himself, touching the water and breaking through the surface.

379

Lights and noise.

A face, bending over him.

Another.

Both bewildered. One with tears dripping, tears that touched his own face.

A word, formed in his head, bubbled into being. 'Mam.'

Chaos.

## 60

FRED CAME OVER that night with a bottle of champagne. Jim let him in and took two glasses down from the press. Running them under the tap, he tried to locate a tea towel. The only one he could find was a rather mouldy one that had been in the press from before Owen had gone into hospital.

'Aw Jaysus,' Fred looked in disgust at the towel. 'Here, give the glasses here.' He took them and rubbed them on his shirt sleeve. 'I dunno, Jimbo, this place needs a woman's touch.'

'I've hardly been in it for the last five weeks,' Jim said. 'Can't bleedin' do everything.'

'And sure it's not as if you'll be here much longer.' Fred poured two generous glasses of champagne.

'Another week and then it's London,' Jim agreed.

'Ummm.' Fred handed Jim his glass. Raising his own in the air, he said, 'To your job and to Clinton and Owen.' Clinton was his baby son's name.

'Job, Clinton and Owen,' Jim said.

'So how is Owen?' Fred asked. 'He came home from hospital today – yeah?'

Jim nodded. 'He's great. He'll recover completely, the doc says. It's a big relief.'

Fred nodded sagely. 'I never really understood how awful it must've been on yez to lose Matt,' he said. 'I guess, being a father meself now, I'd have a better idea.'

Jim didn't answer. He drank some more champagne.

'It makes you see stuff differently, doesn't it, Jimbo?'

'Yeah.' Jim drained his glass and held it out for some more.

'Thanks for making me see how stupid I was being,' Fred said.

'No probs. Any time,' Jim grinned.

Fred didn't smile back. 'And I know this is gonna be completely out of character for me, but, well, Gill has told me to say what's on me mind to you.'

'If it's about Debs—'

'Naw, naw, not about her. She thinks she had a lucky escape. Says you love your wife too much.' Fred paused, as if waiting for a reaction.

'And?'

'Well, do you?'

'She won't have me back,' Jim said into his glass. 'I let her down.'

'What? When?'

He'd never voiced it aloud before, never wanted to admit it. 'The time that Matt died.' He had to force the words out. 'D'you remember, you and me left the funeral and went on a bender for a week?'

'*You* went on a bender,' Fred said. 'I made you go home in the end.'

'Yeah. You told me to get my act together and go home.'

'And you did.'

'Naw,' Jim shook his head. 'I just went home. I don't think I've ever got my act together.'

Fred said nothing.

'Jane needed me and I wasn't there. It was the worst thing ever to happen to us, and I wasn't there.'

'But did you not explain to her? You know, tell her why you did it?'

Jim shrugged. '*I* hardly knew why I'd done it. I'd never have explained it to her.'

Fred put down his glass and said sagely, 'Jim, women like explanations. They need to understand things. I mean, Gill wanted to know why I was so afraid of commitment and I found it hard to explain, but eventually we figured it was because of me ma leaving me when I was a kid.'

'Awww, poor baby,' Jim grinned.

'Fuck off, right?' Fred flushed. 'I'm just saying that women like that shit. You have to tell her something, even if it's just to say you made a mistake. And you did make a mistake, didn't you?'

Who the hell was Fred to be advising him? 'Just forget it.'

'I would if you didn't look so bloody miserable.' Fred poured him another glass of champagne. 'Did you never, ever, ever talk about it?'

Christ, Jim thought, Gillian was having a weird effect on Fred. 'D'you know something, I preferred you before you had that baby.'

Fred laughed and drank some more booze. 'All I'm saying is that it's good to talk,' he said.

'It's too late now.'

'It's never too late. Look at me, I thought Gill would tell me to take a flying fuck out of the hospital and did she? Nope.' He punched Jim on the arm. 'You gotta go for what you want in this life, Jimbo. It's too bloody short. I know that from experience.'

All Jim knew was that it was a night for getting smashed.

Jane pulled a bottle of wine out of the press and, uncorking it, set it on the counter to breathe. It was the first night she'd had to herself in a long time. Owen was safely in bed, fast asleep. He was going to be tired for a long time yet, the doctor had told them. But he was alive and healthy and she didn't care how much hard work lay ahead. Di was out with Libby, and her mother – who had insisted on staying around while Owen was in hospital – had retired to bed. She'd been a revelation, Jane thought, the way she'd looked after Di. OK, so she'd wrecked all their clothes in the hot wash, and anything that had been lucky enough to survive had scorch marks from the iron, but she'd tried.

Di hadn't seen it quite that way and there'd been a bit of a scene, but Jane had promised her new stuff.

Her mother was going home the following day and Jane actually thought that she would miss her.

As she pulled a glass out of the press, the doorbell rang. She wondered who it was, if maybe it was Jim. He'd offered to stay the night to help with Owen, but she'd told him to go. It hurt having him around.

From the frosted glass in the hall door, Jane made out the silhouette of a woman. Maybe it was one of the neighbours, they'd been so good to her these last few weeks. It'd be nice to share the wine with someone.

She unlocked the door and was startled to see Mir standing on the doorstep. Her surprise must have shown in her face because Mir began to back away. 'If this is a bad time,' she began, 'I'm sorry, I can—'

'No, no, it's not. Come in.' Hastily, she opened the door wider. 'Please.'

'Sure?' Miranda looked questioningly at her. She was terrified, Jane could see it in the way she kept fidgeting with her hands. Mir had never been like that in all the years she'd known her.

'Of course I am,' Jane said in a softer voice. 'It's great to see you.'

Mir stepped into the hallway. Holding a bag out to Jane, she said shyly, 'For Owen. I heard he came home.'

'Thanks.' Jane smiled at her. 'Today.'

They stood looking at each other.

Breaking the silence, Mir said, 'I rang you at the salon the day after the competition to see how you'd done, a sort of peace offering, and Patrick told me about Owen. I didn't want to come any earlier.' She paused. 'I thought you'd have enough on your plate.' She stared at a point over Jane's shoulder.

'I'd have loved to have seen you earlier,' Jane said quietly.

Mir brought her eyes to meet Jane's. To her surprise, Mir's eyes were glistening. 'I've been such a bitch, Jane. I know I have. I'm sorry.'

'No.' Jane shook her head.

'Yeah.' Mir brought her hands to her face and hastily scrubbed some tears away. 'Well, that's all I came for.' Her voice broke and she made fumbling motions for the door.

Jane reached out and touched her. 'Don't go. Not yet. Look, I've a bottle of wine open. Stay and have some.'

'You don't want me.' Mir's hand slipped on the door lock.

'True. But I reckon you're the best I'll get tonight.'

As Mir spun around to see if she was serious, Jane gave a hesitant smile. 'Come on,' she began to walk to the kitchen.

Her eyes strayed to a photo of Matt that Di had put on the hall table. Life was too short for fights. Way too short.


Fred showed Jim snapshots of his son before he left.

The pictures seemed to mock him, Jim thought. Fred's happy smiling family. Gillian, looking radiant, holding by turns the 'cleverest', the 'strongest', the 'most gorgeous' son in the world.

'Who ever thought that a kid could be so interesting, huh, Jimbo?' Fred kept saying. 'We're getting a video camera next week. Nothing like live action, I say.'

Jim smiled, remembering how many pictures they'd taken of Di when she was born. They hadn't taken as many of Owen. And as for Matt – they were lucky to have a baby picture of him. If only they'd known . . .

'Anyway, have ta go,' Fred broke into his thoughts. Tucking his pictures into his jacket, he zipped it up. 'I'll call around soon, we'll head out for a few jars before you go – huh?'

'Sure.'

Jim watched as Fred, with half a bottle of champagne and three cans inside him, made unsteady progress down the hall. Jesus, he envied him starting out on a whole new life. Looking

385

at his suitcases, which he'd bought for his move to London, he guessed that he'd be starting out on a new life too.

'I hit rock bottom when Harry told me he didn't want to be my friend,' Mir said, downing her glass of wine in one gulp.

Jane refilled it. 'He didn't mean it, though,' she said, her mind going back to the last time she'd seen Harry, staring dejectedly into his pint.

'He did.' Mir gave a bitter laugh. 'Serves me right too. I treated him like dirt. I always have. Serves me right.'

'What happened?'

There was a slight pause before Mir said, 'The day after you called, I went around to his place – just for a few beers, as I'd nothing else to do – and he told me that he was going out and he didn't want to see me. So I called the next day and the next day and it was the same thing every time. Eventually I snapped. I mean, you were gone, Pat was gone and I was losing him too, Jane. I did a complete psycho on it. I started yelling at Harry, through his letter box, telling him that he was a prick for not seeing me.'

'You didn't!' Jane could just imagine it. A small grin curled her mouth.

Mir smiled uncomfortably and said sheepishly, 'Yeah, well, it has always worked before. He'd usually be on bended knees the minute I'd raise my voice. This time though, he opened the door and he gave me a look that would have stopped two rabbits shagging.'

Jane grinned, despite Mir's doleful tone.

'He said, right, that he wasn't as much of a prick as I was a cold selfish bitch.'

'That was awful!'

'No, it was true.' Mir shook her head and managed a watery grin. 'He told me that I was always blaming someone else for the way I acted. He said that maybe if I grew up, I'd realise that. He said that I, well, that I was a slapper.'

Jane handed her a piece of kitchen paper.

'Thanks.' Mir dabbed her face. Looking at Jane, she whispered, 'He was right. I mean, I picked up every shithead in Dublin 'cause I think, well, I think I felt superior to them or maybe, I dunno, maybe I felt I didn't deserve much better.'

'But you do.'

'I know,' Mir gulped, 'and I didn't realise it until it was too late.'

'That's when most of us realise things,' Jane said softly. 'You don't have to tell me all this, you know.'

'I do, I owe it to you. I said some awful things to you, and then when Pat rang I really went to town on him. Called him all sorts.'

'Nothing he hasn't heard before.'

'Yeah. Well . . .' Mir took a gulp of wine and when her voice was slightly stronger, went on, 'When I finally realised that I'd lost Harry, I understood how bloody lucky I'd been all along. It was that simple. I had a job, friends, a nice place. But I just wasn't happy with that. I dunno why. I've always wanted more. I wanted the husband, the kids, anything I hadn't got. Guess that's why I picked up the dregs, they were the excuse for my life not being the way it should have been.'

'What?'

'Well, I guess if I never made the effort, I could still have my dreams, you know?'

Jane nodded slowly. 'You didn't want to fail.'

'Yep. But I failed anyhow. I think that's why Rosemary got up my nose so much, she was so enthusiastic and ambitious and bloody *happy*. I used to think, Jesus, how can anyone be happy looking like her?'

Jane grinned, despite herself.

'But she's happy because she's trying,' Mir said. Then added wryly, 'Very trying.'

Jane laughed.

'I'm only joking,' Mir said.

387

'You haven't failed, you know.' Jane poured her some more wine. 'You're here, aren't you? You've still got me. And I know Pat will have you back like a shot at the salon. He's only got a temp until the end of the week. All you've got to do is ask.'

'I've never been much good at asking for things.'

'And then you trot around to Harry and apologise. Get down on your knees and yell through his letter box.'

'Oh, I couldn't.'

'You have to go for what you want, Mir. At least you can always say you tried.'

And it was true, Jane realised. It was better to try to fix things than ignore them.

Jim switched off his mobile and grinned. The billboard posters were being delivered on Tuesday. When Jane saw the photos she was sure to guess. Maybe, just maybe she might give him a second chance. There'd be no need for any talk then.

It was the first time in months he felt he'd done something right.

In bed that night, Jane felt calmer than she had in months. Mir coming around had made her see that maybe if you faced things head on they could be sorted out. It gave her the courage to face something else she'd been putting off these last few weeks.

# 61

S HE CHOSE A time when there was little chance of them being disturbed. Di was at school and her mother was packing her thousands of belongings in readiness for going home.

Owen was watching the telly, sitting on the sofa with a duvet thrown over him. He'd lost weight in hospital and his once handsome face looked pinched and old. His black eyes seemed to have sunk deep into their sockets and there was a scar on his forehead where his head had hit the road. Jane's heart twisted as she looked in at him.

She laid a glass of orange juice on the table beside him.

'Ta.' He gave her a smile.

Her hands clammy, Jane sat at the end of the sofa and took Owen's feet on to her lap. She began, absently, to rub his toes. 'Owen,' she said casually, though her heart was pounding, 'can I ask you something?'

His gaze flitted from the telly and rested on her. His eyes were wary. 'What?'

'Why did you steal from the off-licence?'

Owen jerked. 'Dunno.' His gaze returned to the telly, but he wasn't really watching it. He pulled his feet from her grasp and picked up his orange juice. 'Dunno,' he repeated.

'Did it give you a . . .' Jane sought for the word Charlotte had used, 'buzz?'

Owen didn't answer. His profile gave nothing away.

389

'Please, Owen, tell me. I need to understand – don't you see?' When he still made no reply, she got up and stood in front of him. 'Just tell me why you did it – please?'

Nothing.

And then, from way back, she remembered something he'd said about why he'd bunked off school. Hunkering down, so that he could see only her face and not the TV screen, she asked softly, 'Is it to do with Matt?'

His brother's name sparked something. Owen screwed his eyes up and shook his head. 'Ma, please—'

'Owen, you've got to tell me. I'm going out of my mind here. It's not like you to steal stuff.'

Owen bit his lip. He stared her in the face. 'Yeah, yeah it is, Ma. I've been doing it for ages. I've stolen drink from you, sweets and crisps and drink and fags from shops.'

'No!'

'Yeah.'

'Why?'

He looked dejectedly at her. 'The buzz. The high. Makes me feel . . .' he took a breath, '. . . alive.'

Jane didn't understand. 'Alive?' she repeated.

Owen nodded and stared over her shoulder to the wall beyond. 'Ever since Matt,' he began haltingly, 'ever since he died I've been scared. So scared.'

'Scared?' Jane could only stare dumbly at him.

'Yeah. Like he got up that day and ate his breakfast and then by lunchtime he was dead. How did he not know, Ma? How did he not know that he was going to die?'

'Aw, Owen—'

'It's such a *big* thing Ma.'

'I know.'

They gazed at each other. Owen broke the silence. 'And after that, Ma, well, nothing seemed to make sense any more. I mean, I could die any time. And, well, I dunno, I just couldn't take anything seriously. And not taking stuff seriously meant that

390

nothing mattered. And then I just needed to feel as if stuff *did* matter, you know?'

She didn't.

'I stole just to *feel* something. I climbed trees just to be dizzy. I drank to laugh.' He bit his lip. 'I bunked off 'cause what did school matter in the end anyway?'

Jane touched his hand. 'You should have told me,' she gulped.

'You were too sad. You wouldn't have understood. I didn't really, not then. And afterwards, it was too hard.'

'You mean with me and your dad?'

'Uh-huh.'

'We let you down, didn't we?'

'Naw.'

'And now,' Jane touched his damp hair. 'How are you now? Still scared?'

Owen didn't answer for a bit. Then he said softly, 'Since the accident I know I want to live.'

'Good.' Jane sat down on the sofa beside him. She rubbed his arm and said fervently, 'Know this, Owen, no one knows when they're to die. I wish I could make it easy for you, but I can't. No one can.' She gulped. 'Mattie just died, his little life was over, there was no sense to it, but it happened. We have to accept it. You, on the other hand, are very much alive.' She cupped his face with her hands. 'So *brilliantly* alive. Just live, please. Just do that for me and I promise, I'll listen to you and be there for you and never let you down again. It's my fault for not talking about it with you at the time. I should have, I know that now. Di gave me grief over it at the hospital.'

'No one better than her to do that.' Owen gave a shaky grin.

'You'd better believe it,' Jane smiled back.

'I'm sorry, Ma,' Owen said.

'No,' Jane cuddled him to her, 'no, I'm the one who's sorry.'


Sheila looked up as Jane came into the kitchen. Her daughter looked exhausted. 'There's tea in the pot, dahling,' she said.

'Ta.' Jane poured herself a cup and sat opposite Sheila at the table.

Really, Sheila thought, Jane had to sort herself out. If she kept going the way she was, she'd be nothing but a shadow. Her hair was a mess, you'd never think she was a hairdresser, and all that stuff she'd just said to Owen – she wondered if . . .

'What?' Jane asked. 'Why do you keep looking at me?'

'Did you mean what you said to Owen in there?' Sheila hadn't planned to ask that, it just popped out.

Jane's eyes narrowed. 'What?'

'When you told Owen that he had to accept that Matt was dead?'

'Were you listening? You had—'

'I was bringing you a cup of tea, dahling, and I heard all the emotion, so I decided not to intrude, but nevertheless, I did hear you tell Owen that he had to accept things.'

'You had no right—'

'Maybe not, but still, I heard you tell Owen that,' Sheila's eyes glistened slightly, 'well, that Mattie's life was over and that though it didn't make sense he had to accept it.'

'You must have glued your ear to the door,' Jane muttered.

Sheila said nothing.

'Well, it's true,' Jane snapped. 'Makes things easier.'

Sheila reached across and patted Jane's hand. She said quietly, 'So why don't you also accept it, dahling, and make things easier on yourself?'

'What?'

'You heard.'

'Mam, I don't need . . .' Jane didn't finish. She pushed her cup away from her and stood up.

Sheila blocked her way. It was about time someone said something. 'Don't run away now, dahling,' she said.

'It's harder to accept things when you're responsible for them happening,' Jane said, trying to push past. 'It's my fault he died, how can I accept that – huh?'

'Making him wear his helmet wouldn't have saved that child.'

'Looking for it would have.'

'Maybe. Maybe not.' Sheila caught Jane by the arm. There was no way Jane was leaving the kitchen until she faced facts. 'But you said it yourself to Owen. Matt just died. There was no sense to it.' Tightening her grip on Jane, she continued, 'You can't keep blaming yourself any more than you can blame Owen or Jim. It's *ruining* you, dahling.'

'Let – me – go.' Jane tried to wrench herself free.

'You can't take responsibility for everything, Jane. You can't sort everything out with a phone call or by wishing it never happened, you know. You have to accept that some things happen that are no one's fault.'

Jane twisted her face away. '*Stop.*'

'You are *not* to blame.'

'I am.' Jane pushed against her, trying to free herself.

Despite her angry face, there were tears in her eyes and Sheila was determined to make her shed them. She'd only seen Jane cry once for Matt and then that waster of a husband had gone and left and Jane hadn't cried or talked about Matt since. Instead she'd turned all her unhappiness in on herself. 'Jane, dahling,' she said, 'look at me and I'll let you go.' At first she thought that Jane wouldn't, then slowly, her daughter brought her eyes up to her face. 'You are *now* looking at a hopeless mother,' Sheila said. 'You, dahling, are a shining light by comparison.'

Jane gulped out a laugh but shook her head. 'No.'

'Yes!' Sheila said emphatically. 'I know I neglected you terribly when you were growing up, Jane. The truth was, I just didn't know what to do with you. I mean, if you were a dress or something, there'd have been no problem. And then, off you went and had Di, and I couldn't believe the way you were with her. You shamed me. I knew how bad I'd been, but that was me. And now, now I'm trying to be a good mother, so for God's sake don't ruin it for me!' She shook Jane gently. 'You are *not* to blame. And, dahling, you have to let people back in again.

Di and Owen need you – you know that. You've been great with them, but they need more than you just keeping it together. They need someone who's living fully in the world. And your father and I have always needed you. I think even Jim needs you, though,' she sniffed, 'that's not surprising.'

'He doesn't need me. He shut me out. I killed his son.'

Sheila shook her gently again. 'Well, if he thinks that, then he's the fool I always said he was,' she said with passion. 'You are a *great* mother and you learnt it all on your own. You are not to blame.'

'I am. I should have looked after him – I was his mother.'

'You still are, wherever he is, you still are.' She pulled Jane to her. It was lovely to feel her so close. 'It's time now to go on and make the best of what's left. Accepting things makes you free, you know, it stops you fighting stuff you just can't change.'

Patrick had said that to her once. Jane closed her eyes to squeeze away the tears. 'I try, but I can't . . .'

'You have to. Look at me and your father. I'm making the best of the fact that he can't perform and he's making the best of the fact that I'm going to spend all his money when I get back. But we accept . . .' Sheila stopped. Against her, Jane was sobbing, her shoulders heaving.

Sheila, only vaguely aware that tear stains would not come out of the suit she was wearing, pulled Jane tighter. 'Let it out,' she soothed. 'Just *cry* for God's sake.'

# 62

IT WAS HER first day back at work since the accident and Jane was looking forward to it, despite the fact that she'd probably spend all day worrying about Owen. She'd made him promise to ring her if he needed anything and he'd rolled his eyes and said that all he needed was for her to stop nagging him. He'd changed since they'd had their talk, Jane had to admit. Even though he still looked ill, there was a brightness to his eyes that had been missing for a long time. And he'd begun fighting with Di, which was another good sign.

Jane too felt different. Lighter somehow. The only black cloud on the horizon was that Gooey had begun sniffing around again. However, Di was now relying heavily on her nana for advice, so it was highly unlikely they'd get back together.

Jane parked her car and made her way to the salon. Despite the fact that she hadn't been to work for almost six weeks, nothing about the road had changed. Lisa's was open and a sign in the window announced that Sexy Sheila's rolls were on sale. A picture of her mother, taken at least thirty years ago, was plastered to the window. Jane grinned and carried on down, past Cutting Edge, where she noted that their prices had reverted to normal. Ha. Ha. Finally she arrived outside her own place.

She stood still, savouring the fact that this was her salon. Her little business. The prices were still the same, the posters of their 'Winning' hair were still up in the windows. A new, funky one of Rosemary had been added. 'IHF prize-winner' was scrawled in bright green along the side of it. It looked cool and modern.

Inside the salon, Jane could see Mir escorting one of the customers to a seat. She was chatting and laughing and it was a Monday. Patrick was studying something at the reception desk and Rosemary was washing some poor victim's hair. Taking a deep breath, Jane pushed open the doors of the salon and walked in.

All activity stopped. There was a moment's silence before Patrick ran to embrace her.

'Welcome back! Welcome back!' He beamed delightedly into her face and, grasping her hand, tugged her up the salon. 'Hey, everybody, Jane is back,' he called.

Eileen Simms was the first over. Grasping Jane's arms in a vice-like grip, she said passionately, 'I'm so glad about your son, *so* glad.'

'Ta.'

Rosemary's client managed a wave before beginning to cough violently. Rosemary, in her excitement, had squirted what had to be at least half a pint of water over the woman's face and into her mouth. Rosemary, oblivious to her client's distress, rushed towards Jane, stood in front of her and then, unsure of what to do, stood beaming stupidly up at her. 'It's great to have you back, Jane,' she eventually gasped out.

'You're drowning Mrs Lyons,' Patrick said in disbelief as water squirted everywhere.

'Ohhhh.' Her hands splayed out in panic, Rosemary rushed off.

'Fucking idiot,' Mir muttered darkly as she came abreast of Jane. They smiled at each other. 'Hiya boss,' Mir smiled. 'It's great you're back.'

'It's great to be back,' Jane grinned.

Patrick was doing big pointy things with his fingers. Dancing from foot to foot, he was pointing at Mir.

'What?' Jane asked.

Mir rolled her eyes and held out her hand. On it, a ring inset with a row of diamonds gleamed.

Jane grasped her hand. 'Is this what I think it is?' she asked delightedly. 'Is it?'

'Nope.' Mir rolled her eyes again. 'It's a friendship ring. Harry bought it for me.'

'My arse it's a friendship ring,' Patrick chuckled. 'The man just wants everyone to think you're engaged to him, that's all. And it'll double as an engagement ring when the time comes.'

'It is *not* an engagement ring.' Mir sounded fed-up. Patrick had obviously been saying the same thing to her for days. 'What part of "not" don't you understand, Pat?'

'Ohhh, touchy.' Patrick rubbed his hands gleefully and headed back up to the reception desk.

Jane turned to Mir. 'So, what? Harry is back on the scene, is he?'

'And it's all thanks to you.' Mir blushed. It was the first time Jane could ever remember her doing that. 'Come over here and I'll tell you.'

In-between cutting her customer's hair, Mir told Jane that she'd gone to Harry's and yelled through his letter box that the cold, selfish bitch wanted to try to apologise.

'He was a bit off at first, but I just said that all I could do was apologise, isn't that right, Jane?'

'Yep.'

'I mean, I couldn't change the past, but I could make the future a lot more enjoyable for both of us. It was the "enjoyable" part that got him in the end. I think he liked the idea of that.' Mir gave a dirty laugh.

Jane smiled. 'Well done.'

'Hey,' Patrick sauntered over, 'what do you think of this as a billboard poster?'

He held up a picture of a grinning Rosemary with an enormous yellow lollipop in her hand. Her head was tilted to one side and her hair was the funky mix of colours that Jane had done. The picture was laid against a brilliant green background. *Hair To Dye For* was the caption.

'Well?' Patrick asked.

'Cool, yeah,' Mir nodded.

'It's me!' Rosemary squealed. 'I'm going to be up on a bill-board.'

It was like the one outside, Jane thought. Very quirky, very modern. Very Jim. The thought came unbidden, but as soon as it hit her, she knew. 'Jim did that, didn't he?' she asked slowly. 'That's one of his, I'd know his design ideas anywhere.'

Patrick flushed. 'No, Barney arranged—'

'Patrick!' Her voice was sharp. He hated when she sounded like that. 'Tell me the truth.'

'He didn't want you to know.' Patrick looked guilty.

'What? What? That you'd used him to do up a billboard?'

No answer.

'Well?'

No answer.

'Has he been helping you and Barney from the start?' Jane asked incredulously. 'Did you ask him to?'

'No!' Patrick said hastily. 'Well, he rang me, see. Apparently one of the kids told him the place was in a bit of trouble and, well, he gave me a few ideas.' He smiled ruefully. 'He almost flipped when I told him we'd slashed our prices. He's a bit of a tyrant, your Jim. He told me I was a complete idiot and to hike the prices up pronto.'

'That was Jim's idea?'

'Uh-huh.'

'And the coffee and biscuits? And the posters in the window?'

'All Jim's.' Patrick gave a nervous laugh.

'So Barney was never a part of it?'

'Well,' Patrick bit his lip. 'He agreed to pretend that he was, you know, in case you ever met him.'

'No wonder he always sounded different on the phone,' Mir said. 'One day he'd sound dead sexy and the next, well,' she giggled, 'well, he'd sound like Jim.'

She laughed as Jane belted her one.

'I'm sorry, honey chicks,' Patrick said contritely. 'I didn't like keeping things from you, but, well, you'd never have agreed and Jim, well, he's good at marketing, isn't he?'

'You should have told me,' Jane said flatly.

'He made me swear not to.' Patrick rolled up the poster. 'And anyway, it's dead nice of him, isn't it?'

'He's just dead.' Jane made her way to the door.

'Where are you going?' Patrick asked alarmed.

'To see my husband.'

'But, but, we've customers booked in for you.'

'Get *Barney* to help.'

She dialled Jim and told him she wanted to meet him. He told her he was in the flat packing away a few things and she said she'd meet him there.

Jim's apartment block was very nice, she thought as she pulled into the visitor car park around the back. The gardens were well taken care of and the whole place had an air of newness about it. Now, what apartment number was he again? 3b or something? Oh well, she thought, as she pressed 3b, even if it wasn't his they'd be sure to know where he was.

'Hi,' a woman's voice answered. 'Is that Jane?'

A woman? A bloody woman!

'Yes.'

'Come on up.' She was buzzed in.

She stood in the foyer, uncertain about what she should do. Was that Debbie? Was it back on between them? Huh, she wouldn't be a bit surprised if it was. Jim was easily swayed like that. Well, she decided, she might as well get a dekko at the woman who'd managed to replace her. She wished she'd worn something a bit more exciting though. Her jeans were just boring blue ones and her T-shirt was the only clean one she'd been able to find that morning and it didn't really do her justice. But, feck it! She ran her hands through her hair, squared her shoulders and gave the brass bell of 3b the most aggressive ring she could.

A 'Fuck's sake' was heard.

Someone opened the door and it wasn't Jim. It wasn't Debbie either. It took a second for her to realise that it was Fred. She hadn't seen him in ages.

'Jane,' he managed some sort of a grimace, 'come in. We're just going.'

Jane, feeling awkward, entered the bare room. Well, it was bare except for a sofa and two chairs. 'Hiya Fred,' she mumbled.

'This is Gill.' Fred indicated a bushy-haired, slightly plump girl with a friendly smile.

*Not Debbie, Gill. Whoever that was.*

'Gee, hiya.' The girl held out her hand. 'So you're Jane. You look different to what I expected.'

'Naw, honey.' Fred gave her a nudge. 'I wasn't serious when I said she had a black hat and a broomstick.'

Gillian looked mortified as Fred laughed. 'Underdeveloped sense of humour,' Gillian said. 'Comes from his mother leaving him when he was a kid.'

More like his mother dropping him from a height when he was a kid, Jane thought mutinously. Still, she managed to smile politely. Where the hell was Jim? she wondered.

As if reading her mind, Gillian said, 'He's just nipped out to buy biscuits seeing as you were calling. I was just feeding junior here while he was gone.' She indicated the sofa where a small baby lay curled up in a white baby blanket. Jane hadn't noticed the baby at all because there was a pile of boxes blocking her view. 'A baby?' she said. 'Yours?'

'Mine and Freddie's,' Gillian said proudly.

'Well, congratulations.' Fred a father, the very idea sent shivers up her spine.

'You wanna see him?' Gillian didn't wait for an answer. Dying to show her child off, she placed him gently into Jane's arms.

He was beautiful, Jane thought. All clean and innocent, with that gorgeous baby smell. She put her nose against his scalp and inhaled the sweet scent. 'He's lovely,' she said softly. 'Really lovely.'

'He is, isn't he?' Fred peered in at the baby too. 'The blanket sort of ruins him, though. Gill bought lovely clothes for him and he looks nicer when you can see his clothes.'

Gillian giggled.

Jane smiled.

The door opened and Jim walked in. He stopped dead at the sight of her holding the baby.

'Jim,' she said, not able to make her voice sound as hard as she wanted because the baby had now opened the most navy blue eyes she had ever seen, and was staring at her.

'Jane. Hiya,' he muttered.

'Let us get out of your way.' Fred gently took the baby from Jane and after gathering their bits and pieces they left.

Jane and Jim stood looking at each other.

'So Fred's a daddy,' she said at last.

He nodded. 'Scary, isn't it?'

They smiled at each other. Briefly.

'So, what's the occasion?' Jim walked past her and into the kitchen. 'Come to say goodbye?'

'No, actually.' Her anger flared again. 'Just came to tell you that I don't appreciate you butting into my business.'

'What?' He began to fill up the kettle.

'You helped Patrick market the salon.'

He actually had the nerve to smile at her. 'Yeah.'

'Well, you had no right!'

His grin faltered. 'Sorry?'

'So you should be! It's my salon. Not yours. If I'd wanted your help I'd have asked for it. I don't appreciate being kept in the dark by my own partner. Being made a fool of by my own husband.'

'I wasn't making a fool of you.' He genuinely looked bewildered. 'I was only trying to help. To show—'

'The thing is, I don't want your help. I don't want anything from you.'

401

'Fine.'

'Good.'

The kettle flicked off.

'Do you even want tea?'

The question caught her off guard. She smiled. Then stopped. 'No. I'd better go.'

She wasn't prepared for the look of devastation on his face. 'OK.'

There was a pause.

She indicated his boxes. They looked so final. So lonely. 'Good luck with the new job.'

'Ta.'

She was leaving. Walking out without even having a cup of tea. And he'd bloody well gone and bought her favourite biscuits and everything. Her hand was on the door. Now she was pulling the door open. *And* she was mad at him.

That wasn't meant to happen.

He stood by helplessly as the door began to swing shut behind her.

'No!' His voice seemed to work all by itself. His legs, of their own accord, sprinted across to the door and he yanked it back open. 'Jane! Jesus, don't go.'

She turned to face him, puzzled.

Silence descended.

Damn it. Why couldn't he ever say what he wanted?

'Yeah?' she asked.

'I only did it because I couldn't think of any other way to tell you that I loved you,' he said.

'What?' She thought he was mental.

'The posters and marketing and stuff,' he said. 'At first I, well, I did it 'cause Di was upset. But, well, I wanted to do it. There was no other way I could make you see that I still cared. You shut me out, see, and, well . . .' He stopped.

Fucking words.

402

'No,' she said simply. 'You left me.'

He ran his hands over his face and gulped. 'Yeah. Yeah, I know.' Why did everything always have to come back to that? 'I made a mistake. A big mistake.'

To his surprise, her eyes filled with tears.

'Aw, Jane, Jesus, don't.'

'I didn't mean to let him go out without his helmet,' she said, blinking really hard. 'It was an accident.'

'Jesus, yeah. Yeah. I know *that*.' He didn't know if he should hold her or leave her. 'I know that.'

'So why did you blame me? Why did you leave me, Jim?'

'I didn't blame you.' Not this again. She never believed him.

Women like to talk. To know things. Fred's voice cut in on his thoughts.

But he couldn't explain to Jane. He'd never explained to anyone. It hurt too much.

'Then why?'

He looked up at the ceiling then down at his trainers. His heart began to pound, sweat broke out on his forehead. 'I couldn't cope,' he said eventually. 'When Matt died, I just couldn't cope.'

Jane stared at him. He couldn't cope. He'd never admitted that before. Instead, he'd shut off, or change the subject, or walk out of the room. Or leave.

'Talk to me, Jim,' she said. 'Please.'

There was no other way. If he had to have a shot at getting her back he had to talk. He couldn't just do stuff and hope she'd understand. How had he ever thought that would work anyway? For the first time in his life, it looked like Fred was right.

He opened the door wider and stood aside to let Jane walk back inside. Taking a deep breath, he followed her.

Jane sat on the sofa while Jim took a chair.

There was an expectant silence.

He bowed his head, clasped his hands between his knees and haltingly said, 'I just couldn't cope when Matt died, Jane. You

403

were crying and the kids were crying and I didn't know what I should be doing.'

She didn't say anything.

Jim looked quickly at her. Said, 'I couldn't cry. I felt bad. So I left with Fred.'

'But I wouldn't have cared if you hadn't cried, as long as you were with me,' Jane said softly. 'I thought you couldn't bear to be near me.'

'Naw.' He shook his head. 'Don't put that on me. It's not true. All I ever wanted was to be with you.' He gave her a half-smile.

She smiled a bit in return.

He closed his eyes. He'd never really told Jane much about his family and she, knowing how valuable his privacy was, had never really pushed him. He'd liked that about her. But now, well, that had to change. 'See,' he stopped, then started again. 'See . . . I never knew my dad. And when me ma died, my gran, she wouldn't let me cry. She told me that big boys didn't cry.' He gave a bitter laugh. 'I was only seven, you know.'

'Jim.'

He shook off the pity in her voice. 'And I went to live with her then. You were lucky you never knew her, Jane. Fred called her The Ball-breaker and she was. I couldn't cry, get mad, get upset, nothing.' He looked at her. 'I don't think I've ever cried in my whole life, Jane.'

She looked upset.

'The point is, right, that no one ever talked to me about any of it. And then when Matt died, I wanted to cry, but I didn't know how. I wanted to talk to you and I didn't know how. It was like,' his eyes closed, 'well, like I was trapped in myself . . . words just, you know, wouldn't come.'

'Oh Jim, I'm so sorry.' She crossed towards him and knelt down beside him. 'I thought it was me, see, and I—'

'No.' He reached for her hand and she clasped his. 'Never. I've always loved you, you know, but I let you down. I know I

404

did. And, God, I'm so fucking sorry.' He wiped her hair from her face and let his palm caress her cheek. 'I know it sounds crap, but it's all I can say. I can't change the past.'

Neither of them could, she realised. 'Nope,' she said. 'But we can try to change the future, can't we?'

It was like coming home, feeling her arms around him again. Feeling her hair against his face. He'd lost so much in his life that to find her again was better than finding her for the first time – a cute brunette with hair dye under her fingernails. His lips sought hers and he felt her tears on his face.

He was crying, Jane realised. She could taste the salt of his tears on her lips. He was holding her fiercely and telling her how much he loved her, and he was crying.

At long last.

## 63

THEY TALKED NON-STOP all the way to the graveyard. She made him laugh when she told him about the card Cutting Edge had sent congratulating them on their second placing in the IHFs.

'He'd written on it that he was looking forward to beating us next year and Patrick sent him a card back saying that as the standard of entry was so low, he didn't know whether he'd bother entering next year.'

'Well, at least Patrick is a bit smarter with his comments than he is as a marketing agent. Jesus, he was bloody hopeless, you know.'

'Not like you, eh?'

Jim grinned modestly.

Since turning down the job with Incredible Crisps, he'd been headhunted by every firm in town. He was finally doing the kind of stuff he'd always wanted to do. 'Great thing I'm working on now,' he said, beginning to tell her all about it.

Jane smiled at the enthusiasm with which he talked. He was like a kid that had seen something wonderful for the first time.

He paused mid-sentence and looked at her with sparkling eyes, 'I'm boring you, amn't I?'

'Naw,' she smiled back. 'I'm just thinking of how much I love you.'

His eyes grew sombre. 'We'll always be like this, won't we, Jane? Let's never mess up again.'

She put her arm around his waist and he slung his arm over her shoulder. They kissed softly.

The grave was neat and tidy. Together they began replacing old flowers with fresh ones, talking quietly as they did so and touching off each other as much as they could. It was like the thrill of new love all over again.

'Sorry, excuse me,' a tearful voice said.

Together they looked up and a woman who couldn't have been more than twenty-five was gazing down at them. 'Sorry for disturbing you,' she said, 'but I come here every week and I couldn't help seeing that your boy was only six when he died.'

'That's right,' Jane said quietly. 'Why?'

'Well,' the woman pointed to the grave that backed on to Matt's. 'My baby died a few months ago. She was almost three and, well . . .' Her eyes filled up, 'I was just wondering how you cope. I'm not, you see. Not at all.'

Jane jumped up, flowers falling from her lap. She took the woman's hand and pressed it. 'You are,' she said. She moved nearer the woman and said more firmly, 'Believe it or not, you are. It takes time—'

'But you two seem so happy,' the woman whispered, looking from one to the other. 'Me and my partner aren't like that.'

Jane put her arm around the woman's shoulders. 'Come on,' she said, 'Jim can cope here. I'll buy you a coffee and a danish in this coffee shop outside and then . . .' She looked at Jim, who smiled up at her. Turning back to the woman she said softly, 'And then, I'll tell you a story . . .'

**Other bestselling titles available by mail:**

| | | |
|---|---|---|
| ☐ Something Borrowed | Tina Reilly | £5.99 |
| ☐ The Rebel Fairy | Deborah Wright | £6.99 |
| ☐ Under My Spell | Deborah Wright | £5.99 |
| ☐ Lazy Ways to Make a Living | Abigail Bosanko | £6.99 |
| ☐ A Nice Girl Like Me | Abigail Bosanko | £6.99 |
| ☐ Playing James | Sarah Mason | £6.99 |
| ☐ The Party Season | Sarah Mason | £5.99 |
| ☐ High Society | Sarah Mason | £5.99 |

*The prices shown above are correct at time of going to press. However, the publishers reserve the right to increase prices on covers from those previously advertised without prior notice.*

———————————————— sphere ————————————————

**SPHERE**
**PO Box 121, Kettering, Northants NN14 4ZQ**
**Tel: 01832 737525, Fax: 01832 733076**
**Email: aspenhouse@FSBDial.co.uk**

**POST AND PACKING:**
Payments can be made as follows: cheque, postal order (payable to Sphere), credit card or Maestro. Do not send cash or currency.
All UK Orders        **FREE OF CHARGE**
EU & Overseas        25% of order value

Name (BLOCK LETTERS) . . . . . . . . . . . . . . . . . . . . . . . . . . . . . . . . . . . . . .

Address . . . . . . . . . . . . . . . . . . . . . . . . . . . . . . . . . . . . . . . . . . . . . . . . . .

. . . . . . . . . . . . . . . . . . . . . . . . . . . . . . . . . . . . . . . . . . . . . . . . . . . . . . . . .

Post/zip code: . . . . . . . . . . . . . . . . . . . . . . . . . . . . . . . . . . . . . . . . . . . . .

☐ Please keep me in touch with future Sphere publications

☐ I enclose my remittance £ . . . . . . . . .

☐ I wish to pay by Visa/Mastercard/Eurocard/Maestro

☐☐☐☐☐☐☐☐☐☐☐☐☐☐☐☐☐☐

Card Expiry Date ☐☐☐☐        Maestro Issue No. ☐☐